The Shape of Things to Come...?

"Let my brother go first," I pleaded.

O'Shaughnessy laughed. He crooked one leg around Don's ankle and simultaneously pushed. O'Shaughnessy advanced on me with hands outstretched. Two of his fingers were bloody.

"The ball and the gimmick," he demanded, "or it's your turn, punk."

"The only gimmick's inside my head," I said. "But you can have the ball."

I drove the rubber sphere at him with all my psychokinetic strength. His nose shattered and the ball burst its bladder. Help me get him Donnie!

The torn and flattened ball like some writhing marine organism clamping itself across a horror-stricken face. Savage sounds and big hands clawing and punching at me. Then a grotesque figure like a scarecrow, its head a red-smeared dented globe. Go for it Donnie man HEY togethernow allezallez SLAMDUNK THE BASTARD...

D0954098

By Julian May
Published by Ballantine Books:

The SAGA OF PLIOCENE EXILE:
Vol. I: The Many-Colored Land
Vol. II: The Golden Torc
Vol. III: The Nonborn King
Vol. IV: The Adversary

A PLIOCENE COMPANION

THE SURVEILLANCE
Book One of *Intervention*

THE METACONCERT
Book Two of *Intervention*

THE SURVEILLANCE

BOOK ONE OF
INTERVENTION

A Root Tale to the Galactic Milieu
and a
Vinculum
between it and
The Saga of
Pliocene Exile

JULIAN MAY

A Del Rey Book

BALLANTINE BOOKS ● NEW YORK

A Del Rey Book
Published by Ballantine Books

Copyright © 1987 by Julian May

All rights reserved under International and Pan-American Copyright Conventions. Published in the United States of America by Ballantine Books, a division of Random House, Inc., New York, and simultaneously in Canada by Random House of Canada Limited, Toronto.

No part of this work may be reproduced or transmitted in any form or by any means, electronic or mechanical, including photocopying and recording, or by any information storage or retrieval system, except as may be expressly permitted by the 1976 Copyright Act or in writing from the publisher. Requests for permission should be addressed in writing to Houghton Mifflin Company, 2 Park Street, Boston, Massachusetts 02108.

While many of the institutions and organizations depicted in this book, including those devoted to parapsychology, actually do exist, the characters are entirely products of the author's imagination.

The quotation on page vii is from "Burnt Norton" in *Four Quartets* by T. S. Eliot, copyright 1943 by T. S. Eliot; renewed 1971 by Esme Valerie Eliot. Reprinted by permission of Harcourt Brace Jovanovich, Inc.

Library of Congress Catalog Card Number: 87-4021

ISBN 0-345-35523-7

First published by Houghton Mifflin Company. Reprinted by permission of Houghton Mifflin Company.

Manufactured in the United States of America

First Ballantine Books Edition: December 1988

Cover Art by Michael Herring

To Robie Macauley

INTERVENTION

Evolutionary creativity always renders invalid the "law of large numbers" and acts in an elitist way.

> —Erich Jantsch
> *The Self-Organizing Universe*

At the still point of the turning world. Neither flesh nor
    fleshless;
Neither from nor towards; at the still point, there the dance is,
But neither arrest nor movement. And do not call it fixity,
Where past and future are gathered. Neither movement from
    nor towards,
Neither ascent nor decline. Except for the point, the still
    point,
There would be no dance, and there is only the dance.

> —T. S. Eliot
> "Burnt Norton"

CONTENTS

PROLOGUE • 1

PART I • The Surveillance • 13

PART II • The Disclosure • 161

The Remillard Family Tree • 349

PROLOGUE

HANOVER, NEW HAMPSHIRE, EARTH
17 FEBRUARY 2113

THE PROVERBIAL FEBRUARY THAW DID NOT MATERIALIZE FOR THE 203rd annual Dartmouth Winter Carnival, and the temperature was around −10° Celsius when Uncle Rogi Remillard emerged from the sanctuary of the Peter Christian Tavern into a blustery, festive night. Cheered by a late supper of turkey-apple soup and a Vermont cheddar omelette, not to mention a liberal intake of spirits, he was damned if he would let the Family Ghost keep him from the fireworks display. The thing couldn't possibly do anything blatant in the midst of such a mob.

The northeast wind blew leftover snow about thronged Main Street and down the tavern's stairwell. Rogi had to push past revelers who tried to crowd down the steps as he climbed up. When the full blast caught him, he gave his long red-wool muffler an extra twist to wrap it partially about his head. Thick grizzled hair stuck out of the scarf folds like a scraggly fright wig. Uncle Rogi was tall, skinny, and slightly stooped. His youthful face was disfigured by great bags under the eyes and a slightly mashed nose, which dripped when forced to inhale the arctic air of unmodified New Hampshire winters. More fastidious Remillards had long since given up pleading with Rogi to fix himself up. The family image? Ça ne chie pas!

1

He stood in the partial shelter of the tavern building and looked warily around. The melting grids for both the streets and sidewalks of downtown Hanover had been turned off to preserve a properly old-fashioned atmosphere for the celebration. A six-horse team pulling a snow-roller had tamped down the worst ruts; and now sleighs, farm wagons full of hay and carousing students, and chuffing antique autos equipped with antique tire chains drove toward the College Green in anticipation of the pyrotechnics display. No modern vehicles were in sight. One could imagine it was the 1990s again ... except that among the human pedestrians in their reproduction winter gear from L. L. Bean and Eddie Bauer were slower-moving groups of exotic tourists from the nonhuman worlds of the Galactic Milieu. All but the hardy little Poltroyans were snugly sealed inside environmental suits with visors closed against the harsh Earth weather. The Poltroyans romped and chortled in the stinging cold, and wore fish-fur mukluks and oversized Dartmouth souvenir sweat shirts over their traditional robes.

Rogi searched the night, using his watering eyes rather than his farscan ultrasense. The damn Ghost was too clever a screener to be spotted with the mind's eye—or at least *his* mind's eye. Perhaps the thing had given up and gone away. God, he hoped so! After leaving him in peace for thirty years it had given him a nasty shock, accosting him there in the bookshop just as he was getting ready to close up. He had fled out into the street and it had followed, importuning him, all the way to the Peter Christian Tavern.

"Are you still here, mon fantôme?" Rogi muttered into his scarf. "Or did it get too cold for you, waiting outside? Silly thing. Who'd notice a ghost in a crowded bar with mulled cider and hot buttered rum flowing like Ammonoosuc Falls? Who'd notice a dozen ghosts?"

Something insubstantial stirred in the tiny plaza fronting the Nugget Cinema just south of the tavern. Whirling powder snow seemed for a moment to slide over and around a certain volume of empty air.

Bon sang! It had waited for him, all right. Rogi farspoke it:

Hello again. Beats me, Ghost, why you don't simply put on a psychocreative body and sit down to supper with me like a civilized being. Other Lylmik do it.

The Ghost said: There are too many alumni operants in the Peter Christian tonight. Even a Grand Master or two. In their cups, the older ones might be unpredictably insightful.

"And that would never do, eh? Some really big operator might see through you in the worst way!" Rogi's whisper was scathing and his mental façade, fortified with Dutch courage, no longer betrayed a hint of unease. "Well, I'm going over to watch the fireworks. How about you?"

The mysterious presence drifted closer, exuding restrained co-ercion. Oh, yes—it could force its will on him anytime it liked; the fact that it didn't had ominous implications. It needed whole-hearted cooperation in some scheme again, the sneaky bastard, and very likely over some considerable span of time. Fat chance!

The Ghost's mind-voice was insistent: We must talk.

"Talk between skyrockets," Rogi told it rudely. "Nobody invited you here tonight. I've been waiting for this all winter. Why should I give up my fun?"

He turned his back and set off into the crowd. Nothing re-strained him physically or mentally, but he was aware of the thing following. Bells in the Baker Library tower struck ten. A brass band was playing "Eleazar Wheelock" over in front of the brilliantly lit Hanover Inn. The leafless branches of the ancient elms, maples, and locust trees around the snowy quadrangle were trimmed in twinkling starlights. Streetlamps had been dimmed so the pseudoflames of the energy torches set up around the campus were the major source of illumination. They cast a mellow glow over the cheerful waiting throng and the ranks of huge snow sculptures in front of the college residence halls. In this centennial year of the Great Intervention, whimsical takeoffs on Milieu themes predominated. There was a flying saucer with its Simbiari crew marching down the gangplank, each exotic carrying a bucket of frozen green Jell-O. A hideous effigy of a Krondaku held out a tentacle to take a candy cane from a smiling human snow-child. Gi engaged in their favorite pursuit were posed in a Kama Sutra ensemble. Sigma Kappa had produced Snow White and the Seven Poltroyans. Out in the middle of the College Green was the festival's monumental theme sculpture: a bizarre armored humanoid like a fairy-tale knight, astride a rampant charger that was almost—but not quite—a horse. This statue was almost eight meters high.

The Ghost observed: A fair likeness of Kuhal, but the chaliko's a bit off the mark.

"The Outing Club tried to get him to be grand marshal of the cross-country ski parade," Rogi said, "but Cloud put her foot down. Spoilsport. And you can't fool me, Ghost. I know why you showed up tonight instead of some other time. You wanted to see the Winter Carnival yourself." He groped inside his disreputable old blanket-coat and found a leather-bound flask of Wild Turkey.

There was a *choong* from a cleared area over beyond Wentworth Street. The first rocket went up and burst into an umbrella of pink, silver, and blue tinsel extending from horizon to horizon. The crowd yelled and applauded. Rogi moved into the lee of a giant elm trunk to escape the wind. He held out the flask. "Une larme de booze?"

Nobody noticed when the container left his gloved hand, tilted in the air, and then returned to its owner.

Good stuff, said the Family Ghost.

"As if a damned alien Lylmik would know," Rogi retorted. "Gotcha!" He took three hefty swallows.

Still seeking solace in the bottle instead of the Unity, I see.

"What's it to you?" Rogi drank again.

I love you. I wish you joy and peace.

"So you always said . . . just before you gave me a new load of shit to shovel." He took another snort, capped the flask, and put it away. The expression on his face as he watched scarlet fireflowers bloom above black branches was both cunning and reckless. "Level with me. What are you, really? A living person or just a manifestation of my own superego?"

The Ghost sighed and said: We're not going to start that all over again, are we?

"You're the one who started it—by coming back to bug me."

Don't be afraid of me, Rogi. I know there were difficult times in the past—

"Damn right! Least you can do is satisfy my curiosity, settle my mind before you start in all over again with the botheration. Put on an astral body like your damn Lylmik compères. Show yourself!"

No.

Rogi gave a derisive sniff. He took a bandanna handkerchief from his pocket and mopped his nose. "It figures. You're not a real Lylmik anymore than you're a real ghost." Wind-chill tears blurred the purple and orange comets that chased each other overhead like she-elves with their hair on fire.

The Ghost said: I am a Lylmik. I am the entity charged with the guidance of the Family Remillard through your agency, just as I've always claimed to be. And now I come to you with one last task—

"Shit—I knew it!" Rogi howled in mortal anguish. Three stunning detonations from aerial bombs announced a flock of golden pinwheels. They zoomed heavenward in a tight formation, fissioned into hundreds of small replicas of themselves, then rained down toward the skeletal treetops, whirling and whistling like demented birds. There were vocal and telepathic cheers from the crowd. The brass band in front of the inn played louder. Metapsychic operants among the students were mindshouting the final verse of the old college song with drunken exuberance:

Eleazar and the Big Chief harangued and gesticulated.
And they founded Dartmouth College, and the Big Chief
     matriculated.
Eleazar was the fac-cul-tee, and the whole curriculum
Was five hundred gallons of New England rum!

"All my life," Rogi moaned, "haunted by a damn exotic busybody masquerading as the Family Ghost. Why me? Just a quiet man, not very clever, hardly any metabilities worth mentioning. No world-shaker, just a harmless bookseller. Most insignificant member of the high and mighty Remillard Dynasty. Why me? Persecuted! Pushed around without any common consideration. Forced into one dangerous situation after another just to carry out your damn Lylmik schemes and forward the manifest destiny of humanity . . . unless it all hatched in my own unconscious."

Like starry dandelion puffs, colossal pompoms of Dartmouth green and white exploded high over the Old Row. The wind strengthened, stirring more and more snow into the air.

Patiently, the Ghost said: You and your family were the key that opened the Galactic Milieu to the human race. The work required an exotic mentor because of the psychosocial immaturity of Earth's people and the pivotal role of you Remillards. And while I admit that you were called upon to endure mental and physical hardship—

"You should be ashamed, using me that way. Playing goddam God." Rogi gave a maudlin snuffle. He had the flask out again and emptied it with a single pull. "Nobody ever knew I was the one—your catspaw. Always another pot you wanted stirred, another piece of manipulation, meddling with this Remillard or that one. Uncle Rogi, galactic agent provocateur! And you used every dirty trick in the book to keep me in line, tu bâton merdeux."

The Ghost said: Your family would have been aware if we had tried to coerce them, and they never would have accepted direct counsel from nonhumans—especially in the pre-intervention years. We had to work through you. You were the perfect solution. And you survived.

A cascade of white fire poured from the sky behind the library, silhouetting its lovely Georgian Revival tower. Psychokinetic adepts among the spectators took hold of the falling sparks and formed them into Greek letters and other emblems of college fellowship. The crystal dust of the blown snow began to mix with heavier flakes running ahead of the predicted storm.

Rogi's eyes glittered with fresh moisture. "Yes, I survived it all. A hundred and sixty-eight winters and still going strong. But good old Denis had to die before he ever reached Unity, and Paul and his poor Teresa . . . and Jack! My Ti-Jean, the one you exotics call a saint—for what good it does him. You could have prevented all their deaths, and the billions of deaths in the Rebellion! You could have had me warn Marc, shown me some way to stop him. You could have used me properly, you cold-hearted monster, and nipped the conspiracy in the bud before it ever came to war!"

The Ghost said: It had to happen as it happened. And in your own heart, Rogatien Remillard, you know that the tragedies brought about a greater good.

"Not for Marc! Not for poor Marc the damned one. Why did he have to end that way? My little boy! I think he loved me more than his own father—nearly as much as he loved Ti-Jean. He almost grew up in my bookstore. My God, he teethed on a mint copy of Otto Willi Gail's *By Rocket to the Moon*!"

The Ghost said: So he did . . . I remember watching him.

"And yet you stood by and let him become the greatest mass murderer in human history—that brilliant misguided man who could have done so much good, if only you'd guided *him* instead of using an impotent old fart like me as your puppet."

The fireworks were reaching a crescendo. Great jets of vermilion fire rose from the four points of the compass behind the trees and nearly converged overhead. In the dark at the zenith, in the midst of the glare, there appeared a dazzling white star. It vibrated and split in two and the paired lights began to orbit a common center, drawing intricate figures like laser projections. The stars split again and again; each set drew more detailed designs about the central focus until the sky was covered with a blazing mandala, a magical pattern of spinning wheels within ornate wheels, white tracery in ever-changing motion.

Then it froze. It was fire-lace for a moment, then broke into fine shards of silver that still held the wondrous pattern. The night was webbed in a giant constellation of impossible intricacy. Down on the campus the crowd released a pent-up breath. The tiny diamond-points faded to darkness. The show was over.

Uncle Rogi shivered and pulled his muffler tighter. People were hurrying away in all directions now, fleeing the cold. The band finished playing "The Winter Song" and withdrew into the shelter of the Hanover Inn, there to drink the health of Eleazar Wheelock and many another Dartmouth worthy. Sleigh bells jingled, the wind roared in the white pines, and fresh falling snow curtained off the tall sculpture of the Tanu knight on the Dartmouth College Green.

"Whatever you want," Rogi told the Ghost, "I won't do it."

He darted off across rutted Wheelock Street, dodging a Model A Ford, a wasp-colored Ski-Doo, and a replica post-coach of 1820 vintage carrying a party of riotous Poltroyans.

The unseen presence dogged Rogi's heels. It said: This is the centennial year of the Intervention, 2113, and a year significant in other ways as well.

"Et alors?" sneered Rogi loftily. He headed back on Main Street alongside the hotel.

The Ghost was cajoling: You must undertake this last assignment, and then I promise you that these visitations will end . . . if at the end you wish it so.

"The devil you say!" The bookseller came to a sudden stop on the brightly lit sidewalk. There were roisterers all around, shouting to one another and filling the aether with farspoken nonsense. The celebrating students and visitors ignored Rogi and he in turn shut out all perception of them as he strained his mental vision to get a clear view of his tormentor. As always, he failed. Frustration brought new tears to his eyes. He addressed the Ghost on its intimate mode:

Thirty goddam years! Yes, thirty years now you've let me alone, only to come back and say you want to start all over again. I suppose it's to do with Hagen and Cloud. Well, I won't help you manipulate those poor young folks—not even if you bring a whole planetful of Lylmiks to lay siege to my bookshop. You exotics don't know how stubborn an Earthling can be till you try to cross an old Canuck! To hell with you and your last assignment—et va te faire foutre!

The Ghost laughed. And the laugh was so different from its characteristic dispassionate expressions of amusement, so warm, so nearly human, that Rogi felt his fear and antagonism waver. He was overcome by a peculiar sense of déjà vu.

Then he was startled to discover that they had already reached South Street and were just across from The Eloquent Page, his bookshop. In this part of town, away from the college buildings and drinking establishments, the sidewalks were nearly deserted. The historic Gates House, with his shop on the first-floor corner and the white clapboard of the upper storeys blending into the thickening storm, had only a single lighted window in the north dormer: the sitting room of his third-floor apartment. He hustled up the steps into the entry on Main Street, pulled off a glove, and thumbed the warm glowing key-pad of the lock. The outer door swung open. He looked over his shoulder into the swirling snow. The laughter of the Ghost still rang in his mind.

"Are you still there, damn you?"

From inside the hallway, the Ghost said: Yes. You will not refuse me, Rogi.

The bookseller cursed under his breath, stepped inside, and slammed the door. Stamping his feet, he shook himself like an old hound and untwined the red muffler. "Go ahead—coerce me! But sooner or later I'll break away, and then I'll sic the Magistratum on your self-righteous, scheming ass! I'm a Milieu citizen and I've got my rights. Not even the Lylmik can violate the Statutes of Freedom and get away with it."

The Ghost said: You're half drunk and wholly ridiculous. You've worked yourself into a frenzy without even knowing what my request is.

Rogi rushed up the stairs, past the doors of darkened offices on the second floor, until he came to his own aerie. He fumbled in his pocket for the famous key ring with its gleaming red fob.

"You've set your sights on Hagen and Cloud—or on their kids!" he said wildly. He flung the door open and nearly tripped over Marcel, his great shaggy Maine Coon cat.

The Ghost said: My request does concern them, but only indirectly.

Outside, the snow hissed against the double-glazed windows. The old wooden building responded to the storm's pressure with dozens of secret little noises. Rogi slouched into his sitting room.

He dropped his coat and scarf over a battered trestle bench, sat down in the cretonne-covered armchair in front of the standing stove, and began to take off his boots. Marcel circled the bench purposefully, bushy tail waving. He broadcast remarks at his master in the feline telepathic mode.

"In the right coat pocket, probably frozen stiff," Rogi told the cat. Marcel rose on his great hind legs, rummaged with a forepaw that would have done credit to a Canada lynx, and hooked a doggie-bag of French fries left over from Rogi's supper. Uttering a faint miaow, incongruous for such a large animal, he transferred the booty to his jaws and streaked out of the room.

The Ghost said: Can it be the same Marcel, food-thief extraordinaire?

"The ninth of his line," Rogi replied. *What do you want?*

Once again the strangely evocative laughter invaded Rogi's mind, along with reassurance:

You have nothing to be afraid of this time. Believe me. What we want you to do is something you yourself have contemplated doing from time to time over the past twenty years. But since you're such a hopeless old flemmard, you've put it off. I've come to make sure you do your duty. You will write your memoirs.

The bookseller gasped. "My . . . my memoirs?"

Exactly. The full history of your remarkable family. The chronicle of the Remillards as you have known them.

Rogi began to giggle helplessly.

The Ghost went on: You'll hold nothing back, gloss over no faults, tell the entire truth, show your own hidden role in the drama clearly. Now is the appropriate time for you to do this. You may no longer procrastinate. The entire Milieu will be indebted to you for your intimate view of the rise of galactic humanity—to say nothing of Hagen and Cloud and their children. There are important reasons why you must undertake the task immediately.

Rogi was shaking his head slowly, staring at dancing pseudo-flames behind the glass door of the stove. Marcel strolled back into the room, licking his chops, and rubbed against his master's stockinged ankles.

"My memoirs. You mean, that's *all*?"

It will be quite enough. They should be detailed.

Again the old man shook his head. He was silent for several minutes, stroking the cat. He did not bother to attempt a thought-screen. If the Ghost was real, it could penetrate his barrier with ease; if it was not real, what difference did it make? "You're no fool, Ghost. You know why I never got around to doing the job before."

The Ghost's mental tone was compassionate: I know.

"Then let Lucille do it. Or Philip, or Marie. Or write the damned thing yourself. You were there spying on us from the beginning."

You are the only suitable author. And this is the suitable time for the story to be told.

Rogi let out a groan and dropped his head into his hands. "God—to rake up all that ancient history! You'd think the painful parts would have faded by now, wouldn't you? But those are the most vivid. It's the better times that I seem to have the most trouble recalling. And the overall picture—I still can't make complete sense of it. I never was much good at psychosynthesis. Maybe that's why I get so little consolation from the Unity. Just a natural operant, an old-style bootstrap head, not one of your preceptor-trained adepts with perfect memorecall."

Who knows you better than I? That's why I'm here myself to make this request. To give help when it's needed—

"No!" Rogi cried out. The big gray cat leapt back and crouched with flattened ears. Rogi stared pointedly at the spot where the Ghost seemed to be. "You mean that? You intend to stay around here prompting me and filling in the gaps?"

I'll try to be unobtrusive. With my help, you'll find your own view of the family history clarifying. At the end, you should understand.

"I'll do it," Rogi said abruptly, "if you show yourself to me. Face to face."

Your request is impossible.

"Of course it is . . . because you don't exist! You're nothing but a fuckin' figment, a high-order hallucination. Denis thought so, and he was right about the other loonies in the family, about Don and Victor and Maddy. You tell me to write my memoirs because some part of my mind wants to justify the things I did. Ease my conscience."

Would that be so terrible?

Rogi gave a bitter laugh. The cat Marcel crept back on enormous furry feet and bumped his forehead affectionately against his master's leg. One of Rogi's hands automatically dropped to scratch the animal's neck beneath its ruff. "If you're a delusion,

Ghost, then it means that the triumph of Unified Humanity was nothing but the result of an old fool's schizophrenia. A cosmic joke."

I am what I say I am—a Lylmik.

"Then show yourself! You owe it to me, damn you."

Rogi . . . nobody sees the Lylmik as they really are, unless that person is also a Lylmik. We are fully perceptible only to minds functioning on the third level of consciousness—the next great step in mental evolution, which you younger races of the Milieu have yet to attain. I tell you this—which is known to no other human—to prove my commitment to you. My love. I could show you any one of a number of simulacrum bodies, but the demonstration would be meaningless. You must believe me when I say that if you saw me truly, with either the mind's eye or that of the body, your sanity would be forfeit.

"Horse-puckey. You don't show yourself, I don't write the memoirs." A tight little smile of satisfaction thinned Rogi's lips. He patted his lap and Marcel leapt up, purring. The old man watched the dancing artificial flames. He whispered, "I've had my suspicions about you for years, Ghost. You just *knew* too much. No probability analysis, no proleptic metafunction can account for what you knew."

The Seth Thomas tambour clock that had belonged to Rogi's mother struck twelve with familiar soft chimes. Outside, the storm winds assaulted the north wall of the building with mounting vigor, making the aged timbers groan and the clapboards snap. Marcel snuggled against Rogi's stomach, closed his wildcat eyes, and slept.

"I'm bound and determined to know the truth about you, Ghost. Read my mind! I'm wide open. You can see I mean what I say. I'll work with you and write the memoirs only if you come out in the open at last—whatever the consequences."

Rogi, you're incorrigible.

"Take it or leave it." The old man relaxed in the armchair, fingering a silken cat's ear and toasting his feet at the stove.

Let me propose a sublethal compromise. I'll let you see me the way I *was*.

"You got a deal!"

Rogi realized that the thing was invading his mind, flooding him with the artificial calm of redactive impulses, taking advantage of the liquor's depressant effect, triggering endorphins and God knew what-all to bolster him in anticipation.

And then Rogi saw. He said, "Ha." Then he laughed a little and added, "Goddam."

Are you satisfied?

Rogi held out a trembling hand. "Are you going to tell me the way you worked it?"

Not until you complete your own story.

"But—"

We have a deal. And now, good night. We'll begin the family history tomorrow, after lunch.

PART I

THE
SURVEILLANCE

1

FROM THE MEMOIRS OF
ROGATIEN REMILLARD

I WENT DOWN TO WALK ALONG THE ICEBOUND CONNECTICUT River very early today before beginning this chronicle. My wits were more than usually muddled from overindulgence, and I had received an emotional shock as well—call it a waking dream!— that now seemed quite impossible out here in the fresh air and the revitalizing aetheric resonances of the rising sun. As I went west along Maple Street the pavements were still patchy wet and steaming; the melting network had been turned back on precisely at 0200 hours. In the business district and throughout most of the college precincts the $-25°$ chill would be gentled by area heaters, but in this residential part of Hanover it was still fast winter. The night's brief storm had given us an additional ten or fifteen cents of snow, piling small drifts in the lee of fences and shrubs. Out here only a few wealthy eccentrics had force-field bubbles over their houses to screen out the elements. It was early enough so that the gravo-magnetic ground-cars and flying eggs were still locked away in their garages.

Down in the sheltered strip of woodland alongside frozen Mink Brook the scene was even more reminiscent of the New England I knew when I was a kid in the 1940s. The snow under the tall hemlocks and birches was almost knee-deep and level as a

marble floor. I'd brought decamole snowshoes in my coat pocket
and it took only a moment to inflate them, slip them on, and go
slogging down to the shore path that paralleled the silent Connecticut.

The great deep river was locked under a thick ice mantle,
reminding me that winters are colder now than in my youth—if
not always so picturesque. Thanks to the storm, the snow-cover
of the Connecticut was again without blemish, swept clean of the
tracks of skis and power toboggans and the footprints of foolish
rabbits seeking a better climate on the other bank, over in Vermont. I 'shoed north for nearly two and a half kloms, passing
under Wheelock Street Bridge and skirting the Ledyard Canoe
Club. Finally I reached that awesome patch of forest preserve
where white pines tower eighty meters high and little siskins and
nuthatches whisper mysteriously in the brush thickets. The scent
of conifer resin was intense. As so often happens, the odor triggered memory more strongly than any effort of will ever could.

This snow-girt woods I had not visited for three decades was
the place where the boys used to come.

The Gilman Biomedical Center of the college was only a few
blocks away—and the Metapsychic Institute, and the hospital.
Young Marc, an undergraduate already showing the promise that
would someday make him a Paramount Grand Master, used to
coerce the nursing staff in the intensive care unit and take Jack
away. The beloved baby brother, slowly dying of intractable
cancers that would devour his body and leave only his great brain
untouched, rode in an ingeniously modified backpack. Marc and
Jack would spend a morning or an afternoon talking, laughing,
arguing. Stolen, pitiable hours of pine and pain and the conten-
tion of those brother-minds! It was then the rivalry was born that
would bring thousands of inhabited planets to the brink of ruin,
and threaten not only the evolution of the Human Mind but also
that of the five exotic races who had welcomed us into their
peaceful Galactic Milieu . . .

Close to the shore where the snow lies drifted, it is not easy to
tell where granite ends and the frozen river begins. The juncture
is veiled. Molecules of water have slowed to the solidity of stone,
apparently immutable. My deep-sight easily sees through the
snow to tell the difference, just as it pierces the icy lid of the
Connecticut to perceive black water flowing beneath. But I am
not strong-minded enough to see the subtler flux of the ice molecules themselves, or the vibration of the crystals within the gran-

ite boulders, or the subatomic dance of the bits of matter and energy among the nodes of the dynamic-field lattices that weave the *reality* of ice and gray rock in the cosmic All. My vision of the winter river in its bed remains limited, in spite of the abstract knowledge science lends me.

And how much more difficult it is to apprehend the greater pattern! We know we are free, even though constraints hedge us. We cannot see the unus mundus, the entirety that we know must exist, but are forced to live each event rushing through space and time. Our efforts seem to us as random as the Brownian movement of molecules in a single drop of ultramagnified water.

Nevertheless the water droplets come together to make a stream, and then a river that flows to the sea where the individual drops—to say nothing of the molecules!—are apparently lost in a vast and random pooling. The sea not only has a life and identity of its own, but it engenders other, higher lives, a role denied to water molecules alone. Later, after the sun draws them up, the molecules condense into new water drops or snowflakes and fall, and sustain life on the land before draining away to the sea again in the cycle that has prevailed since the biogenesis. No molecule evades its destiny, its role in the great pattern. Neither do we, although we may deny that a pattern exists, since it is so difficult to envision. But sometimes, usually at a far remove of time, we may be granted the insight that our actions, our lives, were not pointless after all. Those (and I am one) who have never experienced cosmic consciousness may find consolation in simple instinct. I know in my heart—as Einstein did, and he was justified in the long view if not in the short—that the universe is not a game of chance but a design, and beautiful.

The great white cold takes hold of the amorphous water droplet and turns it into an ice crystal of elegant form. Can I organize my memories into an orderly ensemble and give coherence to the tangled story of the Family Remillard? I have been assured that I can . . . but you, the entity reading this, may decide otherwise.

C'est bien ça.

The chronicle will begin in New Hampshire and conclude in interstellar space. Its time-span, willy-nilly, will be that of my own life; but I will tell the story from a number of different viewpoints—not all of them human. My personal role in the drama has not always been prominent, and certain Milieu historians have forgotten that I existed, except for grudging footnotes! But I was Don's fraternal twin and close to his wife and children,

I was with Denis and Lucille at the Intervention, and I know what drove Victor and the Sons of Earth to their infamy. I was privy to the secrets of the "Remillard Dynasty" and to those of the Founding Human Magnates. I watched Paul "sell" New Hampshire as the human capital of the Milieu. I stood by Teresa throughout her tragedy. I know what kind of demons possessed Madeleine. I can tell the story of Diamond Mask, since her life was inextricably entwined with that of my family. Marc's tormented presence and his Metapsychic Rebellion will pervade these memoirs and climax them.

Above all, however, this will have to be the story of Jon Remillard, whom I called Ti-Jean and the Milieu named Jack the Bodiless. Even though he was born after the Intervention, his life is prefigured in the struggles and triumphs of the people I will write about in this book: the first human beings to have full use of their higher mind-powers. But Jack would be their culmination. He would show us the awful and wonderful course our human evolution must take. He was the first Mental Man. Terrified, we saw in him what we will eventually become.

Saint Jean le Désincarné, priez pour nous! But please—let us not have to follow your example for at least another million years.

2

OBSERVATION VESSEL CHASSTI
[SIMB 16-10110]
9 AUGUST 1945

"LOOK THERE," CRIED ADALASSTAM SICH. "THEY'VE DONE IT again!"

The urban survey monitoring system had zeroed in on the terrible event at the moment of the bomb's detonation, and at once Adalasstam stabbed the key that would transfer the enhanced image from his console to the large wall-screen. The other two Simbiari on duty saw the fungoid growth of the death-cloud. A blast wave spread away from it, obliterating the beautiful harbor.

"O calamity! O day of despond! O hope-wreck!" intoned Elder Laricham Ashassi. Thin green mucus poured from the scrobiculi of his fissured countenance and outstretched palms. Being the senior member of his race present, it was his duty to express the sorrow and vexation of all Simbiari at the catastrophic sight—and its implications. The telepathic overtones of his keening brought the observers of the other Milieu races on watch hurrying into the oversight chamber.

The two little humanoid Poltroyan mates, Rimi and Pilti, who had been at work in EM Modulation Records next door, were followed closely by the monstrous bulk of Doka'eloo, the Krondak Scrutator of Psychosocial Trends and a magnate of the Concilium. The horror unfolding on the wall-screen was so riveting that none of the entities thought to prevent the entry of the ship Gi, NupNup Nunl, until it was too late. The creature's great yellow eyes rolled back into its skull as the mass death-shout from the holocaust filled the chamber. NupNup Nunl uttered a wail in a piercing progression of minor sixths, lost consciousness from shock, and proceeded to collapse. Doka'eloo caught it with his psychokinesis and lowered it gently to the deck, where it lay in a disheveled heap of silky filoplumage, gangling limbs, and pallid genitalia. Aware that their supersensitive colleague's mind had withdrawn safely into the consolation of the Unity, the others paid no more attention to it.

Elder Laricham, still dripping in ritual mourning, let dismay sharpen into indignation. "One atomic bombing was dire enough. But to devastate *two* cities—! And with peace feelers already sent forth by the wretched Islanders!"

"Barbaric beyond belief," agreed Chirish Ala Malissotam; but she held her green, as did her spouse Adalasstam. "But it was just about what one might expect of humanity, given the escalation of atrocities among all participants in this war."

"By using this appalling weapon," Adalasstam said, "the Westerners prove they are no less savage and immoral than the Island warmongers."

"I do not agree," Doka'eloo said ponderously. He paused, and the others knew they were in for a lecture; but the Krondaku was their superior officer as well as a magnate of the Concilium, so they steeled themselves. "While it is true that the Islanders at this time have expressed a certain inclination to sue for peace, prompted by the first display of atomic weaponry, their gesture was by no means wholehearted. The Island military leaders remain determined to continue hostilities—as our Krondak analysis of their high-level signals has confirmed. The Westerners are partially aware of this intelligence. Even without it, however, given the Islanders' record of perfidy in past dealings, plus the warrior-ethic forbidding honorable surrender, one might hold the West justified in thinking that the Islander High Command required a second stimulus"—he nodded at the fire-storm on the screen—"to bring the truth of their situation home to them beyond the shadow of a doubt."

"Bring home indeed!" exclaimed the scandalized Chirish Ala. "Oh, I agree that this second atomic bombing will end the stupid war, Doka'eloo Eebak. But by taking this course the planet Earth has signed its metapsychic death-warrant. No world utilizing atomic weaponry prior to its cooperative advent into space has ever escaped destruction of its primary civilized population component. The coadunation of the global Mind has been set back at least six thousand years. They'll revert to hunter-gatherer!"

"We might as well pack up the mission and go home right now," old Laricham said. The other two Simbiari murmured agreement.

"Precedent tends to support your pessimism," said the imperturbable Krondaku. "Nevertheless, we will await the decision of the Concilium. Debate has been lively since the atomic bombing of the first Island city. This second incident, which I farspoke to Orb promptly, should elicit a vote of confidence concerning our Earth involvement."

"The Concilium's vote is a foregone conclusion," Adalasstam said. "The Earthlings are bound to blast themselves to a postatomic Paleolithic within the next fifty orbits or so, given their abysmal state of sociopolitical immaturity."

"Perhaps not!" the male Poltroyan, Rimi, piped up. He and his mate had been watching the mushroom cloud hand in hand, with tears in their ruby eyes and their minds locked in mutual commiseration. But now they showed signs of cheering up.

Pilti, the female Poltroyan, said, "Earthlings have been atypical in their accelerated scientific progress as well as in their aggressive tendencies. Certain segments responded to this war with a great upsurge of solidarity, setting aside petty differences for

the first time in human history as they worked together to oppose
a clearly immoral antagonist."

"By Galactic standards, they're ethical primitives," Rimi said.
"But they have *amazing* metapsychic potential. Isn't that right,
Doka'eloo Eebak?"

"You speak truly," the monstrous being assented.

Now the fallen Gi began to stir. It opened its enormous eyes
while keeping its mind well screened from distressing resonances. "I do hope we won't have to write Earth off," NupNup
Nunl fluted. "It has such gorgeous cloud formations and oceanic
shadings—and its inventory of presapient life is rich beyond
measure and quite resplendent. The birds and butterflies! The
oceanic microflora and the glorious sea-slugs!"

"Pity the sea-slugs aren't candidates for induction into the Milieu," snorted Adalasstam.

NupNup Nunl climbed to its feet, assisted by kindly Rimi.
The Gi settled its plumage and untangled its testicular peduncles.
"Human beings are quarrelsome and vindictive," it conceded.
"They persecute intellectual innovators and mess up the ecology.
But who can deny that their music is the most marvelous in the
known universe? Gregorian chant! Bach counterpoint! Strauss
waltzes! Indian ragas! Cole Porter!"

"You Gi!" Elder Laricham exclaimed. "So hopelessly sentimental. What matter if the human race is an aesthetic wonder—
when it so obstinately resists the evolution of its Mind?"
Laricham turned to the two Poltroyans. "And your optimistic assessment, Rimi and Pilti, is supported by nothing more than a
naive view of the synchronicity lattices. The Arch-College of
Simb has recognized Earth's unsuitability from the very start of
this futile surveillance."

"How fortunate for humanity," Rimi remarked suavely, "that
our federation of worlds outranks *yours* in the Concilium."

Chirish Ala could not resist saying, "Poltroyans empathize
with Earthlings merely because both races are so revoltingly fe-
cund."

"So speed the great day of Earth's Coadunate Number," Pilti
said, lowering her eyes in piety. And then she grinned at the
female Simb. "By the way, my dear, did I tell you I was pregnant
again?"

"Is this a time for vulgar levity?" cried Adalasstam, gesturing
at the wall-screen.

"No," Pilti said. "But not a time for despair, either."

Rimi said, "The Amalgam of Poltroy has confidence that the human race will pull back from the brink of Mind destruction. In friendship, let me point out to our esteemed Simbiari Uniates that we of Poltroy belong to a very old race. We have studied many more emerging worlds than you have. There has been at least one exception to the correlation between atomic weaponry and racial suicide. Us."

The three green-skinned entities assumed a long-suffering mental linkage. Elder Laricham acknowledged the point with cool formality.

"Oh, that's so true!" burbled the Gi. It wore a sunny smile, and its pseudomammary areolae, which had been bleached and shrunken by its horrific experience, began to re-engorge and assume their normal electric pink color. "I'd forgotten what bloodthirsty brutes you Poltroyans were in your primitive years. No wonder you feel a psychic affinity to the Earthlings."

"And no wonder *we* don't," Elder Laricham growled. He crinkled his features to stem the flow of green. "Earth is a lost cause, I tell you." He pointed melodramatically to the screen. "The principals in the current conflict, Islanders and Westerners, are certain to remain deadly antagonists for the next three generations at the very least. There will be fresh wars of vengeance and retaliation between these two nations so highly charged with ethnic dynamism, then global annihilation. The Galactic Milieu's overly subtle educative effort has been in vain. We will surely have to abandon Earth—at least until its next cycle of high civilization."

"It's the Concilium's decision, not yours," Rimi said flatly. "Any word yet, Doka'eloo Eebak?"

The fearsome-looking officer sat motionless except for a single tentacle that flicked emerald mucus blobs toward the floor scuppers in nonjudgmental but relentless tidiness. Doka'eloo opened his stupendous farsensing faculty to the others so that they might envision the Concilium Orb, a hollow planetoid more than four thousand light-years away in the Orion Arm of the Milky Way. In the central sanctum of the Orb, the governing body of the Coadunate Galactic Milieu had finally completed its deliberation upon the fate of Earth's Mind. The data had been analyzed and a poll of magnates was taken. The result flashed to the receptor ultrasense of Doka'eloo with the speed of thought.

He said, "The Poltroyan Amalgam voted in favor of maintaining the Milieu's involvement with Earth. The Krondak, Gi, and Simbiari magnates voted to discontinue our guidance—giving a majority in favor of disengagement."

"There!" exclaimed Adalasstam. "What did I tell you?"

"We can't let their music die," NupNup Nunl grieved. "Not Sibelius! Not Schoenberg and Duke Ellington!"

But the Krondaku was not finished. "This negative verdict of the Concilium magnates was summarily vetoed by the Lylmik Supervisory Body."

"Sacred Truth and Beauty!" whispered Elder Laricham. "The *Lylmik* intervened in such a trivial affair? Astounding!"

"But wonderful," cried the two little Poltroyans, embracing.

The Gi shook its fluffy head. Its ovarian externalia trembled on the verge of cerise. "A Lylmik veto! I can't think when such a thing ever happened before."

"Long before your race attained coadunation," Doka'eloo told the hermaphrodite. "Before the Poltroyans and Simbiari learned to use stone tools and fire. That is to say, three hundred forty-two thousand, nine hundred and sixty-two standard years ago."

In the awestruck mental silence that followed, the Krondaku signaled Adalasstam to change the image on the wall-screen. The picture of the devastated Island city melted into a longer view of Earth as seen from the Milieu observation vessel. The sun shone full on it and it was blue and white, suspended like a brilliant agate against the foaming silver breaker of the galactic plane.

"There is more," Doka'eloo said. "The Lylmik order us observers to commence a thirty-year phase of intensified overt manifestation. The people of Earth are to be familiarized with the concept of interstellar society—as a preliminary to possible Intervention."

The three affronted Simbiari fell to choking on green phlegm. The Poltroyan couple clapped their hands and trilled.

NupNup Nunl controlled itself heroically, quieting its reproductive organs to the magenta state, and uttered a luxurious sigh. "I'm so glad. It's really a fascinating world, and there *is* a statistically significant chance that the people will shape up. Very long odds, but by no means hopeless..."

It extended a six-jointed digit and activated the ambient audio system, which was patched to Vienna radio. The climaxing strains of "Verklärte Nacht" filled the oversight chamber of the exotic space vessel.

Invisible, it continued the Milieu's surveillance of over sixty thousand years.

3

FROM THE MEMOIRS OF ROGATIEN REMILLARD

I WAS BORN IN 1945, IN THE NORTHERN NEW HAMPSHIRE MILL town of Berlin. My twin brother Donatien and I took our first breaths on 12 August, two days after Japan opened the peace negotiations that would end World War II. Our mother, Adèle, was stricken with labor pains at early Sunday Mass, but with the stubbornness so characteristic of our clan gave no indication of it until the last notes of the recessional hymn had been sung. Then her brother-in-law Louis and his wife drove her to St. Luke's, where she was delivered of us and died. Our father Joseph had perished six months earlier at the Battle of Iwo Jima.

On the day of our birth, clouds of radioactivity from the bombing of Hiroshima and Nagasaki were still being carried around the world by the jet-stream winds. But they had nothing to do with our mutations. The genes for metapsychic operancy lay dormant in many other families besides ours. The immortality gene, however, was apparently unique. Neither trait would be recognized for what it was until many years had gone by.

Don and I, husky orphans, had a legacy from our mother of a GI insurance policy and an antique mantelpiece clock. We were taken in by Onc' Louie and Tante Lorraine. It meant two more mouths to feed in a family that already included six children, but Louis Remillard was a foreman at the big Berlin paper mill that also employed other males of our clan (and would employ Don and me, in good time). He was a stocky, powerful man with one leg slightly shorter than the other, and he earned good wages and owned a two-storey frame apartment on Second Street that was old but well maintained. We lived on the ground floor, and Oncle Alain and Tante Grace and their even larger brood lived upstairs. Life was cheerful, if extremely noisy. My brother and I seemed to be quite ordinary children. Like most Franco-Americans of the region, we grew up speaking French to our kinfolk, but used English quite readily in our dealings with non-Francophone neighbors and playmates, who were in the majority.

The Family Ghost, when I first met it, also spoke French.

It happened on an unforgettable day when I was five. A gang of us cousins piled into the back of an old pickup truck owned by Gerard, the eldest. We had a collection of pots and pans and pails, and were off on a raspberry-picking expedition into the National Forest west of town, a cut-over wilderness beyond the York Pond fish hatchery. The berries were sparse that year and we scattered widely, working a maze of overgrown logging tracks. Don and I had been warned to stick close to our cousin Cecile, who was fourteen and very responsible, but she was a slow and methodical picker while we two skipped from patch to patch, skimming the easily reached fruit and not bothering with berries that were harder to get.

Then we got lost. We were separated not only from Cecile and the other cousins but from each other. It was one of the first times I can remember being really apart from my twin brother, and it was very frightening. I wandered around whimpering for more than an hour. I was afraid that if I gave in to panic and bawled, I would be punished by having no whipped cream on my raspberry slump at supper.

It began to get dark. I called feebly but there was no response. Then I came into an area that was a dense tangle of brambles, all laden with luscious berries. And there, not ten meters away, stood a big black bear, chomping and slurping.

"Donnie! Donnie!" I screamed, dropping my little berry pail. I took to my heels. The bear did not follow.

I stumbled over decaying slash and undergrowth, dodged around rotted stumps, and came to a place where sapling paper birches had sprung up. Their crowded trunks were like white broom-handles. I could scarcely push my way through. Perhaps I would be safe there from the bear.

"Donnie, where are you?" I yelled, still terror-stricken.

I seemed to hear him say: Over here.

"Where?" I was weeping and nearly blind. "I'm lost! Where are you?"

He said: Right here. I can hear you even though it's quiet. Isn't that funny?

I howled. I shrieked. It was *not* funny. "A bear is after me!"

He said: I think I see you. But I don't see the bear. I can only see you when I close my eyes, though. That's funny, too. Can you see me, Rogi?

"No, no," I wept. Not only did I not see him, but I began to realize that I didn't really *hear* him, either—except in some strange way that had nothing to do with my ears. Again and again I screamed my brother's name. I wandered out of the birch grove into more rocky, open land and started to run.

I heard Don say: Here's Cecile and Joe and Gerard. Let's find out if they can see you, too.

The voice in my mind was drowned out by my own sobbing. It was twilight—entre chien et loup, as we used to say. I was crying my heart out, not looking where I was going, running between two great rock outcroppings . . .

"Arrête!" commanded a loud voice. At the same time something grabbed me by the back of my overall straps, yanking me off my feet. I gave a shattering screech, flailed my arms, and twisted my neck to look over my shoulder, expecting to see black fur and tusks.

There was nothing there.

I hung in the air for an instant, too stupefied to utter a sound. Then I was lowered gently to earth and the same adult voice said, "Bon courage, ti-frère. Maintenant c'est tr'bien."

The invisible thing was telling me not to be afraid, that everything was now all right. What a hope! I burst into hysterical whoops and wet my underpants.

The voice soothed me in familiar Canuckois, sounding rather like my younger uncle Alain. An unseen hand smoothed my touseled black curls. I screwed my eyes shut. A ghost! It was a ghost that had snatched me up! It would feed me to the bear!

"No, no," the voice insisted. "I won't harm you, little one. I want to help you. Look here, beyond the two large rocks. A very steep ravine. You would have fallen and hurt yourself badly. You might have been killed. And yet I know nothing of the sort happened . . . so I saved you myself. Ainsi le début du paradoxe!"

"A ghost!" I wailed. "You're a ghost!"

I can hear the thing's mind-voice laughing even now as it said:

Exactement! Mais un fantôme familier . . .

Thus I was introduced to the being who would help me, advise me—and bedevil me—at many critical points in my life. The Family Ghost took my hand and drew me along a shadowy, twisted game trail, making me run so fast I was left nearly breathless and forgot to cry. It reassured me but warned me not to mention our meeting to anyone, since I would not be believed. All too probably brother and cousins would laugh at me, call me a baby. It would be much better to tell them how bravely I had faced the bear.

As the first stars began to show, I emerged from the forest onto the road near the fish hatchery where the pickup truck stood. My cousins and the fish men were there and welcomed me with relieved shouts. I told them I had flung my berry bucket in a bear's face, cleverly gaining time to make my escape. None of them noticed that I stank slightly of pipi. My brother Don did look at me strangely, and I was aware of a question hovering just behind his lips. But then he scowled and was silent.

I got double whipped cream on my raspberry slump that night. I told nobody about the Family Ghost.

To understand the mind of our family, you should know something of our heritage.

The Remillards are members of that New England ethnic group, descended from French-Canadians, who are variously called Franco-American, Canado-Américaine, or more simply Canuck. The family name is a fairly common one, now pronounced REM-ih-lard in a straightforward Yankee way. As far as I have been able to discover, no other branches of the family harbored so precocious a set of supravital genetic traits for high metafunction and self-rejuvenation. (The "bodiless" mutagene came from poor Teresa, as I shall relate in due time.)

Our ancestors settled in Québec in the middle 1600s and worked the land as French peasants have done from time immemorial. Like their neighbors they were an industrious, rather bloody-minded folk who looked with scorn upon such novelties as crop rotation and fertilization of the soil. At the same time they were fervent Roman Catholics who regarded it as their sacred duty to have large families. The predictable result, in the harsh climate of the St. Lawrence River Valley, was economic disaster. By the mid-nineteenth century the worn-out, much-subdivided land provided no more than a bare subsistence, no matter how hard the farmers worked. In addition to the struggle required to earn a living, there was also political oppression from the English-speaking government of Canada. An insurrection among the habitants in 1837 was mercilessly crushed by the Canadian army.

But one must not think of these hardy, troublesome people as miserable or downtrodden. Au contraire! They remained indomitable, lusty, and intensely individualistic, cherishing their large families and their stern parish priests. Their devotion to home and religion was more than strong—it was fierce, leading to that solidarity (a species of the coerceive metafaculty) that Milieu anthropologists call ethnic dynamism. The Québec habitants not only survived persecution and a grim environment, they even managed to increase and multiply in it.

At the same time that the French-Canadian population was outstripping the resources of the North, the Industrial Revolution came to the United States. New England rivers were harnessed to provide power for the booming textile mills and there was a great demand for laborers who would work long hours for low salaries. Some of these jobs were taken by the immigrant Irish, themselves refugees from political oppression and economic woe, who were also formidably dynamic. But French-Canadians also responded to the lure of the factories and flocked southward by the tens of thousands to seek their fortunes. The migratory trend continued well into the 1900s.

"Little Canadas" sprang up in Massachusetts, New Hampshire, Vermont, Maine, and Rhode Island. The newcomers clung to their French language and to much of their traditional culture, and most especially to their Catholic faith. They were thrifty and diligent and their numerous offspring followed the parents into the family occupation. They became American citizens and worked not only as mill-hands but also as carpenters, mechanics, lumberjacks, and keepers of small shops. Most often, only those children who became priests or nuns received higher education. Gradually the French-Canadians began to blend into the American mainstream as other ethnic groups had done. They might have been quite rapidly assimilated—if it hadn't been for the Irish.

Ah, how we Franco-Americans hated the Irish! (You citizens of the Milieu who read this, knowing what you do of the principal human bloodlines for metapsychic operancy, will appreciate the irony.) Both the Irish and the French minorities in New Eng-

land were Celts, of a passionate and contentious temperament.
Both were, in the later nineteenth and early twentieth centuries,
rivals for the same types of low-status employment. Both had
endured persecution in their homelands and social and religious
discrimination in America because of their Catholic faith. But the
Irish were much more numerous, and they had the tremendous
social advantage of speaking the English language—with a rare
flair, at that! The Irish parlayed their genius for politicking and
self-aggrandizement into domination of the New England Catholic hierarchy, and even took over entire city governments. We
Francos were more aloof, politically naive, lacking in what Yankees called "team spirit" because with us it was the family that
came first. With our stubbornly held traditions and French language, we became an embarrassment and a political liability to
our more ambitious coreligionists. It was an era fraught with
anti-Catholic sentiment, in which all Catholics were suspected of
being "un-American." So the shrewd Irish-American bishops de-
creed that stiff-necked Canucks must be forcibly submerged in
the great melting-pot. They tried to abolish those parishes and
parochial schools where the French language was given first
place. They said that we must become like other Americans, let
ourselves be assimilated as the other ethnic groups were doing.

Assimilate—intermarry—and the genes for metapsychic
operancy would be diluted all unawares! But the great pattern
was not to be denied.

We Francos fought the proposed changes with the same ob-
stinacy that had made us the despair of the British Canadians.
The actions of those arrogant Irish bishops during the nineteenth
century made us more determined than ever to cling to our heritage. And we did. Eventually, the bishops saved face with what
were termed "compromises." But we kept our French churches,
our schools, and our language. For the most part we continued to
marry our own, increasing our homozygosity—concentrating
those remarkable genes that would put us in the vanguard of
humanity's next great evolutionary leap.

It was not until World War II smashed the old American social
structures and prejudices that the Canucks of New England were
truly assimilated. Our ethnocentricity melted away almost pain-
lessly in those postwar years of my early childhood. But it had
prevailed long enough to produce Don and me . . . and the others
whose existence we never suspected until long after we reached
adulthood.

4

SOUTH BOSTON, MASSACHUSETTS, EARTH
2 AUGUST 1953

HE WAS ON HIS WAY HOME FROM THE TEN-O'CLOCK AT OUR LADY, toting Sunday papers and some groceries Pa had remembered they were out of, when he got the familiar awful feeling and said to himself: No! I'm outside, away from her. It can't be!

But it was. Sour spit came up in his throat and his knees went wobbly and the shared pain started glowing blue inside his head, the pain of somebody dying who would take him along if he wasn't careful.

But he was outside, in the sunshine. More than six blocks from home, far beyond her reach. It couldn't be her hurting and demanding. Not out here. It never happened out here . . .

It happened in a dark room, cluttered and musty, where a candle in a blue-glass cup burned in front of one Sorrowful Mother (the one with seven swords through her naked pink heart), and the other one lay on her bed with the beads tangled in her bony fingers and her mind entreating him: *Pray a miracle Kier it's a test you see he always lets those he loves best suffer pray hard you must you must if you don't there'll be no miracle he won't listen . . .*

The full force of the transmitted agony took hold of him as he turned the corner onto D Street. Traffic was fairly heavy even at this early hour, when most of the Southie drowsed or marked time until the last Mass let out and the sandlot ballgames got underway and the taverns opened; but there wasn't another person in sight on the dirty sidewalks—nobody who could be hurting demanding calling—

Not a person. An animal dying.

He saw it halfway down the block, in the gutter in front of McNulty's Dry Cleaning & Alterations. A dog, hit by a car most likely. And Jeez he'd have to go right by it unless he went around by the playground, and the groceries were so heavy, and it was so rotten hot, and the pleading was irresistible, and he *did* want to see.

It was a mutt without a collar, a white terrier mix with its coat all smeared red and brown with blood and sticky stuff from its insides. Intelligent trustful eyes looked up at him, letting pain flood out. A few yards away in the street was a dark splotch where it had been hit. It had dragged itself to the curb, hindquarters hopelessly crushed.

Kieran O'Connor, nine years old and dressed in his shabby Sunday best, gulped hard to keep from vomiting. The dog was dying. It had to be, the way it was squashed. (Her dying was inside her, not nearly so messy.)

"Hey, fella. Hey, boy. Poor old boy."

The dog's mind projected hurtful love, begging help. He asked it: "You want a miracle?" But it couldn't understand that, of course.

The dog said to him: *Flies.*

They were all over the wounded parts, feeding on the clotted blood and shit, and Kieran grunted in revulsion. He could do something about them, at least.

"No miracle," he muttered. He set the bag of groceries and the paper down carefully on the sidewalk and hunkered over the dog, concentrating. As he focused, the iridescent swarm panicked and took wing, and he let them have it in midair. The small greenbacked bodies fell onto the hot pavement, lifeless, and Kieran O'Connor smiled through his tears and repeated: "No miracle."

The dog was grateful. Its mind said: *Thirst.*

"Say—I got milk!" Kieran pulled the quart bottle out of the grocery bag, tore off the crimped foil cap, and lifted the paper lid, which he licked clean and stowed in his shirt pocket for later. Crouching over the ruined body in the sunshine, holding his breath and letting the pain lose itself inside his own head, he dripped cool milk into the dog's mouth.

"Get well. Stop hurting. Don't die."

The animal made a groaning sound. It was unable to swallow and a white puddle spread under its open jaws. From the brain came a medley of apology and agony, and it clung to him. "Don't," he whispered, afraid. "Please don't. I'm *trying*—"

A shadow fell over the boy and the dog. Kieran looked up, wild-eyed with terror. But it was only Mr. Dugan, a middle-aged bald man in a sweat-rumpled brown suit.

"Oh," said Dugan shortly. "So it's you." He scowled.

"I didn't do it, Mr. Dugan. A car hit it!"

"Well, can't I see that with my own two eyes? And what are you doing messing with it? It's a goner, as any fool can see, and if you don't watch out, it'll bite."

"It won't—"

"Don't sass me, boy! And stop wasting good milk on it. I'll phone the Humane Society when I get home and they'll come and put it out of its misery."

Kieran began to recap the bottle of milk. Tears ran down his flushed face. "How?" he asked.

Dugan threw up his hands impatiently. "Give it something. Put it down, for God's sake. Now get away from it, or I'll be telling your Pa."

No! Kieran said. *You go away! Right now!*

Dugan straightened up, turned, and walked away, leaving Kieran kneeling in the filthy gutter, shielding the dog from the sun.

"Put you out of your misery," Kieran whispered, amazed that it could be so simple. (Why did Mom try to make it complicated?) He'd never thought of it that way before. Bugs, yes; he didn't care a hoot about them. The rats, either. But a dog or even a person . . .

"You wouldn't take me along, would you?" Kieran asked it warily. The pain-filled eyes widened. "Stop loving me and I'll do it. Let go. Lay off." But the dog persisted in its hold, so finally he reached out and rested his fingertips on its head, between its ears, and did it. Oddly, all of the hairs on the dog's body stiffened for an instant, then went flat. The animal coughed and lay still, and all pain ceased.

Kieran wondered if he should say a prayer. But he felt really rotten, so in the end he just covered the body with the want-ad section of the newspaper. His Pa never bothered with that part.

5

FROM THE MEMOIRS OF
ROGATIEN REMILLARD

I WAS NOT TO EXPERIENCE ANOTHER MANIFESTATION OF THE FAMily Ghost for nearly sixteen years. That first encounter in the twilit woods took on a dreamlike aspect. It might have been forgotten, I suppose, had not the memory been rekindled every time I smelled raspberries or the distinctive pungency of bear scats. But I did not brood on it. Truth to tell, I had more important matters to occupy me: my own developing metafunctions and those of my brother.

I have already mentioned that Don and I were fraternal twins, no more closely related than any singleton brothers. Many years later, Denis told me that if we had both hatched from a single egg, our brains might have been consonant enough to have attained harmonious mental intercourse, instead of the clouded and antagonistic relationship that ultimately prevailed between us. As it was, we were of very different temperaments. Don was always more outgoing and aggressive, while I was introspective. In adulthood we both were tormented by the psychological chasm separating us from normal humanity. I learned to live with it, but Don could not. In this we were like many other natural operants who came after us, our successes and tragedies blending into the ongoing evolutionary trend of the planetary Mind studied so dispassionately by the scientists of the Galactic Milieu.

In our early childhood, following that initial stress-provoked incident of farspeech and farsight out in the woods, we experienced other near-involuntary telepathic interchanges. Once Don scalded himself with hot soup and I, in the next room, jumped up screaming. I would have a furious argument with a cousin and Don would come running up, knowing exactly what the fight was about. We sometimes dreamed the same dreams and shared unspoken jokes. Eventually, we attained crude telepathic communication as well as a kind of shared farsight and mutual sensitivity. We experimented, "calling" to each other over greater and greater distances, and exercised our farsight with variations on games such as hide-and-seek and hide-the-thimble. Our cousins were blasé about our talents, ascribing them to the acknowledged freakishness of twins. They learned early not to play card games with us, and casually utilized our farsensing abilities to track down lost items and anticipate impending adult interference in illicit activities. We were a little weird, but we were useful. No big thing.

On one of our first days at school I was cornered by a bully and commanded to hand over my milk money, or suffer a beating. I broadcast a mental cry for help. Don came racing into the schoolyard alcove where I had been trapped, radiating coercive fury and saying not a single word. The bully, nearly twice Don's size, fled. My brother and I stood close together until the bell rang, bonded in fraternal love. This would happen often while we were young, when each of us was the other's best friend. It became rarer as we approached adolescence and ended altogether after we reached puberty.

By the time we were nine (the age, Denis later explained to me, when the brain attains its adult size and the metafunctions tend to "solidify," resisting further expansion unless painful educational techniques stimulate them artificially), Don and I had become fairly adept in what is now called farspeech on the intimate mode. We could communicate across distances of two or three kilometers, sharing a wide range of nuance and emotional content. Our farscanning ability was weaker, requiring intense concentration in the transmission of any but the simplest images. By mutual agreement, we never told anyone explicit details of our telepathic talent, and we became increasingly wary of demonstrating metapsychic tricks to our cousins. Like all children, we wanted to be thought "normal." Nevertheless there was a good deal of fun to be had using the powers, and we couldn't resist playing with them surreptitiously in spite of vague notions that such mind-games might be dangerous.

In the lower grades of grammar school we drove the good sisters crazy as we traded farspoken wisecracks and then snickered enigmatically out loud. We sometimes recited in eerie unison or antiphonally. We traded answers to test questions until we were placed in separate classrooms, and even then we still managed to cooperate in uncanny disruptive pranks. We were tagged fairly early as troublemakers and were easily bored and inattentive. To our contemporaries we were the Crazy Twins, ready to do the outrageous to attract attention—just as in our baby years we had vied to attract the notice of hard-working, hard-drinking Onc' Louie and kind but distracted Tante Lorraine. (But our foster parents had three additional children of their own after our arrival, for a total of nine, and we were lost in the crowd of cousins.)

As we grew older we developed a small repertoire of other metafaculties. I was the first to learn how to raise a mental wall to keep my inmost thoughts private from Don, and I was always better at weaving mind-screens than he. It provoked his anger when I retreated into my private shell, and he would exercise his coercive power in almost frantic attempts to break me down. His mental assaults on me were at first without malice; it was rather as if he were afraid to be left "alone." When I finally learned to block him out completely he sulked, then revealed that he was genuinely hurt. I had to promise that I would let him back into my mind "if he really needed me." When I promised, he seemed to forget the whole matter.

Don amused himself by attempting to coerce others, a game I instinctively abhorred and rarely attempted. He had some small success, especially with persons who were distracted. Poor Tante Lorraine was an easy mark for gifts of kitchen goodies while she was cooking, for example; but it was next to impossible to coerce the redoubtable nuns who were our teachers. Both of us experimented in trying to read the minds of others. Don had little luck, except in the perception of generalized emotions. I was more skilled in probing and occasionally picked up skeins of subliminal thought, those "talking to oneself" mumblings that form the superficial layer of consciousness; but I was never able to read the deeper thoughts of any person but my twin brother, a limitation I eventually learned to thank God for.

We developed a modest self-redaction that enabled us to speed the healing of our smaller wounds, bruises, and blisters. Curing germ-based illness, however, even the common cold, was beyond us. We also practiced psychokinesis and learned to move small objects by mind-power alone. I remember how we looted coin telephones throughout two glorious summer weeks, squandering the money on ice cream, pop, and bootleg cigarettes. Then, because we were still good Catholic Franco-American boys at heart, we had qualms of conscience. In confession Father Racine gave us the dismal news that stealing from New England Bell (we didn't reveal our modus operandi) was just as much of a sin as stealing from real human beings. Any notions we might have had of becoming metapsychic master-thieves died aborning. Perhaps because of our upbringing, perhaps because of our lack of criminal imagination, we were never tempted along these lines again. Our fatal flaws lay in other directions.

The first indications of them came when we were ten years old.

It was late on a dreary winter day. School was over, and Don and I were fooling around in what we thought was an empty school gym, making a basketball perform impossible tricks. An older boy named O'Shaughnessy, newly come to the school from a tough neighborhood in Boston, happened to come along and spot us working our psychokinetic magic. He didn't know what he was seeing—but he decided it must be something big and sauntered out to confront us.

"You two," he said in a harsh, wheedling voice, "have got a *secret gimmick*—and I want in on it!"

"Comment? Comment? Qu'est-ce que c'est?" we babbled, backing away. I had the basketball.

"Don't gimme that Frog talk—I know you speak English!" He grabbed Don by the jersey. "I been watching and I seen you gimmick the ball, make it stop in midair and dribble all over your bodies and go into the hoop in crazy ways. Whatcha got—radio control?"

"No! Hey, leggo!" Don struggled in the big kid's grip and O'Shaughnessy struck him a savage, sharp-knuckled blow in the face that made my own nerves cringe. Both of us yelled.

"Shaddup!" hissed O'Shaughnessy. His right hand still clenched Don's shirt. The left, grubby and broken-nailed, seized Don's nose in some terrible street-fighter grip with two fingers thrust up the nostrils and the thumbnail dug into the bridge. Don sucked in a ragged agonized breath through his mouth, but before he could utter another sound the brute said:

"Not a squeak, cocksucker—and your brother better hold off if he knows what's good for the botha you!" The fingers jammed deeper into Don's nose. I experienced a hideous burst of sympathetic pain. "I push just a little harder, see, I could *pop out his eyeballs*. Hey, punk! You wanna see your brother's eyeballs rollin' on the gym floor? Where I could *step* on 'em?"

Queasily, I shook my head.

"Right." O'Shaughnessy relaxed a little. "Now you just calm down and do a repeat of that cute trick I saw you doing when I came in. The in-and-outer long bomb."

My mind cried out to my brother: "DonnieDonniewhatgonnaDO?

TricktrickDOit! DOitGodsake—

Thenhe'llKNOW—

O'Shaughnessy growled, "You stalling?" He dug in. I felt pain and nausea and the peripheral area of the gym had become a dark-red fog.

"Don't hurt him! I'll do it."

Trembling, I held the ball between my hands and faced the basket at the opposite end of the court. It was fully sixty feet away, more than eighteen meters. I made a gentle toss. The ball soared in a great arc as though it were jet-propelled and dropped into the distant basket. When it hit the floor it bounced mightily, came up through the hoop from beneath, and neatly returned to my waiting hands.

"Jeez!" said O'Shaughnessy. "Radio control! I knew it. Thing's a gold mine!" Raw greed glared out of his eyes. "Awright, punk, hand over the ball and the gimmick."

"Gimmick?" I repeated stupidly.

"The thing!" he raged. "The thing that controls the ball! Dumb little fart-face frog! Don't you know a ball-control gimmick like that's gotta be worth a fortune? Get me outa this backwoods hole and back to Beantown and my Uncle Dan and—never mind! Hand it over."

"Let my brother go first," I pleaded.

The big kid laughed. He crooked one leg around Don's ankle and simultaneously pushed. My brother sprawled helplessly on the floor, gagging and groaning. O'Shaughnessy advanced on me with hands outstretched. Two of his fingers were bloody.

"The ball and the gimmick," he demanded, "or it's your turn, punk."

"The only gimmick's inside my head," I said. "But you can have the ball."

I drove the rubber sphere at him with all my psychokinetic strength, hitting him full in his grinning face. His nose shattered with the impact and the ball burst its bladder. I heard a gargling scream from O'Shaughnessy and a throaty noise like a Malamute snarl from somebody else.

Help me *get* him Donnie!

The torn and flattened ball like some writhing marine organism clamping itself across a horror-stricken face. Savage sounds and big hands clawing and punching at me. The brother mind poured out its own PK spontaneously to meld with mine, strength magnified manyfold, cemented with mutual loathing, fear, and creative solidarity. Somebody shrieking as the three of us struggled beneath the basket. Then a grotesque figure like a scarecrow, its head a red-smeared dented globe. Go for it Donnie man HEY togethernow togethernow allezallez SLAM-DUNK THE BASTARD...

They found O'Shaughnessy bloody-nosed and half out of his mind with terror, stuffed headfirst into the basket so that the hoop imprisoned his upper arms. The broken basketball encased his head and muffled his cries a little, but he was never in any real danger of suffocating. We had been caught, literally red-handed, trying to sneak out of the gymnasium. O'Shaughnessy blamed us, of course, and told the story pretty much as it had happened —leaving out his own extortion attempt and assault with intent to maim. He also accused us of owning a mysterious electronic device "that the FBI'd be *real* interested in hearing about."

His tale was too outlandish to be credited, even against us, the Crazy Twins. We maintained that we had found him in his weird predicament and attempted to help. Since we were obviously both too small to have boosted a hulking lout three meters above floor-level, it was evident that O'Shaughnessy had lied. His reputation was even more dubious than ours: he was a bad hat who had been shipped off to relatives in the New Hampshire boondocks in the vain hope of keeping him out of a Boston reformatory. Following the incident with us he was retransported with alacrity and never heard from again.

We, on the other hand, were clearly not telling all we knew.

Many questions were asked. Odd bits of circumstantial evidence were noted and pondered. In the midst of the uproar we remained tight as quahog clams. Our cousins who knew (or could deduce) a thing or two rallied round loyally. The family came first—especially against the Irish saloperie! After some weeks the incident was forgotten.

But Don and I didn't forget. We hashed over and over the glorious experience of metaconcert, the two-minds-working-as-one that had produced an action greater than the sum of its parts, giving us transcendent power over a hated enemy. We tried to figure out how we had done it. We knew that if we could repro-

duce the effect at will we would never have to be afraid of anyone again.

We thought about nothing else and our schoolwork was totally
neglected; but we were never able to mesh our minds that way
again, no matter how hard we tried. Some of the fault lay in our
imperfect metapsychic development, but the greater failure was
grounded in a mutual lack of trust. Our peril at O'Shaughnessy's
hands had been sufficient to cancel our jealous individuality; but
once the danger was lifted, we reverted to our deeper mind-sets
—Don the driven, domineering coercer and I the one who
thought too much, whose imagination even at that young age
whispered where the abuse of power might lead.

Each of us blamed the other for the metaconcert failure. We
ended up locking each other out in a fury of disappointment,
thwarted ambition, and fear—and we barely missed flunking the
fifth grade.

Onc' Louie called us to him on a certain spring evening and
displayed the fatal report cards. Our cousins were all outside
playing in the warm dusk. We heard their laughter and shrieks as
they played Red Rover in a vacant lot while we stood sulkily
before our uncle and faced the time of reckoning.

"Haven't I done my best to rear you properly? Aren't you as
dear to me as any of my own children?" He brandished the cards
and his beer-tinged breath washed over us. "A few failing grades,
one could understand. But this? The sisters say that you must
make up these failed subjects or repeat a year. All summer long,
you must go to the public school in the morning. What a disgrace! Such a thing has never happened before in this family. You
shame the Remillards!"

We mumbled something about being sorry.

"Oh, my boys," he said sorrowfully. "What would your poor
parents say? Think of them, watching from heaven, so disappointed. It's not as though you were blockheads who could do no
better. You have good brains, both of you! To waste them is an
insult to the good God who made you."

We began to sniffle.

"You will do better?"

"Yes, Onc' Louie."

"Bon." He heaved a great sigh, turned away from us, and
went to the sideboard where he kept the whiskey. "Now go out
and play for a while before bedtime."

As we fled onto the front porch we heard the clink of glassware.

"Now he can get stinko in peace," Don hissed bitterly. "Rotten old drunk. Never expect him to understand. He talks about *us* being a disgrace—"

We sat together on the bottom step, putting aside our enmity. It was quite dark. The other kids were dodging around under the streetlights. We had no wish to join them.

I said, "Plenty of people flunk. He didn't have to drag Papa and Maman into it . . . or God."

"God!" Don made the word a curse. "When you come right down to it, the whole darn mess is his fault."

Horrified at the sacrilege, I could only gape at him.

He was whispering, but his mental voice seemed to shout inside my skull. "God made us, didn't he? Okay—our parents made our bodies, but didn't *he* make our souls? Isn't that what the nuns say? And what's a soul anyhow, Rogi? A mind!"

"Yes, but—"

"God made these weird minds of ours, so it's his fault we have all this trouble. How can we help it?"

"Gee, I don't know," I began doubtfully.

He grabbed me by the shoulders. The voices of the kids mingled with crickets and traffic noises and the sound of a television program that Onc' Louie had turned on inside.

"Didn't you ever stop to think about it, dummy?" Don asked me. "Why are we like this? Why aren't there any other people in the world like us? When God made us, what in hell did he think he was doing?"

"What kind of a dumb question is that? That's the dumbest thing you ever said! It's probably some kind of sin, even. You better shut your stupid trap, Donnie!"

He started to laugh, then, a smothered squeaky sound loaded with an awful triumph, and he mind-screamed at me:

He did it it's not our fault we didn't ask for this he can't blame us nobody can hell with all of them hell! hell! hell! . . .

I closed my mind to him, slamming the barrier into place as though I were locking the door of a cellar that threatened to spew out black nightmares, and then he began to snivel and beg me to open up to him again, but I got up from the steps and went back into the house, into the kitchen where Tante Lorraine was baking something and the lights were bright, and I sat at the table and pretended to do my homework.

6

OBSERVATION VESSEL
SPON-SU-BREVON [PoL 41-11000]
10 NOVEMBER 1957

THE POLTROYAN COMMANDER'S RUBY EYES LOST THEIR TWINKLE and his urbane smile faded to a grimace of incredulity. "Surely you jest, Dispensator Ma'elfoo! Personnel from my ship?"

The Krondaku's mind displayed a replay of the incident, complete with close-ups of the miscreant Simbiari scouts taken flagrante delicto. "As you see, Commander Vorpimin-Limopila-kadafin."

"Call me Vorpi. Do you mind telling me what you were doing in the vicinity of the satellite anyhow?"

"My spouse, Taka'edoo Rok, and I were doing an unscheduled survey in order to include details of its fascinatingly crude design in a report we have prepared. Our transport module was totally screened, as is the invariable custom of the Krondak Xenocultural Bureau when visiting pre-emergent solar systems. The scout craft with the Simbiari was also screened heavily, but this presented no particular obstacle to Grand Master farsensors such as Taka'edoo and myself. We considered replacing the stolen property. However, the scouts had meddled with the biomonitoring equipment, and there was a chance that the satellite might have transmitted some anomalous signal to the Earthside control station. And so we contented ourselves with taking the scouts in charge, together with their booty, and bringing them to you."

"Love's Oath," groaned Commander Vorpi. "Our tour's nearly over, and we had an almost perfect disciplinary record—up to now."

"My condolences." The Krondaku politely refrained from stating the obvious: When vessels of his own methodical race were in charge of planetary Mind observations, nothing *ever* went wrong.

"I must request that you testify at the disciplinary hearing,"

41

Vorpi said. "And perhaps you have suggestions for redress."

"Our time is limited, Commander Vorpi. We are due back on Dranra-Two in the Thirty-Second Sector for a conference on primitive orbital biohabitats, derelict and functional. We postponed presentation of our paper and sped here at maximum displacement factor when we learned that Sol-Three had just entered this phase of astronautic achievement. (Most of our investigations have involved the orbiters of extinct civilizations.) However, it will not be convenient to prolong our stay..."

"Oh, I'll call the silly buggers on the carpet right now." Vorpi sent out a thought on the imperative mode: GupGup Zuzl! Have Enforcer Amichass bring in those two scouts on report. And don't forget the contraband. I'll need you to log the hearing. Snapsnapsnap!

Dispensator Ma'elfoo glanced about the commander's directorium. "A handsomely appointed chamber," he remarked politely. "The artifacts are from Earth?" One tentacle palpated the multicolored animal-fiber carpet while another lifted an Orrefors crystal vase from Vorpi's monitoring desk.

"Souvenirs." Vorpi waved a violet-tinted hand. "The drapery textiles from the serictery secretions of certain insect larvae; the rug painstakingly knotted by hand-laborers in a desert region; the paintings by Matisse and Kandinsky, rescued from a Parisian fence; the settee by Sears Roebuck; the liquor-dispensing cabinet by Harrods. May I offer you some refreshment, by the way?"

"I would esteem some Bowmore Scotch," the Krondaku said. "My deep-sight perceives a bottle hidden away."

Vorpi chuckled as he left his desk to do the honors. "Distinctive treatment of alcohol, the Scotches. I predict a wide market for them in the Milieu—provided the Intervention does take place. Mixer?"

"Just a splash of liquid petrolatum." The two entities toasted one another. After savoring his drink, Ma'elfoo exhaled gustily. "Yes, it is as I remembered. Two orbits ago I visited Sol-Three to participate in a comparative study of aircraft evolution. We went on a survey to the British Isles and I acquired a taste for this beverage, among others. Earth technology has developed apace; but one can be grateful that the distilleries cling to tradition."

The connoisseurs enjoyed a momentary mental rapport. "Have you ever sampled the genuine rareties?" Vorpi asked softly. "Bunnahabhain? Bruichladdich? Lagavulin? Caol Ila?"

The fearsome Krondaku uttered a whimper of ecstasy. "You're

not joshing me, you fire-eyed little pipsqueak? *Caol Ila?*"

Vorpi lifted his shoulders, let a tiny smile crease his lips.

The door of the directorium slid open. The Gi GupGup Zuzl, secretary of the mission, stalked in, followed by two very young Simbiari scouts and an enforcer of the same race. Vorpi went back to his desk and sat down. The Gi declaimed:

"Commander, the prisoners taken by Grand Masters Ma'elfoo and Taka'edoo Rok herewith submit to disciplinary inquiry. Defendant names: Scout Misstiliss Abaram and Scout Bali Ala Chamirish. Charges: On this Galactic Day La-Prime 1-344-207, the defendants, on a routine inspection of the Second Earth Orbital Vehicle, did mischievously interfere with said orbiter in contravention of divers Milieu statutes and regulations, removing its subsapient passenger with intent to smuggle said creature on board the Spon-su-Brevon."

The male and the female scouts stood at attention with screened minds and dry, impassive faces. Bali Ala had a harder time of it than her comrade because the small animal in her arms was squirming wildly and resisting her attempts at coercion. The Simbiari enforcer scowled and added his coercive quotient, but the beast only struggled harder, gave a sharp yap, and jumped free. It made a dash for the still-open door and would have escaped if Ma'elfoo had not zapped its brainstem very gently, paralyzing it in its tracks.

Enforcer Amichass, mortified and glistening with green sweat, retrieved the creature and set it like a stuffed toy beside the two crewmen on report. "I'm sorry about that, Commander. A recalcitrant species that resists—"

"Never mind," Vorpi sighed. "Get on with it. What do you two have to say for yourselves? Of all the sophomoric idiocies—pinching the damn Russian dog!"

"Her name is Laika," Misstiliss said.

Bali Ala said, "The power-source of the vehicle's environmental system was almost exhausted. The animal was about to perish from oxygen lack. We—we shorted out the biomonitoring equipment and took Laika after making certain that Soviet ground control would have no indication of any anomaly."

Misstiliss added, "The orbit of the satellite is very eccentric and decaying rapidly. Sputnik II will burn up on re-entry, obliterating any trace of our interference. Laika has endured nearly a week in orbit, and we thought she might provide us with valuable research data—"

"Half-masticated lumpukit!" swore the Poltroyan commander. "You wanted to take the thing back with you as a souvenir! As a pet!"

A green droplet hung from Misstiliss's nose. He fixed his gaze on a point where the wall behind Commander Vorpi met the ceiling. "You are correct, of course, sir. We admit our guilt fully, repent of the infraction, and stand ready to accept discipline at the Commander's pleasure."

"So say I also," Bali Ala murmured. "But we really didn't do any harm."

"Won't you youngsters ever learn?" Vorpi was out of his chair and pacing in front of the pair and the dog, waving his glass of Scotch by way of punctuation. "We realize that these long surveillance tours of exotic worlds can be tedious—especially to youths who, like yourselves, belong to a race imperfectly attuned to Unity. But think of the importance of our work! Think of the Milieu's noble scheme for planet Earth and our hope that its unique Mind may eventually enrich the Galaxy!"

The Krondaku addressed Commander Vorpi on his intimate mode: *At least that's what the Lylmik keep telling us.*

"Young people," Vorpi went on, "remember your history. Think of your poor planet Yanalon, Friin-Six, that was hurled back to barbarism on the very threshold of coadunation merely because a careless botanist on a Milieu survey vessel contravened regulations and picked a single piece of fruit and spat out the pips..."

She was a Poltroyan, as I recall, said Ma'elfoo.

"The work we do, coaxing these primitive worlds toward metapsychic operancy and coadunation with our Milieu, is excruciatingly delicate. It can be jeopardized by a single thoughtless action, even one that seems harmless. This is why every infraction of the Guidance Statutes for Overt Intervention must be considered a most serious matter. One doesn't meddle frivolously with the destiny of a sapient race."

And tell that to the Lylmik as well! Ma'elfoo suggested.

His peroration at an end, Vorpi resumed his seat and said, "Now you may respond."

"We would not deliberately contravene any scheme of the Concilium," Bali Ala said stiffly, "even in the case of a patently unworthy world such as Earth, which has been showered with far more Milieu assistance than it deserves. But... the Earthlings will never know that we saved the little dog, and it has a very appealing personality. Far more appealing than that of the average human, when it comes to that! We farspoke Laika on all three of our inspection tours of the satellite, and I admit that we both became bonded to her."

The Gi smiled and whiffled its cryptomammaries. "It really *is* adorable."

Misstiliss said, "When we saw that the planetside controllers meant to let Laika die, we were outraged—and we acted. I'm sorry we violated the Guidance Statutes, but not sorry we saved the little dog."

Commander Vorpi tapped the side of the empty Scotch glass with the talon of his little finger. "A grave matter. Yet, as you said, it would seem no harm was done."

"I haven't yet logged the hearing," GupGup Zuzl insinuated slyly. "And we have enjoyed a perfect duty tour up until now . . ."

Vorpi fixed the Krondak scientist with a meaningful gaze. "However, the violation was witnessed and reported by two citizens of unimpeachable status."

Did you say Caol Ila, my dear Vorpi?

I only have two bottles.

One for me and one for Taka'edoo Rok.

"What is your disposition of this case, Commander?" the Gi secretary inquired formally.

"I don't find any infraction of Milieu statutes," Vorpi replied, "but these crewmen are clearly derelict in not having filed a report on their last inspection of the satellite Sputnik II. Let a reprimand be entered in their files, and they are sentenced to six days each on waste-water-recycling system maintenance. The animal can keep them company. Dismissed."

The Krondaku canceled his coercive grip on the dog, which came to its senses. Misstiliss scooped it up. It lapped at the Simb's glistening green face.

"Likes the way we taste," the scout said sheepishly. He and Bali Ala saluted and hurried away, taking Laika with them.

7

FROM THE MEMOIRS OF
ROGATIEN REMILLARD

BELATEDLY, AT THE AGE OF TWELVE, I DISCOVERED THAT I LIKED
to read. It was early in 1958 and every American kid was
passionately interested in the new "race for space." Our older
cousins bought science-fiction magazines and left them lying
around, and I picked them up and immediately became addicted.
They were much more exciting than comic books. But it was not
the tales of space travel that fascinated me so much as the stories
that dealt with extrasensory perception.

ESP! For the first time I was able to put a name to the powers
that made Don and me aliens in our own country. I got all worked
up over the discovery and made Don read some of the stories,
too; but his reaction was cynical. What did that stuff have to do
with us? It was fiction. *Somebody had made it up*.

I ventured beyond the magazines, to the Berlin Public Library.
When I looked up ESP and related topics in the encyclopedias,
my heart sank. One and all, the reference books acknowledged
that "certain persons" believed in the existence of mental faculties such as telepathy, clairvoyance, and psychokinesis. One and
all, the books declared that there was no valid scientific evidence
whatsoever for such belief.

I went through all the books in the juvenile department that
dealt with the brain, then checked the adult shelves. None of the
books even mentioned the mind-powers that Don and I had. The
Berlin library was rather small and it had no serious volumes
about parapsychology, only a few crank books listed under "Occult Phenomena" in the card catalog. Hesitantly, I went to the
librarian and asked if she could help me find books about people
who had extraordinary mind-powers. She thought very hard for a
moment, and then said, "I know the very book!"

She gave me one of the old Viking Portable Novel collections

46

and pointed out Olaf Stapledon's *Odd John* to me. Concealing my disappointment at the fiction format, I dutifully took it home, read it, and had the living hell scared out of me.

The book's hero was a mutant of singular appearance and extremely high mental power. He was Homo superior, a genius as well as an operant metapsychic, trapped in a world full of drab, commonplace normals, most of whom did their fumbling best to understand him but failed. Odd John wasn't persecuted by ordinary humans; there were even those who loved him. And yet he was tormented by loneliness and the knowledge of his uniqueness. In one chilling passage, he described his attitude toward other people:

> I was living in a world of phantoms, or animated masks. No one seemed really alive. I had a queer notion that if I pricked any of you, there would be no bleeding, but only a gush of wind. And I couldn't make out *why* you were like that, what it was that I missed in you. The trouble really was that I did not clearly know what it was in *myself* that made me different from you.

John's alienation led him to set up his own self-centered moral code. He financed his ambitions by becoming a ten-year-old burglar; and when he was caught at it by the friendly neighborhood policeman, he had no compunction about murdering the man to escape detection.

Later, when John was in his teens, he merely treated other people as pets or useful tools. He thought great thoughts, used his remarkable talents to make a lot of money, and traveled around the world in search of other mutant geniuses like himself. He found a fair number and proceeded to establish a secret colony on an island in the South Seas. (The inconvenient original inhabitants of the place were coerced into mass suicide; but the superfolk held a nice feast for them first.) Once John and his mutant friends were secure on their island, they set out to organize a combination Garden of Eden (they were all very young) and technocratic wonderland. They were able to utilize atomic energy by "abolishing" certain nuclear forces through mental activity. They had all kinds of sophisticated equipment at their command, yet chose to live in rustic simplicity, often linked telepathically to an Asian guru of like mind who had remained at home in his lamasery in Xizang.

The colony made plans for the reproduction of Homo superior.

The young mutants "reviewed their position relative to the universe," attained a transcendental quasi-Unity called astronomical consciousness, embraced the exotic mentalities inhabiting other star-systems—and discovered that they were doomed.

A British survey vessel stumbled onto John's island in spite of the metapsychic camouflaging efforts of the colonists. Once the secret was out, the military powers of the world sent warships to investigate. Some nations saw the colony as a menace; others coveted its assets and schemed to use the young geniuses as political pawns. Attempts at negotiation between Homo sapiens and Homo superior broke down permanently when the Japanese delegate put his finger on the basic dilemma:

> This lad [Odd John] and his companions have strange powers which Europe does not understand. But we understand. I have felt them. I have fought against them. I have not been tricked. I can see that these are not boys and girls; they are devils. If they are left, some day they will destroy us. The world will be for them, not for us.

The negotiating party withdrew and the world powers agreed that assassins should be landed on the island, to pick off the supranormals with guerrilla tactics.

Odd John and his companions had a weapon, a photon beam similar to an X-laser, that they might have used to fend off an invasion attempt; but they decided not to resist, since then "there would be no peace until we had conquered the world" and that would take a long time, as well as leaving them "distorted in spirit." So the young mutants gathered together, focused their minds upon their atomic power station, and obliterated the entire island in a fireball . . .

"You've got to read this story, Don," I pleaded, with my mind leaking the more sinister plot overtones that had frightened me— the hero's icy immorality that contradicted everything I had ever been taught, his awful loneliness, his totally pessimistic view of ordinary mankind faced with the challenge of superior minds.

Don refused. He said he didn't have time and that I shouldn't get worked up over a dumb, old-fashioned book. It had been written in 1935, and by an Englishman! I said it wasn't the story itself but what it said about *people like us* that was important. I bugged him about it and finally wore him down, and he waded through the novel over a period of two weeks, keeping his mind tight shut against me all that time. When he finished he said:

"We're not like that."

"What d'you mean, we're not? Okay—so we aren't geniuses and we'll never be able to make a million bucks on the stock market before we're seventeen like John did, or invent all that stuff or found a colony on an island. But there are things we do that other people would think were dangerous. Not just the PK, but the coercion. You're a lot better at it than me, so you ought to know what I'm talking about."

"Big deal. So I fend off guys in hockey or nudge Onc' Louie to cough up a little money when he's half lit."

"And the girls," I accused him.

He only snickered, dropped the book into my hands, and turned to walk away.

I said: DonnieDonnie when people find out they'll hate us just like they did OddJohn!

He said: Make sure they *don't* find out.

Don and I were late bloomers physically, puny until we graduated from grammar school—after which we shot up like ragweed plants in July. He was much better looking and more muscular, with a flashing grin and dark eyes that went through you like snapshots from a .30-06. His use of the coercive metafunction that used to be called animal magnetism was instinctive and devastating. From the time he was fourteen girls were crazy for him. Don Remillard became the Casanova of Berlin High, as irresistible as he was heartless. I was his shadow, cast by a low-watt bulb. Don was husky and I was gangling. His hair was blue-black and curled over his forehead like that of some pop singer, while mine was lackluster and cowlicky. He had a clear olive skin, a dimpled chin, and a fine aquiline nose. I suffered acne and sinus trouble, and my nose, broken in a hockey game, healed rapidly but askew.

As our bodies changed into those of men, our minds drifted further apart. Don was increasingly impatient with my spiritual agonizing, my manifest insecurity, and my bookish tendencies. In high school my grades were excellent in the humanities, adequate in math and science. Don's academic standing was low, but this did not affect his popularity since he excelled in football and hockey, augmenting genuine sports prowess with artful PK and coercion.

Don tried to educate me in that great Franco-American sport, girl-chasing, but our double-dating was not a success. I was by nature modest and inhibited while Don was the opposite, afire with fresh masculine fervor. The urges awakened in me by the new flood of male hormones disturbed me almost as much as my repressed metafunctions. In Catholic school, we had been lectured about the wickedness of "impure actions." I was tormented by guilt when I could no longer resist the temptation to relieve my sexual tensions manually and carried a burden of "mortal sin" until I had the courage to confess my transgression to Father Racine. This good man, far in advance of most Catholic clergy of that time, lifted the burden from my conscience in a straightforward and sensible way: "I know what the sisters have told you, that such actions bring damnation. But it cannot be, for every boy entering manhood has experiences such as this because all male bodies are made the same. And who is harmed by such actions? No one. The only person who could be harmed is you, and the only way such harm could come is if the actions become an obsession—as occasionally happens when a boy is very unhappy and shut away from other sources of pleasure. Keep that in mind, for we owe God the proper care of our bodies. But these actions that seem necessary from time to time are not sinful, and especially not mortally sinful, because they are not a serious matter. You recall your catechism definition of mortal sin: the matter must be *serious*. What you do is not serious, unless you let it hurt you. So be at peace, my child. You should be far more concerned with the sins of cheating on school exams and acting uncharitably toward your aunt and uncle than with these involuntary urgings of the flesh. Now make a good act of contrition . . ."

When I was sixteen, in 1961, I emerged a bit from my broody shell and had occasional chaste dates with a quiet, pretty girl named Marie-Madeleine Fabré, whom I had met in the library. She shared my love of science fiction. We would walk along the banks of the beautiful Androscoggin River north of the pulp mills, ignoring the sulfurous stench and taking simple joy in the dark mirrored water, the flaming maples in autumn, and the low mountains that enclosed our New Hampshire valley. She taught me to bird-watch. I forgot my nightmares of Odd John and learned to react with forbearance when Don mocked my lack of sexual daring.

There were still five of us living at home: Don and I and our younger cousins Albert, Jeanne, and Marguerite. That year we played host to a grand Remillard family reunion. Relatives came from all over New Hampshire, Vermont, and Maine—including the other six children of Onc' Louie and Tante Lorraine, who had married and moved away and had children of their own. The old house on Second Street was jammed. After Midnight Mass on Christmas Eve there was the traditional réveillon with wine, maple candy and barber-poles, croque-cignols and tourtìeres, and meat pies made of fat pork. Tiny children rushed about shrieking and waving toys, then fell asleep on the floor amid a litter of gifts and colored wrappings. As fast as the big old-fashioned Christmas tree lights burnt out, assiduous boy electricians replaced them. Girls passed trays of food. Adolescents and adults drank toast after toast. Even frail, white-haired Tante Lorraine got happily enivrée. Everyone agreed that nothing was so wonderful as having the whole family under one roof for the holidays.

Seventeen days later, when the Christmas decorations had long been taken down, there was a belated present from little Cousin Tom of Auburn, Maine. We came down with the mumps.

At first we considered it a joke, in spite of the discomfort. Don and I and Al and Jeanne and Margie looked like a woeful gang of chipmunks. It was an excuse to stay home from school during the worst part of the winter, when Berlin was wrapped in frigid fog from the pulp-mill stacks and the dirty snow was knee-deep. Marie-Madeleine brought my class assignments every day, slipping them through the mail slot in the front door while the younger cousins tittered. Don's covey of cheerleaders kept the phone tied up for hours. He did no homework. He was urged by the high school coach to rest and conserve his strength.

Everyone got better inside of a week except me.

I was prostrate and in agony from what Dr. LaPlante said was a rare complication of mumps. The virus had moved to my testicles and I had something called bilateral orchitis. The nuns had been right after all! I was being punished.

I was treated to a useless course of antibiotics and lay moaning with an ice bag on my groin while Tante Lorraine hushed the solicitous inquiries of little Jeanne and Margie. Don slept at a friend's house, making some excuse, because I couldn't help communicating my pain and irrational guilt telepathically. Marie-Madeleine lit candles to St. Joseph and prayed for me to get well. Father Racine's common sense pooh-poohed my guilt and Dr. LaPlante assured me that I was going to be as good as new.

In my heart, I knew better.

8

VERKHNYAYA BZYB, ABKHAZIYA ASSR,
EARTH
28 SEPTEMBER 1963

THE PHYSICIAN PYOTR SERGEYEVICH SAKHVADZE AND HIS FIVE-year-old daughter Tamara drove south from Sochi on the Black Sea Highway into that unique part of the Soviet Union called Abkhaziya by the geographers. Local people have another name for it: Apsny, the Land of the Soul. Its mountain villages are famed for the advanced age attained by the inhabitants, some of whom are reliably estimated at being more than 120 years old. The unusual mental traits of the isolated Abkhazians are less publicized; and if questioned, the people themselves generally laugh and call the old stories outworn superstition.

Dr. Pyotr Sakhvadze's wife Vera had done so until less than a week ago, on the day she died.

Still numb with grief, Pyotr drove like an automaton, no longer even bothering to question the compulsion that had taken hold of him. It was very hot in the semitropical lowlands and Tamara slept for a time on the back seat of the brand-new Volga sedan. The highway led through tobacco fields and citrus groves and stands of palm and eucalyptus, trending farther inland south of Gagra, where the mountains receded from the coast in the delta of the great River Bzyb. The road map showed no Upper Bzyb village, but it had to lie somewhere in the valley. Pyotr turned off the highway onto the Lake Ritsa road and pulled in at a village store at the lower end of the gorge.

"I'll buy us some bottles of fruit soda here," Pyotr said, "and ask the way. We don't want to get lost in the mountains."

"We wouldn't," Tamara assured him gravely.

Pyotr's laugh was uneasy. "Just the same, I'll ask."

But the woman in the store shook her head at his inquiry. "Upper Bzyb village? Oh, there's nothing for tourists there, and the road is nothing but a goat-track, suitable only for farm trucks. Better to go to the lovely resort at Lake Ritsa."

When Pyotr persisted she gave vague directions, all the while maintaining that the place was very hard to find and not worth the trip, and the people odd and unfriendly to boot. Pyotr thanked her and returned to the car wearing a grim expression. He handed his daughter her soda. "I have been told that the road to Upper Bzyb is impossible. We simply can't risk it, Tamara."

"Papa, don't worry. They won't let anything happen to us. They're expecting us."

"Expecting—! But I never wrote or telephoned—"

"Mamenka told them we'd come. And they told me."

"That's nonsense," he said, his voice trembling. What was he thinking of, coming here? It was madness! Perhaps he was un-hinged by sorrow! Aloud, he said, "We'll turn around at once and go home."

He started up the car, slammed it into reverse gear, and stamped on the accelerator so abruptly that the engine died. He cursed under his breath and tried again and again to start it. Damn the thing! What was wrong with it? With *him*? Was he losing his mind?

"You've only forgotten your promise," the little girl said.

Aghast, Pyotr turned around. "Promise? What promise?"

Tamara stared at him without speaking. His gaze slid away from hers and after a moment he covered his face with his hand-kerchief. Vera! If only you had confided in me. I would have tried to understand. I'm a man of science, but not narrow-minded. It's just that one doesn't dream that members of one's own family can be—

"Papa, we must go," Tamara said. "It's a long way, and we'll have to drive slowly."

"The car won't start," he said dully.

"Yes it will. Try."

He did, and the Volga purred into instant life. "Yes, I see!

This was also their doing? The old ones waiting for us in Verkh-nyaya Bzyb?"

"No, you did it, Papa. But it's all right now." The little girl settled back in her seat, drinking the soda, and Pyotr Sakhvadze guided the car back onto the gorge road that led deep into the front ranges of the Caucasus.

The promise.

In the motor wreck a week earlier, as Vera lay dying in her husband's arms, she had said: "It's happened, Petya, just as little Tamara said. She told us not to go on this trip! Poor baby . . . now what will become of her? I was such a fool! Why didn't I listen to them? . . . Why didn't I listen to her? Now I'll die, and she'll be alone and frightened . . . Ah! Of course, that's the answer!"

"Hush," the distraught Pyotr told her. "You will not die. The ambulance is on its way—"

"I cannot see as far as Tamara," his wife interrupted him, "but I do know that this is the end for me. Petya, listen. You must promise me something."

"Anything! You know I'd do anything for you."

"A solemn promise. Come close, Petya. If you love me, you must do as I ask."

He cradled her head. The bystanders at the accident scene drew back in respect and she spoke so low that only he could hear. "You must take Tamara to my people—to the old ones in my ancestral town of Upper Bzyb—and allow them to rear her for at least four years, until she is nine years old. Then her mind will be turned toward peace, her soul secure. You may visit Tamara there as often as you wish, but you must not take her away during that time."

"Send our little girl away?" The physician was astounded. "Away from Sochi, where she has a beautiful home and every advantage? . . . And what relatives are you talking about? You told me that all of your people perished in the Great Patriotic War!"

"I lied to you, Petya, as I lied to myself." Vera's extraordinary dark eyes were growing dim; but as always they held Pyotr captive, bewitching him. He knew his wife's last request was outrageous. Send their delicate child prodigy to live with strangers, ignorant mountain peasants? Impossible!

Vera's whisper was labored. She held his hand tightly. "I

know what you think. But Tamara must go so that she will not be alone during the critical years of mental formation. I . . . I helped her as best I could. But I was consumed with guilt because I had turned my back on the heritage. You know . . . that both Tamara and I are strange. Fey. You have read Vasiliev's books and laughed . . . but he writes the truth, Petya. And there are those who will pervert the powers! Our great dream of a socialist paradise has been swallowed by ambitious and greedy men. I thought . . . you and I together, when Tamara was older . . . I was a fool. The old ones were right when they counseled watchful patience . . . Take Tamara to them, to the village of Verkhnyaya Bzyb, deep in the Abkhazian mountains. They say they will care for her . . ."

"Vera! Darling Vera, you must not excite yourself—"

"Promise me! Promise me you will take Tamara to them!" Her voice broke, and her breath came in harsh gasps. "Promise!"

What could he do? "Of course. Yes, I promise."

She smiled with pallid lips and her eyes closed. Around them the gawkers murmured and the traffic roared, detouring around the accident on the busy Chernomorskoye Chaussée just south of Matsesta. In the distance the ambulance from Sochi was hooting, too late to be of any use. Vera's hands relaxed and her breathing stopped, but Pyotr seemed to hear her say:

The few years we have had together were good, Petya. And our daughter is a marvel. Some day she will be a hero of the people! Take care of her well when she returns from the village. Help her fulfill her great destiny.

Pyotr bent and kissed Vera's lips. He was calm as he looked up at the medical attendants with their equipment, introduced himself, and gave instructions for the body to be taken to the medical center for the last formalities. With his wife's death, the enchantment was broken. Dr. Sakhvadze put aside the morbid fancy that had taken hold of poor Vera and himself and resumed rational thinking. The promise? Mere comfort for a dying woman. Little Tamara would stay home where she belonged with her father, the distinguished head of the Sochi Institute of Mental Health. Later, after the child had received appropriate therapy to assuage grief, they would scatter Vera's ashes together over the calm sea. But for the present, it would be best if Tamara was spared . . .

When Pyotr came at last to his home that evening, the old housekeeper greeted him with eyes that were red from weeping and a frightened, apologetic manner. "She forced me to do it, Comrade Doctor! It wasn't my fault. I couldn't help it!"

"What are you babbling about?" he barked. "You haven't broken the news to the child, have you? Not after I instructed you to leave it to me?"

"I didn't! I swear I said nothing, but somehow . . . the little one knew! No sooner had I put the telephone down after your call, than she came into the room weeping. She said, 'I know what has happened, Mamushka. My mother is dead. I told her not to go on the trip. Now *I* will have to go away.'"

"Idiot!" shouted the doctor. "She must have overhead something!"

"I swear! I swear not! Her knowledge was uncanny. Terrible! After an hour or so she became very calm and remained so for the rest of the day. But before going to bed tonight she—she forced me to do it! You must believe me!" Burying her face in her apron, the housekeeper rushed away.

Pyotr Sakhvadze went to his daughter's room, where he found her sleeping peacefully. At the foot of Tamara's bed were two large valises, packed and ready to go. Her plush bear, Misha, sat on top of them.

The Lake Ritsa Road followed the Bzyb River gorge into the low range called the Bzybskiy Khrebet, a humid wilderness thick with hanging vines and ferns and misted by waterfalls. At one place, Tamara pointed off into the forest and said, "In there is a cave. People lived there and dreamed when the ice came." Again, as they passed some ruins: "Here a prince of the old ones had his fortress. He guarded the way against soul-enemies more than a thousand years ago, but the small minds overcame him and the old ones were scattered far and wide." And when they arrived at a small lake, glowing azure even under a suddenly cloudy sky: "The lake is that color because its bottom is made of a precious blue stone. Long ago the old ones dug up the stone from the hills around the lake and made jewelry from it. But now all that's left is underwater, where people can't get at it."

"How does she know this?" muttered Pyotr. "She is only five and she has never been in this region. God help me—it's enough to make one take Vasiliev's mentalist nonsense seriously!"

Up beyond the power station the paved route continued directly to Lake Ritsa via the Gega River gorge; but the storekeeper had told Pyotr to be on the lookout for an obscure side road just beyond the big bridge, one that angled off eastward, following the main channel of the Bzyb. He slowed the car to a snail's pace and vainly scanned the dense woods. Finally he pulled off onto the exiguous verge and said to Tamara:

"You see? There's nothing here at all. No road to your fairy-tale village. I was told that the turning was here, but there's no trace of it. We'll have to go back."

She sat holding Misha the plush bear, and she was smiling for the first time since Vera's death. "I love it here, Papa! They're telling us, 'Welcome!' They say to go on just a bit more. Please."

He didn't want to, but he did. And the featureless wall of green parted to reveal a double-rut track all clogged and overhung with ferns and sedges and ground-ivy. There was no signpost, no milestone, no indication that the way was anything more than a disused logging road.

"That can't be it," Pyotr exclaimed. "If we go in there, we'll rip the bottom right out of the car!"

Tamara laughed. "No we won't. Not if we go slow." She clambered into the front seat. "I want to be here with you where I can see everything—and so does Misha. Let's go!"

"Fasten your seat belt," the doctor sighed.

Shifting into the lowest gear, Pyotr turned off. The wilderness engulfed them, and for the next two hours they bounced and crawled through a cloud-forest of dripping beeches and tall coni-fers, testing the suspension of the Volga sedan to the utmost. The track traversed mountain bogs on a narrow surface of rotting puncheons and spanned brawling streams on log bridges that rumbled ominously as the car inched across. Then they came to a section of the road that was hewn from living rock and snaked up the gorge at horrific gradients. Pyotr drove with sweat pouring down the back of his neck while Tamara, delighted with the spec-tacular view, peered out of her window at the foaming rapids of the Bzyb below. After they had gone more than thirty-five kilo-meters the canyon narrowed so greatly that Pyotr despaired. There could not possibly be human habitation in such a desolate place! Perhaps they had missed a turning somewhere back in the mist-blanketed woods.

"Just five minutes more," he warned his daughter. "If we don't find signs of life in another kilometer or so, we're giving up."

But suddenly they began to ascend a series of switchbacks leading out of the gorge. At the top the landscape opened miraculously to a verdant plateau girt with forested uplands that soared in the east to snowy Mount Pshysh, thirty-eight hundred meters high, source of the turbulent Bzyb. The track improved, winding through alpine meadows down into a deep valley guarded by stands of black Caucasian pine. Stone walls now marked the boundaries of small cultivated fields, and in the pastures were flocks of goats and sheep. The track dead-ended in a cluster of white-painted buildings sheltered by enormous old oak trees. Twenty or thirty adults stood waiting in a tight group as Pyotr drove the last half kilometer into Verkhnyaya Bzyb and braked to a stop in a cloud of dust.

In this place the sun shone and the air had an invigorating sparkle. Weak with fatigue and tension, Pyotr sat unable to move. A tall stately figure detached itself from the gathering of villagers and approached the sedan. It was a very old man with a princely bearing, dressed in the festive regalia of the Abkhazian hills: black karakul hat, black Cossack-style coat, breeches, polished boots, a white neck-scarf, and a silver-trimmed belt with a long knife carried in an ornamented silver scabbard with blue stones. His smiling face was creased with countless wrinkles. He had a white mustache and black brows above deep-set, piercing eyes. Eyes like Vera's.

"Welcome," the elder said. "I am Seliac Eshba, the great-great-grandfather of your late wife. She left us under sad circumstances. But her marriage to you was happy and fruitful, and I perceive that you, Pyotr Sergeyevich Sakhvadze, also share the blood and soul of the old ones—even though you are unaware of it. This gives us a double cause to rejoice in your coming."

Pyotr, craning out the car window at the old man, managed to mumble some response to the greeting. He unsnapped his seat belt and Tamara's and opened the car door. Seliac Eshba held it with courtesy, then started around to Tamara's side; but the little girl had already opened her door and bounded out, still keeping a tight grip on Misha the bear. At that same moment more than a dozen young children carrying bouquets of late-summer flowers dashed out from behind the crowd of adults calling Tamara's name.

She ran to meet them, shouting gleefully. "Nadya! Zurab! Ksenia! It's me! I'm finally here! Hello, Akaky—what pretty flowers. I'm so hungry I could almost eat them! But first, take me to the little house before I burst!" Giggling and chattering, the children led Tamara away.

Pyotr, white-faced, said to Seliac, "She knows their names! Holy Mother, she knows their names."

"Your daughter is very special," Seliac said. "We will care for her like a precious jewel. Be of good heart, grandson. I'll tell you everything you must know about us in due time. But first let me take you to a place where you can refresh yourself after your long drive. Then we invite you to join us for the special meal that we have prepared in your honor—and Tamara's."

It was not until the middle of the afternoon that the last toast was raised by Great-Great-Grandfather Seliac, the tamadar.

"To the soul—which now must pass from the old ones to the young!"

"To the soul!" chorused the banqueting villagers, lifting their glasses. But then Dariya Abshili, who was Tamara's great-great-aunt and the chief organizer of the feast, exclaimed: "Hold! The children must also drink this time."

"Yes, yes, the children!" everybody shouted. The young ones, who had been segregated at their own table in the outdoor dining pavilion, where they bounced up and down and celebrated in their own fashion during the long meal, now left their seats and filed solemnly up to stand on either side of Seliac. Grand-Uncle Valeryan Abshili, a stalwart of seventy years, poured a small portion of rich Buket Abkhaziy wine into each child's glass, coming finally to Tamara, who had the place of honor closest to Seliac. The old man bent and kissed the girl's brow, then let his electric gaze sweep over the assembly.

"Let us drink now to the soul . . . and to this little one, the daughter of our poor lost Vera, who is destined to announce our ancient secret to the world and open the door to peace."

This time the villagers responded without words. Pyotr, befuddled with a surfeit of wine and food, was surprised to find that he had no difficulty at all hearing them:

To the soul. To Tamara. To the secret. To peace.

They drank, and there was much cheering and clapping, and a few of the oldest women wiped their eyes. Then the indefatigable Dariya began to direct the clearing of the table. Younger men drifted off to attend to certain necessary chores before the next phase of the celebration, which would include dancing and singing. Old folks ambled out of the open-air shelter to take their ease, the men replenishing their pipes and the women gossiping softly, like pigeons. When Pyotr thought to look about in search of Tamara, he discovered that she had run off into the golden sunshine together with the other youngsters. A pang of loss touched his heart as he realized that she belonged to the village now. She was part of the soul.

Seliac arose from the table and beckoned Pyotr to come for a stroll. "There are still some questions of yours that I must answer, grandson. And a few that I would ask you."

They followed a path among the houses that led into a grove of venerable walnut trees, their branches heavy with green-husked fruit. Pyotr said, "I will have to begin my return journey soon. The thought of negotiating that road in darkness freezes my balls."

"But you must stay the night! I offer you my own bed."

"You are very kind," Pyotr said with distant formality. "But I must return to my duties in Sochi. There are patients at the Institute for Mental Health requiring my urgent attention. I bear heavy responsibilities and the—the loss of Vera will make my workload that much greater until adjustments can be made."

"She was your comrade as well as your wife." The old man nodded slowly. "I understand. You were well suited to each other both in temperament and in the blood. Instinctively, Vera chose well even as she defied us. The ways of God are ingenious."

The two walked in silence for a few minutes. Somewhere a horse whinnied and children let out squeals of laughter. Then the old man asked, "Are you of Georgian heritage entirely, grandson? Your flame-colored hair and fair complexion suggest the Cherkess."

"I am descended from both races," Pyotr said stiffly. His spectacular hair, now mercifully graying, had been somewhat of an embarrassment to him throughout his professional life. He had passed it on to Tamara, who gloried in it.

"The Caucasian peoples are all rich in soul," Seliac observed, "even though some of the tribes scanted its nurturing as modern ways overcame the ancient customs . . . And is it not true that one of your ancestors belonged to a group even more brilliantly ensouled than the folk of Apsny? I am speaking of the Rom. The Wanderers."

Pyotr looked startled. "There was an old scandal whispered about my maternal grandmother, that she had been impregnated by a gypsy lover before her marriage. But how *you* should know that—"

"Oh, grandson," laughed the 123-year-old patriarch of Verkh-nyaya Bzyb. "Surely you have guessed by now why I know it, just as you know what kind of special human being your late wife was, and what your daughter is, and why you were commanded to bring her to us."

Pyotr stopped dead, turning away from the old man in a fury, willing himself to be sober again, free of the thrall of this be-witched village Vera had rebelled against so many years earlier, when she had run away to the Black Sea Coast and civiliza-tion . . .

"Vera left us," Seliac said, "because she did not love the man we chose to be her husband. And she took seriously the tenets of dialectical materialism presented in the schoolbooks, with their naive, romantic view of the perfectability of human nature through a mere socialist revolution. Vera came to believe that our ancient soul-way was superstition, reactionary and elitist, contra-vening the basic socialist philosophy. And so she denied her birthright and went to Sochi just before the Great Patriotic War. She threw herself into hospital work and studies, remained a val-iant maiden, and seemed wed to Party loyalty and her profession of healing. She almost managed to forget what she had been, as others have done when distracted by the turmoil of modern times. Over the years we called out to her, but there was never an an-swer. We mourned her as lost. But all unknown to us, quite late in life she had found you, her ideal mate, and when she was forty-two your marvelous child was born."

"Tamara . . ."

Pyotr still refused to face the village elder. He stood on the stony bank of a brook at the edge of the walnut grove, looking over the countryside. The steep little fields and pastures were a green and golden patchwork on the slopes. Crowded against their low rock walls were hundreds of white-painted hives, piled high like miniature apartment complexes, the homes of mild-tempered Caucasian bees that flew about everywhere gathering late-season nectar for the aromatic honey that provided the village with its principal income. Thyme was still blooming, and hogweed and melilot and red clover, filling the crisp air with fragrance. Grass-hoppers sang their last song of doom before the frost, which had already whitened the highest northern ridges below the spine of the Bokovoi Range. It was here in these mountains that Jason had sought the Golden Fleece; and here that Prometheus stole the divine fire; and here that defiant tribes guided by sturdy centenarians withstood wave after wave of conquering outlanders: Apsny, Land of the Soul, a place of legends, where human minds were said to accomplish wonders that conventional science deemed impossible! But not all scientists scoffed, Pyotr recalled. There were other believers besides the egregious Vasiliev. The great Nikolai Nikolayevich Semyonov, who had won the 1956 Nobel Prize for Chemistry, had spoken in favor of psychic research, and it was studied seriously in Britain and America. But even if such things as telepathy and psychokinesis did exist, did they have *pragmatic* value?

Seliac Eshba bent and picked up a green walnut fruit from the ground. "Does this?" he inquired, his dark eyes twinkling. "It is a thing with a tough husk; and if you break into it, it stains the fingers badly, and then there is a second inner shell that must be cracked before the meat is reached. But the walnut is sweet and nourishing, and if a man is patient and long-sighted he may even plant it in the ground and someday reap a thousandfold." Seliac scrutinized the green ball and frowned. "Ouff! A weevil has been at this one." Cocking his arm, he flung the useless thing over the brook into the pasture. "Perhaps the goats will eat it ... but for the finest trees, one must choose the best possible seed."

"As you have?" Pyotr's laugh was bitter. "You draw a striking analogy. But even if it's a valid one ... Tamara is only one little girl."

"But a mental titan. And there are others—not many yet, but increasing in numbers—all over the world."

Pyotr whirled about to lock eyes with the village elder. "You can't possibly know that!"

"We do know."

"I suppose you claim some kind of telepathy—"

"Only a little of that, and not over great distances. The real knowledge comes because of our close rapport with the earth, with her seasons and rhythms, those of the year and those of the aeon. This land round about you with its hidden fertile valleys and secret caves is the place where humanity first learned to dream. Yes! It happened here, in the Caucasus, as the great winter ebbed and flowed and primitive people honed their minds yearning for the glories of spring. The hardships they endured forced them toward the long fruition. Do you know that walnut trees will not bear fruit in the tropics? They need the winter. In the old days, they needed it twice! Once to stimulate the fruit to form, and again to rot the thick husks so that the inner nut would be set free to germinate. Our human cycle is much longer, but we, too, have passed through our first great winter and attained the power of self-reflection. Over the ages our minds have ripened slowly, giving us greater and greater mastery over the physical world, and over our lower nature."

"Oh, very good! And now I suppose the superior nuts are ready to fall! The winter of nuclear war that threatens—is this what will bring about your mental revolution? Are we to look forward to supermen levitating over glowing ashes, singing telepathic dirges?"

"It might work out that way," the old man admitted. "But think: One doesn't have to wait for the walnut husks to rot naturally, not if one is determined—and not afraid of stained hands. Work with us, grandson. Help us prepare Tamara to meet her peers, to use her great gifts worthily. There will be a price you and I must pay, but we dare not wait passively for the terrible season to do our work for us . . ."

Seliac held out his brown-dyed hand to Pyotr, smiled, and waited.

9

BERLIN, NEW HAMPSHIRE, EARTH
21 OCTOBER 1966

THE NOTION OF KILLING DON INSINUATED ITSELF INTO HIS MIND AS he was clocking out of the paper mill that Friday afternoon, and the other office workers called out to him.

The women: "Night, Rogi! Save a pew for us at the wedding."

The men: "See you at the Blue Ox tonight. We'll give that big stud a sendoff he'll never forget!"

And the snide crack from Kelly the Purchasing Agent, Rogi's boss: "Hey—don't look so down in the mouth, fella. The best man always wins, even when he loses!"

Rogi grinned lamely and muttered something, then plunged into the stream of exiting employees with long strides.

After the bachelor party. He could do it then. Don would be so drunk that his mental defenses would be shaky and his offensive coercion and reflexes slowed. The two of them would have to cross the bridge over the Androscoggin on the way back to the rooming house.

(Am I going crazy? My God, am I seriously considering killing my own brother?)

My PK would be strong enough. It had been the last time, when the fishing boat tipped in Umbagog Lake. Only my *will* had been too weak.

(An accident! Of course it had been an accident. And unthinkable not to haul Don up from the depths, swim with him to shore, and pump life back into him . . .)

A car went by Rogi as he walked through the parking lot, windows down and radio playing. His throat constricted. The song was "Sunny," and that had been his private, precious name for her. But she had willingly surrendered it to Don along with all the rest.

Rogi went down to walk along the wide river. It was a fine evening, with the sun just gone behind Mount Forist and the trees touched with color from the first light frosts: the kind of evening they had loved to share, beginning with the days they had walked back from the library. There was a certain grove of trees down by the shore, on the other side of the CN tracks, and a large flat rock. The trees muffled the noise from the traffic along Main Street and gave an illusion of privacy.

He found himself coming upon the place, and she was waiting for him.

"Hello, Rogi. I hoped you'd come. I—I wished you would."

And my mind's ear heard you!

He only nodded, keeping his eyes on the ground.

"Please," she begged him. "You've avoided me for so long and now there's no more time. You must understand. I want tomorrow to be a happy day."

"I wish you every happiness, Sunny . . . Marie-Madeleine. Always."

Mentally, he saw her hold out supplicating hands. "But it'll all be spoiled if you're miserable at the wedding, Rogi. If you blame Don. He couldn't help what happened any more than I could.

Love is without rules. Quand le coup de foudre frappe . . ."

He laughed sadly. "You're even willing to use French when you talk about him. But with me, you pretended you didn't understand. It made me bold. I said things to you that I'd never dare say in English. Very casually, so the tone wouldn't give me away. Sneaking les mots d'amour into ordinary conversation and thinking what a sly devil I was."

"You were very sweet."

"And of course you really did know how I felt. From the start."

"Of course. And I learned to love you. I mean—to love being with you. No! Oh, Rogi, try to understand! With Don it was so different. The way I feel about him—"

He clenched his teeth, not trusting himself to speak. His eyes lifted and met hers, those innocent blue eyes lustrous with tears. His mind cried out to her:

You were mine! It went without saying. All we had to do was wait until we were old enough. That was sensible, wasn't it? And he had so many others to choose from, so many other girls he could have taken. *Did* take. Why did he need you, too, Sunny?

She said, "Rogi, I always want you to be my dearest friend. My brother. Please."

The temptation had been strong but now it became overwhelming, a compulsion thundering in his brain that battered away the camouflage of abstraction he had erected to disguise it. Kill Don. Tonight.

He said, "Don't worry about me, Sunny. It'll be all right."

She was weeping, clutching the strap of her shoulder bag in both hands and shrinking away from him. "Rogi, I'm so sorry. But I love him so much."

He wanted to take her in his arms and dry her tears. He wanted to shout: You only think you love him! You don't realize that he's bewitched you—coerced you. When he's dead you'll come to your senses and realize that the one you really love is me. You'll cry bitter tears for him, but in time you'll forget that you ever loved anyone but me.

Aloud he said, "I understand. Believe me."

She smiled through the tears. "Be his best man tomorrow, Rogi, and dance with me at the wedding. We'll all drink champagne and be happy. Please tell me that you will."

He took her gently by the shoulders and kissed the top of her head. The smooth hair was as pale and shining as cornsilk. "I'll do whatever it takes to make you happy, Sunny. Goodbye."

Dave Valois nearly ruined the plan when he insisted on driving the two of them home after the bachelor bash at the Blue Ox. But Rogi pointed out that walking a mile in the fresh air was just what Don needed to sober up.

"Gotta burn off some of that booze. Ol' Donnie's got such a skinful, he'll be in a coma tomorrow 'less he walks it off. Father Racine won't 'preciate a zombie groom. No, sir! You just leave ol' Don to me."

It was three in the morning, the Ox was closed tight, and the gang was dispersing in dribs and drabs, bidding farewell with honks and convivial hollering. Valois and some others protested a bit, but gave in when Rogi took his twin's arm and started slowly down Main Street with him. Don was all but unconscious. Only Rogi's coercion kept him upright and plodding along the sidewalk. Dave circled the block in his Ford and came back to yell, "You *sure* you don't want a ride?"

"Damn sure," said Rogi. "See you in church."

A few minutes later, he and Don were virtually alone, walking slowly toward the bridge. It was a chilly night with no wind. The Androscoggin was a wide pool of ink reflecting a flawless duplicate of upside-down streetlights and the omnipresent pillars of steam that rose from the pulp mills.

Under his breath, Rogi chanted: "Pick 'em up and lay 'em down. Pick 'em up and lay 'em down. Attaboy, Donnie. Just keep slogging."

"Argh," said Don. His mind was a merry-go-round of fractured images and emotions—hilarity, triumph, anticipation, and erotic scenarios featuring Sunny and himself. He didn't suspect a thing. Rogi had thrown off most of the effects of inebriation and was concentrating on maintaining his mental shield and keeping Don moving. The two of them made slow progress to the center of the bridge. A few cars drove along Main Street, but none made the turn to cross the river.

Rogi came to a halt. "Hey—looky here, man! Look where we are."

Don uttered an interrogatory grunt.

"On the bridge, kid," Rogi caroled. "The good old bridge.

Hey, remember what we used to do in high school? Walk the rail! Drive the other guys nuts. They didn't know we could use our PK to balance."

Don summoned concentration with a mighty effort. He giggled, exuding good-natured contempt. "Yeah, I 'member. You were chicken, though, till I showed you how."

"I'm not chicken now, Don," Rogi said softly. "But I bet you are."

The railing was not exceptionally high. It was of metal, wide and pipelike, interrupted every nine meters or so by a lamp stanchion. The two young men stood by one of those stanchions now and Rogi wrapped Don's arm around it so he wouldn't fall down.

"Watch this!" Grasping the lamppost in one hand, Rogi vaulted up. "I'm gonna do it now, Don. Watch!" He extended his arms, teetered a little, then began walking steadily along the pipe. The deep Androscoggin was a star-flecked black mirror nearly twenty meters below. Don could swim, but not strongly. It wouldn't take much mental strength to keep him under in his present condition. The tricky part was getting him off the bridge without laying a hand on him.

"Wah-hoo! Boy, that's a kick!" Rogi skipped along the pipe, which was a hand's span in width. When he reached the next stanchion he hugged it and swung himself around and around, cackling madly. "Oh, that's great! C'mon, Donnie. Now it's your turn."

Rogi jumped to the pavement and faced his brother, tensing.

Don blinked. His teeth gleamed in a crooked grin. "Don't wanna."

Rogi's guts lurched sickeningly. God! Had he leaked the hostility after all? Given himself away? "Aw. What'sa matter, Don? You too scared to walk the rail? Or maybe your li'l heart's throbbin' too hard, thinkin' about Sunny."

"Ain't my heart throbbin'," Don said, leering.

Rogi kept a grip on himself. "Then you're chicken."

"Nope. Just drunk 's a skunk."

"Well, so'm I—but I walked the rail. I'm just as smashed as you and I walked the fucker. Thing is, I don't lose the power when I've got a snootful—and you do."

"Like hell!" Don balled a fist. "Famme ta guêle!"

"I'll shut up when you walk, pansy!"

Don gave a bellow, seized the stanchion in both hands, and

hauled himself up. It was perfect. Even if someone saw them there could be no suspicion of foul play. Rogi was ten meters away and Don had taken his first step.

"So long, Don," Rogi said. "I'll take good care of Sunny."

He exerted both PK and coercion with all his strength.

Don screamed and his feet flew out from under him. For a split second he hung unsupported except by his own panic. Then he fell, but he caught the railing and clung to it, kicking. His heavy boots clanged against the ironwork. Rogi concentrated on his brother's hands, lifting the fingers from the dew-slippery metal one by one.

Don was crying his name and cursing. His fingernails broke and his hands slid down the uprights and scrabbled to the toe-plates and the rough concrete footing. Black blood from his lacerated skin splattered the front of his windbreaker. There was a long cut across his right cheek. Don's PK seemed to have deserted him but he still clung to the bridge with all his considerable physical strength, no longer wasting energy in kicking. Waves of rage and imperfectly aimed coercion spewed from his brain.

"Let go, damn you!" Rogi cried. He felt his own powers beginning to weaken. His skull seemed about to burst. He would have to take a chance—get up close and stamp on Don's hands—

He was blind. Deprived of both vision and farsight.

A voice said: No, Rogi.

Unable to perceive his target, Rogi found that his coercion and psychokinesis were useless. He let out a shout of despair and relief and dropped like a dead man to the pavement. The voice that addressed him was calm and remote:

Once more it seems that I am fated to intervene. How interesting. One might conjecture that Don survived in some other fashion, and yet the proleptic foci show no asymmetry as a result of my obtrusion . . .

Rogi lifted his head and groaned. "You! You again."

It said: Your brother must live, Rogi. He must wed Marie-Madeleine Fabré and beget children of her according to the great pattern. One of those children will become a man of high destiny. He will not only possess mental powers more extraordinary than his father's, but he will understand them—and help the whole human race to understand them. This child unborn will have to overcome great hardship. He will need consolation and guidance that his parents will be unable to supply, and the friendship of another operant metapsychic. *You* will be that child's friend and mentor, Rogi. Now get up.

Nonono goaway let me kill him Imustonlyway must KILL—

Rogi, get up.

Better perhaps weboth die freaks damned unrealmen unrealhuman kill them kill them BOTH intowaterdowndowndissolve—

Du calme, mon infant.

Best. Would be best.

You know nothing. Nothing! Get up, Rogi. You will remember everything I have said and you will act upon it at the appropriate time.

"You're not *my* Ghost at all." The realization filled him with irrational sorrow.

The thing said: All of you are my responsibility and my expiation. Your entire family. Your entire race.

With great difficulty, Rogi climbed to his feet. He was no longer blind and he could see Don standing under a lamp, swaying, one hand over his face. Poor old Donnie.

The Ghost said: Your brother has forgotten your attack. His injuries are healed. Take him home, put him to bed, and get him to the church on time.

Rogi began to laugh. He rocked and roared and stamped his feet and howled. He wouldn't have to do it after all, and he wouldn't be damned. Only poor Donnie, not him. The Ghost, that meddling shit, had turned "Thou shalt not" into "Thou canst not" and set him free! Oh, it was so funny. He couldn't stop laughing . . .

The Ghost waited patiently.

Rogi finally said to it, "So I let Don have his way. Then later on I become a kind of godfather to his child prodigy."

Yes.

Fury took hold of him suddenly. "But you couldn't let *me* be the kid's father! You couldn't let me marry Sunny and beget the superbrat myself. Don's genes are Homo superior and mine are—"

The Ghost said: You are sterile.

Don was walking shakily toward him. A single car turned off Main Street onto the bridge, slowed as it passed them, then accelerated again when Don waved mockingly at it.

"I'm sterile . . ."

The Ghost said: The orchitis you suffered five years ago destroyed the semeniferous tubules. Your self-redactive faculty was inadequate to repair the damage. You function as a male but will sire no offspring.

No little Odd Johns to dandle on his knee? Rogi was quite unconcerned. The responsibility for unleashing the freaks on the world would be Don's, not his! But pride made him say, "Heal me! You could. I know it."

It is not possible, nor is it appropriate. When the design is complete you'll understand. For now, let it be. But take heart, because you have a long life to live and important work ahead of you.

It was drunken lunacy! A nightmare. And all at once Rogi was deathly tired. "I don't know what the hell you're talking about. Go away. For God's sake, leave me alone!"

I'll go for now, but I'll be back... when I'm needed. Au 'voir, cher Rogi.

Don came stumbling up, a bleary smile on his face. "Hey, Rogi, you look bad, man. Never could hold your liquor. Not like me. C'mon, man, let's go home."

"Right," Rogi said. He draped an arm over his brother's shoulder. Supporting each other, the two of them went off into the night.

10

EXCERPTS FROM:
ADDRESS GIVEN BY DR. J. B. RHINE
AT THE ANNUAL CONVENTION OF THE
AMERICAN PSYCHOLOGY
ASSOCIATION
WASHINGTON, DC, EARTH
4 SEPTEMBER 1967

SOME IMPRESSION OF THE SPREAD OF PSI RESEARCH OVER THE world in recent years can be had from facts connected with the McDougall Award. This annual event, like the Parapsychological Association, was initiated at Duke in 1957 and was later adopted by the Institute for Parapsychology when it took over the laboratory. The Award is granted each year by the Institute staff for the most outstanding contribution to parapsychology published during the preceding year by workers not on the staff of the Institute. During the ten years in which the awards have been made, two have been given for American contributions and two for British, with one divided between the two countries; one award each was made to Czechoslovakia, India, the Netherlands, South Africa, and Sweden.

Another indication of the expansion of parapsychology may be had from the establishment of new research centers. A number of these have had the sponsorship of psychiatry, such as the one at Maimonides Hospital in Brooklyn, one at the Department of Psychiatry at the University of Virginia, and a third at the Neuropsychiatric Institute at the University of California at Los Angeles. Others with more physically and technologically oriented connections are located at the Newark College of Engineering in New Jersey, the Department of Biophysics at the University of Pittsburgh, and the Boeing Research Laboratories in Seattle.

The center in Leningrad is in the department of physiology; that at Strasbourg, in psychophysiology; and the laboratory at St. Joseph's College in Philadelphia, in the department of biology. Psychology-centered psi research in the university is found mainly in foreign countries rather than in the U.S. City College in New York has what may rightly be called a center; and at Clemson University, as well as at branches of the University of California (Los Angeles, Berkeley, Davis), psychologists are allowed to do psi research. But something more like centers have long existed in Europe at Utrecht and Freiburg. More recently work has begun that seems firmly planted in psychology departments at the Japanese Defense Academy and the Universities of Edinburgh, Lund, and Andhra (India). Some recognized research, of course, is not connected with any institution whatever, as, for example, the work of Forwald in Sweden and that of Ryzl while still in Prague.

One of the noteworthy changes taking place in the present period is the development of more teamwork with workers in other branches and the use of skills, knowledge, and equipment of many other research areas. Some of the psi workers today are working with physiological equipment or with computer analyses; others are depending on electronic apparatus in the measurement of psi performance or utilizing new devices in statistics. Numbers of them are using psychological tests or perhaps working in a laboratory of microphysics, or of animal behavior. . . .

Psi research is obviously of special concern to those who are interested in the full range of the unexplored nature of man, over and above the existing subdivisions of science. As has happened already in many of the smaller branches, parapsychology is certain to find itself grouped sooner or later with other fields in one or more of those composite sciences which are reshaping the modern structure of knowledge—groupings such as the space sciences, the earth sciences, the microbiological sciences, or such major disciplines as medicine, education, and the like. When we come eventually to the state when the *sciences of man* take a pre-eminent position, we shall find that one of the places around the conference table will have to be reserved for parapsychology.

If the findings are as important as they seem to workers in this field, we shall need no great concern over future recognition by the academic world, by the larger bodies of the sciences, and by other institutions that matter. Rather, the urgent needs today have to do with holding on to the firm beginning psi research has made. This research science needs to operate for the present mainly in the freer terrain of the independent institute or center, or with such semiautonomous attachments as may be found in hospitals, clinics, engineering schools, smaller colleges, and industrial research laboratories. In time its own roots will make the attachments that are right, and proper, and lasting. Such growth is slow, but it can be assisted by careful effort and understanding and by recognition of its significance.

11

FROM THE MEMOIRS OF ROGATIEN REMILLARD

AFTER THE WEDDING OF DON AND SUNNY I WAS MISERABLE FOR months. I toyed with the notion of moving out of town and went so far as to peruse the "Help Wanted" column in the Manchester and Portland newspapers. But by Christmas the entire family knew that Sunny was pregnant, and I presumed that my subconscious was in thrall to the Ghost and its great expectations for the unborn—and so I stayed.

Since that night on the bridge, Don and I had erected virtually impregnable mental bulwarks against each other. Our social relationship was affable on the surface, but mind-to-mind communication was now nonexistent. I avoided Don and Sunny as much as I decently could. It wasn't difficult, since they had moved into a circle that included mostly young married couples like themselves. I saw them during holiday get-togethers and at the funeral of Tante Lorraine late in March. They seemed to be happy.

I continued at my job in the purchasing department of the mill and Don worked in shipping, some distance away in another building. I feel certain that he was doing as I was during those days: trying to live as much like "normal" as possible. I no longer used psychokinesis, and I confined my coercive manipulations to feather-light nudges of the office manager, a dour Yankee named Galusha Pratt, who looked upon me as hard-working, ingratiating, and deserving of advancement when the right spot came along.

During my leisure hours I practiced cross-country skiing and went hiking in the mountains, and I continued to read whatever books I could find that dealt seriously with paranormal mental activity. My researches were still on the impoverished side, however, and would remain so until the 1970s, when the legitimate science establishment finally began to concede that "mind" might be more than an enigma best left to philosophers and theologians.

The child was born on 17 May 1967, some seven and a half months after his parents' wedding. He was a small baby with an oversized head and the charitable consensus was that he was premature. My first sight of him was eleven days later, when I drove him to church for the baptism. He looked pink, adequately fleshed, and not at all unfinished. Sunny's sister Linda and I renounced Satan and all his works on behalf of the infant, and then Father Racine trickled cold water over the hairless, swollen little skull and baptized him Denis Rogatien.

Little blue eyes with shocked, dilated pupils flew wide open. The baby sucked air and let it out in a wail.

And his mind clutched at me.

What I did was instinctive. I projected: [Comfort.]

He protested: *!!!* [cold] + [wet] = [discomfort] *CRY!*

I said: [Discomfort.] CRY. [Reassurance.]

He was dubious: ? !! *CRY!*

I amplified: Soon MOTHERyou soon youMOTHER. [Comfort.]

He was figuring it out. [Heartbeatwarmsecuregraspmilksuck-LOVE] = MOTHER? Cry...

I said: [Affirmation.] MotherGOOD CRY. [Comfort + reassurance.]

He said: LoveYOU. [Acceptance trust peace.]

Then he went back to sleep, leaving me reeling.

It amazed me when the baby demonstrated telepathic ability at such an early age; but I didn't realize just what *else* was amazing until I thought the thing over lying in bed that night, and did a crude replay of the incident. There in the church, distracted by the ceremony and the relatives standing around, I had not been consciously aware of the feedback taking place between my mind and the infant's. But the replay made it clear—and explained why I still felt an uncanny closeness to that small mind asleep in its crib on the other side of town.

I jumped out of bed, turned on the lights, and rooted through my boxes of books until I found several on developmental psychology. They confirmed my suspicion. Not only was my nephew a telepath, but he was also a *precocious* telepath. His mind had displayed a synthesizing ability, an intellectual grasp far above that of normal newborn infants. He was hardly out of the womb, and yet he was thinking, drawing conclusions in a logical manner.

I knew what I was going to have to do. I spent the rest of the night thrashing and cursing the Family Ghost, and in the morning I called in sick at work. Then I walked to the little rented house on School Street to tell Sunny what kind of a brother-in-law she had, and what kind of a husband, and what kind of a baby son.

It was a glorious day. Spring flowers bloomed in the little front yards and even dingy Berlin looked picturesque instead of shabby. She came to the door with the baby in her arms, an eighteen-year-old Madonna with long fair hair and an unsuspecting smile of welcome. We sat in the kitchen—bright yellow and white enamel, café curtains, Formica counters, and the scent of chocolate cake in the oven—and I told her how Don and I discovered we were telepaths.

I wanted to make the revelation as gentle as possible, so I did it in the form of a life history, starting with the incident of the bear in the raspberry patch. (I left out the Ghost.) I explained how my brother and I only gradually came to understand our singularity, how we experimented with mindspeech and image projection and deep-sight even before we started school. I demonstrated how easy it is to cheat on exams when farsight enables you to read a paper lying open ten feet away—behind you. I told her about psychokinesis and revealed the secret of how young O'Shaughnessy got stuffed into the basketball hoop. I discreetly moved a kitchen chair around the floor to demonstrate the PK facility. (She only smiled.) I explained why Don and I had early decided to keep our abilities secret. I went into detail about *Odd John* and my fearful reaction to it. Some instinct warned me not to mention the coercive metafaculty to her—and of course I said nothing about my conviction that Don had used some mesmerizing power to win her away from me. Of the terrible events that took place on the eve of the wedding I spoke not at all.

My long recital took most of the morning. She listened to it almost without speaking but I could feel the tides of conflicting emotion sweeping over her—affection for me and fear for my sanity, disbelief coupled with profound unease, fascination overlaid by a growing dismay. As I talked, she made us lunch and fed the baby. When I finally finished and sat back exhausted in my chair, she smiled in her sweet way, laid her hand over mine, and said:

"Poor dear Rogi. You've been awfully troubled these past months, haven't you? And we hardly saw you, so we didn't know. But now we'll see—Don and I—that you get help."

Behind those dear blue eyes was a flat refusal to even consider the truth of what I had told her. Adamant denial. And worse than that was a new kind of fear. Of me.

God . . . I'd bungled it. I projected meekness, nonthreat, pure love. Sunny, don't be afraid! Not of this thing. Not of me.

Very quietly I said, "I can't blame you for being skeptical, Sunny. Lord knows it took years for Don and me to come to terms with our special mind-powers. It's no wonder that the notion seems outrageous to you. Crazy. Frightening, even. But . . . I'm the same old Rogi, and Don is still Don. The fact that we can talk without opening our mouths or move a thing around without touching it doesn't make us monsters."

As I said it, I knew I was lying.

She frowned, wanting to be fair. Early-afternoon sun streamed into the small kitchen. On the table were cups with dregs of cold tea, and plates with cake crumbs, and a bowl of fragrant lilacs making a barrier between us. She said, "I read once about some studies that were made at a college. Extrasensory perception experiments with flash cards."

I seized the opening eagerly. "Dr. Rhine, at Duke University! You see? It's respectable science. I have books I can show you—"

"But no one can read another person's mind! It's impossible!" Her panic stung me like a whip and there was outrage, too, at the possibility of mental violation. "I couldn't bear it if you knew my secret thoughts. If Don did!"

I summoned all sincerity. "We can't, Sunny. It's not like that. You normals—I mean, people like you—are closed books to telepaths. We can feel your strongest emotions and sometimes we receive images when you think about something very intensely. But we can't read your secret thoughts at all. Even with Don, I can only receive the farspeech he *wants* to transmit."

Partial truth. It was very difficult to decipher the innermost thoughts of normals, but often enough they were vaguely readable, especially when highlighted by strong feelings. And then many persons "subvocalized"—mumbled silently to themselves —when they weren't talking out loud. We could pick up this kind of stuff rather easily. The problem was to sort it, to make sense of the conceptual-emotional hash that floated like pond-scum at the vestibule of an undisciplined mind, confusing and concealing the inner thoughts. Most of the time, you instinctively shut all that mental static out to keep from being driven crazy.

I said, "You never have to worry that I'd spy on you and Don through his mind, either. We put up mind-screens automatically now to shut one another out. It's a trick we learned years ago. I'd never pry into your life with him, Sunny. Never . . ."

She flushed, and I knew I'd seen through to at least one of her great fears. She was a conventional, modest young wife and I loved her for it.

"These so-called superpowers," I said, "aren't really any more unusual than being able to play the piano well, or paint beautiful pictures. They're just something we were born with, something we can't help. You've read about people who seem to predict the future. And—and water-dowsers! My God, that's an old New England thing that nobody around these parts thinks twice about, but it must seem like black magic to people who aren't used to it. I think there may be lots of other telepaths, too, and psychokinetics, but they're afraid to admit having the powers because of the way normals would react."

(But if there were others, why hadn't we been able to contact them? And why hadn't researchers like Rhine found them—instead of the unreliable and ambiguously talented "psychics" who participated in his experiments?)

Sunny said, "I *want* to believe you, Rogi."

"There was a particular reason why I came here today. It wasn't just to unburden my own mind. I'd never have intruded on you for my own sake. Not even for Don's. But now there's Denis."

She sat there frozen with fresh disbelief. "Denis?"

"Yesterday at the christening I felt a wonderful thing. The baby's mind communicated with me. No—don't look shocked. It was marvelous! He was startled by the water poured on him and I reached out telepathically without thinking, used the kind of mental soothing Don and I used to share when we were little kids. And Denis responded. He did more than that! There was—a kind of creative flash, something very special. At first I only transmitted formless feelings to him, trying to calm him and make him stop crying. He grabbed at the comfort but it wasn't enough, so I let my mind say, 'Soon you're going to be back with your mother, and everything will be all right.' Only I said it in the kind of mental shorthand that Don and I sometimes use, not projecting real words, just the concept of mother and baby together and happy. And do you know what Denis did? He made a connection in his mind between his own notion of mother and the image I projected! It's what psychologists call a mental synthesis, a putting together. But . . . a baby as young as Denis shouldn't have been able to do that yet. He's too young. In another month or two, yes. But not yet."

She said coldly, "My baby did nothing of the kind."

"But he did, Sunny. I'm certain of it."

"You're imagining things. It's ridiculous."

"Look," I said reasonably. "You go get Denis and I'll try to show you. He's not even asleep in there. He's listening—"

"No!" She radiated a fierce, protective maternal aura. "My baby's normal! There's nothing wrong with him!"

"He's more than normal, Sunny. Don't you see? He's probably some kind of ESP genius! If you really want proof, you could probably have him tested at one of the colleges or hospitals that are doing—"

"No, no, no! He's just an ordinary baby!" She jumped to her feet and the fear came pouring out of her like a cataract of ice. "How can you say these things to me, Rogi? You're sick! Sick with jealousy because I married Don and had his child. Oh, go away! Leave us alone!"

Exasperated, I began to shout at her. "You can't hide your head in the sand! You know I'm not crazy and you know that what I've told you is the truth! Your own mind gives you away!"

"No!" she screamed.

I gestured. The vase of lilacs on the table rose two feet in the air. I sent it soaring across the kitchen to the bowl of the sink and let it fall with a crash. In another room, the baby let out a terrible cry. Sunny came at me like a tigress with her hands clenched into fists and her eyes blazing.

·"You freak! You bastard! Get out of my house!"

I had never in my life touched her with my coercion, but there was nothing else to do.

Sit down.

Her voice choked off and she turned into a statue, except for her widening eyes. Her face was a tragic mask, open-mouthed in silent screaming.

Sit down.

Somewhere the baby was howling like a wild thing, reacting to the emotion of his mother. Sunny's eyes implored me but I held her fast. Two tears rolled down her frozen cheeks. She let her eyelids close and volition evaporated. She sank slowly onto one of the chairs. Her head fell forward, veiled by the long blond hair, and she wept without making a sound.

Don't be afraid. Stay right there.

She wasn't hearing my precise telepathic words, of course, only their meaning filtered through the larger coercive impulse. I went and got Denis, wrapped him in a blanket, and handed him carefully to his mother. Then I freed her mind from the compulsion and projected reassurance at the baby.

CRY. [Tranquility.] "It's okay, Denis. Maman's fine now."

His wails ceased abruptly. He hiccupped and sniffed.

I extended my hand to the child, pointing my index finger, and exerted the lightest invitation. The baby's eyes were still swimming but his tiny mouth curved in a smile. A bare doll-like arm came out from under the blanket, reached unerringly, and clasped the end of my finger in a firm grip. I said:

ROGI [touch] DENIS. I/Rogi—you/Denis. Rogi [love] Denis.

There was a sudden radiant concordance. Even Sunny must have sensed it for she gave a slight gasp. The baby cooed.

"Your name is Denis," I said.

The baby made a small sound.

"Denis," I repeated.

The little face shone. His mind said: DENIS! His voice uttered the same funny little noise.

"He's trying to say his name," I explained to Sunny, "but his vocal cords and tongue really aren't hooked up properly to his brain yet. But his mind knows that he's called Denis."

Sunny rocked the child without speaking. She was still weeping softly but the horror was gone, leaving only bewilderment and reproach. Oh, Sunny, I'm so sorry you were afraid, so sorry for my clumsiness . . .

"But I had to do it," I told her, no longer coercing but pleading for understanding. "I couldn't let you go on denying. It wouldn't be fair to Denis. You're going to have to be brave for his sake. He's a *responsibility*. He probably has all the special mental abilities that Don and I have—plus more. I think he has superior intelligence, too. If that giant brain of his has a chance to develop properly, he'll grow up to be a great man."

She was now entirely calm. The infant basked in self-satisfaction and yawned. She held him tightly against her breast. "What am I going to do, Rogi? Will—will they take him away from me?"

"Of course not! For God's sake, Sunny—when I said you could have him tested by scientists, I only meant that you could do it if you felt you had to. To prove he was—what I said. But nobody can force you to give Denis up for experiments. No way! Not in this country. If he was my son—"

She looked at me expectantly.

I was standing so close to her and the child that their combined aura enveloped me. There was relief and dependency emanating from her, and from the baby a strengthening variant of the harmonious bond I had felt earlier.

Denis [love] Rogi.

Oh, Denis, you can't! You're not mine. She's not mine. It's Don you have to imprint on. Your real father. Not me . . .

She asked quietly, "What would you do if Denis was your son?"

I heard myself speaking dispassionately. "The people who run those ESP labs wouldn't have the faintest idea how to give this baby what he needs. They're only normals. They've only dealt with normals. Denis needs to be taught by others like himself. Only his father and I are able to mindspeak him, so Don will have to—will have to—"

DENIS/ROGI!

Mind to mind the bond was forging, whether I willed it or not. The child was catching me just as he had earlier caught his mother, as all babies form a linkage with their nearest and dearest.

Denis, no! Not me! (Bless me, Father, for I have sinned. Attempted murder. Yes, we'd both been drinking. Yes, I was out of my mind for love of her. Yes, I'm sorry sorry sorry . . . Thank you. No, Don never even knew. It was all in my mind? No, I don't think so, but perhaps—perhaps—I don't know. Two months' fast and abstinence and a good act of contrition and it's over and gone and I'll never forget never . . .)

Sunny was saying, "Don help me teach the baby? Well, I suppose we could ask him. He loves Denis, of course, but he's terribly old-fashioned. I can't get him to change diapers or even give Denis his bottle. What would Don have to do?"

My heart sank. I might have known. The Family Ghost knew all along, of course. If it *was* a ghost.

"Well, Don would have to spend time with the baby. Talk to him, mind to mind. Show him mental pictures. Help him learn control of his faculties."

She made a dubious little moue. "I suppose I can try."

"This is important, Sunny! Listen. When Don and I were babies, Tante Lorraine hardly had time to give us the love and attention ordinary babies need—and God knows she wasn't a telepath. So we grew up stunted."

Sunny opened her mouth to protest, but I held up my hand and rushed on.

"Stunted in our use of the ESP powers, I mean. Look. Have you ever read about feral children, ones raised by animals or locked away from human contact by criminal parents? When they get out at last into the normal world they're hardly human at all because they were deprived of a certain kind of education they needed when their young minds were most impressionable. Don and I seem to be normal men—but we're really cripples, too. We should have had somebody to teach us how to use our special mind-powers when we were tiny babies. All my psychology books say that the first three years of life are critical for mental development. That must hold true for special powers even more than for ordinary ones. Don and I discovered our powers accidentally and developed them in a haphazard way. We've never been comfortable with them. Don doesn't understand them at all and I'm—I know a bit more about them than he does, but not enough."

"You would have to explain to Don what had to be done."

"Yes, of course. I'll work out some kind of general outline. Denis would need to interact with both of you. There'd be a lot of things you could do alone, Sunny—reading aloud to him, just talking to him. I have a book by Piaget, a famous French child psychologist, that I'll let you read. It gives the step-by-step process of a baby's learning. Really fascinating."

She nodded, holding the child close. The little boy's eyes were fixed on me and there seemed to be an air of puzzlement about him. I realized then that I had erected a mental barrier against his persistent reaching out. He was rooting against the obstruction like a puppy trying to dig under a wall.

No child no.

ROGI!

He forced himself on me. I tried to break eye contact with him and found that I could not. There was a strength and determination in him that was formidable, for all his immaturity, and I felt myself weakening. Babies! They have ways to insure their survival that even the normals are aware of. Mental ways. Why else do we think a helpless, noisy, smelly, demanding, inconvenient little travesty of a human being is almost irresistibly adorable!

No!

ROGImyROGI. [Love.]

My mental armor was dissolving. And then Denis smiled at me, and the trap closed.

Sunny said, "We mustn't let any outsiders know the truth about Denis for a long time. Not until he's old enough to protect himself from people who might exploit him. We'll teach him to be cautious—and to be *good*." She cuddled his head against her cheek. "Strange little superbaby. How will I ever keep up with him? I wonder how Mama Albert managed?"

"Little Albert was a disappointing child," I told her. "He didn't even speak until he was four."

I went to the sink and began to gather up the broken pieces of the lilac vase. It was quite a mess.

Don came home from work that evening and found Sunny and me sitting with the baby on the front porch. While she made supper, he and I had our first telepathic exchange in more than a year. I told him what I had done, and why.

At first he laughed, and then he was enraged when I told him it was his moral duty to undertake the special education of his son. We got into a shouting match in the living room and Sunny came running to put herself between us. Then she proceeded to beat down every objection Don could think of, all the while radiating such passionate devotion to him and to Denis that I was astounded. It was plain even to a fool like me that coercion was not the force that bound Don and Sunny—nor had it ever been.

As she finished telling him of the plans she and I had worked out for the first course of instruction, Don lifted his powerful arms in a resigned shrug. "All right! You win! I think it's a mistake to treat the kid special—but what the hell. I'll mind-speak him the way you want. But don't expect me to turn into a goddam kindergarten teacher, okay?"

Sunny flung herself against him joyously and kissed him long and hard. When he broke away from her he looked over her head and gave me a sardonic grin.

"This business of working with the kid in the evenings. The flash cards and all that crap. I'd be lousy at it. Tell you what, Rogi. You help Sunny and me teach the kid. It's just the kind of thing you'd be good at—and the whole damn thing is your idea, after all. How about it?"

"What a wonderful idea," Sunny said warmly. "Say you will, Rogi."

From the bedroom came another plea: a formless mental one.

It was hopeless. The Family Ghost had won. I said, "All right."

"Well, that's settled," Don said. "What's for supper, sweetheart?"

12

EXCERPTS FROM:
FINAL REPORT OF THE SCIENTIFIC STUDY OF UNIDENTIFIED FLYING OBJECTS CONDUCTED BY THE UNIVERSITY OF COLORADO UNDER CONTRACT TO THE UNITED STATES AIR FORCE
9 JANUARY 1969

THE IDEA THAT SOME UFOs *MAY BE SPACECRAFT SENT TO EARTH* from another civilization, residing on another planet of the solar system, or on a planet associated with a more distant star than the Sun, is called the extraterrestrial hypothesis (ETH). Some few persons profess to hold a stronger level of belief in the *actuality* of UFOs being visitors from outer space, controlled by intelligent beings, rather than merely of the *possibility*, not yet fully established as an observational fact. We shall call this level of belief ETA, for extraterrestrial actuality. . . .

Direct, convincing, and unequivocal evidence of the truth of ETA would be the greatest single scientific discovery in the history of mankind. Going beyond its interest for science, it would undoubtedly have consequences of surpassing significance for every phase of human life. Some persons who have written speculatively on this subject profess to believe that the supposed extraterrestrial visitors come with beneficent motives, to help humanity clean up the terrible mess that it has made. Others say they believe that the visitors are hostile. Whether their coming would be favorable or unfavorable to mankind, it is almost certain that they would make great changes in the conditions of human existence. . . .

The question of ETA would be settled in a few minutes if a flying saucer were to land on the lawn of a hotel where a convention of the American Physical Society was in progress, and its occupants were to emerge and present a special paper to the assembled physicists, revealing where they came from, and the technology of how their craft operated. Searching questions from the audience would follow.

In saying that thus far no convincing evidence exists for the truth of ETA, no prediction is made about the future. If evidence appears soon after this report is published, that will not alter the truth of the statement that we do not *now* have such evidence. If new evidence appears later, this report can be appropriately revised in a second printing. . . .

Whether there is intelligent life elsewhere (ILE) in the Universe is a question that has received a great deal of serious speculative attention in recent years. . . . Thus far we have no observational evidence whatsoever on the question, so therefore it remains open. . . . The ILE question has some relation to the ETH or ETA for UFOs as discussed in the preceding section. Clearly, if ETH is true, then ILE must also be true because some UFOs have then to come from some unearthly civilization. Conversely, if we could know conclusively that ILE does not exist, then ETH could not be true. But even if ILE exists, it does not follow that the ETH is true.

For it could be true that the ILE, though existent, might not have reached a stage of development in which the beings have the mechanical capacity or the desire to visit the Earth's surface. . . . We have no right to assume that in life-communities everywhere there is a steady evolution in the directions of both greater intelligence and greater technological competence. Human beings now know enough to destroy all life on Earth, and they may lack the intelligence to work out social controls to keep themselves from doing so. If other civilizations have the same limitation, then it might be that they develop to the point where they destroy themselves utterly before they have developed the technology needed to enable them to make long space voyages.

Another possibility is that the growth of intelligence precedes the growth of technology in such a way that by the time a society would be technically capable of interstellar space travel, it would have reached a level of intelligence at which it had not the slightest interest in interstellar travel. We must not assume that we are capable of imagining now the scope and extent of future technological development of our own or any other civilization, and so we must guard against assuming that we have any capacity to imagine what a more advanced society would regard as intelligent conduct.

In addition to the great distances involved, and the difficulties which they present to interstellar space travel, there is still another problem. If we assume that civilizations annihilate themselves in such a way that their effective intelligent life span is less than, say, one hundred thousand years, then such a short time span also works against the likelihood of successful interstellar communication. The different civilizations would probably reach the culmination of their development at different epochs in cosmic history. . . .

In view of the foregoing, we consider that it is safe to assume that no ILE outside of our solar system has any possibility of visiting Earth in the next ten thousand years.

13

LENINGRAD, USSR, EARTH
5 MARCH 1969

"WE HAVE SAVED THE BEST FOR THE LAST, COMRADE ADMIRAL. Please be seated here at this table with the microphones . . . You other comrades may take the chairs nearer the observation window. Dr. Valentina Lubezhny, our specialist in biocommunications phenomena, will bring the subject into the Faraday cage in just a moment. There is a small delay." Danilov offered an apologetic smirk. "The little girl was very nervous."

Kolinsky gave a curt nod and lowered his ample buttocks to the hard wooden chair. Scared children! And you are the most frightened of all, Comrade Doctor Asslicker, and rightly so, considering the flimsy quality of entertainment offered thus far in your extremely expensive laboratory. Dull demonstrations of the human bioenergetic field. A Chukchi shaman able to stop the heart of a rat (but not the heart of any creature weighing more than four hundred grams). A neurasthenic blind youth reading printed matter with his fingertips. A modern Rasputin (sanitized) laying hands on tortured rabbits and healing their wounds. A housewife doing psychokinetic tricks with cigarettes and water glasses. A gypsy who peers into a Polaroid camera lens and produces blurry "astral photos" of the Petropavlovskaya Fortress, the Bronze Horseman, and other local landmarks. (That one had looked promising—until Danilov admitted that the subject could only "envision" places where he had been. So much for psychic espionage!)

Sternly, Kolinsky said, "We have been most interested to see how far you have progressed in the area of pure research, Comrade Danilov. Still, it was not the *existence* of psychic powers that we hoped to prove. Unlike the skeptics of the West, we are quite willing to concede that the human brain is capable of such activities. However, we had hoped that after five years of work you might have uncovered a bioenergetic effect of more immediate military significance."

Danilov fiddled with the microphones, set out a pad of paper and marker-pens, saw that the naval aides Guslin and Ulyanov and the GRU attaché Artimovich were settled in. "In just a few minutes we will demonstrate the talents of our most remarkable subject. I don't think you'll be disappointed, Comrade Admiral. By no means!"

Down in the test chamber on the other side of the glass a door opened. A white-coated female scientist appeared with a red-headed girl wearing a school uniform. The child had an extraordinarily pretty face. She eyed the men in the observation booth with a certain apprehension.

Danilov hurriedly addressed the admiral and the other officers. "The girl is very sensitive to adverse mental attitudes— even more so than the other subjects you have seen today. For this experiment to succeed, we must have an atmosphere pervaded with kindness and goodwill. Please try to banish all doubts from your minds. Cultivate a positive attitude."

Commander Guslin coughed. Ulyanov lit a cigarette. Artimovich, the intelligence man, sat bolt upright with a fixed smile on his face.

Danilov picked up a microphone with blue tape wrapped around its stand. "I will introduce you, Comrade Admiral, and then perhaps you will speak a few words to the child and reassure her."

Kolinsky, who had seven grandchildren, sighed. "As you wish."

Danilov pressed the microphone stud. "All ready now, Tamara?"

The girl's voice came to them over a ceiling speaker. "Yes, Comrade Doctor."

"We have a special guest here today, Tamara. He is Admiral Ivan Kolinsky, a great hero of the Soviet Navy. He is eager to see how well you do your biocommunication exercise. The Admiral would also enjoy talking to you." The scientist made a formal gesture. "Admiral Kolinsky, may I present Tamara Sakhvadze."

Kolinsky took the microphone and winked at the child. "Now, you must not be nervous, devushka. We will leave the nervousness to Dr. Danilov." The child giggled. She had marvelous white teeth. "How old are you, Tamara?"

"Eleven, Comrade Admiral." Great dark eyes, rose-petal mouth.

"You have a Georgian name. Where is your home?"

"I live in Sochi—I mean, I used to live there before they found me and brought me here to work and go to school. Sochi is on the Black Sea."

Ah, yes—a Celtic Caucasian girl, one of that ancient breed famed through history for their beauty and bewitching ways! "I know Sochi very well, Tamara. I have a vacation villa there, a very pretty place. It must be spring in Sochi now, with flowers blooming and birds singing in the palm trees. What a pity both of us are here in wintry Leningrad instead of in your pleasant hometown."

And if I were there, I could sail my little boat—or sit at a small table in Riviyera Park, sipping a cold mix of Georgian champagne and orange juice and baking my tired bones in the sunshine. Gorgeous young things (your older sisters or cousins, Tamara!) would stroll by, tall and barelegged and bold of eye, and I would admire and remember old pleasures. When that palled I would plot the destruction of Gorshkov, that prick on wheels, and the KGB schemer Andropov, whose hobbyhorse this whole bioenergetics farce is, and put an end to it, and get on with the Extremely Low Frequency Broadcaster, just as the Yankees have done. Psychic forces as weapons! What superstitious peasants we Russians remain, in spite of our thin veneer of science and culture. One might as well speak of enlisting the terrible Baba Yaga and her hut on fowl's legs . . .

The girl laughed out loud. "You're so silly, Comrade Admiral!"

The woman scientist standing beside Tamara stiffened. Danilov said hastily, "The child is overexcited. Please excuse her rudeness. Let us begin the experiment—"

Kolinsky studied the girl narrowly. "Tamara and I have not yet finished our little talk. Tell me, devushka, what special talent do you have that interests the doctors at this Institute?"

"I read thoughts. At a distance. Sometimes."

"Can you read mine?" the admiral asked softly.

Tamara now looked frightened. "No!"

Danilov implored him. "It is most important that the child be calm, comrade! If we could begin now . . ."

"Very well." Kolinsky put the blue-marked microphone down.

Danilov signaled to his colleague. The woman took Tamara by the hand and led her to a large cubicle of copper screening that stood in the center of the test chamber. Inside it was a plain wooden chair.

"The enclosure is called a Faraday cage," Danilov explained. "It is proof against most forms of electromagnetic radiation. We have found that Tamara works best when shielded in this way. The emanations from her mind do not seem to be in any way connected to the energies of the electromagnetic spectrum, however. The 'bioenergetic halo effect' that we monitored for you earlier on your tour seems to be a side effect of the life-energies rather than part of their primary manifestation."

Kolinsky nodded, barely concealing his impatience. Within the test chamber, the girl Tamara was now completely enclosed in the copper-screen cage, sitting with her hands clasped in her lap. Dr. Lubezhny had withdrawn, and within a few minutes came into the observation booth.

"All is in readiness," she reported. "Tamara feels confident."

Danilov picked up a second microphone from the table. The tape marking it was bright scarlet. Activating it, he said, "Danilov here. Are you standing by?"

Masculine accents overlaid by static responded. "This is the diving tender Peygalitsa awaiting your instructions."

"Please give us your approximate position," Danilov requested.

"We are standing approximately nine kilometers due west of Kronshtadt Base in the Gulf of Finland."

"The divers are ready?"

"Sublieutenant Nazimov and the Polish youth are suspended at the required depth of ninety meters and awaiting your bioenergetic transmission."

"Okhuyevayushchiy!" exclaimed Commander Ulyanov.

Danilov flapped a frantic hand. "Please! No extraneous remarks! All of you—think the most refined and peaceable thoughts."

Commander Guslin smothered a chuckle.

"Stand by, Peygalitsa, we are prepared to transmit." Danilov set the red-marked microphone down.

The admiral murmured, "You are a man of surprises, Dr. Danilov."

"The experiment has worked before," the scientist said in a strained voice, "and it will work again—given the proper conditions." He glared at the two aides and the GRU man.

Kolinsky wagged his right index finger at the trio. "Not a peep from you, minetchiki."

The scientist expelled a noisy breath. He explained rapidly, "The girl Tamara is what we call an inductor. A telepathic broadcaster, the most talented we have ever found. The percipient or receiver is a seventeen-year-old Polish lad named Jerzy Gawrys, another gifted sensitive. Gawrys wears cold-water diving dress. He is holding an underwater writing pad and a stylus, but he is *not* equipped with telephone apparatus, as is his companion, Sublieutenant Nazimov. The only way that the boy Gawrys may communicate is by writing on his pad. Nazimov will relay the pad's message to the tender. The tender's radio operator will relay the data to us. Our own receiver picks it up and broadcasts it through the room speaker."

"Understood," said Kolinsky. "And what data are to be transmitted?"

Danilov lifted his chin proudly. "The data of your choice."

The aides muttered fresh exclamations of amazement.

Danilov said, "May I suggest that you start with a few simple shapes—stars, circles, squares—then pictures, then a few words. Use the pad of paper in front of you and the ink-marker. As you finish each sheet, hold it up so that Tamara can see it . . . and send the message."

Kolinsky compressed his lips, and bent to the pad. He drew a five-pointed star, raised the paper, and smiled at Tamara.

The girl stared intently.

"Star," said the diving tender Peygalitsa.

The admiral drew an arrow.

"Arrow," said the faraway relay operator.

The admiral drew a clumsy cat in profile.

"Cow," the speaker reported.

Everybody in the booth laughed. Kolinsky shrugged and drew a circle with pointed rays around it.

"Sun."

The admiral waved jovially at Tamara. She smiled and waved back. He wrote the seven Cyrillic letters that spelled a familiar greeting in Russian and held it up. The girl concentrated on them for some time.

The speaker cleared its throat, then said: "We receive from Sublieutenant Nazimov the letters zeh-deh-oh-er-oh-uncertain-oh."

Danilov picked up the red microphone. "Stand by, Peygalitsa." He told Kolinsky, "You must remain mindful that our percipient is Polish. It may be difficult for him to receive complex messages written in our script. Please keep the words as simple as possible." He alerted the boat to receive the next message.

Kolinsky printed carefully, "Tamara sends greetings." The words were returned, letter by letter, over the speaker.

"May I congratulate you, Dr. Danilov, Dr. Lubezhny." The admiral beamed on the scientists. "A splendid breakthrough!" And so Andropov had been right after all. A billion-to-one gamble seemed to have paid off and he, Kolinsky, would have to eat his ration of shit. If Tamara's talent could be taught to others, the Soviet Navy could scrub its own Extremely Low Frequency Broadcaster Project. Let the Americans use the long-wave radio system to send messages to deep-lying missile submarines—a system that worked, but was so slow that a three-letter word might take nearly a half hour to transmit. The Soviet Union would talk to its submarines via mental telepathy, in moments! As to the KGB's use of psychic powers, the less said . . .

Danilov was babbling. "You are very kind, Comrade Admiral! I know that little Tamara and the boy Jerzy Gawrys, who have worked so hard, will also be gratified by your praise. Perhaps you would like to tell them so yourself."

Kolinsky said, "First we will test one other message." He bent to the pad, then held it up to Tamara. The lovely little face glowed at him through the copper mesh, so pleased that everything had gone well, so eager to show her skill.

She saw: FIRE MISSILES.

Tamara sat still. Her dark eyes opened wider, like those of a cornered doe.

Admiral Kolinsky tapped a finger firmly against the paper.

They waited.

Finally, Danilov addressed the red microphone. "Attention, Peygalitsa. Do you have a message to reply?"

"No message," said the loudspeaker.

Kolinsky regarded the little girl without expression. So that's the way of it, little Tamara! Can one blame you? You have hardly lived at all, and the true purpose of your work did not occur to you. You are shocked and revolted. You shrink from adult wickedness. But one day, will you see such wickedness as duty? As patriotism?

"No message," said the loudspeaker.

Danilov apologized. "Perhaps the girl is tiring. Perhaps Jerzy has temporarily suffered diminished sensitivity—"

"No message," said the loudspeaker.

"I will go and speak to her," Dr. Lubezhny suggested.

"No," Admiral Kolinsky said. "Don't be concerned. I've seen quite enough for today. Please be assured that I will urge full funding of your continuing efforts here at the Institute, and I will commend your work most highly to the Council for National Defense." The admiral rose from his seat, tore the sheet of paper into small pieces, and let them sift from his hand onto the table. He beckoned to his aides and strode out the door after having given one last wave to the motionless little girl.

Dr. Danilov's eyes met those of Dr. Lubezhny. The woman said, "If only she were younger. Then it would be a game."

"She will bend to larger considerations in time," Danilov said. He picked up the red microphone and keyed it. "Attention, Peygalitsa. The experiment is ended. Thank you for your cooperation."

"Message coming through," said the loudspeaker.

Danilov almost dropped the microphone. "What's that?"

The amplified voice was brisk. "We receive another set of letters. It spells . . . nyet."

"Nyet?" exclaimed Danilov and Lubezhny in unison.

Down in the Faraday cage, Tamara Sakhvadze looked at them and slowly nodded her head.

14

FROM THE MEMOIRS OF
ROGATIEN REMILLARD

I CAME TO DON AND SUNNY'S HOUSE EVERY TUESDAY, THURSday, and Sunday evening for nearly three years. We would have supper, and Sunny would stack the dishes. Then she would bring little Denis into the living room for the educational sessions that we came to call "head-lessons."

At first Don tried to work along with me. But he had very little empathy with the infantile mind and his attempts at telepathic rapport were so crude as to be little more than mental puppet-training. Here it is, kid—learn or else! He couldn't resist teasing the baby, looking upon our work with him as an amusement rather than serious business, treating the child like some glorified pet or a sophisticated toy. The occasional mental quantum leaps made by the boy could be very exciting, and then Don was all praise and affection. But there were tedious times as well, the nuts and bolts of teaching that Don found to be a colossal bore. He would put pressure on Denis, and more often than not the session would end with the child crying, or else stubbornly withdrawn in the face of his father's mocking laughter.

As I expected, Don got tired of the teaching game after only a few weeks. Not even Sunny's pleas would move him to continue serious participation. So he watched television while Sunny and I worked with the child, and looked in with a proprietary condescension during commercial breaks. This might have been a satisfactory solution—except that babies have no tact, and little Denis couldn't help showing how much he preferred my mental tutelage to that of his father. Don's pride was hurt and he began to broadcast bad vibes that the sensitive baby reacted to, setting up a kind of mind-screen that threatened to cut him off not only from his father but also from me. I had to tell Don what was happening, dreading his reaction. He surprised me, however, and said, "What the hell! Teaching kids is no job for a man like me." And he began going out to the Blue Ox right after supper, leaving me alone with his wife and son.

I found out some time later that a burly tavern habitué named Ted Kowalski dared to make a suggestive crack about this unorthodox domestic arrangement. Don decked him with a single uppercut. Then he made a little speech to the awed onlookers at the Ox:

"My egghead brother Rogi is writing a book. It's about the way that little kids' minds work. Me and Sunny are letting him use our son Denis as a kind of guinea pig. Rogi runs tests on the kid using blocks and beads and pictures cut from magazines and other suchlike crap. Sunny helps. I used to help, too, but it was dull as dishwater. That's why I'm here, and why my brother and my wife and kid are at home. Now would anybody besides the late Kowalski care to comment?"

Nobody did, then or ever.

Don got so fond of the Blue Ox that he took to spending evenings there even when there were no head-lessons scheduled. Sunny was sorry about that but she never reproached him. She did cook especially fine meals for him on the nights that I visited, and kept urging him to stay with us and see what Denis had learned. When Don refused, as he almost invariably did, she kissed him lovingly goodbye. When he returned two hours later in a haze of alcohol, she kissed him lovingly hello. His drinking became heavier as the months went by and the baby made spectacular progress.

At Remillard family gatherings, Don boasted to one and all that he was proud as hell of his son, the genius. Denis, carefully coached by me, let the relatives see him as a child who was plainly above average—yet not so advanced as to appear bizarre. We let him start speaking in public when he was thirteen months old, three months after he had actually mastered speech. He learned to walk when he was a year old; in this and in other purely physical developments he was very nearly normal. In his appearance he favored the Fabré side of his family, having Sunny's fair skin and intensely blue eyes but lacking her beauty. He was never sick, even though he had a deceptively frail look about him. His temperament was shy and withdrawn (which was a vast disappointment to Don), and I believe that he was by far the most intellectually gifted of all the Remillards, not even excluding such metapsychic giants as Jack and Marc. There are some Milieu historians, I know, who mistook his gentleness for weakness and his innate caution for vacillation, and who say that without the psychic impetus furnished by his wife, Lucille Cartier, Denis's great work might have remained unaccomplished. To counter these critics I can only present this picture of the young Denis as I knew him, surmounting the emotional trials of his youth with quiet courage—and almost always facing those problems alone, since I was only able to aid him during his earliest years, and circumstances conspired to separate us during his latter childhood and adolescence.

I must not minimize the role that Sunny played. Denis learned to read before he was two, and she saved her housekeeping money in order to buy him an encyclopedia. Since the child had a never-ending thirst for novel sensations and experiences, she wheeled him all over Berlin in a stroller during the warm months and toted him on a sled in the winter. Later, she drove him about the countryside in the family car, until the rising cost of gasoline and Don's precarious financial situation put an end to her expeditions, and their growing family left her less and less time to spare.

The metapsychic training of Denis was left almost entirely to me. I worked hard, if inexpertly, in the development of his farsenses and wasn't surprised when his abilities quickly surpassed my own. He learned the art of long-sight amplification all by himself—and tried in vain to pass the skill on to me. His mental screening function very early became so formidable that neither Don nor I could penetrate it; aside from that, Denis seemed untalented in coercion. Psychokinesis didn't interest him much either, except as an adjunct to manipulation when his little fingers were inadequate for handling some tool, or for supporting books too heavy to be held comfortably. It was an eerie thing to come upon the child, not yet three years old, still sucking his thumb as he pursued a levitated volume of the *World Book Encyclopedia*; or perhaps sitting in unconsidered wet diapers, studying a disassembled transistor radio while a cloud of electronic components and a hot soldering iron floated in thin air within easy reach.

But I had even more disquieting experiences in store for me.

One February night in 1970 Don returned from the tavern a bit early. He was no drunker than usual, and unaccustomedly cheerful. He said he had a surprise for me, and admonished me and

Sunny to stay right where we were with Denis. He went into the kitchen and closed the door.

Denis was deeply engrossed in a new book on the calculus that I had just bought, thinking we might learn it together. Sunny was knitting. Outside the little house on School Street a frigid wind from Canada howled down the Androscoggin Valley and solidified the old snowdrifts into masses like dirty white styrofoam. I hated to think of walking home.

Don came back into the living room sans outdoor wear, carrying a cup of steaming hot cocoa. Grinning, he held it out to me. "Just what you need, Rogi mon vieux, to warm you on a truly rotten night."

My brother making a cup of cocoa was an event about as unprecedented as me doing a tap dance on the bar at the Blue Ox. I probed his mind, but the usual barriers were in place. What was he up to?

Little Denis looked up from his differentiation formulas. His eyes went first to his father, then to his mother. His expression was puzzled.

Sunny gasped.

Don held out the cup to me.

"No!" Sunny cried. She sprang from her chair and slapped the cup from Don's hand. It made an ugly brown splash on the wall. I was flabbergasted.

Denis asked me gravely, "Uncle Rogi, will *you* tell me why lysergic acid diethylamide makes cocoa taste better?"

Don started to giggle. Sunny regarded him with a terrible expression of outrage. His mind-screen, shaken by her unexpected action, wavered just enough to let me see what kind of joke he had intended to play on me. Little Denis had had no trouble penetrating Don's psychic barricade when it was still firm, and he had perceived the name of the drug emblazoned on his father's short-term memory trace as on a lighted theatre marquee.

But how had Sunny known?

Don's laughter was louder, more unsteady. "Hey, it was only a gag! This hippie came into the Ox lookin' to deal, and we were ready to throw him out on his ass when I remembered ol' Rogi jabbering about altered states of consciousness. And I thought—hey! Whole lotta talk about the wild side of the mind, but never any action. That's you, Rog."

I said, "You were going to slip the LSD into me and supervise my trip."

His grin became a grimace of pure hate. "You been experimenting. I figured it was my turn."

Sunny grabbed his arm. "You're drunk and you don't know what you're saying!"

He shook Sunny off as though she were some importunate kitten and took one step toward me, big hands opening and closing. Denis whimpered, abandoned his book, and scuttled aside.

"I know exactly what I'm saying," Don blustered. "You and your fuckin' mind-games! You turned my own kid against me! And my wife—my wife—" He faltered, looked at Sunny in a dazed fashion. His mind-walls were down and I could see the wheels turning as he made the connection about the cup of cocoa and Sunny's frustration of his plan.

"You *knew*," he accused her. His tone was confused, the anger momentarily sidetracked. "But how?"

She straightened. "Denis asked me about the LSD before he asked Rogi. Our son has been teaching me telepathy. It was to be a surprise for you and Rogi."

I was stunned. None of my books on parapsychology had prepared me for a mind capable of exercising psychoredaction, the "mental editing" faculty that is so taken for granted in Milieu pedagogy and psychiatry. I cried:

Sunny—is it true?

She didn't respond.

Denis said: Mommy can only mindspeak me. She can't hear you or Papa. You aren't strong enough.

Don looked down incredulously at the little toddler in corduroy overalls and a miniature lumberjack shirt. Denis was on his hands and knees. His lower lip trembled.

"I'm not strong enough?" Don roared. He stooped to seize the child, ready to shake him, to slap him—

Sunny sensed what was coming and I saw it clearly in Don's mind. We both started to intercept him. But it wasn't necessary.

"Papa won't hurt me," Denis said. He climbed to his feet and stood in front of his father. His head was about on a level with Don's knees. "You won't ever hurt me, will you Papa." It wasn't a question. The boy's magnetic blue eyes were rock-steady as he looked up.

"No," said Don. "No."

Sunny and I let out suppressed breath. She bent down and lifted Denis in her arms.

Don turned to me. He moved like a man in a dream, or one in

an extremity of pain. His mental walls were back in place. I had no idea what message Denis had transmitted, what coercive interdict the child had used. I knew that Denis would never be harmed by his father—but the protective aegis did *not* extend to me.

Don said, "You won't have to bother coming over in the evening anymore, Rogi."

"I suppose not," I said.

The child reached out to comfort and reassure me. In those days I knew nothing of the intimate mode of farspeech, that which tunes directly to the personal mind-signature of the recipient; nevertheless, I was aware that Denis spoke to my mind alone when he said:

We will find a way to continue.

"Denis has had enough coddling," Don said, "and Sunny's going to be too busy to play games with you two. Did she tell you she's expecting again?"

She held Denis close, her eyes brimming with tears. She hadn't. And I'd never noticed the knitting. "Congratulations," I said in a level voice.

Don was at the front closet getting my coat and things. He held them out to me, a defiant smile twisting up one side of his mouth, his thoughts unreadable.

He said, "I plan to take care of the next kid's training myself."

15

EDINBURGH, SCOTLAND, EARTH
28 JANUARY 1972

HE CLIMBED, AS HE OFTEN DID WHEN THE TENSIONS BECAME TOO great, clutching at slippery rocks and gnarled heather stems with frostbitten hands gone numb.

HALLOO!

Reveling in the height, the separation from the world of ordinary mortals, he scrabbled for precarious footholds. His mud-clotted, soggy waffle-stompers abraded the fresh blisters on his heels, adding to the welcome ensemble of pain.

HALLOO OUT THERE!

His heart was banging in his throat fit to brast. The wintry gusts blowing into the steep defile called the Guttit Haddi froze his hurdies and his ears and his chin and his nose.

HALLOO! OI! IS THERE A BODY CAN HEAR ME?

He climbed like a man pursued by demons invisible, never looking down. The spreading sea of city lights seemed to undulate dizzily below—glittering currents of traffic, dirty backwaters of tenements and shops, the up-thrust reefs of church steeples and castle ramparts and the perilous shoals of the University.

HALLOO!

Down there ran the Pleasance and on it stood the building with the laboratory. It had a grand name: the Parapsychology Unit of the Department of Psychology of the University of Edinburgh; but it was only a big dreary room up under the eaves, partitioned into cramped wee offices and carrels for the endless testing. It was presided over by the eminent Dr. Graham Finlay Dunlap, whose staff—alas!—consisted only of two graduate assistants, William Erskine and Nigel Weinstein, and him: James Somerled MacGregor, a silly gowk of twenty, by virtue of his fey talents awarded a bursary at one of the finest universities in Britain—and for all that bored and wretched and wanting only to go home to Islay in the Hebrides.

HALLOO! WHAT'S NEW? DAFT JAMIE SAYS: SOD YOU!

Climb up laughing at the uselessness of it. Climb above the winterfast reeky city toward a louring sky still scarlet in the west. Climb up the steepest, most dangerous way in shifty twilight, hurting all the while. Scramble up rocks. Creep along the igneous ridge all frosty and windblasted. Climb finally to the top of that ancient crag, that sentinel of Dun Eadain beloved of tourists and sentimentalists and trysting lovers. Climb up to Arthur's Seat!

HALLOO! HURRAW! EXCELSIOR!...

The near-gale blowing up the Forth from the North Sea now smote him squarely. To escape he sprawled bellyflaught, face cradled in his arms, and let rattling gasps from his parched throat soften while his heart tripped over itself and slowed. He licked cracked lips and tasted salt from wind-tears and wool from his sweater. The sheepy taste and the ocean taste and the smell of wet cold stone and moorland! The thrill of climbing in the high air, the pain of it, the happiness . . . and see—the humor was coming on him again, just as it used to so easily in the early days when he was still excited with the novelty of demonstrating his uncanny powers to the psychologists. He felt it coming. He knew that he was going to be able to do it again.

The thing he thought he'd lost. What they'd been coaxing him vainly to do again down in the damned laboratory for nigh on a year.

The out-of-body thing.

I'M AWAY!

Oh, aye, it was grand! To soar up and see himself left prone below, a husk without a soul. He sped into the sunset, across West Lothian's black fells and crouching Glasgow and the Firth of Clyde, over Arran and Kintyre and tiny Gigha, beyond the sea to home. To Islay, to his private place. Like a sea bird he hovered, seeing the surf crash against the shoulder of Tòn Mhór. A few sheep skirted the bog on their way downhill. Somewhere one of the dogs was barking. The ruins of the old croft near the bay sheltered a shaggy red longhorn stot. In his own snug home the lights were on and a thread of smoke rose from the chimney. Suppertime on a winter's Friday night, and Granny portioning out the sweet while Mum dished up savory haddock and fried potatoes. Dad and Colin and old Iain came trampling in tired and famished and red-cheeked.

He watched them, full of joy and with all pain abolished. Then he concentrated on the well-known dear aura. He said:

It's me! I'm here!

Granny looked up from the trifle she'd made that day for a special treat: Jamie my dear laddie. It's been so long. And how are you then?

Ah Gran I'm that miserable here at university I could die I think!

Such blether.

No no they're all fools and Dr. Dunlap the biggest of all with his testing testing testing as if he didn't *know* my powers exist but had to prove it over and over endlessly with his damned statistics and I get so tired and impatient and I feel the hostility from the other undergrads because I'm a privileged character and allowed my special academic track here in the Psychology Department and Gran dear Gran this queer mind of mine sometimes does its tricks and sometimes not but what's the use it's not as though I could use the Sight or the Speech or the Out-of-Body Thing to earn a good living as a bookie or a blackmailer or a spy Lord knows the powers are too unreliable and me too conscience-tender for that but Gran I'm beginning to think I don't want to be a psychologist either not even to study the powers if it means this endless dull dull testing not only of me but of *common* folk and Dunlap and his two assistants nattering on about "extrachance performance" and the "psi-missing effect" (which means can you believe it test results so rotten that the psi experts have decided they must be significant!) and they keep trying to find a theory in physics to fit the powers and nothing works and still they write their papers and look wise and pretend it all *means* something when we know it doesn't have to and what I'd really like to do is chuck the whole thing and go off and be a stage magician or a mind reader on the telly and make a packet like Uri Geller or the Amazing Kreskin . . .

Jamie Jamie ungrateful gorlin the time's come to stop playing with the powers selfishly as I've told ye for now they must be put to use for all mankind. And if the good Professor can't solve the problem of making the powers fit into real science then maybe the job's meant for YOU Daft Jamie MacGregor!

Ah Gran. Dunlap's department doesn't have the money to do the job proper. Ah you should see what a threadbare wee place this Parapsychology Unit is. If we were in America now it might be different for there all the colleges are rich but here in Edinburgh the two doctoral candidates working under Dunlap must live on cheese sandwiches and beer I'm all right of course eating in the Pollock dining room but—

It's time for us to eat here as well so stop your whinging. You must fulfill your part of the bargain so bear with Professor Dunlap and his perjinkities and study hard and be a credit to us. Then later if you can't abide parapsychology you can shrink silly neurotics and get rich.

Ah Gran.

Ah Jamie. Go back now. Your poor body's freezing in the haar and one of your good friends has come searching for you . . .

He opened his eyes. He was back in Holyrood Park on the pinnacle of Arthur's Seat and stiff as an iced halibut. He stood upright, tottering in the east wind, tucked his bare hands into his warm crutch, and stamped his feet. The pins-and-needles effect was exhilarating.

It was too dark now to climb down the way he'd come, for the western side of the small mountain was steep and trackless down the Haddie. And besides, the lights of Edinburgh were turning yellow and fuzzy. It was the haar, as Granny had warned him, sneaking in from the Firth to swaddle the city in freezing mizzle. He'd have to go back the long way, down the easy east path to Dunsapie Loch, and then along the Queen's Drive to the Dalkeith entrance to the park where he'd come in. A dreary mile and a half, but there was no helping it.

He came down the east side of the knoll into thickening fog. The temperature was dropping and he moved as rapidly as he could along the footpath, comforting himself with the thought that antibiotics easily cured pneumonia these days—

"Jamie!"

He heard the thin shout from below. Gran had said a friend was looking for him, hadn't she? But nobody knew where he'd gone! He cantered down a precipitous stretch of track and saw an amber light bobbing about: someone with a torch coming up to meet him.

"Oi!" he shouted. "I'm here!"

And there was a familiar stocky figure pouring out vibes of relief only slightly tainted by peevish mutterings.

"Nigel!" Jamie exclaimed delightedly. "Did you track me with psi? The hill's strongly magnetic, you know. I would've thought that—"

"Oh, put a sock in it, you young idiot, and let's get down to the car before we both freeze." Nigel Weinstein unwound a long striped muffler from his own neck, flung it at Jamie, and glowered. "You and your magnetism! Dunlap was pissed to the wide when Wee Wully Erskine told him you'd aborted the afternoon magnetometer session and run off. You bloody ass! We had a devil of a time getting that test set up with the physics boys—and now, thanks to your silly-buggery, we can go back to square one."

"I'm sorry, Nigel." The two of them came to the road. Dunsapie Loch was lost in the murk. They turned right and hurried toward the car-park at the south end. "Were you really worried about me?"

"You might have broken your neck," the graduate assistant snapped. "Where would we find another test subject with your talent? You know we're all chewing nails worrying about the new research grant."

The underlying fear leaked through his gruff words: *And who* knows what kind of stupid thing a morose young Celt might get up to on a slippery crag in the dead of winter?

"I'm not *that* depressed," Jamie told him. But thanks for caring. "As for the tests, they'd have been no good anyway. The morning runs wore me down and I just didn't have the heart to keep on. I keep telling Erskine that it's no good endlessly repeating really tough mind maneuvers. I lose motivation and get to swithering and then the powers wonk out. I'm not a bloody computer, you know. And Wee Wully's attitude is no help—Mr. Objectivity, plug me into the circuit and work me like a damn dray-horse!"

Weinstein heaved a sigh. "Dr. Dunlap would say you're suffering from a psi decline. Me—I'd label you a prima donna."

"So'd my Granny," Jamie admitted, grinning.

They found Weinstein's battered Hillman at last and climbed in. There was no traffic at all on the one-way Queen's Drive that encircled Hollyrood Park and the fog was getting so thick that the car's headlamps were worse than useless. Nigel muttered a curse, switched them off, and navigated with the ambers. He drove little faster than a walking pace. Outside was a world of dull-glowing golden cotton wool.

Jamie said, "Tests like those we were doing today are a waste of time. So I try to move drinking straws with psychokinesis and the instrument measures the perturbation of the magnetic field around my head. Super! A needle wiggles, the field gets slightly bent, and it's all recorded for posterity . . . which won't give a tinker's dam."

"The research adds to the body of parapsychological evidence."

Jamie rolled his eyes. "How much evidence do you need, man? It isn't as though the magnetic measurements told you anything *useful*. You still haven't a clue about the nature of mental energy—what forces operate during PK, how telepathic messages are carried, what mechanism enables me to travel without my body. There's no scientific theory for any of it."

"We're still assembling data. Eventually we'll fit psi phenomena and the whole notion of mind into the reality framework."

Jamie huddled closer to the warm air beginning to come from the car heater. "Weird powers have been around since caveman days. How come Australian bushmen and Eskimos and African witch doctors and fire-walking Hindus can use the powers and not worry about it—but scientists can't? Science flies to the moon, but it diddles and daddles and wrings its hands when the mind performs its psychic tricks, and needs to be convinced over and over again that it's not all a sham. As far as useful theory goes, we're not much wiser today in 1972 than we were in 1572 —when people blamed it all on the devil and burnt blokes like me at the stake... For God's sake, why can't we simply buckle down and *use* the powers without the endless havering?"

Weinstein laughed. "Science likes things it can measure. Psi powers are too slippery for comfort. So we must try to analyze them, try to formulate theories and test them. And if psychic research had the kind of financial backing that astronautics has, we'd get results."

"I used to think so," Jamie said slowly, "but I've chewed over the matter a lot lately. And I've about concluded that there may be a basic flaw in the entire concept of psi research—one that makes our kind of research futile."

"Bosh!"

"No—listen to me, Nigel. All over the world scientists have been doing serious studies of psi effects. The Russians are keen on it because they think it might make a weapon. Give them credit for a pragmatic attitude, anyhow! The Yanks are a touch leery just because the Russkies believe in it—but they have quite a few dedicated research groups, and the American Association for the Advancement of Science *did* finally admit the Parapsychological Association to membership. Our British teams are going full throttle. There's good work being done by the Dutch and the Indians and the Finns and the Japs and the Germans. Nobody who matters laughs at us anymore or calls us crackpots. The consensus in scientific circles is that psi effects are real. But... the net *practical* result of nearly twenty years of activity has been just about nil! You still get untrained people finding water with forked sticks, and fakirs treading hot coals, and faith healers laying on hands and curing the sick, and all the rest of the disorganized clamjamphrie of PK and telepathy and precognition and all the rest—unreliable and unexplainable—while trained researchers still have no coherent results from their experiments."

"That's no reason to label our work futile—"

"What if the human race had the eyesight of a mole? Could we develop a science of astronomy? Of course not! The appropriate sense organs would be too weak even to notice the stars, much less organize scientific data concerning them. I think that's the way it is with psi and normal humanity right now. Most human beings have some kind of parapsychological capability, but it's so weak and undependable that it might as well not exist. The few people like me who have stronger powers are still too ill-equipped to demonstrate much that's useful. I think that science won't get off the ground analyzing higher mind-powers until really efficient psychic operators are born."

"You're saying that our data will remain essentially incomplete until . . . mental giants come along. Until the brain evolves further."

"Exactly. When people have full control of their paranormal faculties—whether they're born with it, or develop control through training—*then* we'll be able to do valid testing. Nigel, I know I'm right! I'm one of the flawed ones myself—not totally eyeless, but still only seeing the stars as off-again, on-again blurs . . . Just look at the fog outside this car of yours. Would you know there was a great city all around Arthur's Seat if you spent your entire life in a car, cruising around and around this misty drive, only catching a rare glimpse of the lights outside? And with Edinburgh only a half-seen mystery, would you even dream that other cities existed?"

They glided through mustard-colored murk, searching for the exit road. And then a gust of wind blew the swirling vapors aside for a moment and they saw the junction ahead, and both of them gave exclamations of relief, and Nigel said, "You see? Breakthroughs do happen. Take a lesson, Jamie." He turned the regular headlamps back on and made the turn.

"You want us to keep traveling our research road, no matter how foggy, until we find a way into the hidden city—and maybe a body with radar eyes."

"A muddled metaphor, but thine own."

Jamie grinned at the older man. "You poor buggers working under Dunlap are luckier than most. At least you've got me. Not quite as blind as a mole. More in the hedgehog class, maybe."

Weinstein sighed. "And to think I'm basing my doctoral thesis on you! I'd do better to creep back to the family tog-shop on Duke Street."

Jamie said, "I'll quit mucking up, Nigel. Just promise me . . . when you do get your degree, stay on at the university. Work with me on *useful* experiments, not this codswallop that Dunlap insists on. You came out to get me tonight knowing exactly where I was. We know what that has to mean. Let's train my clairvoyance and yours, too, instead of stifling it with trivia.

Let's show the world that psychic powers are serious business."

"Conceited little twit. All you want is my life, eh? All right—you're on!" Weinstein peered through the windscreen at indistinct blobs of light marking Dalkeith Road. "Now suppose you use your clairvoyance, or your out-of-body faculty, or *some* damn thing to find us a nice pub."

16

RIVER FOREST, ILLINOIS, EARTH
9 JUNE 1973

ALDO "BIG AL" CAMASTRA STEPPED OUT OF HIS AIR-conditioned study into the muggy, music-filled evening and closed the French doors behind him. He was smiling, for the business with the union reps and the party bagmen from Chicago had gone very well indeed. Now he was free to circulate among the guests like a proper host, just as Betty Carolyn had begged him to do. Family business came first, of course; but he wanted to keep her happy on their Twenty-Fifth Anniversary, and besides, there were some people around that he should glad-hand.

Nick and Carlo were patiently waiting on patio chairs, ever alert. Big Al nodded to them. "Party going good?"

"Really swinging, Al," Carlo said. "Joe Porks even brought this broad who sang on the Johnny Carson show. Terrific! Sort of a Cher, but with boobs."

Big Al laughed, adjusted his silk cummerbund, and shot his cuffs so the big gold links just peeked out from the sleeves of his dinner jacket. "Did Rosemary get here?"

"Frankie drove her in from O'Hare about an hour ago," Nick said. "Her plane was delayed. She went to change."

They went down the flagstone steps with Carlo leading and Nick bringing up the rear. The big garden behind the Camastra mansion was lit with skeins of Japanese lanterns in addition to the bronze lamps illuminating the rose beds. A marquee for refreshments had been set up near the west wing and there were throngs of guests moving about inside of it. Another considerable crowd had gathered around the portable dance floor where tables and chairs made an outdoor cabaret flanked by flower beds. The big band was playing "Leaving the Straight Life Behind." Some forty couples gyrated to the music without ever engaging in body contact.

Big Al grimaced contemptuously at the sight of them. "They call that dancing? Everybody doing their own thing, bumping and grinding like a buncha Clark Street hookers?"

The two soldiers guarding the patio steps greeted the Chicago Boss respectfully and stepped aside so he and his bodyguard could enter the crush of the party. The bolder guests began to converge immediately—businessmen and politicians and lobbyists and fellow mobsters and their expensive women. The relatives and smaller fry hung around in the backyard, clutching drinks and waving.

"Happy Silver Anniversary, Al!"

"Mazel tov, Al baby!"

"Wonderful party, Mr. Camastra. Quite a showplace you have here!"

"Lemme get a glassa spumante for you, Al."

"Mr. Camastra, I think we met in Springfield at the last session—"

Shaking hands, smiling, and returning compliments, he wove expertly through the crowd. Nick and Carlo were always a few steps behind. He accepted the best wishes of a Chicago alderman, kissed his wife's sister, gave a polite brush-off to a hollow-eyed banking executive, told a dapper monsignor that he'd be delighted to contribute to the parish carillon fund, and congratulated a visiting New York consigliere of the Montedoro Family for having beaten a federal conspiracy rap.

Then he was at the end of the dance floor, and all the well-wishers and importuners were swept away as if by magic. He kissed his wife Betty Carolyn, who looked terrific in clinging white Bob Mackie evening pajamas with silver fringe, topped off with a coiffure like sculptured meringue. And there was his grown daughter Rosemary, laughing as he swept her up in a bear hug.

"Hey, Rosie, my little princess! You look great. How's the art-gallery business in the Big Apple? We were afraid you'd miss the party with your plane delayed—"

"Al, the most exciting thing!" Betty Carolyn squealed. "Rosemary didn't say anything when she called from the airport so's we wouldn't worry, and anyhow by the time the plane landed it was all over, and her wonderful hero of a boyfriend even cooled off the U.S. Marshals so she and him don't even have to make a statement until tomorrow when the skyjacker is arraigned."

"What?" The word was like a soft explosion. Big Al held his smiling daughter at arm's length. "Your plane was *skyjacked*? Jesus Christ!"

"Poppa, I'm all right. No one was hurt and the skyjacker was captured—thanks to Kieran. Kieran O'Connor, a very dear friend of mine."

Carlo and Nick were still fending off guests, and the band was working itself into incipient apoplexy as it approached the climax of "Jeremiah Was a Bullfrog." Rosemary drew forward a slender dark-haired man who had been standing behind her. He was about thirty years old, clean-cut and with conservatively styled hair. He wore designer jeans and an open shirt with a gold neck-chain, the usual summer formal wear of his generation. His smile was diffident and his eyes cast down as Rosemary said:

"Kieran subdued the skyjacker single-handed, Poppa. He took away the man's gun—and somehow knocked him unconscious with a single blow! Karate or something."

Big Al seized the hand of Kieran O'Connor. "My God! How can I thank you? You gotta tell me everything. My own daughter skyjacked! What's this damn country coming to? Your name's O'Connor? You a frienda Rosie's from New York? Let's find a place to sit down and—"

The band, having brought "Jeremiah" to a rousing conclusion, now blared out a fanfare. People started tinkling their glasses with spoons.

"Ooh," cried Betty Carolyn. "I told the band leader that when you came in, he should quick finish up whatever they were playing and then announce our special dance. Al, you know everybody's been waiting for you to come down. And then we cut the cake—"

"Lay-deez and gentlemen!" The amplified voice of the band leader boomed through the festive summer night. "And now, by special request, in honor of the Silver Wedding Anniversary of Mr. and Mrs. Aldo Camastra . . ."

The opening strains of Big Al's favorite tune, "The Godfather Waltz," throbbed from a single violin. The guests broke into applause and cheers and Betty Carolyn tugged at her husband's left hand. The right one was still in the grip of Kieran O'Connor.

"Al, we gotta dance. Come on!"

But Big Al stood unmoving, his mouth open in an expression of incredulity and his eyes locked upon those of the young man standing before him. Kieran O'Connor's lips were moving, but the noise from the crowd and the now fully instrumented waltz music made his voice inaudible to Betty Carolyn and Rosemary.

Big Al heard every word.

I have wanted to meet you—or someone like you—for a long time, Mr. Camastra. The skyjack was a charade. An introduction and a demonstration. I brought the gun aboard the aircraft myself, and I selected the poor devil who would play the skyjacker role and made certain that he played it. Wouldn't you like to know how I did that, Mr. Camastra? I have a number of other useful talents at my command. If we can come to an amicable arrangement, I am willing to put them at your disposal.

"Malocchio," whispered Big Al. Sweat had broken out on his forehead. "The Evil Eye!" He tried to cry out to Carlo and Nick. The young Irishman's hypnotic voice reproached him.

You don't have to be afraid, Mr. Camastra. My offer is entirely legitimate. I need you, and you stand to profit considerably through use of my special services.

"Al, come on!" said Betty Carolyn.

The voice in his mind was genial. The paralysis that had fettered his body eased, but still that entrancing gaze held him. Malocchio!

I'll let you dance with your lovely wife in just a moment, Mr. Camastra. I just want to assure you that there is no possible way for you to harm me. We are going to be friends. Your daughter and I are already very good friends.

Big Al felt himself being pulled onto the dance floor. Betty Carolyn's body pressed against his and they began to waltz to the sad, lilting melody. Rosemary stood arm in arm with a pleasant, very ordinary looking young man—who still exerted his mental wizardry from more than twenty feet away.

Ever since I finished law school at Harvard I've been researching the economics of the nationwide organization operated by you and your Sicilian colleagues. I found it fascinating. I know every significant detail of the Five Families' operations

*back in New York, including a maneuver currently being orches-
trated to your disadvantage by a certain Mr. "Joe Porks" Porcaro of the Falcone Family. We'll talk about it later. Enjoy your
dance, Mr. Camastra. It's really a great party.*

17

FROM THE MEMOIRS OF
ROGATIEN REMILLARD

I CONTINUED TO ACT AS THE SURREPTITIOUS CONFIDANT OF DENIS
Remillard throughout his early childhood in spite of my brother
Don's antagonism. The boy's long-distance farspeaking ability
improved with each passing year; and my own telepathic faculty,
through our constant interaction and mental symbiosis, also advanced far beyond the level I had previously achieved with Don.

Little Denis soaked up knowledge like a human computer and
my role as simple tutor soon became obsolete. Nevertheless I still
had an important job to do educating Denis in human relation-
ships. At times he seemed almost like some naive little visitor
from an extraterrestrial civilization, overflowing with data about
Earth, its science, its culture, and its people—yet unable to fully
comprehend how the human race *worked*. I could not help but
recall Odd John, who was similarly bewildered. Not that Denis
had any of the fictional character's inhuman alienation—far from
it. But the murkier ins and outs of human psychology—especially the irrational elements playing a part in human decision
making—tended to perplex and bemuse him. Brilliant though he
was, he was handicapped by overly logical attitudes, social inex-
perience, and the inevitably self-centered mind-set of a very
young child. It would have been futile to try to form Denis's
conscience, for instance, by referring him to treatises on ethics or
moral theology; he needed to develop a sense of values by observing the actions of others, analyzing them, and judging their
good or evil in a context that was not only social but personal.
Practically speaking, it amounted to talking things over with me.

Looking back on our relationship from my present perspective, 140 years later, I can only be grateful that at the time I did not fully appreciate the crucial importance of what I was doing. If I had, I doubt that I would have had the courage to undertake the job—Ghost or no Ghost.

With the birth of Don and Sunny's second son Victor in 1970, Denis was relieved of a good deal of paternal constriction. Don became obsessed with the new child, who was strapping and handsome and the very image of his father, and lifted his earlier prohibition of contact between Denis and me. With Sunny's co-operation I was able to spend many hours each week with the boy. Our meeting place was the old apartment on Second Street, where aging Onc' Louie still lived with my unmarried cousins Al and Margie.

It was in 1973, when the time came for Denis to enter school, that the next crisis took over. After careful negotiation (and a bit of coercion!) I had managed to wangle a partial scholarship for Denis at Northfield Hall, a prestigious private boarding school in Vermont that specialized in gifted children; but when the time came to finalize the arrangements, Don balked. He was in a precarious financial position. His alcoholism affected his job performance and he had been passed over for promotion. Furthermore, Sunny was pregnant again, and Dr. Laplante predicted twins. Don's share of the tuition at Northfield would entail considerable sacrifice on his part—and he also professed an objection to the philosophical orientation of the school, which was ultraliberal and permissive and not at all congenial to the old-fashioned Catholicism of our family. Don dragged the entire Remillard family into the row. We split into those who wanted the best for Denis (me, Sunny, Al, and Margie), and those who maintained that no educational opportunity was worth "endangering the child's faith at some godless, left-wing school for spoiled rich kids" (Don, Onc' Louie, and about twenty-five other cousins, uncles, aunts, and in-laws).

In vain, I argued that Denis's religious instruction could be assured by special arrangement with a church near Northfield. Don declared that the Berlin parochial school had been good enough for him, and it should be good enough for his older son —genius or no genius. When I volunteered to share the tuition expenses, Don stubbornly refused. A last-ditch attempt on my part to garner a full scholarship for Denis was shattered when

Don made a truculent phone call to the school's headmaster. Northfield washed its hands of us volatile Canucks.

Of course nobody had asked Denis what *he* wanted.

Frustrated and disgusted by the debacle, I decided to go on a weekend backpack in the Mahoosucs to cool off. I could usually restore my spirit by climbing in the mountains, and I have since known many other metas who felt the same way. Perhaps it is merely instinctive for the psychosensitive to ascend as high as possible above the walls and confining rock formations that tend to block the free ranging of our minds; perhaps it is more—a yearning to be where the light is brightest, where the trees merge and the extent and shape of the forest can be known, where mean and mundane concerns are blotted out in flatland haze. I suppose I am moderately devout, but I don't feel impelled to pray in the high places. (I'm more likely to cry out of the depths!) Instead, I climb upward to bask. Skyey energies seem to pour through me when I stand on a peak like a human lightning rod; they renew me, and in some mystical fashion revitalize the Earth I stand upon.

On that day in mid-August I climbed Goose Eye Mountain, a 1170-meter pinnacle some fifteen crow-flight kilometers from Berlin, just across the border in Maine. When I reached the top I farspoke Denis and shared the summit experience with him. For two years now he had begged to accompany me on my wilderness rambles, but Sunny felt he was still too young and frail for strenuous hiking and I reluctantly had to agree. I took Denis with me mentally instead, and he told me it was almost as good.

After I'd let him borrow my senses, I asked: What are you doing?

Baking CAKE allbymyself (OK Mom supervises) Papa goneout so he won't laugh took Victor they lookingfor birthdaypresentPapa outboardmotor tomorrow Papabirthday I make cake Mom&me privatejoke not tell Papa cake goingtobe *magnificent*.

OmyGod forgot completely tomorrow August12. My birthday too 28yearsold just like yourPapa.

![Dismay.] BUT YOU HAVE NO CAKE.

Laughter. Waitwait in backpack gooeycreamfilled Feuilleté! Tomorrow put littletwigs in light sing HappyBirthdaytoMe.

[Mindshout broken off.] Cake done! Goodbye UncleRogi . . .

I'll try to speak you tomorrow MountSuccess. Goodbye Denis.

And he was gone, caught up in his great confectionery adventure. Of course it would have to be kept secret from Don, who would ridicule his little son for doing "women's work." It was typical of my brother that he should take three-year-old Victor, his pet, with him while he shopped for his own expensive birthday present. Small chance he would have saved the money for Denis's education.

I cursed quietly. If only the tuition at Northfield Hall weren't so exorbitantly high. If only the great state of New Hampshire hadn't let the gifted-child program go down the drain in a budget cut. If only the local Catholic school weren't so stodgy and inflexible. Sister Superior was willing to "see what could be done" about assigning Denis some special courses of advanced study, but she was adamant about having him start in first grade just like all the other six-year-olds. It was necessary that he "gain the requisite social skills and learn good work habits."

Denis now probably knew more than I did. And how would *I* like to spend a year twiddling my thumbs in first grade? Doux Jésus!

I slithered down from Goose Eye and picked up the Appalachian Trail. I had intended to spend Saturday and Sunday browsing about this region of the Mahoosucs, a rather modest weekend ramble; but now renewed fury at Don's selfishness and my own inability to help Denis kindled a perverse need to push myself to the limit. I checked my watch. It wasn't quite noon. Sunset would not be until around eight o'clock. My AMC map showed a more challenging itinerary, a fourteen-kilometer hike to Gentian Pond Shelter. That section of the trail was quite rugged, involving the negotiation of steep ridge and valley terrain and several scrambles over areas with great blocks of granite. I was a strong hiker, however, and my legs are long. I figured that by pushing myself I could cover the distance and arrive at Gentian well before dark—dead tired and no doubt chock-full of self-justification.

So I set off.

It was a fine day in spite of the heat. A tricky descent along the southwestern flank of Goose Eye commanded my attention. Then I flushed a few languid spruce grouse down in a hollow, and was further distracted by a harsh call that sounded like a raven, a species formerly rare in New England but now making a comeback. My bird-watcher's instinct perked up and I tramped along more cheerfully. In time I reached Mount Carlo and made my way up its rough northern shoulder. The eminence was as somber as a chunk of Labrador tundra, but there was a good view back to Goose Eye and ahead to Mount Success. I tried to hail Denis telepathically but there was no answer. No doubt Don had returned home and the child had been obliged to take refuge in the mental sanctuary he customarily erected against his father's barbs and disparagements.

Damn Don! He couldn't hurt Denis physically, but he could certainly do enormous emotional damage. The boarding school had seemed the perfect solution, taking the boy out of Don's orbit for nearly nine months of the year and providing him with an environment where he could continue his self-education, while at the same time learning to get along with other bright youngsters and sympathetic adults. With that escape vetoed, there seemed to be only one other solution to Denis's dilemma.

I would have to reveal his metapsychic gifts.

Every instinct in me warned against it. The child would be exploited, pressured, treated as a freak if not a menace. Once the truth came out, the psi laboratories at the various institutions would squabble over him. And I had read recently about a psi research facility at the U.S. Army's Aberdeen Center...

No. There had to be another way.

I hiked on, agonizing, entertaining one preposterous idea after another. I would steal Denis away. I would poison Don's liquor just enough to put him in bed, under my coercive thumb. I would confide Denis's secret to the nuns at school and enlist their help. (But the truth would leak out. The unsophisticated sisters could never deal with it.) I would write to Dr. Rhine himself! To our bishop. To the Governor of New Hampshire. To President Nixon. To *The New York Times*!

Occupied with these thoughts, I crossed the steep notch of Carlo Col and slogged into New Hampshire again, beginning the long climb to Mount Success, that ironically named central point of the little Mahoosuc Range. Success wasn't very difficult to master. It wasn't high, only interminably broad. Up around the summit were treacherous patches of thinly crusted bog where a false step put you boot-top-deep in black muck. I finally snapped out of my distraction when I missed my footing and fell headlong into a pocket of the stuff. It was only by the skin of my teeth that I missed tumbling over a kind of rock-slab retaining wall into a lethally steep ravine.

I had managed to wrench my knee, I was half soaked, and clinging black glop slathered me from stem to gudgeon.

I crawled out swearing at my own stupidity—and at the whimsical topography of my native state, where bogs appeared at the tops of otherwise arid mountains. They were a consequent of the local weather pattern, formed when moist air driven by strong winds collided with the small peaks. In summer there might be thick mist or drizzle or even sleet at the higher elevations while the lower slopes remained warm and dry. The same terrain and weather factors made for extremely violent thunderstorms.

I recalled this as I sat on top of Mount Success changing my wet pants and socks in a rising wind while towering cumulus clouds billowed up behind the two Bald Caps in the west. Now I knew why I had met so few hikers during the last three hours—and those hiking in the opposite direction. Anybody with brains was already holed up in a shelter; but I was caught halfway between the Carlo Col hut and Gentian Pond. It was almost five in the afternoon, my knee hurt like hell, I had no tent in my pack, and shelter was four hours away in either direction...for an able-bodied hiker.

I limped off in the direction of Gentian, moving as fast as the knee permitted. As the clouds humped higher and darker, I looked for a likely bivouac. I found nothing but windswept open ledges, knee-high tangles of scrub spruce and balsam (but no wood large enough to cut into a walking stick), and tumbled rocky slopes that had to be traversed with the utmost caution. Clouds hid the sun and wind whipped the miniature evergreens viciously in a prelude to the arrival of the storm front. Off in the southwest, the sky was purplish black.

As I slid downhill into a brushy washout my knee buckled. I went over sideways, but managed to land on my pack. The pain was intense. I lay there with my eyes shut listening to a tinkle of a tiny rivulet a few meters away. Then came a faint grumble of thunder, raindrops splattered my face, and I said, "Oh, shit."

Now what? I was going to have to get out of that ravine, for starters, since it would probably become a torrent once the storm began in earnest. Shedding my pack, I hobbled around gathering sticks to splint the knee. When the joint was immobilized I rested for a few minutes, trying to concentrate my metapsychic healing ability on the injury. But it was no good. I was too distracted and anxious to focus my mind properly. I put on my Gore-Tex jacket, the only rainwear I had, shouldered my backpack again, and began a long and awkward climb.

The rain came on fast and so did the fireworks. There was a

real danger of being zapped by lightning if one remained in an exposed position during one of these big storms, and an outside chance of getting killed on the slippery granite rocks. I was still a good hour and a half away from Gentian Pond Shelter and I didn't have a hope of making it before nightfall. I'd have to hole up somewhere; but as I rummaged frantically in my memory trying to recall this section of the trail from my last-year's hike, it seemed that there was no real refuge to be had, not along the trail proper. And if I went sidetracking in the dusk I would certainly get lost.

I stood still in the driving downpour and I tried to exert my farsight, seeking some cranny or marmot hole where I could gain at least minimal shelter. My ultrasense refused to function. Perhaps it was the lightning that blazed all around me; perhaps it was the pain of my sprained knee, or sheer funk. Whatever—I farsaw nothing. I remember crying out mentally to little Denis in my desperation, having some notion that his superior brain might be able to locate a hiding place where mine had failed. But Denis didn't respond. I suppose my telepathic howl was too feeble and too circumscribed by the dense granite rock that surrounded me. I was stuck.

Alors—j'y suis, j'y reste! Unless . . .

What happened next seems, in retrospect, to be almost a prefiguring—if not a parody—of the great event that would take place forty years later. Trapped on that damned mountain in a thundering deluge, I lifted my head to the sky and yelled:

"Ghost! Get me *out* of this!"

Between lightning blasts, the landscape was now nearly pitch black. I cried out to the Fantôme Familier a second time. The wind roared and my knee gave me hell. I was drenched all over again in spite of the Gore-Tex, since the rain was somehow blowing uphill. I unfastened my pack and sat on the streaming rocks, my splinted leg jutting awkwardly.

"Ghost, you son of a bitch! Where are you when I need you?"

And it said: *Here.*

I gave a violent start. Hallucination? But the wind had fallen off abruptly and the rain spigot was turned off. I was aware of a hazy glow surrounding me. The lightning's glare was almost lost in it, only visible now as slightly brighter pulses of light in an overarching luminescence.

I whispered, "Ghost?"

À vos ordres.

"Is it really you?"

Poor Rogi! When you have legitimate need of me, you have only to call. Someone will hear and summon me. I thought you understood this.

I cursed the mysterious presence roundly in French and English, then demanded that it do something about my knee. Voilà! The injury healed instantly. Giddy with triumph, I told it, "Now dry me off—if you can."

Nothing easier.

Pouf! Clouds of vapor poured out of the sleeves and from under the lower edge of my rain jacket. I pulled the thing off and watched my pants and sweater steam dry in a couple of minutes. Even my socks dried.

"Hot damn!" I chortled. "Now let's have a nice cup of tea with plenty of brandy in it."

The Ghost's mind-voice was slightly caustic: I believe you've used up the customary three wishes. You have your Bluet stove and the makings in your pack.

Laughing like a loon, I pulled out the things and got cooking. The Ghost had charitably dried off a few rocks in the immediate vicinity so I just sat where I was, waiting for the pot to boil and munching a Granola bar. The glow from what I now know was a psychocreative bubble cast a friendly light over the dripping skunk-currant bushes.

After I had managed to calm down a little I said, "It's a good thing you did show up. A man could die in this kind of a mess. Poor little Denis has had enough hard luck without losing his favorite uncle, too."

The Ghost seemed surprised: Hard luck?

"The boarding-school thing I arranged for him fell through. Don and most of the family are dead-set against it. I should think you'd know."

I have been ... elsewhere. Do you mean to tell me that Don objects to Denis being taught by the Jesuits?

"Jesuits! Hell, no. He objects to the kid going to that school for budding geniuses in Vermont—Northfield Hall."

The Ghost seemed to be ruminating: So! It seems that further direct intervention is called for, with the probability loci focused by this minor contretemps of yours. An interesting manifestation of synchronicity! Of course Denis never spoke of this failed arrangement, so how was one to know?

The thing's jabbering made no sense so I brewed tea and

tossed in a hefty slug of Christian Brothers. Half joking, I held out the small plastic flask. "I don't suppose you'd care for a nip?"

It said: Merci beau.

The flask floated away, tipped briefly, and returned. I hastily swilled my tea and had a fit of coughing. If the Ghost was a delusion, as I was beginning to suspect, my unconscious mind had a rare imaginative flair. I said: "What's this about the Jebbies?"

It said: Two priests named Jared Ellsworth and Frank Dubois are opening an experimental school intended to serve gifted children from low-income families. It is called Brebeuf Academy and it is located just outside Concord, on the grounds of a small Jesuit college. You will find that the fathers will readily accept Denis, under full scholarship. You yourself will take care of the boy's incidental expenses. Don will give his consent.

A euphoric warmth, not from the brandy, began to suffuse me. "Didn't I read something about Ellsworth in *Newsweek* a while back?"

But it ignored me and continued: After Denis has attended Brebeuf Academy for one year, you will tell Father Ellsworth the full truth about the boy's supranormal mental faculties. He will know what steps must be taken to protect Denis during his minority. You may then safely leave the boy's guidance in this priest's hands.

My brain spun. For over six years I'd devoted almost every moment of my spare time to the education and encouragement of my nephew. The rest of the time I'd merely worried myself sick over him. Was the Ghost telling me my job was done?

It said: Not done. Denis will always need your friendship. But you have fulfilled very well the first charge I placed on you, Rogi, and for a while you'll have time for yourself.

For a while?

Peace! Ne vous tracassez pas. There are years yet.

I shouted, "How can I believe you? What *are* you?"

You may as well know. It won't hurt. I am a being from another world, from another star. I am your friend and Denis's friend—the special guardian of the entire Remillard family, for reasons that will eventually be made clear to you. Now I will see to your safety before I go. The storm will last far into the night.

All I could think of were the flying-saucer flaps going on all over the world for the past several years. And my Ghost was some kind of extraterrestrial?

I blurted out, "What *did* happen to Betty and Barney Hill on the old Franconia Highway?"

The Ghost uttered its dry little laugh: Perhaps we can discuss it another time! I must go now. Adieu, cher Rogi . . .

Glowing mist closed in about me. I was captive for a few moments inside a pearly sphere and then there was a dazzling lightning bolt and a clap of thunder. Rain sprayed me as though I'd stepped beneath a waterfall and the terrain was completely different. I was standing about three meters away from a log cabin with lighted windows that was perched on a rock shelf above a wind-whipped little body of water. People moved around inside. A sound of singing and concertina music drifted through the night.

I was still holding my teacup, which was now half full of rainwater. My backpack lay at my feet. I dumped the cup and retrieved the pack, then strode up to the Gentian Pond Shelter and pounded on the door.

18

OBSERVATION VESSEL
KRAK NA'AM [KRON 96-101010]
24 JUNE 1974

RA'EDROO SLITHERED INTO THE SURVEILLANCE CHAMBER, SA-luted her Krondak superior on the intimate racial mode, and bid the other three entities on duty a courteous vocal "High thoughts, colleagues." An unspoken query was prominent in her mind's vestibulum: Why have you summoned me, Umk'ai? The Russian Salyut space laboratory is not scheduled to be launched for at least another five hours.

Thula'ekoo said aloud, "That is true, Ra'edroo. But another event is about to take place below, one that happens every year . . . in New Hampshire."

The Simb and the Gi who were working at the think tank laughed at some private joke.

Thula'ekoo reproved the pair with the slightest mental tap on their itch-receptors. He addressed Ra'edroo and a young Pol-troyan who had a puzzled smile on his grayish-purple, humanoid face. "I know that both you and Trosimo-Finabindin are keen amateur xenopsychologists. Since you two are new to the Earth tour, you'll be interested in this rather typical example of the current North American mind-set with respect to exotic en-counters."

"Perhaps not *wholly* typical," sniffed the Simb, who was a statistician and inclined to be overpunctilious. "Our current sam-pling among Status Seven Earth indigenes shows that 49.22 per-cent believe that UFOs do exist, and that they originated on other inhabited planets. Some 9.91 percent think they have personally seen one."

A brief wave of amusement passed over the Gi, DriDri Vuvl. "We're getting to be positively old hat. I suppose it was inevita-ble."

"I should think," Ra'edroo said, "that those figures demon-strate that the thirty-year familiarization scheme has been a re-sounding success."

"You've got a lot to learn about Earthlings, colleague," said the Simb.

DriDri Vuvl added, "These Americans, for instance. Their capacity for ennui in the face of the marvelous is mind-boggling. Why, they've very nearly lost interest in their space program! Major funding was cut off in order to finance some idiotic war. And now all their leaders seem concerned about is a tacky politi-cal scandal and threats by Status Three nations to cut off the petroleum supply. *Petroleum!* I ask you."

The Simb passed judgment. "Excretory orifices, the lot of them. How can they be expected to coadunate their world Mind?"

Thula'ekoo was busy at the monitor and chose to ignore the crude chaffing. When the image was well centered, fully dimen-sioned, and computer-enhanced for all eight Krondak senses (a pity young Trosi would miss out on the pla'akst, which enriched this type of observation so; but that was life), he transferred the scene to the large wall-screen.

Twenty-three humans, fourteen men and nine women, sat in a circle on the weathered rocks near the summit of Mount Adams in New Hampshire's Presidential Range. It was 5° Celsius with a cutting westerly wind, overcast skies, and visibility of about twenty kilometers. The people were dressed in nondescript out-door gear obviously chosen for warmth. Most of them were talking quietly, with three or four engaged in solitary meditation. One woman offered plastic cups of hot cocoa from a thermos and had a few takers.

"Down from last year's gathering," the Simb noted with wry satisfaction. "Way down."

The Gi rolled its saucer eyes. "The faithful are defecting to macrobiotics, pacifism, and whale watching."

"Silence!" said Thula'ekoo. "They are about to begin."

Ra'edroo and the Poltroyan, Trosi, were completely absorbed in the scene. The human leader, a female of commanding aspect, had directed members of the circle to join hands. She said:

"Fellow Aetherians, the time has come. Empty your minds of all earthly thought. Prepare to divorce yourselves from your fleshy bodies and take on the astromental configuration. Banish all physical discomfort. Close your eyes. Shut out all sounds except that of my voice. Feel nothing but the Presence of the Universe. Join with me as I call to it. Let our thoughts arise with a single voice. Call out! The Universe sees us and loves us. It is alive with powerful and friendly spirits who are watching us even at this moment. If we only have faith and strength of will, these extraterrestrial beings will answer when we call. They will come and save our world from the death that threatens us. Call out! Bid the otherworld creatures come! Let them know they are welcome. Together, now, with me . . ."

Come.

"Why, she's a borderline suboperant!" Ra'edroo exclaimed. "The others are hopelessly latent, but what meager faculties they can project are actually in a loose mind-meld with the leader. How extremely interesting!"

Come.

Trosi was radiant. "The dear things—what a splendid effort!" His voice broke with compassion. "What a pity that the subsidiary humans are so inferior in mind to the leader."

Thula'ekoo said, "All humans possess latent metafaculties to a greater or lesser degree. In this case, only the leader has the projective farspeech capacity to penetrate the ionosphere. At this distance, none but the Krondaku and the Poltroyans can detect the metapsychic emanations of the subordinates in the meld."

"Thanks be to Sacred Truth and Beauty," muttered the Simb.

"I agree with Trosi," offered Ra'edroo, "that the effort of this little group is most affecting, a foreshadowing of the metaconcerted request that must take place before Intervention."

COME.

"Hah!" scoffed the Simb. "A futile mockery of such an effort, rather. One might as well compare a chorus of chirping insects to a symphonic ensemble. These poor things are one of a handful of cranks who periodically attempt to make mental contact with exotic beings—what they so quaintly call extraterrestrials. They are only unique in having a meagerly talented latent as their leader, which is about what one might expect in New Hampshire."

COME!

"Again I detect overtones of satire in your remark, colleague," Ra'edroo said.

"Oh, the place is crawling with latents. Even imperfect operants. It's one of the irruptive metapsychic nuclei of the planet. This world's Mind isn't evolving overall, but breaking out in spots. Quite grotesque. Makes it devilish hard for the immatures. It's a wonder any of them reach adulthood sane."

COME!

The sentimental Gi clapped a hand over its central heart. Its intromittent organ glowed crimson in empathetic passion. "Oh, feel the goodwill in the female entity's cry, citizens. The yearning! One longs so to console her."

Come come come.

"Hold your honey, colleague," the Simb jeered, "until you've traveled down below the planet's ionic shell as we Simbiari have, and experienced the full unsavoriness of its puny knots of consciousness—the selfishness, the irrational suspicion separating one nation from another, the perverted male sex-dynamic that keeps them endlessly at war."

"What you say may be true, Salishiss," little Trosi said, "but the fact remains that these people have the greatest metapsychic potential in the galaxy, according to the Lylmik."

"The Lylmik tell us a lot of things they never bother to prove," grumped the Simb. "I'm no magnate of the Concilium, only a lowly number-cruncher. But my trade gives me a certain insight into social dynamics. Left to itself, this world Mind would inevitably destroy itself."

Come. Please come.

"So far humans have refrained from using atomic weapons in battle," DriDri Vuvl noted, "even though they've had them for thirty years. They keep making more and bigger weapons, but they don't use them. It seems to be a sort of threat-display mechanism."

"Oh, yes?" Salishiss gesticulated at the view-screen. "What do you think that group on the mountain is so worked up about? They're convinced that only a galactic civilization can rescue their world from atomic suicide. That's why they call out to us in this pathetic fashion. Of course, they have no conception of what Intervention would *really* mean, with the vast majority of Earth's population still metapsychically latent and socially infantile. Why, we'd have to occupy the planet and play nanny to it for more than a hundred orbits until its Mind matured—and the humans would oppose our proctorship almost every step of the way. The very thought of it makes me cringe."

The Krondak officer, Thula'ekoo said, "The picture is by no means as bleak as you paint it, Salishiss. Large numbers of Earthlings already experience feelings of universal fellowship, the precursor to true coadunation. And the Lylmik profess to be gratified by the accelerating mental evolution."

"And who would dare question the ineffable judgment of the oldest and wisest race in the galaxy?" the Simb inquired archly. "Those architects of the Milieu, those masters of absent-minded subtlety? Hard luck for the rest of us that Lylmik reasoning is sometimes just as ethereal as their bodies . . ."

Come!

"The human leader is weakening," said Ra'edroo. "It must be very stressful on that cold mountaintop for such high-metabolism creatures."

"So few in the little group now." DriDri Vuvl shook its ruff of filoplumage sadly. "They may not show up at all next Midsummer Day."

Come oh come.

Trosi the Poltroyan leaked compassion from every neuron. "If only we could encourage them—let them know that we're out here, and we really do care."

Great Thula'ekoo responded with implacable authority. "Even if every human being now living on Earth called out to us, we could not answer. It would violate the scheme of the Concilium."

"Just some tiny gesture," Trosi begged. "Something that wouldn't warp the probability lattices. Love's Oath—we do enough manipulation of them, what with the mental analyses and the technical experiments and the flybys. How about a simple gesture of friendliness for a change?"

"Statute Blue-4-001," Ra'edroo said respectfully to her superior, "gives the officer of the watch certain discretionary powers. Thou and I, Umk'ai, have the expertise to direct a most delicate farspeech beam in metaconcert."

The circle of humans still held hands and had their faces raised to the clouded sky. Their attempt at mental synergy was crumbling. The leader urged them to one last effort.

Come!

Opaque membranes flicked over the accessory eyeballs of Thula'ekoo. His primary optics glowed an intense blue and seemed to suck in the willing psyches of his fellow Krondaku, the eager Poltroyan, and the Gi. After a nanosecond's hesitation, the Simb Salishiss blended into the fivefold brain, and it broadcast a mental chord that blended tranquillity with patience—and the merest hint of Unity:

Persevere.

For just an instant, the uplifted human faces were transfigured. Then the spell was broken and the twenty-three startled people turned to each other with whispers. The female leader buried her head in her arms. Several others crowded around her anxiously, touching her. She finally looked up, not seeing her companions, lifted an arm to the sky, and smiled.

Then she started off down the Star Lake Trail to the Madison Huts. The others came straggling after.

19

BRETTON WOODS, NEW HAMPSHIRE, EARTH
25 JUNE 1974

"WAKE UP, DENIS. WE'RE HERE."

The Volkswagen Beetle slowed for the left turn and swung into the hotel entrance road. The seven-year-old boy was immediately alert, straining against his seat belt to see over the dashboard of the car. Ahead of them to the east was a majestic panorama, several hundred acres of rolling lawn fronting a wooded rise that hid a tantalizing glimpse of white and red. Beyond this, a vast slope that stretched almost from horizon to horizon culminated in a mountain rampart, dark with timber in the middle reaches and a gleaming pewter along bare summit peaks that reflected the early-morning sun. This was the Presidential Range of the White Mountains. Even though it had been ground down by ice-age glaciers, it was still the highest part of northeastern North America.

The child cried: Wherehotel? Wherecograilway? Look thatmountain SNOW top in June!

That's Mount Washington. The one we're riding to top of today.

Studied allmountain names let's see: JeffersonClayWashington MonroeFranklinEisenhowerClinton north/south. (Notall presidents!) Why Eisenhower so dinky UncleRogi?

He got his mountain last and beggars can't be choosers. State changed name MountPleasant to Eisenhower. Once tried change name MountClinton to MountPierce honor only president born NewHampshire. Try never amounted to much. Neither did PresidentPierce. People still call mountain Clinton.

Laughter. Why thesemountains look bigger from here than from Berlin? What that funnystreak MountWashington? When we see yourHOTEL?

Rogi laughed out loud. "Take it easy. You've got three whole days to ask questions. Batège! I'd nearly forgotten what a frantic little quiz-kid you are."

"You haven't forgotten at all." The child was complacent. "I see inside your mind how much you missed me. And I missed you, too."

The car slowed beside a guard kiosk painted a spotless white, decorated with window boxes of scarlet petunias. The old watchman stuck his head out. "Morning, Roger. Got your nevvy here all safe and sound, I see. Plenty time yet for breakfast."

"Morning, Norm. Yup—give him a treat before we go up the cog. Say hi to Mr. Redmond, Denis."

"Hello, Mr. Redmond." Why hecallyou ROGER UncleRogi?

"See you, Norm." Because that myname here: Roger Remillard. Bettername man works bighotel easier people remember&pronounce than Rogatien. (And Rogi sounds naughty.)

Appreciative mirth.

The car swung around a long curve and the famous old White Mountain Resort Hotel came into view. At first it looked as though it must be a toy castle, or a chateau made from white spun sugar with the glistening roofs of the towers and wings colored like cherry jam. The hotel had more tiny windows than you could count, and little flags flying, and a candy-spill of flower gardens amidst miniature trees in front. The actual size of the place only gradually became evident as the driveway seemed to stretch on and on, with the hotel growing steadily larger until it blotted out the mountain vista entirely. The five-storey building was made of white stuccoed wood. It had a two-tiered colonnaded verandah curving from the central porte-cochère all around the entire south wing.

"It's a palace," exclaimed the overawed boy. "Are you really the boss?"

Rogi shook his head, laughing. "Hardly. I'm only the assistant convention manager." [Explanatory image.] "But I get to live here where I work, and I like this job much better than the one I had at the paper mill. It pays better, too."

They drove past the grand main entrance, which was crowded with autos and tour buses and guests and bellmen scurrying to load and unload people's luggage, and pulled into the employees' parking lot behind a screen of tall shrubs. Denis insisted on carrying his small suitcase himself. They entered an annex building that housed resident staff members. A man dressed in a white jacket and bow tie hurried past them, greeting Rogi and mussing Denis's mousy brown hair.

Rogi said, "That was Ron, one of the waiter captains. Just wait until you see the dining room here. There are two of them, but we'll eat in the biggest one where Ron works this morning." They climbed carpeted stairs.

"You like it here a lot, don't you, Uncle Rogi." There was a tinge of dejection in the boy, imperfectly screened.

"Yes. But I can come visit you in Berlin while you're home for the summer. It isn't even an hour's drive."

"I know. Only. . ." UncleRogi I miss you. Miss mindspeech. Miss friendadult questionanswers fearcalming. Teachers at Brebeuf nice kids notbad but not same YOU.

Comfort. Denis you know grownups must work sometimes goaway oldhome.

Understand. But can't speak you through mountains down Concord school can't speak you from Berlin whileyou here either.

There's your Maman & littlebrotherVictor to bespeak.

Denis stopped at the top of the stairs. He averted his eyes, clumsily trying to conceal a dark emotional coloration. "Mom's changed since last fall. When I came home from school last week she could hardly mindspeak me at all anymore. She was like that when I went home at Easter, too, but I thought it was just because of the new babies. Now she—she just doesn't *want* to share her thoughts with me the way she used to. She kisses me and says she's busy and tells me to go play."

"Your mother has a lot to do taking care of Jeanette and Laurette. Twin babies are a terrible handful unless you have older children as ready-made baby-sitters, the way Tante Lorraine had with your Papa and me . . . Have you been able to mindspeak with your Papa?"

"Not very much. I thought he'd be pleased at the way things worked out at the academy. My good grades, and the way I was auditing classes with the college kids, and how Father Ellsworth has been getting me parapsychology books and publications from the library at Brown University, and how I'm learning archery, and how to play the piano. But he wasn't much interested. He doesn't like me, you know. Not like he does Victor."

The hallway was deserted and quiet. Rogi knelt down to face the boy. "Your father does love you, Denis. The thing is—Victor's only a little boy and he needs more attention right now."

But Victor*dumber*thanme! Weak farspeech/farsight/farhearing/ PK. (Strong coercion though.) And he fights and swipes things and mindpinches new babysisters awful when thinks nobody looking. Tried mindpinch me HA! myshield reflected pinch back *him*.

"Victor is probably jealous of his new sisters. Maybe even jealous of you now that you're going to school. Four-year-olds are still pretty uncivilized. It takes time for them to learn right from wrong."

"He already knows," Denis said darkly. "I can tell. He hurts the little twins anyway whenever their minds make telepathic noises that bug him. You know how little babies are."

Rogi made a comical grimace. "I remember."

"Jeanette and Laurette can't help being pests sometimes. But Victor doesn't seem to be any good at putting up a protective mental shield, so the baby-thoughts drive him crazy. I told Mom how he was tormenting the twins and she told him to stop—but there's really not much she can do about it."

"I see." (Poor Sunny, retreating into fatalism and saying her beads and watching soap operas on television! Inside of a year she would be enceinte once again.)

"I tried to explain to Papa why Victor shouldn't harass the babies. I told him it would discourage them from developing their own ultrafaculties—maybe even make them *normal*. He laughed."

Rogi stood up, keeping a tight lid over his own thoughts. "I'll talk things over with your father when I take you back. Don't worry."

Denis smiled at him. "I knew you'd help."

"My room's right down here. Let's hurry. We want time for breakfast, and the shuttle bus to the cog is at ten." (And what *can* I say to Don to show him how he's poisoning his younger son and endangering his daughters and breaking the older boy's heart? The only time he opens to me is when he's drunk. His precious Victor can do no wrong.)

They went into the small suite that was Rogi's apartment and left Denis's suitcase on the rollaway bed that had been brought in for his visit. The child inspected the premises gravely and admired the sweeping vista from the windows.

"That's a view that costs the hotel guests at least two hundred dollars a day," Rogi told his nephew, "but I get it for free. Of course this place of mine is pretty small, and I have to walk up a lot of stairs. But I have a nice office over in the main part of the hotel with room for my books, and when I sit up here and watch the storms play around the mountains I have a show that beats anything on television."

They went downstairs, crossed a courtyard, and entered the hotel's north wing through a side door. Denis's eyes popped at the sight of apparently endless corridors with pillars and chandeliers, ornate Edwardian furniture, potted palms, gilt-framed mirrors, and fireplaces—large enough for a boy to stand in—that now had bouquets of red and yellow peonies in the grates instead of flaming logs. They looked into a great ballroom with green velvet drapes and standing silver candlesticks as big as hat-trees. Two men ran polishing machines across a floor that looked shiny enough to ice-skate on. Rogi told Denis there would be a Midsummer Night Ball there that evening. Another salon, lush with ferns and tropical flowers, overlooked a golf course and the approach to Mount Washington.

When they came at last to the dining room, Denis was struck

dumb. It was fancier than any restaurant he had ever seen in his life. Ron, the captain who seated them, treated Denis like a grown man and called him Sir when he gave him a menu. There were weird things for breakfast like kippers and steak, and eight different ways of having eggs, and twelve varieties of fresh fruit including New Zealand gooseberries. The table was set with crystal and shining silver and monogrammed damask napery. There was a vase with a single mauve rose, so perfect in form and so outré in color that Denis had to touch it to be certain it was real. The sugar came in hard lumps wrapped in embossed gold paper. (Denis stole two.) Milk was served in a faceted goblet, sitting on its own small plate with a paper doily underneath. They ate eggs Benedict and had mini-croissants and strawberries Wilhelmine, and were served funny little cups of espresso, which Denis drank politely but didn't much care for.

When they had finished, Denis sighed and said, "I expect you'll stay here forever."

Rogi laughed and touched his lips with his napkin. "I'll tell you a secret. What I'd really like to do is save my money until I have enough to buy a little bookstore in a nice quiet college town. I could stay in a place like *that* forever."

The check came. Rogi signed it and he and Denis stood to go. The boy said, "That doesn't sound very exciting—a bookstore."

"I'm afraid I'm not a very exciting man, Denis. Most people aren't, you know. Movies and television shows and books are full of heroes, but they aren't too common in real life anymore."

The boy thought about this as they walked through the lobby. It was crowded with guests on their way to the day's activities, most of them middle-aged or elderly, but with a sprinkling of young couples and well-dressed parents with children. There were people in tennis togs and riding breeches and hiking boots, and a group of little old ladies in polyester pantsuits carrying shawls and heavy sweaters, and old men in loud sports jackets hung about with camera bags and bincoulars. A pretty tour guide was callling for their attention, please.

"I used to think it would be neat to be a hero when I was just a little kid," Denis said. "An astronaut or a jungle explorer or a hockey star like Bobby Clarke or Gil Perreault. But I guess I'm not a very exciting person either. Father Dubois kids me about it sometimes. He says I should quit sitting around like a stuffed owl, contemplating the infinite." The boy chuckled. "But the infinite's *interesting*."

They went out the front door of the hotel to the shuttle bus. Rogi said, "Don't take his teasing seriously. Be what you are. You've got a brain—maybe one like nobody else in the whole world. Explore that."

The mob of old folks and the tour guide followed Rogi and Denis into the bus. The guide counted her charges, then signaled the driver. The bus drove off.

Denis said, "There are doctors who study the brain—take it apart and poke needles and things into it to find out how it works. But I don't want to do just that. What I want to learn about isn't how the brain works but *why*. Why do those electrical impulses and chemical exchanges result in thinking? No electroencephalograph shows the thoughts in a person's mind. And how do brains control bodies? It's not my brain that commands my fingers to grab this bus seat, *it's me*. A brain is nothing but a lump of meat."

"With a mind in it."

"That's right," the boy agreed. "Mind! That's what I want to learn about. A mind isn't the same as a brain."

"Some scientists would argue the point—but I don't think the two are identical."

Denis said: People like you&me would give scientists fits! How mybrain speak yourbrain? No radiowaves other energy pass between us! Through whatmedium propagates coercion/PK/farspeech? How farsight/hearing/smell/taste/touch impulses transmitted? Received? What energysource powers PK? Why can't farsense through granite? Why easier farsense at night? How mymind influence another in coercion? How mymind heal mybody? ...I know mymind controls mymind. This means: mymind controls chemistry&electricity in brain. The nonmatterenergything dominates the matterenergything! How?

Rogi said: Denisdearchild find out! Explore your mind and mine and Don's and Victor's. Explore other minds as well minds of normals find way bridge gap separating them/us. What an adventure... more exciting than mountaineering deepdiving oceantraveling flyouterspace!

[Good-humored juvenile skepticism.] But not anything like as dangerous.

Rogi squeezed the thin little shoulder. Aloud, he said, "Of course not."

The bus bounced over the frost-heaved macadam road that twisted through a forest of maples and hemlocks. Around Rogi and Denis, the little old ladies twittered like wrens.

The cog railway that ascends the western slope of Mount Washington is unique in North America, one of those mad Yankee notions that never should have worked but somehow did, for more than a hundred years. Denis took one look at the chunky coal-fired locomotive, oddly lopsided on level track since its boiler was designed to be horizontal when the train climbed the steep grade, and cried: "It's the Little Engine That Could!"

The old folks simpered fondly.

There were many other tourists of all ages waiting at the base station to board the train. The engine pushed a single car, painted bright yellow. Traction came from a rack-and-pinion mechanism beneath. Between the regular narrow-gauge rails was a central track that resembled an endless ladder of thumb-thick iron rods four inches long. This rack was gripped by twin cog gears on the engine's drive mechanism, which powered the train up the mountain with an earsplitting clatter while the engine chugged and hissed and belched an air-polluting cloud of ebony smoke such as Denis had never seen before in his life.

As they crept upward through scrubby trees the entire Bretton Woods area was visible behind them. "This is neat!" Denis yelled over the racket. "Look down there—it's your hotel!"

Rogi said: I watch little trains go up&down mountain from my window. Sometimes when cloud clamps down on summit trains look like they're heading into sky never to return . . . Man who invented train went to state legislature in 1858 asked it to grant charter so he could build railroad. Lawmaker proposed amendment permitting inventor to build railroad to Moon after he finish one up MountWashington.

Laughter. Getting really cold. Glad brought jacket. Glad we can mindspeak can hardly hear WOW whatanoise!

You know about mountainweather? It can change in flash: bright sunshine to freezing cold even now in June. Snow any month. Wind blows hurricanefast on summit ⅓ days year.

Yes I read book school worldclass record MountWashington

wind 231 mph! Know also Indians thought mountain home GreatSpirit afraid to climb no wonder.

You hear story ChiefPassaconaway?

?

Lived NewHampshire early colonial times. Great wise leader also famed wonderworking magic allkinds wizard tricks. When Chief Passaconaway died legend says wolves pulled body on sled to top MountWashington. There fiery coach carried him away into sky.

Like *flyingsaucer*? Awww...

Lots of other stories. You ever hear Great Carbuncle?

?

Supposed tobe huge shining red jewel hidden mountain worth zillions. Glowing ruby light lures greedy people come search for it. They follow light get trapped terrible storms never able to get hold carbuncle. Die. NathanielHawthorne used legend in story.

I'll get book BerlinLibrary this summer... UncleRogi you don't believe flyingsaucers do you?

Never saw one. But Elmer Peabody man drives tractormower at hotel says he did. Sensible man Elmer. Lots of reputable people say they see UFOs. Funny. NewHampshire seems have awfullot those things confounded UFO plague!

I read two books kindof scary. Onebook man&woman driving FranconiaNotch just west here say they abducted by saucermen. Doctor got story years later by *hypnotizing* people! Saucerman told lady come faraway star meant noharm. Anotherbook guy saw big saucer with redlights over Exeter nearcoast. Went to police. Police saw it too! Also wholebunch other people. What think?

I think... it may be possible.

Ahh. Littlegreenmen visit Earth but not make official contact? Why they want do such crazything! Why keep secret instead reveal selves rightout to world?

Dearchild *why do we*?

The little train crawled slowly to the region above timberline, leaving behind gnarled and crouching dwarf trees and passing into a place where carpets of subarctic flowers, pink and white and pale yellow, bloomed in the midst of sedge meadows and a desolation of gray crags. There was still snow in shadowed hollows and the western side of the rocks was encrusted with thick hoarfrost. The summit buildings came into view. They passed a cluster of water tanks and saw a simple painted board:

LIZZIE BOURNE
PERISHED 1855

"She was twenty-three," Rogi said. "Nearly seventy other people have died on this mountain—more than on any other peak in North America. Some died from accidents, some from exposure. The mountain is deceptive, you see. People come up on a beautiful day like this, without a cloud in the sky, and decide to take a little hike. Suddenly clouds of icy fog come racing in and you can't see two feet in front of you. There might be snow or hail or freezing rain with a wind-chill factor way below zero. The worst weather on Earth short of the polar regions happens right here in our own state, on a mountain only sixty-two hundred feet high. I've been up here lots of times—on the cog, driving up the eastern side of the Carriage Road, even hiking up from the hotel. But I never feel quite comfortable. The top of Mount Washington is an eerie place."

The train drew to a halt in front of a drab, barnlike wooden building that the trainman proudly identified as the famous Summit House Hotel. He warned the passengers that they would have only forty-five minutes to explore. The return trip, like the journey up the mountain, would take more than an hour.

A strong, cold wind was blowing and Rogi told Denis to watch his step on the slippery gravel. There was very little snow on the ground, but the windward side of every structure, rock, railing, and guy-cable was thick with dazzling white rime. The giant frost crystals looked like otherworldly marine growth, a crust of twisted tabs and plates and knobs and opaque lenses of ice.

The Summit House Hotel held no interest for Denis. He wanted to climb the cone-shaped rock mass that marked the absolute high point of the mountain. Then he raced off to see if the weather observatory or the TV and radio transmitter buildings were open to the public. They weren't. As he squinted up at the ice-wrapped antenna tower, the boy projected to Rogi dramatic imaginary pictures of the way this place might look in a howling blizzard with the wind blowing two hundred miles an hour. His mind was charged with exhilaration as they walked to a rocky spur and looked south, down a leg of the great Appalachian Trail, and saw a group of tiny lakes and a hikers' hut more than a thousand feet below.

"Those are the Lakes of the Clouds," Rogi said. "Maybe on one of your later visits we can hike up to them from the Hotel, on the Ammonoosuc Ravine Trail."

"Wow! That'd be great." Denis squinted, studying the area immediately below the spur. "What are those piles of rocks with yellow paint on top?"

"Cairns marking the trails. You have to watch very carefully for them in some places to keep from getting lost. The trails on this mountain don't look like the woodland paths you're used to—at least not in the high parts. They mostly go over bare rock. That's one of the reasons why Mount Washington can be treacherous."

They went back to the northern area of the summit to see if they could see Berlin. Sure enough, the steam plumes from the paper mills were little tan feathers rising from the Androscoggin Valley. The air was so clear that they could see Umbagog Lake and Bigelow Mountain over in Maine, and the Green Mountains of Vermont to the west, and beyond the White Mountain Resort Hotel was a pimple on the horizon that was really Mount Marcy, 150 miles away in the Adirondacks of New York.

"I see hikers," Denis said, pointing to a line of people toiling up alongside the cog railway line. He instinctively magnified the tiny figures with his farsight and projected the picture into Rogi's mind.

". . . eighteen, nineteen, twenty . . . twenty-three of them."

"It's a popular place to hike. Over there is the main trail leading to Clay and Jefferson and Adams. There are overnight huts between Mount Adams and Mount Madison, too."

Denis shaded his eyes. He was shivering in the unrelenting wind. The vision of the climbers faded from Rogi's ultrasense. And then the child uttered a gasp of disbelief, and there came a surge of fear from him that made Rogi cry out in concern.

"Denis! What's wrong?"

A trembling, bluish finger pointed at the line of people. They disappeared behind the shoulder of the mountain for a moment as the trail dipped, then came into view again. The mental picture was huge.

"Uncle Rogi, the lady in front. I *hear* her."

"What?"

The boy burst into tears. "I hear her mind. She's like us!

Another person like us! Her mind projection is very faint and it doesn't make much sense..."

He dashed the moisture from his eyes and hugged himself as he tried to stop shivering. Swiftly, Rogi unzipped his down-filled jacket and wrapped Denis in it. He knelt beside the child on sharp stones, feeling no cold, only a gut-churning hope. "Concentrate! Try to share the farspeech with me, Denis. Help me hear what you hear." He put his arms around the boy and closed his eyes.

Oh my God.

She was singing a wordless melody, some classical fragment that Rogi was unable to recognize. A joyful song. Now and then a subvocalization floated above the music like gossamer spider-threads against sunlit air:

Answered ... they answered ... out there ... surely ... the others may doubt but ... answered ...

The clairaudient emanations and her farseen image cut off as the woman followed the trail into another hollow, but his memory would never relinquish that first picture, and whenever he thought of her after she was lost to him, this vision of windblown vitality would always come to mind: a strong-featured face, striking but not conventionally pretty, slightly sunburned across the bridge of the nose; eyes of a blue so pale that they were almost silver; an exultant smile—my God, that smile!—that was the external sign of her mind's rejoicing; strawberry-blond hair escaping from a green woolen watch cap; a body tall, slender, and strong.

Denis was trying to squirm out of his paralyzed arms. "Uncle Rogi—your jacket! You'll freeze!"

He came to himself. The hikers were still out of sight and Denis was looking up at him, face tear-stained and twisted with emotion. Rogi spoke urgently. "That woman. You're certain that the music and farspeech came from her mind?"

"Absolutely certain. She really is another one like us. No— wait! She's not as controlled as we are. Not aware. I don't think she knows what she's doing when she mindspeaks. Perhaps she's never had any other telepaths to speak to. But she *is* like us! Uncle Rogi, we're not all alone..."

"And that she should be the one," Rogi whispered. "C'est un miracle. Un vrai miracle." Sunny's voice came to him, an echo of a long-ago apology: *Quand le coup de foudre frappe—*

The train whistle blew. Once, twice, three times.

"Oh, no!" cried the boy. "We can't just go and leave her."

Rogi lifted Denis in his arms. "The hikers are coming this way, probably heading for Summit House. They should be here in half an hour. We'll wait for them."

"But the train—"

"Another train will come."

Rogi stumbled over the frosty rocks, drunk with happiness, for the first time realizing what Sunny had been trying to tell him about her love for Don. *When the thunderbolt strikes . . .* there is no logic, no resisting. And thus the marvel of the woman hiker's telepathic ability was lost in a greater wonder. He scarcely heard Denis say:

"If there's one mind like hers, there must be lots more! All we have to do is figure a way to find them."

Wind sang in the antenna guy-wires and the humped little engine in front of the hotel renewed its hooting. Tourists called to each other and Denis shivered, radiating a fearful exultation that was almost as intense as Rogi's own. Rogi carried the boy up the stairs into the heavily insulated entry of the small hotel. A bearded man in climbing gear held the door open, concern on his face.

"Little fellow's not hurt, is he?"

Rogi set Denis back on his feet, unwrapped him, and said, "All we both need is a bit of warming up."

"Try the dining room," the man suggested. "Nice fire, fantastic view. You can watch the train go down the mountain while you stoke up with hot food and drink. Best thing."

Thanking the man, Rogi led Denis into the Summit House lobby. The boy was recovering fast and he eyed the souvenir counter with interest. "Can I buy a guidebook and some maps? And maybe we better get some Kleenex. My nose is running and so is yours." The small, wan face looked up with a critical frown. "You should comb your hair before she gets here, too."

Rogi burst out laughing. "Mais naturellement! It wouldn't do to look scruffy."

"I—I just want her to like us," Denis protested.

"If she doesn't, we'll try coercion."

"Be serious, Uncle Rogi! What are we going to *say* to her?"

"We'll have to think about that, won't we? But first, let's clean up and then find something to eat."

Hand in hand, they went looking for the men's room.

20

FROM THE MEMOIRS OF
ROGATIEN REMILLARD

HER NAME WAS ELAINE DONOVAN HARRINGTON.

She was thirty-one years old and separated from her husband, and she lived in a "little country place" just outside the state capital of Concord, where she edited and published a journal for UFO buffs called *Visitant*. I found out later that she had inherited her strawberry-blond hair—and probably her metapsychic traits —from her late father Cole Donovan, a dynamic real-estate entrepreneur. From her late mother, who was of Boston Brahmin stock, she had a legacy of natural elegance and sufficient old money to support a lifestyle far above any that Remillards of that day and age could even imagine.

Scraping an acquaintance with her was the easiest thing in the world, thanks to Denis.

We waited in ambush at a table in the rustic dining room of Summit House; and when Elaine and her party of trail-weary Aetherians arrived, the boy picked her brains. In retrospect, I am appalled at his redactive expertise, for I realize now that he must have been able to monitor every thought that passed between Elaine and me. But at that time I had nothing but admiration for the child as he trotted up to Elaine all primed with pilfered data from her memory bank and claimed to be a reader of her magazine who had recognized her from her masthead photograph. She was charmed by the precocious, well-spoken lad, and engaged him in conversation on sundry flying-saucerish topics while her friends settled down to order a meal.

At an opportune moment I came up to retrieve my young relative. Denis introduced me, explaining, "My Uncle Rogi— Roger—works at the White Mountain Resort Hotel. Do you know it, Mrs. Harrington? That big old place like a palace down at the western foot of Mount Washington."

"I'm staying there," she said. The corners of her mouth lifted in a little smile. "It's rather a family tradition, the White Mountain Hotel. How do you do, Mr. Remillard?"

I had barricaded my unruly emotions behind the sturdiest mind-screen I could muster; but when that silvery gaze focused on me I might as well have tried to hide behind a shield of cellophane. The rapport was instantaneous and I was unable to utter a word. God only knows what thoughts I projected.

She laughed and enclosed my warm hand between her two chilly ones. "Do you mind? My fingers are still like icicles and you seem to be powered by some sort of atomic furnace."

"I—of course I don't mind," I mumbled idiotically. I had the sense to bring up my other hand to complete the electrifying clasp. Denis was grinning at us like a young chimpanzee and several of Elaine's companions threw quizzical looks in our direction.

When our hands finally fell apart, she asked casually, "What do you do at the hotel?" I told her, and she seemed almost relieved. Being a part of management—even very junior management—gave me at least a minimal cachet. She asked: "Are you interested in cosmic visitations, like your nephew?" I assured her that I was a fervid aficionado of all matters UFOlogical, even though I had unfortunately never come across her magazine. She nodded at that. "We've had such trouble getting general newsstand distribution for *Visitant*. Perhaps I could give you a copy of the latest issue when I get back to the hotel. We'd be so glad to rustle up a new subscriber."

"That would be wonderful! I mean—I'd like that."

The quirky little smile deepened and her eyes had a knowing glint. "It will have to be late . . . Shall we say tonight about ten-thirty, in the Grotto Lounge on the lower level of the hotel?"

Denis piped up, all solemn and regretful. "I'm afraid I'll be in bed by then, Mrs. Harrington."

She gave him an amused look. "Well, I'm sure your Uncle Roger will share the magazine with you tomorrow. And now I must go and eat. I'm dying for some real food after two days of freeze-dried trail rations. So nice to have met you both."

She wafted off, the very embodiment of aetheriality in spite of her heavy climbing boots and insulated jacket, leaving my mind full of voiceless music and my heart hopelessly lost.

* * *

She was only a few minutes late for our rendezvous, and as she entered the crowded rathskeller-style bar, breathtaking in a clinging white floor-length gown with a single bare shoulder, I thanked God for the craftiness of my nephew, who had insisted that I wear black tie rather than the casual jacket and slacks I had thoughtlessly laid out.

"She'll want you to take her to the dance," Denis had said. I didn't bother to ask how he knew. He had nodded his approval when I finished dressing and said, "It's a good thing you're so tall. She likes tall men. And you look so nice in those clothes that it doesn't matter that you're not handsome." I had told him: "Ferme ta boîte, ti-vaurien!" and left him giggling. But he had been right . . .

Elaine and I drank cognac, and I studied the copy of *Visitant* she gave me while she expatiated on the authenticity of UFO visitations and the pigheadedness of the U.S. Air Force, which persisted in denying the "incontrovertible evidence" in favor of extraterrestrial encounters. Her organization, the Aetherians, was about what you would expect: a collection of quasi-mystical fanatics whose zeal outpaced critical judgment. My darling Elaine was as willing to accept the crackpottery of a Von Däniken as she was the serious studies of researchers such as Dr. J. Allen Hynek and Dr. Dennis Hauck. She and her friends were convinced that Earth was under intense surveillance by otherworldly intelligences, entirely benignant, who would reveal themselves to humanity if we would only "have faith" and embrace a pacifistic "astromental" way of life.

She leaned over the small table toward me, enveloped in the intoxicating fragrance of Bal à Versailles, and spoke with surprising coolness. "And you, Roger . . . What do you think of all this? Am I a credulous fool, as my ex-husband and my family have always said? Am I hopelessly romantic and visionary and deluded by swamp gas and moonshine?"

My mind cried out: You are romantic and utterly captivating, and in a crazy backhanded way you're *right*!

But that would never do. Not yet. A false note, and she'd be off. I found myself studying the situation with the detached cunning of a master seducer, my normal awkwardness with women having been somehow miraculously electrocauterized by the thunderbolt. I rolled up the UFO magazine and tapped it meditatively against my balloon glass. What would be the most judicious way of snaring her? Perhaps—the truth?

"Elaine, what I'm about to confess to you I've never dared to tell another person. I was afraid to, afraid of ridicule. There have been so many jokes about spaceships and little green men . . ."

Her face shone. "Roger! Not—an encounter! You've *had* one?"

I let my eyes fall and made a deprecating gesture.

"You have!" she whispered. "Oh, tell me."

I let it out with becoming hesitancy, well edited. "It was last summer. I was in the mountains, hiking, and a violent storm came up. I had hurt my leg. It was rather a serious situation. Night was coming on and I had no shelter. Suddenly there was a strange kind of light and the rain stopped in an unnatural way. And this voice—this inhuman voice—"

"Did you see their spaceship? Did it land?"

The crowded bar all around us had faded to an unfocused blur. Our faces were nearly touching. Her misty red hair was caught back in a smooth chignon and the only jewelry she wore was a pearl and diamond ring on her right little finger. Her deeply tanned skin with its touch of sunburn made a sensuous contrast to the white silk of her simple gown. In the fashion of the times, her breasts were free. The nipples had come alive with the intensity of her emotion.

My composure threatened to disintegrate completely. I took a hasty gulp of cognac and resumed my tale.

"I didn't see any ship. I didn't even see the—the being who spoke to me. Perhaps I was blinded by the light. But he healed my leg instantly. And he told me without equivocation that he came from another star."

And there it is. Dear Elaine, you want so much to believe in marvels. But I could show you marvels that would make flying saucers insignificant, marvels inside your own mind and mine, and within our bodies . . .

"Don't stop—go on!" she pleaded. "What happened next?"

I lifted my shoulders. "I seemed to fall asleep. Perhaps I lost consciousness. It was very confusing. But when I awoke I was standing just outside a trail shelter, although I swear I'd been more than two miles away from it when I had my—my encounter. That's really all there is to it. A very improbable story. I probably dreamed the whole thing."

"Oh, no! It's quite plausible, even the part about your losing consciousness. The aliens may have taken you aboard their craft and *examined* you."

I managed to look startled. "I don't remember any such thing."

"You wouldn't!" She was intense. "Try to put yourself in the aliens' place, Roger. To them, we're a primitive people—easily frightened, scientifically unsophisticated, possibly even dangerous. They'd want to study us but their activities would have to be discreet. They wouldn't want to disrupt our culture . . . Have you ever heard of the Cargo Cults in the South Pacific?"

"Those deluded tribes in New Guinea who thought the military transport planes of World War Two were flown by gods?"

"Exactly. Not only in New Guinea, but in the islands all around it; and the Cult started in the nineteenth century, when the first European traders arrived. The local people saw wonderful cargoes coming off the ships, and later off the aircraft. They wanted things like that for themselves and began to believe that the gods would send miraculous cargoes if everyone prayed hard. Their ancient way of life was completely disrupted by the Cargo Cult."

"You think that extraterrestrials would want to be careful not to touch off a similar reaction among Earthlings?"

"If they're intelligent and have our best interests at heart."

"But the aliens have already disrupted our culture to a certain extent with the flying-saucer flaps . . ."

"Not really, Roger. They've shown their ships to us so that we'll get used to the idea of an interstellar civilization. To prepare us for the day they actually *do* land."

"Do you think it'll be soon?"

She hesitated. "You may know that my group has been coming to these mountains for a number of years now, trying to make contact with the visitors. Mental contact. This year, for the first time, I think we may have been successful."

I did my best to hide my skepticism. Darling, if you want to believe it, then let it be so! I made suitably encouraging comments while she described the experience, which struck me as a patent case of wishful thinking.

"I intend to write it up for the magazine, of course," she said in conclusion, "and I'd like to do an article on your encounter, too, Roger."

I registered bourgeois alarm. "I'd rather you didn't, Elaine. I've never told anyone about it—only you. And you're different from anyone I've ever met."

"So are you, Roger." She smiled and extended her hand as she rose from her chair. God! Had the gambit failed after all? My coercive faculty seemed paralyzed. She said, "Of course I'll keep your story in confidence if you want me to. Do look over my little magazine, though. And if you change your mind—"

"Must you go so soon?" I asked inanely.

The silver eyes twinkled. "Well—we could go upstairs and dance if you like. The rest of the Aetherians were too tired after our mountain expedition, but I feel exhilarated. Would you like to take me dancing, Roger?"

My mind gave a triumphant shout. I bowed over her hand, summoning suavity from God knows where. "Enchanté, chère Madame."

"You're French!" She was delighted.

"Only a Franco-American," I admitted. "Even Canadians make fun of our low accent, and our Yankee neighbors secretly envy our savoir faire—while calling us frogs behind our backs."

"There are frogs who are princes in disguise. Are you one of those?"

Elaine, my beloved, I am indeed! And if my courage doesn't fail me, you may see the fantasy's fulfillment this very night . . .

So we laugh, and we mount the stairs, and we sweep arm in arm into the glittering ballroom while a hundred pairs of eyes watch. The orchestra of the famous old resort has instructions to intersperse contemporary music with a generous leavening of romantic oldies, so we hold each other close as we dance to "Fly Me to the Moon" and "Where or When." With her in my arms I am no longer a lowly Assistant Convention Manager presuming above my station but a dark and debonair hero with a Mysterious Secret, squiring the most lovely woman in the room. The other dancers sense the psychomagnetism. We become the center of attention, the golden couple wrapped in uncanny glamour. Our human race still does not recognize the existence of the higher mental faculties—but it can't help *feeling* them.

Elaine and I dance and smile and begin to open our minds to one another. Charily I lift the curtains hiding her emotions, using a gentle redactive probe, the type I instinctively developed when working with baby Denis. The floating thought-patterns are easily accessible. She has loved before and she has tasted ashes. The coolness is a symptom of unfulfillment and self-doubt. She is idealistic but retains a healthy sense of humor. She is really afraid that her pleasant and affluent world will end in a storm of radioactive fallout.

The musical beat becomes more modern, more compelling, and frankly sexual. Our bodies move to the explicit, angular rhythms, no longer daring to touch. But our minds approach conjunction now and I cannot help communicating my heat to her. It is accepted.

Finally, without a word, she leads me from the ballroom. We take the elevator to her luxurious suite overlooking the moonlit mountain range. We kiss at last and her mouth is velvety and cool, eager to receive my fire, pathetically hopeful of returning it. I hear my mindspeech shouting words of love and desire—and she gasps as her lips break away.

"Roger . . . my dear, it's so strange, but—"

I know. I know. Don't be afraid.

Aloud, I whisper, "You heard a telepathic message from outer space and it didn't frighten you. Will you be frightened if I tell you why you were able to hear that alien message?"

Subconsciously, she already knows.

I hold her more tightly, kissing her brow, her cheeks, her upturned fragrant throat. My flooding passion is channeled into the ultraspeech and breaks through the barrier of her latency.

Elaine! Don't be afraid, I love you and I'll help you. Your mind-powers have lain dormant all your life but they're coming alive now. And here's the funny thing, my darling—I've been dormant, too, in a different way, until you came.

Roger? . . . Roger!

See? It's all true. True and wonderful. Now I'll help you, and later you'll help me.

She bespeaks me, tentatively at first, in clotted emotion-fuzzed utterances that gradually assume coherence. Then she becomes excited to the point of hysteria and I must constantly inject reassuring redactive impulses. When she calms I kiss her bare shoulder, her arms, the palms of her chilled hands. My PK finds the pins that hold her hair knotted. I release it and she cries out:

Roger? Really TRUE? Really HAPPEN? GodGodGod! You&I *minds communicate . . .*

Yes. Special minds. I love you.

Slowly, I undress her. I close the blinds with my PK, leaving only a slender beam of moonlight to illuminate her body. The blood sings in me and I must restrain myself. I say to her:

There are people who are born with extraordinary types of minds. I'm one. So are you. There are a few others that I know about. There must be many more. You've heard of extrasensory perception . . .

She moans in mingled fear and ecstasy, holding out her arms to me. "Come," she begs. "Don't tell me any more. I can't bear it. Just love me."

I am naked myself now, and—yes, a little afraid. I have had so many unfulfilled fantasies about the experience that lies ahead of us, so many dreams. I know what the perfection ought to be, and now I face the challenge of having to create it not only for myself, but also for her—because up until now, my poor Elaine has, like me, known only an empty release.

But she must not be frightened. I say, "Please close your eyes, chérie. Trust me."

My brain and body burn, and I am ready. As in the familiar dream I feel myself hovering above her. I enfold her in my arms, lift her without effort, and enter. Her coolness is shocked by my fever and she cries out. Her eyes open but now we can see only each other. The motion is mutual and quite perfect, for we are suspended together in a bright rapture that endures and swells while our minds seem to fuse. I have ignited her at last. When fulfillment comes and my own brain seems to shatter I feel her faint for the joy of it. Turning in the air, I support her, then let myself descend. We rest together for a long time and I thank God for her. We will stay together forever like this, sharing mind and body, banishing all fear . . .

She awoke with her head on my chest. I was stroking her hair.

"I've never—never—" She was unable to continue.

"Was it good?"

"I wanted you very much, Roger. Now I know why. Does— does the extrasensory thing account for it?"

"That, and my being something of a frog prince."

She laughed giddily and began moving her body in a gentle rhythm, without urgency. "You amazing man. I actually felt as though we were floating—doing it in midair."

I was coming alive again slowly. "I had to wait so long. And then, when I finally found you, I wasn't sure I could . . . the way I had dreamed it. But it happened. At last."

She lifted her head and regarded me with astonished eyes. My mental sight caressed every plane of her face. Before she could ask the question I closed her lips with mine.

"You couldn't be!" she whispered when she finally broke free.

It was my turn to laugh. "I warned you I had been dormant,

waiting patiently on my lily pad for a complaisant princess. A veritable virgin frog."

"I don't believe you. Is it some religious thing, then? No normal man—"

My coercion silenced her. I opened my mind and showed her the truth. To my amazement, she began to weep.

"My poor, darling Roger. Oh, my dear. And if we hadn't found each other—?"

"I don't know. As you saw, my first experience with love ended rather badly. I was mistaken about the depth of her feeling because she was unable to open her mind to me. I couldn't risk that again. Do you understand?"

"And you're sure about me." It was a statement.

"You went to the heart of the matter when you started to tell me that I wasn't normal. Of course I'm not. Luckily for me, neither are you. That's why you're going to marry me." I was grinning at her in the moonlight and my fingers traced tickling pathways up and down the luscious curve of her spine.

She said, "Oh, no!"

"You won't marry me?"

"Of course I will, fool." She clung to me. "I meant—perhaps we shouldn't do it again quite so soon. You destroyed me. Do you realize that?"

I gave a sinister chuckle. "The prince is not to be denied. He has princely prerogatives—et un boute-joie princier!"

"But I don't know whether I can *live* through it a second time tonight!" Even as she made false protest, she was encouraging my renaissance. "If they find my poor little dead body in here tomorrow, you'll be the prime suspect. Think of your embarrassment when the prosecutor demands that you produce the weapon in court! Think of the vulgar sensationalism, the requests for autographs—aah!"

Shush.

Oh my darling oh Roger.

Have no fear. If you're really concerned, this time we'll do it on the bed.

Elaine rented a house in Bretton Woods and transferred the one-woman editorial office of her little magazine to its front bedroom. We made good use of the other one all throughout that enchanted summer and planned to marry in November, when her divorce action would be finalized. In those years the Catholic Church was ambivalent in its recognition of such marriages, and sexual liaisons such as ours were considered to be sinful; but I was ready to defy a regiment of archangels for Elaine's sake, and the guilt that must accompany the violation of one's principles was banished to the deepest part of my unconscious. Only those of you, reading this, who are yourselves operant metapsychics can understand the inevitability of our sexual merging, our excitement at the increasingly profound bonding that we experienced—the soul-mating that lovers have sought and celebrated throughout all the ages. Even though Elaine never attained full operancy in relation to other minds, she did become fully consonant with me. We spoke to each other without words, knew each other's moods and needs through telepathic interchange, shared sensations, even reinforced each other's ecstatic submersion. You lovers in the Unity would no doubt think our efforts pitifully naive and maladroit; but we thought ourselves in wonderland. Elaine's previous partners, most especially her insensitive husband, had failed to arouse her; her inhibitions had restrained her from any attempt at remedy. But when she was with me there was no need for any crass éclaircissement. I *knew* her from the very beginning. It was the most amazing part of our love, and it also precipitated the ending because I was not wise enough to know the hazards of entering another's most private place while utterly disarmed.

The four short months with Elaine were the happiest time of my life. Without her I would become a hollow thing—a mere spectator when I was not a puppet. Looking back, I can see that our separation helped bring the great scheme to fruition; but whether the Lylmik engineered it deliberately or whether they simply took advantage of our little tragedy must remain an unanswered question. The Ghost surely knows, but it is silent, just as heaven was silent when I prayed for the strength of character that might have carried me beyond fury and pride to the forgiveness that would be so easy to give now, nearly 140 years too late . . .

But let me tell the story quickly. First, the happy memories:

Champagne picnics and love on an old Hudson's Bay blanket in the deep woods beside Devil's Elbow Brook.

A moonlit tennis game played in the middle of the night on a court at the White Mountain Hotel—and all the staff knowing about Elaine and me, and not daring to say a word because she was Somebody.

Pub-crawling with her in lowest Montréal on a Canadian holiday weekend, and defending her honor in a riot of psychokinetically smashed glassware when she was insulted by canaille even more drunk than we were.

Going down to Boston together, staying at the Ritz-Carlton, sitting on the grass for open-air Pops concerts, messing around the market, and never but *never* eating baked beans.

Taking jaunts to the Donovan family's summer home at Rye where she tried to teach me to sail, then browsing for antiques among the tourist-trappy little coast villages until it was time to finish the day with a clambake or lobster-broil and love on the beach.

Sitting petrified beside her as she drove her red Porsche like a demon through the Maine woods, playing tag with highballing log trucks going eighty-six miles an hour.

Lovemaking on a stormy afternoon in my ancient Volkswagen stalled in the middle of a Vermont covered bridge.

Lovemaking in a meadow above her house at Concord, while monarch butterflies reeled around us, driven berserk by the aetheric vibes.

Love in a misty forest cascade during an August heat wave.

Love in my hotel office at noon behind locked doors.

Love on a twilit picnic table, interrupted by voyeur bears.

Mad psychokinetic love in thirty-three postural variations.

Love after a quarrel.

Hilarious love.

Marathon love.

Tired, comfortable love.

And toward the end, a desperate love that did hold fear and doubt at bay for a little while . . .

There are memories of another type altogether, which I must deal with more briskly:

One of the most disquieting was my realization that she would never be able to overcome the mental blockages causing her latency. She could converse telepathically with me, and Denis could "hear" her as well as probe her memories; but she was never functionally operant with others except when she was experiencing extraordinary psychic stress. Elaine's mind thus seemed to belong to me almost by default, and I felt the first stirrings of real guilt: we were *not* one mind but two, and to pretend otherwise was to court disaster.

She was able to keep very few things secret from me. This

gave me numerous opportunities to learn how to mask from her my own reaction of shock or chagrin—as, for instance, when I found out just how wealthy she really was. She cheerfully made plans for my gainful employment in Donovan Enterprises "after you give up your tedious little job at the hotel." She had all kinds of ideas on how I might capitalize on my metapsychic talents (and how Denis could go far if we only liberated him from the clutches of the Jesuits). She wanted to expand *Visitant* magazine into a rallying vehicle for as-yet-undiscovered superminds. When I balked at these and similar enthusiasms she was hurt, resentful, and unrepententely calculating.

Elaine's loyalty was ardent. Nevertheless she was unable to disguise her disappointment when I was less than a success at a meeting with her brother the eminent Congressman, her other brother the wheeler-dealer land developer, and her sister the Back Bay socialite do-gooder. Elaine plainly regretted my lower-class origins, my lack of appreciation for the cosmological bullshit espoused by her Aetherian clique, and my persistently old-fashioned religious faith—which wasn't at all like the trendy version of Catholicism made socially acceptable by the Kennedy clan.

I introduced Elaine to the Remillards at a disastrous Fourth of July barbecue in Berlin thrown by Cousin Gerard. Poor Elaine! Her clothes were too chic, her manners too high-bred, and the covered dish she contributed to the rustic buffet too haute cuisine. She compounded the debacle by speaking elegant Parisian French to old Onc' Louie and the other Canuck elders, and by admitting that her family were Irish Protestants. The only Remillards who weren't scandalized were little Denis and my brother Don. Don was, if anything, too damned friendly toward her. She assured me that there was no telepathic communication between the two of them; but I recalled his coercive exploits of yesteryear and couldn't help feeling doubt at the same time that I cursed myself for being a jealous fool.

Later that summer, when we would briefly visit Don and Sunny to pick up or drop off Denis, whom we often took on outings, Elaine was distant or even covertly antagonistic toward my brother. At the same time she claimed to pity him and pressed me to "see that he got help" in combating his alcoholism. I knew that any effort on my part would be worse than useless and refused to interfere—which provoked one of our few serious quarrels. Another took place in early September, when I took Denis back to Brebeuf Academy and revealed his metapsychic abilities to Father Jared Ellsworth, as the Ghost had instructed me to do. Elaine was irrationally convinced that the Jesuits would "exploit" Denis in some nameless way. I assured her that Ellsworth had reacted with sympathy and equanimity to the revelation (he had even deduced some of the boy's mental talents already); but Elaine persisted in her fretting over Denis, and her attitude toward him was so oddly colored and tortuous that I was unable to make sense of it until long after the end.

The end. God, how I remember it.

It was late in October on a day when the New Hampshire hills were purple and scarlet with the autumn climacteric. We had gone on a season-end pilgrimage to the Great Stone Face, just she and I, and finished up at a secluded country inn near Franconia. It was one of those terminally quaint establishments that still draw Galactic tourists to New England, featuring squeaky floors, crooked walls, and a pleasant clutter of colonial American artifacts, many of which were for sale at ridiculous prices. The food and drink were splendid and the proprietors discreet. After our meal we retired to a gabled bedroom suite and nestled side by side on a sofa with lumpy cushions, watching sparks from a birchwood fire fly up the chimney while rain tapped gently on the roof.

We had been talking about our wedding plans and sipping a rare Aszu Tokay that the host reserved for well-heeled cognoscenti. It was to be a simple civil ceremony down in Concord, with one of her distinguished Donovan uncles officiating. Later we would have a small supper "for the wedding party only," which effectively meant no Remillards except me. I listened to her with only half an ear, drowsy from the wine.

And then Elaine told me she was pregnant.

I recall a thunderous sound. It may have come from the storm outside the inn, or it may have been purely mental, my psychic screens crashing into place. I remember a fixed-frame vision of my hand, frozen in the act of reaching for the decanter. I can still hear Elaine's voice prattling on about how she was so glad it had happened, how she had always wanted children while her ex-husband had not, how our child was certain to be a paragon of "astromental" achievement, perhaps even more brilliant than Denis.

Incapable of speech or even a rational thought, I sat gripped by a grand refusal. It could not be. She had not said it. I think I prayed like a child, entreating God to cancel this thing, to save

my love and my life. I would repeat the same futile supplications
later through the bleak winter months as I tried in vain to conquer
myself and return to her; but always love would be obliterated as
it was at that hellish moment, wiped out by a blast of volcanic
rage and fatally wounded pride.

Of course I knew who the father was.

I finally turned my face to her, and I know I was without
expression, my howling despair inaudible beyond the closet of
my skull. Elaine cowered back against the cushions, shrinking
from the exhalation of pain and menace.

"Roger, what is it?"

Her mind was, as always, completely open to me. And now
that her thoughts concentrated on the certainty of the life growing
within her, I could perceive a complex skein of memories woven
about the embryonic node. The confirmation would be there.

I knew I should leave those memories of her untouched. It
was the only forlorn hope left to me. I must not look into the
secret place but seal it forever, pretend that the child's father was
someone else. Anyone else.

The secret places. All rational beings have them and guard
them—not only for their own sakes but for those of others. Who
but God would love us if all the secret places of our minds lay
exposed? I knew how to conceal my own heart of darkness; it is
one of the first things an operant metapsychic learns, whether he
is bootstrap or preceptor-trained. Only a few poor souls remain
vulnerable always, trapped in the shadow-country between latency and conscious control of their high mental powers. Elaine
was one. Open. Without secrets.

"Roger," she pleaded. "Answer me. For God's sake, darling,
what's the matter?"

Don't look. She loves you, not him. To look would be a sin
—against her and against yourself. You aren't a truth-seeker,
you're a fool. Don't look. Don't look.

I looked. Our love had been sinful, and I must be punished.

She was calm as I lifted my barriers at last, showing her the
incontrovertible fact of my own sterility, and the theft of her
secret, and what made her betrayal impossible to forgive.

"If it had been anyone but him," I said. "Anyone. But, you
see, I wouldn't be able to live with it."

She looked me full in the face. "Once. It happened once—
that first time you took me to meet your family, at that silly
Fourth of July barbecue. It was madness. I don't know what

came over me. It happened before I realized—without my wanting it."

No secret place. Poor Elaine. You *had* wanted it.

I saw the entire episode etched in her memory and knew I'd see it forever. Don focusing the full force of his coercion, her fascination and willing surrender, Don laughing as he took her by the rockets' red glare, kindling in her a stupendous series of orgasms like chain lightning. And his child.

"I can't live with it," I told her.

"Once, Roger. Only once. And now I hate him."

No secrets at all . . . Anyone but him. Damn the mind-powers. Damn him! But never her.

"Roger, I love you. I know how much this must hurt. I *feel* the hurt. But I honestly thought the child was yours . . . that the thing with your brother was a piece of idiocy better left forgotten." She tried to smile, showed me a glowing mental image. "You love little Denis. He's Don's child."

"I couldn't help it. Denis is different. Sunny was different."

"I'm only fifteen weeks gone. I could—"

"No!"

She nodded. "Yes, I see. It wouldn't make any difference, would it? It would make matters worse."

I let the wretched contents of my mind seep out: The child *will* be brilliant. Don's mental faculties are far more impressive than mine, in spite of his flaws. As you know. Goodbye, Elaine.

"Roger, I love you. For the love of God, don't do this!"

I must. I love you I will always love you but I must.

I walked to the door and opened it. Aloud, I said, "I'm going to take your Porsche back to the White Mountain Hotel. In the morning, I'll send one of our drivers back here with it. There are a few things I must get from the house in Bretton Woods, but I should be out of it before noon. I'll leave my key."

"You *fool*," she said.

"Yes."

I went out and softly closed the door after me.

Elaine married Stanton Latimer, a prominent Concord attorney, that November. He gave her child, Annarita, his name and they were a happy family until his death in 1992. The distractions of motherhood—and the decline in flying-saucer sightings after 1975—led Elaine to abandon *Visitant*. She turned her leadership talents to environmental activism and campaigned against acid rain. In time she decided that she had imagined the more improbable facets of our liaison.

Annarita Latimer grew up to be an actress of vibrant and unforgettable presence who had a triumphant, tempestuous career. Like her mother, she was a powerful suboperant. Annarita's third husband was Bernard Kendall, the astrophysicist, who sired her only child, the fully operant Teresa—known to historians of the Galactic Milieu as the mother of Marc Remillard and Jack the Bodiless.

21

SUPERVISORY CRUISER NOUMENON
[LYL 1−0000]
10 MAY 1975

THE SIMB SHUTTLE SAUCER MADE ITS INGRESS INTO THE IMMENSE Lylmik vessel in the manner of a lentil being swallowed by a whale, and the four senior members of the Earth Oversight Authority gathered in the shuttle's airlock to watch the curious docking maneuvers.

"I hate coming aboard Lylmik spacecraft. One is so likely to become overstimulated." The Gi representative, RipRip Muml, whiffled its plumage in a gesture of libido suppression and sealed off four of its eight sensory circuits. "Strange that the Supervisory Body should want to meet with us here in Earth orbit instead of simply transmitting its instructions mentally."

The Simb magnate, Lashi Ala Adassti, watched the scene outside the viewport with rapt fascination. In spite of her high position in the Oversight organization, she had never before been invited to visit a Lylmik cruiser. "I've given up trying to fathom the motives of the Supervisors, especially those relating to *this* perverse little planet . . . Sacred Truth and Beauty! Will you look what's happening out there in the parking bay?"

"An interesting spectacle, but hardly unnerving," remarked the Krondaku, Rola'eroo.

"I've seen it a dozen or so times myself." The Poltroyan magnate shook his head. "But it still rattles me. It's as though we were being digested!"

The saucer rested on a kind of animated turf, pearly tendrils that rippled in peristaltic waves as they propelled the small spacecraft slowly along. A few meters away, on either side of the shuttle's path, plantlike excrescences apparently made of luminous jelly were sprouting up with graceful regularity; they unfurled pallid leafy ribbons and undulated in a questing fashion in the direction of the passing ship. Some of the larger plants "fruited," producing crystalline structures that opened to discharge glittering powder that swirled around the shuttle viewports like saffron smoke. Behind these pseudo-organisms were rising much taller ones that resembled glassy tree-ferns and opalescent feather-palms. These soon formed an impenetrable jungle alongside the saucer, a bright corridor with purple obscurity lying ahead. The smaller ribbon-bearers became more and more numerous and their appendages reached out to caress the moving vessel's sides. It was like sailing underwater through a twisting tunnel alive with glowing albino kelp.

"By their spacecraft ye shall know them," the poetical Gi murmured. "Ours are preposterous and ramshackle, and their operation is so circumscribed by the reproductive habits of our crews that no other entities dare ride in them. Krondak ships are bleakly functional and those of the Poltroyans cozy and baroque, while Simbiari craft like this one we are riding in are paragons of high technology. But how can one classify the Lylmik ships?"

"Peculiar," suggested Rola'eroo, "like the race that produced them."

The others laughed uneasily.

The Poltroyan, a dapper little humanoid wearing heavily bejeweled robes, shared his meditation. "We never really see the Lylmik, even though they must inhabit forms that are manifestations of the matter-energy lattices. They are not pure mind, as some have speculated—and yet they enjoy a mentality unfathomably above our own. They will tell us very little of their history—nothing of their nature. They are infallibly kind. Their zeal in furthering the evolution of the Galactic Mind is formidable, but they often seem capricious. Their logic is not our logic. As RipRip Muml has noted, this ship of theirs is an embodiment of the Lylmik enigma: it is lush, extravagant, playful. Certain of our xenologists have speculated that the enormous cruisers are themselves aspects of Lylmik life, symbionts of the minds they transport. We know that these beings are the Galaxy's most ancient coadunate race, but their actual age and their origin remain a mystery. Our Poltroyan folklore says that the Lylmik home-star Nodyt was once a dying red giant, which the population rejuvenated into a G3 by a metapsychic infusion of fresh hydrogen sixty million years ago. But such a feat is beyond Milieu science, contradicting the Universal Field Theory."

"Our legends," the Krondak monster said, "are even more absurd. They suggest that the Lylmik are survivors of the Big Bang—that they date from the previous universe. A totally ridiculous notion."

"No sillier than ours," said RipRip Muml. "The more simpleminded Gi believe that the Lylmik are angels—pseudocorporeal messengers of the Cosmic All. An unlikely hypothesis, but not inappropriate for mentors of our Galactic Mind."

An impatient frown had been deepening on Lashi Ala's emerald features. "We Simbiari don't tell fairy-tales about the Lylmik. We accept their guidance at the same time as we resent their arrogant condescension. Look how determined they are to give these Earthlings favored treatment. The planet is a Lylmik pet! And yet the Supervisory Body seems blithely ignorant about just how unready for Intervention Earth is. How many times during the Thirty-Year Surveillance have we Simbiari been obliged to save the barbarians from *accidentally* touching off an atomic war? How many more times will we have to rescue the planetary ass during the upcoming pre-Intervention phase? All of us know that there is no way this world's Mind can achieve full coadunation prior to Intervention. Earth will be admitted to the Milieu in advance of its psychosocial maturation! Sheer lunacy!"

The Krondaku remained stolid. "Should the Earth Mind deliberately opt for nuclear warfare during the next forty years, you know that the Intervention will be cancelled. Furthermore, Intervention is contingent upon a certain minimal metaconcerted action by human operants. If they cannot rise above egocentrism to the lowest rung of mental solidarity, not even the Lylmik can force the Milieu to accept them."

Lashi gave a disillusioned grunt. "No other potentially emergent planet ever got such special treatment."

"The Lylmik always have reasons for their actions," the Poltroyan said, "incomprehensible though they may be to us lesser minds. If the Earthlings are destined to be great metapsychic prodigies, as the Lylmik maintain, then the risk of early intervention will be justified."

"You can talk, Falto," Lashi Ala shot back. "Your people haven't been saddled with the bulk of the planetary surveillance and manifestation as we Simbiari have. Why the Lylmik didn't appoint you smug little mauve pricks as prime contractors for Earth, I'll never know! You *like* humans."

Rola'eroo came as close to chuckling as his phlegmatic race was capable. "Perhaps that is the very reason why Poltroy was not given the proctorship. Despite certain imputations of favoritism, I am convinced that the Lylmik desire a fair and just evaluation of humanity. And this"—he offered a magisterial nod to Lashi Ala—"the citizens of the Simbiari Polity will conscientiously provide."

"Oh, well, of course," she muttered.

RipRip Muml gave a delicate shudder. "Thanks be to the Tranquil Infinite that *we* have been spared close contact with Earth. Its artistic productions are exquisite, but the reverberations of violence and suffering are a sore trial to truly sensitive minds."

"I've noticed," said Lashi sweetly, "that you Gi are too sensitive for any number of tedious but necessary assignments."

The great yellow eyes blinked in innocent reproach.

Falto the Poltroyan interposed diplomatically. "We all do the jobs we're best suited for, given the mind-set of the planet under evaluation."

"And with a race as bumptious as humanity, you Simbiari end up carrying the can!" RipRip gave its phallus a cheerful flourish.

Lashi responded with simple dignity. "We know very well that our people are still imperfectly Unified—and I did not mean to imply that we regretted our first assignment as prime contractor to an emerging Mind. On the contrary, we are honored by the Milieu's mandate." She hesitated, a troubled expression crossing her now glistening face. "But the Oversight Authority concedes that Earth is an anomaly. It seems counter to all logic, therefore, that the Concilium should assign its proctorship to us, the most junior Polity in the Milieu. Surely this difficult and barbaric world would fare better under the more sympathetic guidance of Poltroy—or, even better, under the stern direction that the Krondaku vouchsafed to Gi, Poltroyans, and Simbiari alike."

The Krondak magnate's mind-tone was detached and serene. "My race has proctored more than seventeen thousand planetary Minds since the Lylmik raised us to Unity. Only you three survived to coadunation and membership in the Milieu."

"*We've* never had a winner in seventy-two tries," the Poltroyan admitted, "and we're still smarting over the Yanalon fiasco. A toughminded Simb primacy might have saved that world . . . Don't sell your abilities short, Lashi Ala Adassti."

"You mustn't feel downhearted or put-upon," the hermaphrodite added kindly. "Think how the Unity will rejoice if you succeed! We Gi will never enjoy such a triumph. We're too frivolous and sex-obsessed ever to be appointed planetary proctors. No newborn coadunate Mind will ever call us its foster-parents—and we are the poorer thereby."

A harmonious chord of chimes sounded in the mental ears of the four magnates. Outside the viewports the iridescent glow intensified. The shuttle-craft was approaching the terminus of the overgrown tunnel, an iris gateway of yellow metal that opened slowly like the expanding pupil of a great golden eye.

Welcome. And high thoughts to you, most beloved colleagues. Please debark and join us in the hospitality chamber.

The shuttle had halted at the gateway. Rola'eroo extended a tentacle and activated the hatch mechanism, admitting a billow of warm, superoxygenated atmosphere to the airlock. The four entities toddled, strode, stalked, and slithered down the integral gangway, crossed a short expanse of anemonoid turf flanked by crystal foliage, and entered the Lylmik sanctum. The gate shut behind them.

It was rather dim inside, comfortably so after the brilliant part of the ship they had just traversed. The walls and flooring were gently corrugated, transparent, and seemed to be holding back an encompassing volume of bubbly liquid that swirled slowly in ever-changing eddies of blue and green. In the center of the room was a crescent-shaped table with three seats for the Gi, the Poltroyan, and the Simb—and a squatting spot for the ponderous Krondaku. Besides the furniture, which was austere in design and made of the warm yellow metal, the room contained only a low dais about three meters square, formed by slight exaggerations of the floor ribbing.

The Earth Oversight Authority took their places and waited. Lashi Ala betrayed her apprehension by smearing the table surface with dabs of ichor from her perspiring hands. She tucked them into the sleeves of her uniform, where there were blotting pads, and buffed away the smears with her elbows. The other three Overseers tactfully averted their eyes and veiled their brains.

Above the dais there appeared a small atmospheric maelstrom.

Our heartfelt felicitations to you, dear colleagues, upon the successful completion of Earth's first phase of intensified overt manifestation.

In metaconcert, the Authority responded: We are gratified that the Supervisory Body approves, and herewith present a digest of data relevant to progress in coadunation of the World Mind. [Display.]

The maelstrom was enlarging, spinning in a plane perpendicular to the dais, and five distinct whorls were condensing out of it.

How interesting that the outbreaks of metapsychic operancy among the humans are so widely scattered. Even though the genes for high mental function are present in all racial groups, one notes that its phenotypic expression crops out with special vigor among certain Celtic and Oriental populations.

This has been allowed for in ethnodynamic equations. The sorting factors have a fascinating Darwinian aspect, in that those groups subject to great environmental—as opposed to social—stress tend to manifest the metapsychic traits most strongly. Thus the Georgian, Alpine, Hebridean, and Eastern Canadian Celts tend to become operant more rapidly than their more numerous Irish and French congeners. The same is true of the Asian irruptive locus, with the North Siberian, Mongol, and Hokkaido groups most noteworthy, together with the isolated fractions flourishing in Tibet and Finland. Unfortunately, the Australian aboriginal locus has become nearly extinct, as have the Kalahari and Pigmy concentrations in Africa. The Nilotic group trembles on the brink due to severe social disruption. In any case, these southern populations are now almost too small to be viable reservoirs of operant genotypes.

Tragic. But as we know, operancy must be combined with ethnic dynamism if coadunation of the Mind is to be achieved.

And on Earth, dynamism is largely a Northern function, due to the complex interaction of stress factors.

"Northern hyperfertility isn't to be sneezed at, either," murmured the Poltroyan, ex-concert. "Which is why I put my money on the Canucks in the operancy sweepstakes."

The other three Overseers flinched at the effrontery of their small colleague, but the Lylmik seemed amused.

You are most perceptive, Faltonin-Virminonin! It is indeed from that group, especially the northeastern Franco-Americans, that we expect the largest numbers of natural operants to be born during this critical pre-Intervention phase of proctorship.

The five atmospheric vortices had now assumed a decidedly material aspect. The Gi and the Krondaku, being the most ultrasensitive members of the metaconcert, realized with some excitement that the Supervisors were about to do them the unusual honor of assuming astral bodies—or, at least, astral heads. The news ignited the entire Authority, especially Lashi Ala, who had never experienced a Lylmik vis-à-vis encounter.

They asked: Is it your wish, then, that we devise plans for the special encouragement of these Franco-American operants?

By no means. This is a task reserved for others.

Others? . . . What others?

But before the Oversight Authority could pursue this puzzle further, they were completely distracted by the apparition unfolding before them.

Above the dais now floated five heads. Perhaps in consideration of the Poltroyan, Gi, and Simb representatives, who had largely humanoid features, the heads each developed two eyes and a single smiling mouth. Their psychocreative flesh was roseate with no trace of hair, feathering, scales, or other epidermal outgrowth. The eyes of the central head were gray; those of the four surrounding heads were a brilliant aquamarine green. The Lylmik had no necks, but from their occipital regions trailed multiple ectoplasmic filaments like pale gauzy scarves stirring in a light breeze. Strangely, each of the different Authority magnates thought that the heads were supremely beautiful. Even those who had seen this manifestation of the Lylmik before felt that they could look into those eyes forever without tiring; and poor Lashi Ala, meeting them for the first time, was reduced to bewitched helplessness.

"I am Noetic Concordance," said the uppermost head.

"I am Eupathic Impulse," said the lowest.

"I am Homologous Trend," said the right-hand head.

"I am Asymptotic Essence," said the one on the left.

The central head, which radiated the most overwhelming power of all, had the softest voice. "And I am Atoning Unifex. We of the Supervisory Body embrace you and your organization. We thank you for what you have done, and charge you to carry on your assigned tasks in spite of discouragements, doubts, and difficulties. It is known to us that the small planet we are orbiting at this moment occupies a critical place in the probability lattices. From it may emerge a Mind that will exceed all others in metapsychic potential. It is known to us that this Mind will be capable of destroying our beloved Galactic Milieu. It is further known to us that this Mind will also be capable of magnifying the Milieu immensely, accelerating the Unification of all the inhabited starsystems. For this reason we have directed this extraordinary attempt at Intervention. It involves a great risk. But all evolutionary leaps are hazardous, and without risk-taking there can only be stagnation, the triumph of entropy, and eventual death. Do you understand this, colleagues?"

We understand.

"Mental potential is not actualization. The human race must reach an acceptable level of operancy largely through its own efforts. We can guide, but we cannot force evolution of the Mind. Thus there still exists the possibility that this rising operant population may founder—either through internal or external calamity. There exists another possibility, fortunately diminishing, that the entire world may perish in a suicidal conflict. So Intervention is not certain. But we shall work toward it . . . you in your way and we in ours, full of trust."

We understand.

"Go now and initiate the next Oversight phase. From time to time we will lend special assistance."

We do not understand, but we acquiesce willingly.

The central head nodded. The eyes of all five were ablaze with irresistible psychic energy. The heads began melting away to ectoplasmic vapor, but the eyes remained to focus Unifying power.

Join with us, said the Supervisors, and the minds of the Overseers rushed into the joyous light.

A long time later, when the four awoke in their shuttle-craft, they instinctively came together to gaze out of a viewport at the blue planet rolling below.

"Incredible," said the Krondaku.

"What an experience!" Lashi Ala was still in a state of neartotal bemusement. "I agree—it was quite incredible."

The Gi shook its head, gently corrective. "While Unity with the Lylmik is memorable, it is not the matter that Rola'eroo Mobak finds difficult to believe."

"Certainly not," the monster growled. "It's what they *said*."

The Poltroyan pursed lavender lips and hoisted a single eyebrow in unspoken query.

"The head in the middle." RipRip Muml amplified its speech with a remembered vision. "It said that the Lylmik were going to assist us. That's even *more* unprecedented than their original veto of the Concilium pull-out vote!"

Rola'eroo said, "You will also recall that the Lylmik Supervisors told us that we were not to attempt positive reinforcement of the Franco-American operant group . . . that the task would be undertaken by others."

Both Poltroyan eyebrows shot up and the ruby optics bulged. "Love's Oath! You can't mean it!"

"I conclude that certain human operants are to be shepherded by the Lylmik themselves," Rola'eroo asserted. "By these aloof beings who scarcely ever condescend to participate in the Concilium deliberations, who tantalize us and confuse us when they are not vexing us with their mystical vagary."

"There was nothing vague," Lashi said, "about that crew we met today. That central head was downright blunt."

"Most uncharacteristic," the Krondaku said. "We must ponder the implications strenuously."

The Gi had turned to the port and contemplated the blue planet with a certain foreboding. Its irrepressible genitalia were blanched and subdued. "Earthlings! Do you know—I'm beginning to be quite afraid of them."

"Nonsense!" said Lashi Ala stoutly. "We Simbiari know humanity better than any of you. They don't scare *us*."

The three other entities exchanged thoughts of sudden, shared comprehension.

**THE END OF
PART ONE**

PART II

THE DISCLOSURE

1

NEW YORK CITY, EARTH
21 FEBRUARY 1978

THE FLIGHT FROM CHICAGO HAD BEEN OVER AN HOUR LATE, AND helicopter shuttle service between Kennedy and Manhattan had been disrupted by the same fog that had delayed the airplane. The car-rental counter was mobbed, but here Kieran O'Connor's coercion expedited procurement of a Cadillac limousine. He and Arnold Pakkala, his executive assistant, took the front seat while Jase Cassidy and Adam Grondin got into the back. Then they were off in a squeal of expensive rubber, with the minds of Cassidy and Grondin clearing the way and Pakkala driving like the battle-trained Chicago commuter that he was.

Kieran closed his burning eyes and dreamed while the big black automobile roared up the Van Wyck and Long Island Expressways in defiance of the speed limit. It negotiated the snarl at the Queens-Midtown Tunnel magically and bulldozed its way down 42nd Street. Other vehicles seemed to melt out of its way as it streaked up Avenue of the Americas, ignored by patrolling NYPD cruisers. It turned left onto West 57th against the lights, zigzagged from lane to lane amidst traffic apparently frozen in place, and plunged into the whorl of Columbus Circle like a black shark invading a sluggish shoal of prey species. Here, with vehicles coming at it from six directions, the limousine faced its keenest challenge. The targeting eyes of Cassidy and Grondin flicked to and fro and their minds shouted silent commands to the other drivers: *You stop! You go right! You move left lane! Up the curb bike! Out of the way walkers! Go! Stop! Gangway!* Enchanted buses froze at the curb or lumbered aside; private cars seemed to cower as they yielded; take-out-food delivery boys on bicycles and pedestrians scattered like pigeons before a hawk; even the pugnacious Manhattan taxis were demoralized and swerved out of the limousine's charmed path with tires screeching and brake lights flashing scarlet alarm.

Arnold Pakkala guided the Cadillac with fluid precision through the chaos, ran a red light for the seventeenth time that night, and floored the accelerator when he attained the comparatively unimpeded reach of Central Park West.

Adam Grondin said: Kennedy to Central Park 34 minutes. Beautiful Arnie.

Jase Cassidy said: Time to make it. Chief still asleep?

Pakkala said: Until I tell him to wake up.

A map image of New York City seemed to hover in his peripheral vision off to the right, among the lamplit bare trees of the park. He spotted a police cruiser, but Adam and Jase had already fuzzed the minds of the two officers inside. They knew they couldn't possibly have seen a Caddy doing seventy northbound, and turned their attention to a doorman walking three poodles who was suspiciously unencumbered by a pooper-scooper.

Pakkala said: Only a few blocks more.

The limousine charged across 65th Street on the fag end of the amber light, then hung a left onto 66th virtually riding the rims. For the last time Cassidy and Grondin exerted their coercive powers to stop the modest flow of vehicles on Columbus. The Cadillac took the final corner smoothly, decelerated, and drove up the ramp in front of the Lincoln Center for the Performing Arts. A touch of power brakes brought it to a sedate halt.

Cassidy and Grondin relaxed their overstrained brains with audible groans of relief. Arnold Pakkala's face had gone rigid in the wan light from the instrument panel. Still gripping the steering wheel, he let his head fall back against the padded rest. His eyes closed. The other two men flinched at the orgasmic discharge that energized the interior of the car for an instant, setting their own nerves afire with sympathetic vibration. Seconds later Pakkala was sitting ramrod-straight again, not one white hair out of place, stripping off his leather driving gloves with small, neat motions.

"Jesus, Arnie, I *wish* you wouldn't do that." Grondin ripped open a pack of Marlboros with shaking hands and coaxed one out.

Cassidy wiped his florid face with a handkerchief. "Wouldn't that be a helluva thing for the chief to wake up to? The fallout from your stupid come!"

Pakkala ignored that. "Mr. O'Connor may continue to sleep until I make certain that our subjects are actually inside, in their box. If our informants erred—or if they lied—other plans will have to be made."

"Well, get cracking, dammit," Cassidy snapped. "Don't just sit around here getting your rocks off."

Pakkala's face went rigid again. He seemed to be studying the hub of the steering wheel with blind eyes. Tiny flakes of snow sifted down and melted to pinpoint droplets when they struck the warm windshield. The engine idled soundlessly and Kieran O'Connor exhaled a deep, sighing breath that was almost a sob.

Grondin sucked cigarette smoke fiercely. "Poor bastard."

Cassidy said, "He'll be all right. Just so long as those two dago butchers are in there where we can get at 'em."

Nodding at Pakkala, Grondin said, "Arnie'll find out. Umpteen thousand people in there, but Arnie'll find 'em if they're inside. Helluva head, old Arnie, even if he has his weird moments."

"I still think this is the wrong place for a hit, though," Cassidy said. "I know the chief has to do it before any of the New York crowd expect him to act. But to do it *here* . . ."

Both men looked across Lincoln Plaza, where the five tall arches forming the façade of the Metropolitan Opera House enclosed a scene of festive splendor. They were more than ninety feet high and panelled in transparent glass from top to bottom, framing the four tiers of the house and the golden vaults of the ceiling. Colossal murals by Marc Chagall blazed on either side of a grand double staircase of white marble, carpeted in red. The walls were crimson velvet or gleaming stone, set off by twinkling sconces. In the central arch hung the famous starburst chandeliers, the largest at the top and the smaller satellites offset beneath it like a cluster of crystal galaxies. Rising bright against the black sky of winter, the opera house looked like the open door into a fantasy world, rather than the designated site of a double execution.

Tonight's house was a sellout, a benefit performance of *La Favorita* by Donizetti. The performance was a new and lavish one featuring the superstars Luciano Pavarotti, Shirley Verrett, and Sherill Milnes, a rare treat for aficionados of Italian opera. Among the most devoted of these was a certain New York City business leader named Guido "Big Guy" Montedoro. On most opening nights he was to be found in his regular box with his wife, his grown children, and the spouses of the latter. Tonight, however, his companions were all male. Seated at the rear of the box were four trusted associates of the Montedoro Family, whose rented tuxedos bulged slightly under the arms. In front, next to Don Guido himself, was the honored guest of the evening, Vicenzu Falcone. Don Vicenzu, an old friend of the Big Guy and a fellow music-lover, was being fêted on the occasion of his parole from the federal prison at Lewisburg, Pennsylvania, where he had been serving time for tax evasion. He was accompanied by his deputy, Mike LoPresti, who had kept the Brooklyn narcotics pipeline running more or less efficiently while his superior was hors de combat. LoPresti's brother-in-law, Joseph "Joe Porks" Porcaro, the Falcone enforcer, was also in attendance. It was this same Porcaro who had gone to Chicago three days earlier to execute a contract on the upstart young consigliere of the Chicago Outfit, whose far-reaching activities had encroached once too often upon certain business interests of the boys from Brooklyn.

Porcaro, following LoPresti's orders, had trailed his intended victim to the posh Oakbrook shopping complex in the western suburbs of Chicago. He had smiled as the counselor took pains to park his brand new Mercedes 450SL at some distance from other cars, lest their careless drivers open doors against its immaculate flanks and ding the paint job. When the consigliere went away, Porcaro wired a small bomb to the Mercedes, drove to O'Hare Airport, and was home in Brooklyn in time for a supper of linguini with white clam sauce.

Unfortunately for him—and for Underboss LoPresti, who had ordered the hit on his own authority without consulting Don Vicenzu—the Camastra Family's legal adviser had come to Oakbrook to pick up his wife and children, who had spent the morning shopping with the wife's mother. The young parents and their daughters, aged two and three, had approached the booby-trapped automobile together. But then Shannon, the three-year-old, decided that she had to go to the bathroom. Scolding her just a little, her father took her to a nearby department store while the mother and younger child waited in the car.

It was a cold and blustery February day, and only natural that Rosemary Camastra O'Connor should start the engine of the Mercedes to get the heater going.

[Fireflower!]

Wake up Mr. O'Connor.

[Fireflower!] The dark hallway in the dingy flat in Southie with the emanations from the sickroom hitting him fresh again so that he nearly puked with the pain before he could shut it out *Kier Kier my baby are you back did you pray did you* . . .

Wake up. It's all right. We're at the Opera House.

[Fireflower!] Mom calling in her broken-glass-edge voice the voice only he could hear crying and dying clinging obstinately to her agony and to him *Kier Kier you did receive Holy Communion didn't you Kier you didn't sneak breakfast again did you oh you know you have to pray hard I can't so you must and then there'll be a miracle* . . .

Wake up sir. Open your eyes.

[Fireflower!] The hands dry as newspaper the fingernails blue and broken one hand gripping the tarnished silver-filigree rosary and the other tangled in his old sweater pulling him closer and him fighting to raise a higher and higher wall between the two of them and she calling out to the awful Irish God she loved the one who tortured *Kier Kier he tests the ones he loves best he loves us I love you Kier pray for the miracle pray Jesus it stops Jesus stop it please stop it Kier stop it* . . .

Mr. O'Connor! Wake up!

[Fireflower!] Yes Mom I'll stop it even if damned God won't I know how . . . I know how . . . was it so easy? Blue eyes gone wide and black and empty pain gone mind gone are you really gone? And the boy screams [fireflower!] and the grown man screams [fireflower!] and it expands in thunder under Illinois clouds as gray as Mom's fluffy hair on the coffin's cheap satin pillow and the coffin will have to be closed you understand Mr. O'Connor wake up Mr. O'Connor wake up!

Kieran opened his eyes.

Arnold Pakkala was there, and Adam Grondin, and Jase Cassidy. The loyal ones, the ones he had salvaged and bonded to him, the ones like him: hurt through their own fault, ever hurting.

He asked Arnold: Are Porcaro and LoPresti inside?

"Yes, sir," Pakkala said out loud. "Everything is exactly as Koenig and Matucci told us it would be. The two subjects are here with the dons. There are no women. Four button-men are inside the box and two are on watch outside. The intermission between the Third and Fourth Acts is about to begin. You and Adam and Jason can mingle readily with the crowd."

Kieran unfastened his seat belt and removed his hat, his white silk scarf, and his dark blue cashmere overcoat. Grondin and Cassidy hastily followed his example. All three of them were dressed in black-tie formal evening wear. "Go around to Sixty-fifth Street, by the Juilliard School," Kieran told Arnold. "There's a tunnel on the lower level that goes under the plaza to the stage door. We'll meet you there afterward."

"Yes, sir. Good luck!"

Cassidy and Grondin were already out on the pavement, heading for the broad steps; but Kieran paused, half in and half out of the limousine, and smiled at his executive assistant. A mental picture hovered between them: a drunken derelict being kicked to death by a vicious punk in a Chicago alley, uttering a last telepathic cry for help.

"Luck, Arnold? You of all people should know better than to say that. People like us make our own luck."

Kieran stepped out of the car and slammed the door. The Cadillac's headlights came on like some great animal opening its eyes. Arnold Pakkala raised his hand and said: I'll be waiting.

Kieran nodded. He stood there in spite of the arctic wind knifing through his clothing, until the limousine disappeared around the corner. Yes, we make our own luck. We make our own reality, and when the bill comes due we pay cash on the barrelhead. Arnold and Jase and Adam didn't quite understand that yet, but they would; and so would the others when Kieran found them and bound them.

The Opera House began to shimmer. Thousands of people were pouring from the auditorium and the balconies onto the grand staircase for intermission. Cassidy and Grondin waited patiently, silhouetted against the brilliance.

[Fireflower.]

All right, Kier said to them. This is what I want you to do.

*   *   *

The performance was running long, and Montedoro and Falcone decided to spend this final intermission relaxing in their box, rather than attempt another sortie into the high-society crush out on the Grand Tier lobby. Three of the bodyguard were given permission to take a smoke break and Joe Porks was sent for a magnum of champagne. Mike LoPresti, whose musical tastes ran more toward cabaret singers than divas, appeased his boredom by using the binoculars to inspect the décolletages of the elegant ladies down on the main floor.

The two dons made favorable comments about the rousing curtain-closer ensemble that had ended Act Three. *La Favorita*, they agreed, was somewhat of a potboiler—which explained why the Met hadn't mounted a production since Caruso in 1905 —but it did have some soaring melodies, and Pavarotti was in splendid voice. Vicenzu Falcone was old-fashioned enough to express regret that the heroine was being portrayed by a black soprano.

Montedoro shrugged. "At least she's not fat, and she's got a great legato. So if her color bugs you, close your eyes during the duets."

"Look, Guido, I don't mind a chocolate Carmen or Aïda—but there oughta be limits. When I was in stir I saw Price do *Tosca* on *Live from the Met* and it was fuckin' grotesque! What next? A Jap Rigoletto? It's all the fault of that damn Kraut, Bing. He squanders a bundle building this house, and we got trick chandeliers, no privacy, everything open like a goddam goldfish tank— and the singers gotta blast out their voiceboxes to fill the thing. The old Met was better."

"Nothing stays the same forever, Vince. Us old farts gotta change with the changing times."

"Sez you! You're only sixty-seven and you don't have arteries sludged up like a Jersey backwater at low tide." Falcone lowered his voice and began to speak in Sicilian dialect. "And you don't have a U.S. attorney standing on your testicles, ready to defy God and the Madonna and the Bill of Rights in order to make certain that you die in prison. Piccolomini, that head of a prick! Do you know why he pursues me? He intends to run for senator, and I am to provide him with his ticket to Washington. Illegal wiretaps, suborned witnesses, planted evidence—he doesn't care how he incriminates one. You had better guard your own precious arse, friend Guido."

"I always have," Montedoro said in English. The perfect

acoustics of the auditorium filled the place with white noise during the interval, so the conversation between the two dons was inaudible even to LoPresti and the single remaining bodyguard, who were only a few feet away. Nevertheless, the man whom the newspapers called Boss of Bosses leaned very close to his old friend and spoke in the tongue of secrecy. "Do you think that I'm blind to the government conspiracy against Our Thing? I saw it coming years ago, when that shitter-of-wisdom Robert Kennedy declared war on us. For this very reason, my own Family has diversified, distanced itself from the less savory sources of income. The Montedoro Borgata is legitimate, Vicenzu! Well—very nearly so. My sons, Pasquale and Paolo, have more three-piece-suits on their payroll than a Wall Street brokerage. You don't find cunting zealots like Piccolomini poking into *our* affairs. Not when they can spend their time more profitably pursuing the greatest importer of heroin and cocaine on the East Coast."

"Perhaps I should peddle pizza?" Falcone growled.

Montedoro chuckled. "Why not? See here—I know that your gross profits are tremendous, rising with each passing month. But you are having difficulty laundering the money. And some of your impatient young men complain that their share is slow in filtering down to them. I happen to know that the Sortino Borgata has the same problem, and there are rumors about Calcare's operation, too. It is the unprecedented quantity of money—the drug money—so inconvenient! But there are new methods of handling this embarrassment of riches, Vicenzu—tricks of modern finance."

"Hah! You suggest that we hand the money over to you for safekeeping, my dear old friend?"

"Suppose," Montedoro said softly, "that we revive the Commission? Suppose that the Five Families work together instead of at cross-purposes? The Commission was a good idea—only ahead of its time. But now, with this massive influx of dirty money that must be invested if it is not to be pissed away in bankers' percentages, we need to unify to survive."

"Oh, shit," said Falcone in English. "Now you're startin' to sound just like that Chicago asshole, Camastra."

A troubled look crossed Montedoro's face. "Al Camastra phoned me last night. He knew we'd be getting together. How did he know that, Vince?...And what Al had to say worried me."

The door at the back of the box opened and Joe Porks came in, a tray of empty flute glasses in his hands and a big bottle of champagne tucked under one arm. He nodded deferentially to the dons and went over to LoPresti. The two whispered together. LoPresti, scowling, headed for the door while Joe Porks undid the cork wire on the magnum. There was a juicy *pop*. Joe began to pour.

Falcone was distracted by the actions of his minions. There was a creeping sensation behind his stiffly starched collar, which seemed suddenly to constrict his windpipe. He ran a finger behind the collar and grunted to clear his throat. "Camastra! He always means trouble. Him and that smartass Irish consigliere of his. What kinda crap was he shovelin' this time?"

Before Montedoro could answer, the door to the box opened again. LoPresti stood there, his face gray and drawn, and behind him were three men in evening clothes. The quartet edged inside and the door closed. The lone soldier on guard duty started up from his seat, groping in his armpit, and then crumpled to the floor with a muffled crash. He twitched and lay still.

"Jesus Christ," said Joe Porks. His fingers tightened on the champagne bottle.

"Don't even think of trying it, Porcaro," said one of the shadow men behind LoPresti. "Take his piece, Mike."

The two dons gaped. LoPresti stepped over to his enforcer, who seemed to be paralyzed, and removed a .38 Detective Special from his shoulder holster. Joe Porks stood like a battered mannequin in an After Six display window, a full glass of bubbly in one hand and the big bottle in the other. Sweat poured down his forehead and his acne-pitted cheeks.

Falcone lurched to his feet to confront his Underboss. "Mike, what the fuck's going on here?"

LoPresti's mouth worked as if he were trying to overcome a spasm of lockjaw. There were tears of rage in his eyes. He handed the revolver to one of the men behind him and then went to a seat beside Falcone and slowly lowered himself into it.

The shortest of the three intruders now stepped forward into the light. He was a man in his mid-thirties whose dark hair grew in a widow's peak, and his face wore one of the most compelling and terrifying expressions that the two dons could remember having seen during their unquiet lives.

Montedoro remained seated. "A visitor from Chicago," he said in a neutral tone. "O'Connor, isn't it?"

Yes.

"Al Camastra mentioned your name when we spoke on the phone last night. Do you intend to kill Vince and me?"

No. But I will explain certain matters to you.

Montedoro nodded. His glance took in the sagging LoPresti and motionless Joe Porks, who was teetering a bit with the champagne but didn't spill a drop.

May we sit down? The intermission is nearly over.

Montedoro inclined his head graciously.

Your associates whom we met outside are resting in the men's lounge. They'll probably feel much better after a good night's sleep. The fellow on the floor will require prompt hospitalization. Porcaro and LoPresti, however, will receive their treatment from me.

O'Connor's two companions had gone to Joe Porks and relieved him of his burdens. They guided him to the fourth seat at the front of the box near to LoPresti and sat him down, then retired again to the shadows. The five-minute-warning chime sounded. People began returning to their seats in the boxes to the right and left. They paid no attention to the mobsters and their uninvited guests.

"He's talking," Falcone whispered, his eyes bulging with terror, "but he *ain't* talking."

Montedoro was staring at Kieran with shrewd speculation. "So you're Camastra's edge. No wonder he made you. No wonder he raised you to consigliere."

"I have other talents as well, Don Guido. If you help reorganize the Commission and put it into efficient operation, you may benefit from my unique abilities yourself. And so may Don Vicenzu, and other businessmen of honor." *But first we must settle another matter.*

Falcone said hesitantly, "It wasn't me ordered the hit, O'Connor. You know that, don't you? You're a counselor. Untouchable. But LoPresti was burned because you undercut us on the bidding last year for the Montréal Connection. That was a pipeline he sweat blood to bring in, and the froggies were all ready to deal—until you convinced 'em otherwise." He gave a weak laugh. "Maybe now we know *how* you convinced 'em."

"I'm not a miracle-worker," Kieran said. "My . . . influence isn't longlasting and it certainly doesn't extend over distances. What I offered Montréal was a better deal and safer conditions of transfer, using the Saint Lawrence Seaway. No danger of hijacking, no payoffs to cops or customs, and payment direct to Switzerland. Chapelle explained all that to LoPresti. It was a simple business matter, Don Vicenzu, but your man chose to treat it as a personal affront. He's stupid and shortsighted and vindictive, and so is his animal, Porcaro."

"I agree," said Falcone.

The lights in the Opera House were dimming and the patrons settled down. Applause greeted Maestro López-Cobos as he entered the pit and motioned for the players in the orchestra to rise.

Then there will be peace between Chicago and the Falcone Family, Don Vicenzu?

The don spoke in a harsh whisper. "I swear it. I swear it."

And you are a witness to this, Don Guido?

"I am," said Montedoro.

The hall had become very dark. The conductor raised his baton and the pianissimo notes of an organ began the overture to Act Four of *La Favorita*. LoPresti and Porcaro sat beside Falcone with only the rise and fall of their shirt-fronts signaling life, apparently held in a trance by the two associates of O'Connor who were glaring at the backs of their necks. Kieran rose to his feet and put his right hand on Porcaro's head and his left on LoPresti's. The paralyzed men started violently and O'Connor himself suppressed a groan.

This . . . is not revenge, you understand. Only simple justice. A restoration of order. Don Guido, your men should be able to cope with the disposal of this pair without too much difficulty. It will be an educational experience for them. We will send them in on our way out.

And then O'Connor and the two men with him were gone, and the gold brocade curtain opened on the handsome Ming Cho Lee set of a monastery courtyard in Spain. The stage illumination lit the faces of the audience. Falcone was aware of a faint, peculiar odor. He leaned over and saw that the eye sockets of his hench-men had become streaming wells of dark fluid, and that neither man was breathing even though they both sat very straight in their luxurious chairs.

2

ALMA-ATA, KAZAKH SSR, EARTH
10 JULY 1979

HE WAS THE MOST SELF-EFFACING MEMBER OF THE DELEGATION of Indian parapsychology scholars visiting Kazakh State University, and afterward many staff members at the Bioenergetics Institute (including the Director) denied that he had been there at all. But the truth was that he had been the one who arranged for the tour in the first place, as a pretext for meeting Yuri and Tamara.

The visitors had seen nothing of the laboratory where the young biophysicist and his wife worked, since it was under the Cosmic security classification. Instead they toured the Kirlian facility, where scanning devices purported to monitor the nonphysical aura of living things. Although one or two of the delegates asked indiscreet questions about corona discharge effects and water vapor, most were suitably impressed. In the afternoon there was a tea, presided over by the Director of the Institute, where the delegates were given the opportunity to mingle with the various project supervisors and a few of the percipient subjects whose psychic powers were under analysis. Yuri and Tamara were there, introduced simply as "biocommunications specialists." They said very little and slipped away early, and forgot about the group of Indian scholars almost at once. Their attention was fully occupied by the matter of Abdizhamil Simonov. There were rumors that Andropov himself was taking a personal interest in the KGB's inquiry into the mind-controller's sudden death.

That evening, as Tamara was putting little Valery and Ilya to bed, Yuri received a phone call from the Director.

"A distinguished member of the Indian Paraphysics Association tour group has asked for a personal meeting with you and your wife." The Director's voice was strained and overly formal. "He was told that such an appointment would be difficult to arrange, since it would have to be approved by Moscow. This did not deter him. He ... prevailed upon me to phone the Comrade Academician himself with the request. It was approved."

Yuri could only say, "How unusual!"

"You will meet this Dr. Urgyen Bhotia in the main lobby of the Hotel Kazakhstan as soon as possible. He is a Tibetan resident of Darjeeling, and he wishes to speak to you about certain studies he has made that are relevant to your work. Show him every courtesy." Before Yuri could respond, the Director hung up.

Tamara came out of the children's bedroom with lifted brows.

He transferred the amazing gist of the conversation to her in an instant, adding: I have no idea what this is all about but we are going to have to see this guru and postpone our discussion with Alla and Mukan until later tonight I'll call them while you get Natasha to baby-sit.

When everything was arranged, they took a bus across town to the soaring new hotel on Lenin Avenue, where only the most distinguished visitors were housed. No sooner had they come into the air-conditioned lobby than the strangely influential Tibetan was there bowing. He was a short, sturdy man with very brown skin, dressed in crisply pressed trekker's garb.

"Dr. Gawrys and Madame Gawrys-Sakhvadze, I am Urgyen Bhotia. I thank you profoundly for coming here, and apologize for causing you inconvenience. I hope you will forgive my summoning you in such a precipitate manner, but I have waited nearly five years for this moment." *Shall we stroll outside in the cool of the evening?*

Yuri froze in the act of shaking hands. Tamara said: I think that would be wise. Have you taken the cable car up Koktyube Hill?

Not yet but I hear it provides a marvelous view of the city.

Yuri said: You *know* us and our work? How can this be?

The Tibetan laughed and said, "This is not my first visit to your lovely city of Alma-Ata, but it is my first opportunity to enjoy it with all my physical senses! Let us walk."

He casually took an arm of each of them when they were outside and guided them across Abai Avenue into the gardens of the Lenin Palace of Culture as though he were the host and they the visitors. The fountains were lit with the coming of dusk and the spray from them was cooling and welcome. A heavy scent of flowers arose from the formal gardens and Urgyen paused to admire them.

"So many lush growing things in this splendid, modern city! The aether sings with vitality." He might have been any age from forty to sixty. His head was shaved and his cheeks were such a bright red that they might have been rouged. His teeth were very white and perfect and his eyes, almost hidden in a mass of deep creases when he smiled, were an unusual hazel color.

Tamara said, "It is clear that you are one of the adept—unlike your colleagues. You will please tell us how you came to know of our psychic faculties and of our work, since both are closely guarded state secrets."

"I know you," the Tibetan said, "because I have been blessed with an ability to perceive the bioplasma of the brightest ones across great distances. My vision extends only throughout Asia. But for more than twenty years now, since leaving Tibet, I have studied the soul manifestation by means of what you would call remote-viewing. I saw the two of you for the first time in 1974, when you were newly come to Alma-Ata, a double mind-star more brilliant than any I had found before. Since then I have watched, I rejoiced in the birth of your two brilliantly ensouled sons, and now I anticipate with you the coming of your third child, a daughter."

"It *is* a girl?" Tamara exclaimed.

"Most assuredly." Urgyen searched the faces of the young couple, ruefully acknowledging the mental barricades they had erected against him. "Please do not be afraid of me. My only wish is to help you at this very difficult time, when you two and the many immature minds under your care find yourselves at a moral crossroads."

"You say you have watched us," Yuri stated. "How close has your astral scrutiny been? Have you read our minds?"

"You know from your own remote-viewing studies that such a thing is impossible. Nor can I read them now unless you freely give access. Nevertheless, I am aware of the temptations bedeviling you and the dangers that you face. I asked myself and the Compassionate Lord if it was my duty to advise you."

"And what," Yuri inquired coldly, "did your heavenly oracle say?"

"I was helped to understand that, in spite of certain inhumane actions you have abetted, you are both persons of goodwill. You have rejected the false joy of the great determinism that hands over the individual conscience to a group and evades personal responsibility. You know you are free, and you know you will have to make choices. Too many people of your nation deny this difficult truth. They do not understand that the human mind must cultivate both soul and spirit if it is to be integral."

"You will have to explain that," Yuri said.

They walked on, across the palace concourse and into trees where cicadas were beginning to buzz.

Urgyen said, "A month ago there was a meeting of leaders in Vienna. The President of the United States and the Soviet President Leonid Brezhnev signed a strategic arms limitation treaty. At one of their conferences, which took place in the Soviet embassy in Vienna, a person from your Bioenergetics Institute named Simonov exerted coercive and mind-altering force upon the American President, throwing him into a state of confusion and irrationality that still persists . . . The Chairman of your KGB was so elated by Simonov's success that he made arrangements to send the man to Washington, where he would be able to exert his inimical influence upon other American leaders, as ordered. The plan was aborted when Simonov dropped dead while jogging on the university campus."

"An autopsy showed that his heart was enlarged and weakened," Yuri said. "It is a disability that often accompanies great psychic exertion. I myself am under a physician's care for similar symptoms."

"Exactly," said Urgyen sadly.

They walked in silence. Ahead was the brightly lit funicular station, the goal of many other evening strollers.

Tamara said, "Abdizhamil Simonov was a tribal shaman before he was recruited to the Institute, a petty and vicious man who resisted all our efforts to dissuade him from cooperating in Andropov's scheme. He was half mad, a menace to world peace. The KGB thought they could control him, but we knew they could not."

Urgyen nodded. "There was also Ryrik Volzhsky, a strong coercer and an incorrigible corrupter of children. You have in your special program at the Institute more than sixty youthful psychics. When Volzhsky persuaded your Director to assign him to the pedagogical staff, both of you admonished him to restrain himself. He laughed. Two days later he was found drowned in the Bolshaya Alma-Atinka River."

"The normals can only agonize in their impotence when confronted by evil," Yuri said. "They can only utter foolish curses or wish the destruction of the wicked. We are more fortunate."

"The soul would say so, but not the spirit," said the Tibetan.

They came to the ticket office, where Yuri paid. Then the three of them got into one of the crowded red-and-yellow cable-cars. The other holidaymakers made room for pregnant Tamara near the window, and a moment later they were soaring up the hillside, suspended in the clear air, with the discussion now relegated to telepathy.

Yuri said: So you presume to judge me and castigate me with your pious Eastern word-play . . . Soul and spirit! Talk instead of life and death! Talk of a pair of fearful children become the toys of power-corrupted old men who would use marvelous mind-powers as weapons rather than dedicate them to the good of humanity!

Urgyen said: But if you kill even in a cause that seems just are you any better than your oppressors?

Tamara said: We regretted the deaths bitterly. Yuri acted only after serious reflection.

Urgyen said: In Tibet in the eleventh century the poet Milar-epa had mental powers like yours. He was able to strike his enemies dead from afar. But only after he renounced his usurpa-tion of god-power did he become a saint.

Yuri said: We aren't saints. We are only persons wanting to survive. Yes I killed and because I am a Pole and a Catholic I was tormented and I wish there had been another way but there was not. Once I was timid little Jerzy snatched from my parents in Lodz bullied and cajoled into mental slavery thinking there was no helping it. Then came Tamara! In Leningrad the scientists studied us and tested us and the military men tried to convince us that our duty was unquestioning loyalty and service to the state. But Tamara knew better and helped me to know also. Her dear father was exiled because he dared to protest and publicize the GRU's treatment of us and of other psychics.

Urgyen said: Your unhappy memories are clear to me . . . and I see what you are reluctant to state directly: that even then you thought it necessary to kill . . .

Yuri said: Why can't you understand!

Tamara said: There was a cold-blooded brute the chief of the GRU. Yes he was the first. He would have locked us away treated us as equipment rather than human beings to further his ambition. We were to be his secret weapon to spy with remote-vision on Chairman Andropov of the KGB. When our enemy died the GRU lost control of the psychic-study program. Andropov and Brezhnev became fervent believers in the mind-powers, coopted the project and promised us and the other adepts that we would now be treated as honored Soviet citizens. It was 1974. Six months after Papa's exile. I was 16 and Jerzy/Yuri 22. We were given permission to marry and sent to Alma-Ata.

Yuri said: We expected a barbarous outpost in Central Asia with camel caravans and fierce nomads and bazaars. Imagine our surprise at this green new city with the great university where we could study as well as be studied.

Urgyen said: You have acquired knowledge but not wisdom.

Yuri said: Gawno!

Tamara said: Urgyen Bhotia we are not Indians or Tibetans. Our soul does not flinch at the prospect of violence because our people have survived for centuries in violent lands enduring persecution. We know we face grave choices but we have made glorious plans and we are determined to see them carried out. This means defending ourselves if necessary. Yuri and I are the most powerful of all the minds assembled here in the pilot bioenergetics program. We teach the young ones remote-viewing and convince them to hide their true ability from the KGB evaluators. The program thus seems to progress very slowly. But the children understand that their minds set them apart that they must work for all the world not only for the Soviet Union.

Urgyen said: If you are the teachers it is that much more important that you reform your erring consciences.

"Here we are at the top of the hill," Yuri said. "Come, let us enjoy the view!"

There was an observation platform and a restaurant at the terminus of the cableway, and the other passengers disembarked laughing and exclaiming at the beauty of the panorama. To the north, lost in purple haze, were the steppes of the Virgin Lands, turned into fields and orchards by irrigation. The multicolored lights of the great city were just beginning to twinkle on while the last sunset glow illuminated the eastern foothills. Behind Koktyube, to the south, was the Zailiysky Ala-Tau, a heavily wooded outlier of the high Tien Shan. China lay only three hundred kilometers beyond.

They stood at the railing, looking out over Alma-Ata. Tamara said, "The city's name means Father of Apples. There are orchards everywhere, and vineyards. We have come to love this place. At the university, we are trusted. We say the proper things and are circumspect in the use of our higher mind-powers. We can do so much good, Urgyen . . . and someday when other persons like us in other parts of the world are able to reveal themselves and work openly, we will also. Then we will forever renounce the self-defensive violence that we have been forced to resort to. I swear it."

"You know there are many others, many minds with these powers," Urgyen said. "But do you know that there is a World Mind, of which you and I and the others, whether highly empowered or lowly, partake?"

"We know there is the Great Soul," Tamara said. "My many-times-great-grandfather told me of it when I was a child. Now we would call it the Conscious Field of Humanity. Some persons call it God."

"It is not God," said the Tibetan. "God is spirit and cannot be infected by evil. But the World Soul can . . . and this is why I came to plead with you."

Yuri cried: Soul! Spirit! Tell us plainly what you mean!

"I will try," said the Tibetan. "Years ago, when I was a monk called Urgyen Rimpoche and practiced my mind-powers proudly, I thought I was one blessed by the gods, a living miracle who had the right to command heaven. I was young! In the turmoil that my poor country suffered during the Chinese invasion of the 1950s, my attempts to coerce divinity and repel the invaders were futile. Our little monastery was utterly demolished and we were beaten and called parasites by the Red soldiers. Of course, they were right . . . I had confused soul with spirit. So had my brother monks who had prospered and enjoyed prestige by celebrating my talents. Along with many of my countrymen, I fled to India. After suffering much and losing my psychic abilities because of self-doubts, I began to acquire wisdom. The first thing I took to heart was the realization that the soul and its powers are not supernatural. They are no miracle. They are part of the natural human heritage and all people have them in greater or lesser degree."

"We have also come to that conclusion," said Tamara.

Urgyen said, "The soul is neither physical or spiritual. But it is still part of matter's realm, born with certain coalescences of matter and energy. Even atoms have a minute portion of soul!

Higher organisms have much more. And there is a World Soul—"

"Do you speak of a World Mind?" Yuri asked.

"No, no. That comes later, with the infusion of spirit! But let me go on... The soul feels but it cannot know. It is—as most thinkers have recognized—feminine: life-giving, as patient and enduring as planet Earth whose soul-essence is part of each one of us. Living things form a hierarchy of soul, first tropistic, then sentient. Plants and animals. In us, souls dream and imagine and fantasize and create. They remember and they fear. They are basically passive and amoral. When the soul is properly entuned, its powers may move matter and change it. Sometimes the human soul swells large and begets ultrasenses, or a coercive will, or mental control of matter and energy, or the reorganization of dysfunctioning mind or body that we call healing."

"Tell us how mind relates to soul," Yuri demanded.

"Only in thinking creatures is the soul infused with spirit, making a mind."

"And spirit is what?" Tamara asked.

"It does not belong to the realm of matter. We may call it divine, but it is of a different order of reality. It enkindles the intellect, orders all things in our minds, impels us upward as flames rise. It is masculine: impregnating and driving, engendering discipline, truth, wisdom, and law. It makes thinking creatures yearn toward a higher reality, what I would call the face of God. It knows good and evil. It strives to unite in love with other minds and to form the World Mind. But it can be debased. Its impulse toward increasing organization can be crippled, even halted."

They said: We do not understand. Especially we do not understand why you say WE threaten your World Mind.

"Look around you," Urgyen invited. "You see the terraced mountains with their forests and orchards, and you see a modern city. The mountains were upthrust ages ago, and slowly they are being worn down. The trees and other plant-life spring up from seed and grow—but when growth stops, they will die. The city of Alma-Ata is only the latest of many human settlements in the Valley of the Seven Rivers. Others flourished for a time, but when they stopped growing, they died. Growth! Evolution, if you like, with life and mind organizing itself at ever-higher levels! If Mind does not grow, it will also die. My dear Tamara and Yuri, you are the vanguard of the planetary Mind, together with the others like you. It is so simple: you must be better than those who came before because spirit must grow as well as soul in the evolving World Mind. Without growth, there can only be death. If you, the leading shoots of your growing species, become corrupt, you will tend to corrupt the entire Mind."

Yuri exclaimed: You would have us submit tamely to our enemies? Die rather than kill in self-defense?

Yes.

Tamara said: You want us to be like Mahatma Gandhi. But our system of values says we have a right to kill mortal enemies.

True . . . and yet your Avatar allowed his enemies to kill him.

Yuri said: We are not martyrs! We have a great plan and it requires living leaders. You yourself said it: We are the vanguard we can lead the world to peace!

Never if you kill to prevail. Never if you use the mind-powers that way. Think! What was hard in the beginning becomes more and more easy. Think! The once stricken conscience becomes dulled. Think! Who are you going to lead? Your peers? What of the lesser minds? What if they fear you and will not follow? Will you coerce and kill? Think of your children watching you and learning. Think.

Tamara said: Urgyen your message is hard to hear harder to accept. I don't know if I can accept it. But I do believe it . . .

Her husband rounded on her. "How can you? After all we have suffered together—how can you?"

She placed her hand on her swollen body. Inside, the fetus leapt. "I think it has to do with motherhood," she said.

Urgyen nodded and smiled. "Yes. And fatherhood."

Yuri looked from one to the other in confusion. Both of their minds were open to him, showing. But he still could not understand.

3

SUPERVISORY CRUISER NOUMENON
[LYL 1-0000]
10 JULY 1979

"THE FORMER LAMA SHOWS A COADUNATE SENSITIVITY RARE among humans," said Eupathic Impulse. "How gratifying."

"He typifies an abhorrence of violence found mainly among Easterners of the Buddhist persuasion," Homologous Trend said, "and among the English. The trait is, as one has noted, regrettably uncommon."

"Making the coadunation of the World Mind that much more unlikely," Asymptotic Essence said.

"In the unlikelihood is the greatest glory," said the poet, Noetic Concordance.

"All very well for one to look on the bright side of a situation that's hopeless," Impulse said.

"One supposes that it was inevitable that perverse operants, such as the lamentable O'Connor, would use their higher mind-powers aggressively and for personal gain," Trend observed. "Such flawed personalities, are, after all, outside of the mainstream of mental evolution. But one regrets most deeply that a pivotal operant such as Yuri Gawrys, so estimable in other respects, has seen fit to use his metafaculties to kill."

"The temptation was overwhelming to one of his mind-set," Essence said.

"One fears he does not represent an isolated case," Impulse added. "On the contrary, he is probably typical, given that the most dynamic of the irrupting operant minds share the moral view of the West, not the East. Even Yuri's mate Tamara, inculcated with gentleness and true coadunate principles during her formative years, and assenting intellectually to the truth of the Tibetan's admonition, will undoubtedly succumb to the use of violence under extreme provocation. Human females will kill to

183

defend their children even as they counsel them to embrace peace."

Noetic Concordance radiated sorrow. "Then the Tibetan's warning was in vain?"

"One may hope," Trend said, "that his message will have a positive influence upon other human minds at a more favorable point in mental evolution."

"Strange," Asymptotic Essence mused, "that the lama should have so fortuitously conceived this advanced insight, and gone counter to his naturally retiring disposition to deliver it to Yuri and Tamara. If one had not noted the Tibetan's indubitably authentic mental signature, one might be forgiven for suspecting that he was none other than Unifex, masquerading again in human guise."

"Indeed one might!" Concordance agreed.

"Now there is an oddity," Eupathic Impulse remarked. "That It should take pleasure in simply walking among the lower lifeforms!"

"It empathizes so closely with them," said Concordance. "Should one be surprised when It assumes their physical form?"

"Yes," Impulse said shortly. "Krondaku may do so routinely, but it violates dignity and custom for a Lylmik to take on the material aspect of a client race."

"One is being a bit stuffy," Trend suggested.

"And one should remember," Concordance appended, "that It is in love."

"It is in New Hampshire even now," said Essence, "having completed its contemplation of the supernova in the Soulpto Group that threatened to irradiate the planet of the Shoridai. It saved them by interposing a gas-cloud—then sped back to Earth when It perceived an urgent necessity to harangue its slow-witted catspaw."

"*That* one," said Impulse darkly. "He would have used the powers to kill also, if he had not been restrained. The very agent of Unifex—a reprobate!"

Noetic Concordance's mind smiled. "Oh, I don't know. He rather grows on one."

4

FROM THE MEMOIRS OF
ROGATIEN REMILLARD

MILIEU BIOGRAPHIES OF MY NEPHEW DENIS HAVE COVERED THE latter years of his childhood in considerable detail, thanks not only to his diaries but also the reminiscences of his teachers and fellow students. For this reason I intend to highlight only a few incidents from that time.

First, let me correct a persistent error. Denis was never seriously endangered by Pentagon or CIA zealots seeking to utilize his talents for intelligence gathering or experiments in "psychotronic" aggression. Other young operants *did* suffer from the compulsory enlistment attempts of official (and highly unofficial) groups; but Denis went unharrassed, thanks to his Jesuit protectors at Brebeuf Academy and later to the Dartmouth Coterie, who formed an ad hoc Praetorian Guard as well as a circle of intimate friends during Denis's college years.

One story I must tell deals with the way Denis finally made contact with the Coterie and his other early operant associates, using a method so crude that he was too embarrassed even to mention it when he became a respected academic. His biographers assume that he instinctively used the declamatory mode of farspeech, calling out in a generalized fashion. They seem to think that when his developing powers reached an adequate level, numbers of isolated operants automatically responded.

The truth is otherwise—and much more droll.

After our encounter with Elaine Harrington, Denis was firmly convinced of the existence of other operants, and he made many attempts to contact them via telepathy. Working together, the boy and I checked out his "broadcast range" by the simple expedient of having him bespeak me as I traveled to prearranged New England locales. Although intervening mountain ranges tended to block or interfere with his mental messages, as did the sun and

185

electrical storms, we discovered that Denis could farspeak me reliably over a distance of more than a hundred kilometers. When he operated out of Brebeuf near Concord in central New Hampshire, as he usually did, he could theoretically blanket our own state, plus Vermont, Massachusetts, Rhode Island, and most of Connecticut—as well as a fair-sized chunk of Maine and those parts of upper New York that weren't shielded by the Adirondacks. Our record long-distance exchange during his school years covered 166 kilometers, between Brebeuf and East Hampton, Long Island, where I visited friends in 1977.

Nevertheless, in spite of his success in farspeaking me, Denis had no luck at all in contacting other telepaths using a generalized broad-spectrum hail. His mental CQs remained futile howls into an aetheric rain-barrel, messages lacking addresses, until that day in 1978 when we first tried the seriocomic tactic I dubbed Operation Witch Hazel.

It was in November, when Denis was eleven and in his final term of study at the academy. I had come down on a delicate and rather sticky mission: to break the bad news to Fathers Ellsworth and Dubois that their prize prodigy would not, after all, be matriculating at Georgetown University next year as they had hoped—and quite taken for granted. Denis himself had no objections to attending the Jesuit institution. It had a fine medical school and its faculty, secretly briefed by my nephew's clerical mentors, was quite willing to accommodate a twelve-year-old genius with a supernormal psyche.

But the Ghost had other ideas.

My interview with the good fathers was an uncomfortable one. Following the Ghost's suggestion, I told Ellsworth and Dubois that Georgetown, being situated in Washington, DC, was too susceptible to infiltration by government agents or other parties who might take an unhealthy interest in Denis's talents. (This maneuver of mine was undoubtedly the source of later rumors that Denis was actually pursued by unscrupulous psychological-warfare specialists.) The priests were deeply disappointed when I told them that I had already arranged for Denis to enter Dartmouth College, a venerable Ivy League school in western New Hampshire. My arguments in favor of Dartmouth must have had a paranoid flavor—and even worse, smacked of ingratitude after the special pains taken by the Brebeuf faculty in the first five years of the boy's education. The two priests tried hard to change my mind; but I had my orders, and I prevailed. With Don's total abdication of responsibility, I was Denis's de facto guardian and the decision was mine to make. In the end, I cheered them up. Dartmouth was a small college but it did have a school of medicine sympathetic to the concept of metapsychic research. It was nearby, in the beautiful town of Hanover on the Connecticut River. It had been founded in 1769 and numbered among its alumni such luminaries as Daniel Webster and Dr. Seuss. Above all, because of its quixotic and individualistic atmosphere, it was about the last place in the world likely to be infiltrated by the CIA, the lackeys of the military-industrial establishment—or the KGB. So the matter was settled.

With the Ellsworth-Dubois ordeal behind me, I was glad to escape by taking Denis for a stroll into the gray and leafless woodland adjacent to the Brebeuf campus. The clouds hung low and there was a smell of snow in the air. Early frosts had withered the low-growing plant-life. Fragile rinds of ice crusted the puddles along the path. The boy and I walked for an hour or so, discussing Dartmouth and making plans to visit it over the upcoming Thanksgiving vacation. Then the conversation turned to a vexatious old topic: Denis's continuing futile attempts to farspeak other telepaths.

"I've been thinking over the *theory* of telepathic communication," the boy said. "Trying to discover why you and I can farspeak over long distances—while I have no luck when I call out to others." He detoured so as to walk through a deep drift of maple leaves, kicking them into the air with childish satisfaction. "The first possibility—and the most rotten!—is that there simply aren't any receptive minds within my telepathic radius. I just can't believe that. I *feel* them out there! They're probably unaware of their powers for the most part, but some of them might have a gut conviction that they're different from the rank and file of humanity . . . Now the second possibility: The minds are there but they don't hear me for some reason. I have to find out why my transmissions don't reach them even though I can farspeak you."

Little chickadees, lingering tardily in the woods before their annual withdrawal to town and farmyard during fast winter, sang as we crunched along. I said, "The problem might simply be that your closet telepaths aren't listening! Look how we ignore the sounds made by these birds while we concentrate on each other's voices."

"That's a good point. The unknown out there aren't expecting a telepathic message. They don't think such things are possible. So when farspeech inadvertently reaches them, they may not recognize it for what it is. They could think it was a daydream, or some notion cooked up by their own brains, or even a ghost or something."

"Mm," I said.

"If they were seriously expecting a farspoken message it would be entirely different. You know that our own head-skeds were carefully planned. We were both alert and waiting at the time we'd arranged to communicate—and I knew where you would be. It didn't matter that your mind has a relatively puny receptive faculty—"

"Thank you very much!"

His solemn little face broke into a grin. "Nothing personal. Your mind is a weak telepathic transmitter and you're not a very sensitive receiver. But my mind makes up for it. I put out a high-powered signal that you can read, and I listen for you with an ultrasensitive mental antenna. Theoretically, I should be able to bespeak other weak or untrained telepaths—if only they knew enough to listen for me."

His mind flashed a farcical display advertisement:

TELEPATHS OF THE WORLD!
TUNE IN YOUR MENTAL EARS
WITHOUT FAIL
NEXT TUESDAY, 8:00 P.M. EST
FOR AN IMPORTANT ANNOUNCEMENT!

He added aloud, "Of course we'd never dare do it. And even if we did, the very people we wanted most to reach would ignore it completely."

"Eventually there will be a public acknowledgment," I said. "You *will* be able to discuss the powers openly someday..."

He nodded. "When I'm grown up, and I have my research facility and a suitable aura of academic respectability." The irony on his young face was almost tragic. "But it's so tempting to take a short cut!"

"You're talking like a child."

He wryly agreed. Then he gave me a sidelong look. "You've saved me from making a lot of mistakes, Uncle Rogi. I'm just beginning to understand that. And the way you got me away from Papa—to this school, where I'd be safe and able to grow. Now this business of going to Dartmouth instead of Georgetown. I trust your judgment and you know I'd never try to probe your motivation. But I hope that someday. . ."

All I said was, "At the proper time."

He sighed. We walked along in vocal and mental silence for several minutes, and then he returned to our previous topic of discussion.

"I've thought of another reason why my farspeech might not reach other telepaths: signal incompatible with receiver. The AM/FM thing."

"Could be," I agreed. "Our voices can whisper, talk, yell, sing. Why shouldn't there be different modes of telepathic output?"

"I believe there must be at least two. You know, when we're home in Berlin, how you and I can bespeak each other without Papa or Victor listening in? That's a sort of private mode. But there's a public mode, too—the way we farspeak when the message comes to you and me and Papa and Victor all at once."

He stopped walking, frowned, and cogitated. Then he said, "What if that private kind of telepathy is the most efficient kind? What if it's coherent farspeech, say, sort of like a laser beam of light! Public mode might be more like a streetlamp—casting light in all directions but only illuminating a small, nearby area. You need a tight beam for lighting up faraway objectives. Maybe thoughts need to be beamed, too."

"Makes sense."

His face went gloomy. "But if that's true, then my random telepathic calls can never work. I don't know how I aim the beam . . . I suppose I recognize your mind-pattern and tune to it in some instinctive way when we go private, or when we do long-distance farspeaking. But how will I ever find out the mental signature of unknown telepaths?" He was thinking hard, and in a moment he brightened, "I bet they'd hear me if I spoke in public mode right up close to them! Then I wouldn't need any signature. After all, I heard Elaine okay when she was half a mile away on Mount Washington that first time, and later she could hear me when we were a couple hundred yards apart. Funny, though. I never seemed to be able to go private with her."

I let that one lie. "You can hardly travel all over the country farshouting in crowds, hoping to scratch up other telepaths. It would be prohibitively expensive, slow, and boring beyond belief."

"There ought to be another ultrasense for locating people," the boy growled. "A seekersense."

We were going downhill, toward a little brook. The low ground had moisture-loving hornbeam trees and occasional small thickets of witch hazel. The clouds opened briefly, letting a shaft of sunlight lance down, and from a distance it seemed that the leafless branches were wrapped in a yellow haze. Then I realized the witch hazel shrubs were in bloom. I pointed out the phenomenon mentally to Denis. It was a small bit of botanical sorcery repeated every late fall in the New England woods.

"Weird old witch hazel," Denis said. "No wonder the early folks thought it was magic."

"That's why they used it for dowsing, I guess. You can find water by divining with just about any kind of wooden rod, or even a piece of wire. But the experts say that nothing works quite so well as a branch of witch hazel. I remember reading about one dowser who could find water just by moving a forked witch hazel stick over a *map*."

"It's your mind that does the finding," the boy said absently. "The stick probably just helps you to focus the—" He broke off abruptly. His eyes met mine and we found ourselves mind-shouting in unison:

Seekersense!

"The guy really used a map?" Denis whispered.

I nodded. "Found water on the island of Bermuda, as I recall. From here in the States."

"It's a cockamamie idea. Totally bananas. To think that I might be able to dowse out telepaths with a forked stick and a road map."

"Only," I said pointedly, "if you believe you can. But it can't hurt to try. I have a large-scale Delorme Atlas of New Hampshire in my Volvo . . ."

"Even if I did manage to find people, we'd still have to drive to the place where they were so I could send out a public-type hail. We'd still have to do some hunting."

"It can be managed," I told him, "provided you don't turn up eight hundred prospects." I reached into my pocket for my trusty penknife, and led the giggling boy into a witch hazel thicket to select a suitable forked stick.

* * *

I only saw a water dowsing operation once, and that was on television back in the '50s when I was just a kid. The program was one of those down-around-home local documentaries that were common then, and featured a famous "water-witch" from Hancock in the southern part of the state. I remember being disappointed, after the narrator's exciting build-up, when the witch turned out to be a balding elderly man with a lantern-jawed Yankee face and eyeglasses framed in black plastic. His clothes were unexceptional and his manner laconic—until he took up his forked stick.

In the experiment, a fifty-five-gallon drum full of water had been buried six feet deep in a freshly plowed area of field. The witch held his Y-shaped divining rod by the two short arms and extended the thing ahead of him as he slowly walked up and down the furrows. The camera showed close-ups of his face, staring at the ground with rapt attention, eyes wide behind the eyeglass lenses, sweat beading his forehead. Then the camera pulled back and we saw the witch plodding toward us, stick outstretched.

And the point of the stick suddenly dipped down.

There didn't seem to have been any causative movement of the old man's hands: the stick just revolved a bit and pointed to an area near the witch's feet. The tiniest glimmer of a smile crossed his lips. He backed up, let the stick rise, then walked over the spot once again. A dip. He approached the spot from the sides. As if with a life of its own, the stick turned down perpendicular to the earth.

"I reckon she's there," said the witch.

Two sturdy fellows with shovels stepped forward and the soft dirt began to fly. In a few minutes the drum lay revealed in an open pit; its bung was removed and water gurgled from it. The witch allowed as how he could find water "mebbe eighty percent of the time." He was the fourth generation of his family to have the gift and apparently the last. His children and grandchildren, he said, lacked confidence. Then he added, "But there ain't much call for water-witching nowadays anyhow. Folks feel a little foolish about it. They'd rather call in a geologist—nevvamind he hands 'em a whoppin' bill for his services, so long's he's *scientific*. But the old way still works . . ."

It worked for Denis, too—but only after six months of self-training. I watched him mind-hunting many times, first using the atlas, later poring over a series of aerial photos I'd purchased for him at the cost of an arm and a leg. I had very little seekersense myself (youthful experiments in imitation of the water-witch had proved that), but it was possible for me to share the boy's search by means of our mental rapport. He would sit at a table in a species of trance, the forked twig moving slowly over the surface of the map, and what passed through his mind was almost magical.

We have all flown in aircraft at night and looked down on the scattered jewel-lights that mark towns and settlements. The higher one is, the more indistinct the luminous splotch; but descend, and the individual streetlamps and lighted windows and slowly moving ground-cars become clearly visible. Denis's seeking looked rather like a night flight, when seen by my mind's eye. When he first began to hunt he sensed only bright fuzzy masses that signified concentrations of ordinary mentation: thinking people. But in time he learned to sharpen his focus, to sort the sapient blur into a sparkling collection of separate minds. They were multicolored, bright and dim, large and small. Just as a dowser for water or minerals visualizes the object of his search, then directs his higher senses to find it, so Denis conjured up the quintessence of "operant" mental energy and went hunting for it during a variant of the classic out-of-body experience.

The first operants he viewed, in a targeting operation, were his father and his brother Victor in Berlin. Initially it was hard for him to avoid the instinctive use of their mental signatures; but when he had conquered this technical glitch he was able to see the adult mind and the child only as tiny beacons of higher function, distinct in the miasma of normally talented thought. Don's younger children, who numbered six at that time, glowed dim and latent—a tragedy that Denis and I would understand fully only years laters. But Don was a fitful variable star and nine-year-old Victor burned like a baleful ember hiding in a half-extinguished campfire.

Denis never farspoke them, never hinted to them what kind of a search he was engaged in. "It wouldn't be good for them to know," he told me in that sober, young-old way of his. And of course he was right.

The patient search for kindred spirits began to pay off in June 1979, when he finally located Glenn Dalembert's mind in the congestion of metropolitan Manchester. We set off on a frantic ground-search then, me driving the Volvo and Denis, entranced, sitting beside me with his finger hovering over a tattered aerial survey sheet. (By then he had been able to discard the witch hazel wand, to his manifest relief.) Panic set in when it became evident that our target was on its way *out* of Manchester. A wild chase on the southbound lanes of the turnpike followed, and once we almost lost Glenn; but we bagged him at long last in a hilarious and touching scene at Benson's Wild Animal Park, where he had a summer job coercing elephants in a small circus. The young man reacted to our telepathic revelations with equanimity and took an instant shine to Denis. The boy was stunned to learn that his newfound metapsychic ally was an undergraduate at Dartmouth. Glenn Dalembert became the first member of the now-famed Coterie and would become a champion of metapsychic rights during the dark pre-Intervention years.

A few weeks after finding Glenn, Denis tracked down the second Coterie stalwart, Sally Doyle, in her home at Troy. She was a minor celebrity in her hometown because of a knack for finding lost persons and things. She had graduated valedictorian of her high school class that year, and in the fall (quelle surprise!) she was to enter Dartmouth. Once again Denis was astonished at the coincidence. I, as you might imagine, remained unruffled.

We located only two other operants that summer. One was an elderly invalid, Odette Kleinfelter, whom we nearly frightened into cardiac arrest with our telepathic greeting—and hastily disqualified from recruitment. The other contactee was a Nashua girl a year younger than Denis. When we confronted her, she fixed Denis with a redoubtable glare and snapped: "I suppose you think you're pretty smart!" Except for her metapsychic gifts, which we did not fully appreciate at that time, she seemed a bright but unexceptional child with that streak of mulish stubbornness that occasionally characterizes Franco-American females. Denis was leery of her, and for some years she would remain on the periphery of the growing body of young operants. In 1979 there was no hint of the girl's future role in the metapsychic drama. Her name was Lucille Cartier, and one day she would become Denis's closest colleague, his wife, and the mother of the Seven Founding Magnates of the Human Polity of the Concilium. But that was far in the future, and I will reserve Lucille's story until a later point in this narrative.

That fall, shepherded by Glenn Dalembert and Sally Doyle, Denis entered Dartmouth College. His seekersense quickly pinpointed three other suboperants among the student body, who were gathered into the Coterie through telepathic rapport. Two of these, a senior named Mitch Losier and a sophomore named Colette Roy, had been entirely unaware of their psychic talents until close contact with Denis brought about an accelerated floraison. The third, Tukwila Barnes, was a Puyallup tribesman from Washington state. At the time of Denis's matriculation Tukwila was a seventeen-year-old junior in the college's premed program, a genius well aware of his talent for hands-on healing and soul-travel who was wise enough not to acknowledge his unorthodox skills publicly. He was a wary mind-screener who completely eluded Denis's dowsing, and only revealed himself after observing the activities of the Coterie for more than six months.

As Denis devoured the undergraduate curriculum in three hectic terms, he found time to ferret out three more operants whom he induced to enroll at Dartmouth. Gerard Tremblay was a happy-go-lucky worker in a Vermont granite quarry, nineteen years old, with no idea that he was a suboperant telepath. Gordon McAllister, the only one of the Coterie who would choose physics over psychology or psychiatry, was twenty-six and operating the family potato farm in Maine when he was tapped. He had always known that he was a bit fey, but out of filial piety had repressed his psychic tendencies as frivolous and un-Presbyterian. The final, and oldest, Coterie member was Eric Boutin, who had worked for nearly ten years as the service manager in a Ford dealership in Manchester before Denis discovered him. Boutin's boss wept unashamedly when the most uncanny diagnostician of auto malfunction in the state of New Hampshire enrolled as a Dartmouth freshman at the age of thirty.

Denis received his Bachelor of Arts degree in June of 1980, applauded by me, his Coterie, his mother, and a goodly contingent of Remillard relations. Don did not attend. In 1983, when Denis was a mature and self-possessed sixteen, he was awarded an M.D. from Dartmouth Medical School. This time I escorted to the ceremony not only Sunny but also eight of her children—including the infant, Pauline. Twenty-four other Remillards made the journey to Hanover to celebrate the triumph of the family prodigy. Don, however, suffered a diplomatic attack of flu and remained in Berlin, attended by the adolescent Victor. They were not greatly missed.

Although Denis (as well as his Coterie) kept his extraordinary psychic powers under wraps during his study years, he continued to give his associates informal training. Mitch Losier, a methodical type who quickly became a seekersense adept, continued to trace other suboperants. Many of these were enticed to Dartmouth and eventually helped form the first North American operant nucleus. Denis served his three years' residency in psychiatry at the Mental Health Center associated with the college, and simultaneously took Ph.D. degrees in psychology and mathematics (the latter in the field of cybernetics). His intellectual precocity had attracted considerable public attention, of course, and certain anonymous benefactors helped to finance the first small ESP research facility that he set up and supervised as a postdoctoral fellow.

For the next three years Denis worked with numbers of operant and suboperant metapsychics in this modest little laboratory. Members of his Coterie contrived to join him as they completed their own studies and residencies, sacrificing financial security for the advancement of mental science. During this time of metapsychic pioneering Denis published half a dozen cautious papers and skirted the morass of premature publicity that might have fatally tainted his image. Persistent media snoops—and there were some—were summarily dealt with by the mettlesome Boutin and McAllister, the designated enforcers of the Coterie. More subtle attempts at probing were sidetracked by certain persons high in the administration of the Dartmouth Medical School, who realized what a unique talent the college was harboring.

As rumors of remarkable psychic activities at Dartmouth strengthened, hard-nosed investigators attempted an end run around Denis by importuning his father. Don was then attempting to operate a small logging business, having been fired from the mill for intractable alcoholism. The sensation-seekers were discouraged by bilingual curses and the menaces of Victor, who was by then a hulking youth with a notably malevolent demeanor. Denis had made many attempts to bring Victor into his own circle of young operants, but without success. Victor's coercive faculty had come on strong, together with a raging jealousy of his older brother. He wanted nothing to do with higher education or metapsychic experimentation. Eventually he dropped out of high school and joined Don in the woods.

In 1989, having established himself as one of the premier psychic researchers in the country, Dr. Denis Remillard was admitted to the Dartmouth Medical School faculty as a research associate with the rank of Associate Professor of Psychiatry

(Parapsychology). He was by that time twenty-three years old, almost totally alienated from his father and brother Victor, and committed to the work that would occupy him for the rest of his life . . . until his great mind was lost to humanity and the rest of the Galactic Milieu in the prelude to the Metapsychic Rebellion.

5

ALMA-ATA, KAZAKH SSR, EARTH
18 JANUARY 1984

ONLY OLD PYOTR SAKHVADZE NOTICED THE EARTHQUAKE.

The rest of the spectators and the crowd of ice skaters in Medeo Stadium were completely oblivious. Any faint seismic whisper would have been drowned out by the loudspeakers playing the waltz from *Yevgeniy Onyegin* and the shouting of the children. It is true that the side walls of the gaily ornamented yurta warming tents out on the ice swayed a little, and their horsehair tassels danced; but that might just as easily have been caused by a stray gust from the Zailiyskiy Ala-Tau intruding for a moment into the ice-rink's sheltered bowl.

But Pyotr knew better.

He was newly come to the Central Asian metropolis of Alma-Ata to live with his daughter Tamara and his son-in-law Yuri Gawrys and their three children, after nearly ten years of exile in Ulan-Ude, ministering to the mental-health needs of the Buryat Mongols. On this winter afternoon he was performing grandfatherly duties, shepherding Valery, Ilya, and Anna—who were nine, seven, and four years of age—on a skating outing at Medeo. Pyotr had nearly begged off going because of the sick headache that had plagued him for the past two days; but the youngsters would have been very disappointed, and he wanted so much for them to learn to love him that he pretended he felt better. He drove them in Tamara's red Zhiguli up to the big alpine sports complex in the foothills south of the city. Medeo's rink was world-class, and so cleverly sited that even in midwinter one could usually skate in comfort without bundling up. The three children had joined the throng out on the ice, leaving Pyotr to watch from a front row of the stands.

He had huddled there nursing his headache in silent misery for nearly two hours, feeling cold in spite of the tatty fur greatcoat and shapka he had brought from Siberia. He sipped mint tea from an insulated bottle, felt very sorry for himself, and wondered if he had made a serious mistake allowing his daughter to "rescue" him from exile. Ulan-Ude wasn't the Russian Riviera like Sochi; but the Mongols were a vigorous and good-humored lot and the psychic dabblings of their shamans were strictly apolitical... unlike those of Tamara and her high-strung Polish husband.

The headache grew worse, nauseating him with the pain. At last, when it seemed his poor head would explode, his eyes began to play tricks on him. The sunset-tinged snowy slopes that overhung the stadium started to shimmer, throwing off auroralike beams of an unnatural green color, and the bare rock areas were haloed with eerie violet. He felt the slight vibration of the earth tremor through the sensitive base of his spine and at the same time a lance of white agony seared his vision. He groaned out loud and tottered in his seat, nearly spilling the bottle of tea.

And then, a miracle!

His head cleared and was free of pain. The strange aurora effect cut off abruptly. His muzzy brain snapped into a keen state of cognition. An earthquake! Yes! And accompanied by the same mental phenomena he had experienced twice before, in 1966 at the disastrous psychiatric conference in Tashkent, and just last year in Siberia, when a minor temblor had rocked the Lake Baikal basin.

It could not be a coincidence. It was a species of extrasense! And he shouted:

You see, children? I am one of you after all! This proves that I, too, have the soul-power!

Dizziness overcame him and he lost track of reality until he heard the anxious voice of Valery, his oldest grandson.

"Dedushka? Are you feeling all right? We...we heard you cry out."

Pyotr was aware of the cheerful music again, and he saw the two boys and their little sister standing in front of him in their bright jackets and knit hats with pompons. Their breath was coming in quick cloudy puffs and their dark eyes were wide with astonishment. A couple of adult skaters had also stopped because of the evident concern of the children, and a sturdy woman in a blue speed-suit asked, "Any problem here, comrade?"

"No, I'm fine," Pyotr forced himself to say, giving a chuckle that was nearly giddy. "I nodded off and nearly slid out of my seat. Silly of me."

The adults paid no more attention to him but his grandchildren crowded closer. Pyotr could sense the swift telepathic exchange passing between Valery and Ilya. Their faces were distant, almost frightening in their maturity. But little Anna reached out to him with mittened hands, smiling, her cheeks as shiny as the Aport apples for which Alma-Ata was famous.

"Your head feels better now, doesn't it, Dedushka?"

He squeezed her hands gently. "Much better, little angel. In fact—I think I have made a wonderful discovery!"

Ilya was almost accusing. "We heard your mind shout to us. There was a strange image, too."

"Didn't you feel the ground tremble while you were skating?" Pyotr asked. "There was a small earthquake—and I perceived it with both my body and my mind!"

"I didn't feel anything, Grandfather," Valery said.

"Are you sure you didn't imagine it?" Ilya said.

Anna piped shyly, "I think I felt it, Dedushka. Was it sort of bright, and deep-down?"

"Yes, exactly!" Pyotr swept up the child, skates and all, and kissed her resoundingly. Then he crouched with a serious expression and told the three of them, "I detected the faint preliminaries to the earth tremor with some kind of an extrasense, and the actual shock, the discharge of seismic energy, was translated into a visual phenomenon. It's just as the village elder Seliac said more than twenty years ago: I, too, have the soul! I am one of you! A true extrasensor!"

The children stared at him blankly. Their minds shared subliminal comments that were as incomprehensible to Pyotr as the twittering of bats.

"Don't you see?" the old man said desperately. "My terrible headache was part of it, and I saw colored auras around the rocks as well. The important point is, I've had this type of experience before just prior to earthquakes, but I never realized its significance. Now I'm positive! Yes! It must be some new kind of psychic power—different from the telepathy or psychokinesis or out-of-body travel that your parents study at the Bioenergetics Institute. We must go home at once and tell them about it! It will be a wonderful surprise, and now perhaps they won't feel I'm such a useless burden—"

"You aren't a burden, Grandfather," Valery said, but his smile was remote.

"Do we have to go home?" Ilya's mouth turned down at the corners. "You said we'd stay until eighteen hours. I want to skate some more. I didn't feel any earthquake."

Valery gave him a poke.

Anna threw her arms around Pyotr's legs and peered up at him. "I know you have the soul, Dedushka. Never mind what *they* think."

A coldness crept over Pyotr. The colorful whirl of skaters was growing shadowy as dusk fell, and the music now seemed harsh. All of a sudden the great banks of stadium floodlights flashed on, nearly blinding him with their reflection off the ice. Could he have imagined the entire episode? Was it only the wish-fulfillment of a septuagenarian fool? Or—more ominously—might he have suffered a small stroke? (The symptoms were suggestive, even to a rusty psychiatrist like himself.)

"There was a small earthquake," he said firmly. It was real, my children! Believe me don't shut me out read it in my memories accept my mind-opening accept me . . .

They stood in a row looking at him, opaque—even the dear little Anna—seeming to weigh him among themselves. He tried to relax. He tried with all his heart to love them and not fear them, this new generation for whom he had suffered so much, whose freedom he had championed at the cost of his own liberty and professional advancement. It had been rather easy to do when the truly alien young minds were yet unborn, when there were only Tamara and Yuri (then called Jerzy) and a handful of other frightened, gifted ones in danger of exploitation by the military and the GRU fanatics under Kolinsky. Pyotr had demanded that they be treated as Soviet citizens, not guinea pigs; and through his international professional contacts he had publicized some of the dubious directions that psychic research was taking in his country during the late 1960s and '70s. He had sounded warnings—and he had been silenced. But things changed for the better.

The children stared. Anna smiled first, and then Valery, and finally Ilya, who said:

"Yes, let's go home and tell Mama and Papa."

"Zamechatel'no!" Pyotr whispered, lowering his head so they

would not see his tears. Then they all trooped down to the cloak-room.

When they arrived at the big apartment in the new university quarter of Alma-Ata, the children ran down the hall ahead of Pyotr and burst into the kitchen where Tamara and Yuri were preparing dinner together, as was their custom when Yuri did not feel too exhausted after work. The unmistakable aroma of home-made kielbasa permeated the room, and Tamara was just lifting kachapuri, delectable Georgian cheese tarts, from the oven. With a great deal of shouting and jumping up and down, the children announced their grandfather's claim to a new psychic power. Anna still maintained that she had felt the tremor and experienced the terrestrial aura effect "just like Dedushka."

"Oh, I don't think she did," the old man protested. "Perhaps it was all my imagination after all." He wilted under the barrage of juvenile protest and lifted his hands helplessly. "Now I scarcely know myself whether or not it really happened."

Yuri untied his apron after covering the simmering kettle of sausage and cabbage. "Come along with me, Papa. We'll leave these Red Indians for Tamara to pacify and find something to steady your nerves."

They went into the young biophysicist's cozy, messy little study and closed the door. Pyotr sank into an overstuffed lounge chair while his son-in-law poured brandy into a large glass from a leather-bound bottle.

"Not so much, Yuri! You mustn't waste it on a deluded old fool."

"Drink. Then we'll find out what you've been up to." Gawrys sat down at his desk and shoved aside dog-eared publications and stacks of correspondence. He formed his thin fingers into a stee-ple and studied the bluish nails, his pallid features in repose and his hair falling lankly over his high forehead. He took none of the brandy.

"What we really ought to do," Pyotr mumbled, his face in the glass, "is check with the university to see whether or not there was a small earthquake at about four-thirty this afternoon."

"Tamara is attending to it."

"Oh. Of course." Even after living with them for more than two weeks, he never ceased to be amazed by the domestic inter-action of practicing telepaths. Pyotr took a hefty swig of the brandy. It was Georgian, not Kazakh, mellow and earthy. Pyotr sighed. "It really did happen, you know."

"A psychic response to seismic activity is not unknown to science," Yuri remarked. "Other persons have described similar experiences."

"Then it may be that I *am* a genuine extrasensor?" The old man half rose from his chair in his eagerness.

Yuri Gawrys lifted his eyes. They were dark blue, like the lapis lazuli stones Pyotr remembered inset in the silver knife-scabbard of Seliac Eshba, the patriarch of Verkhnyaya Bzyb. "Would you like to tell me about the other times you sensed impending earthquakes?"

"It happened twice before. The first was in 1966, before I got into trouble fending the jackals off from Tamara. There was a conference on mental health in Tashkent, in April."

"Yes . . . a great quake devastated the city then."

"When I arrived at the airport I began to suffer the same kind of headache, the same vision of ghostly luminosity playing about the earth's surface. And when the first shock occurred, my symptoms vanished. But there was so much confusion in the aftermath—our hotel was damaged, you see—that I never made the connection. Then last year in Ulan-Ude there was a rather small tremor. I read about it the next day in the newspaper and wondered a bit, but at the time I was distracted. It was December, when you suffered your second heart attack, and—"

"Yes, Papa, yes." Yuri made an impatient gesture. "You are very lucky to be a sturdy Georgian rather than a Polack with an unfortunate history of cardiac insufficiency. And there is so much work yet to be done . . . especially now, when we are about to enter into a new, positive phase of psychic research at the university."

Pyotr's jaw dropped. "But the KGB-sponsored programs of bioenergetic weaponry! Surely you will remain locked into them indefinitely—"

"Andropov is dying," said Yuri. "He will not last another month. And when he goes, so will the KGB's stranglehold on our work. He was the one, together with Fleet Admiral Gorshkov, who originally saw aggressive potential in psychic faculties. While Andropov headed the KGB, he took a personal interest in the guidance of psychic research in the Soviet Union. You know, of course, that Secretary Brezhnev was himself treated by a psychic healer, and was completely in accord with Andropov's mind-war schemes."

Pyotr nodded.

"When Andropov finally took over as Party Secretary he was already deathly ill. His grip on us slowly loosened. The awful days of summer 1979, when Simonov and others of his perverted ilk violated the American President's mind during the SALT II signings in Vienna, will not soon come again." Yuri Gawrys's smile was terrible. "We have weeded our mental garden at Kazakh State University's Institute of Bioenergetics. The job was a long one, but it is complete. The last poisonous growth was uprooted only last December. By me, personally."

"Radi Boga! Your heart attack—"

"We all have a certain price to pay, Pyotr Sergeyevich. You have paid yours and I, mine. For the soul."

"What will happen when Andropov goes?" asked the psychiatrist.

"There will be a holding action by the old guard, a caretaker put in place while young Gorbachev and Romanov fight their duel. Whichever wins, we will be safe. They are both well-educated technocrats who have no patience with . . . the unconventional. They will forcibly retire Admiral Gorshkov and we shall probably find that our funding is drastically reduced. It is laser and particle-beam research that will get the rubles now."

"But—" Pyotr hesitated.

"Shall I read your thought?" Yuri inquired, smiling gently now. "This cutback will actually benefit us. The essential work —the gathering together of the psychically gifted here at the Institute—has already been done. We may deplore that these young people were taken from their families, as Tamara and I were, but in the larger view it is all for the best. Now that our minds are linked, we will always remain in contact with one another. The garden, Papa! The garden will grow."

The old man sipped his brandy, unable to respond. After a few minutes the door opened and Tamara came in, buxom and radiant, her bright auburn hair struggling out of its confining chignon.

"I have spoken to Akhmet Ismailov at the Geophysical Observatory. At precisely eighteen-twenty-eight hours there was a minor earth tremor measuring two point four on the Richter

Scale. Its epicenter was about thirty kilometers south of Medeo, in the Zailiyskiy Ala-Tau."

"Ah!" cried Pyotr. "I am one of you! I *am*!"

Tamara kissed the top of his head, where a few sand-colored hairs still grew. "Of course you are. You would be even if your head were stuffed with sawdust, instead of wise old brains that may be very valuable to our work."

"You really think that I can help you, daughter? You aren't simply humoring me?"

Tamara laughed. "Alma-Ata is in a zone of seismic instability. We have minor tremors often, and an occasional large one. Our buildings are specially engineered for safety. If you live here with us, Papa, your extrasense may get more of a workout than you would like. You may end up wishing that you were back in Ulan-Ude, shrinking Mongolian nut-cases! . . . Now please wash up for dinner."

When Pyotr had gone out, Tamara said to her husband, "The faculty is of a certain theoretical interest, and it will help Papa to adjust to us. He was afraid, you know."

Yuri got up from his chair. "I told him—obliquely, but he understood—about our Black Frost."

"Was that wise?"

"He had to know that our group is trustworthy, and that we are not without means of self-defense. I spoke only of my own role in the terminations."

"There must be no more of them! We must find other ways!"

"Hush." He took both her hands and pressed them to his cool lips. "We will find other ways. But above all, we must survive, my darling. Otherwise, the plan will not succeed and it will all have been for nothing."

"The soul," she whispered. "The poor soul of our people. Why must it have this terrible dark side? But it has always been so. We progress only through violence, never through reasoning and love."

"The normals of our nation will have to be taught to love us. It will not be an easy lesson. The plan that we have worked so hard on promises a way, but it cannot be put into force for many years yet. I do not have those years. It will be up to you to be strong. To defend all your mind-children from those who would destroy or pervert them. This Alma-Ata group must survive and link up with the others in other nations, with the World Soul, Tamara.

Until then, the children must endure in a wilderness, defended by a valiant mother." He looked down at her, full of pity. She was twenty-six.

"I will try to find peaceful ways," she said. "If they fail, then I will do as you have taught me."

6

EXCERPTS FROM ADDRESS
GIVEN BY YASUHIRO NAKASONE,
PRIME MINISTER OF JAPAN,
AT THE GENERAL ASSEMBLY
OF THE UNITED NATIONS
UNITED NATIONS, NEW YORK, EARTH
23 OCTOBER 1985

AT THE TIME THE UNITED NATIONS CHARTER WAS SIGNED IN SAN Francisco on 26 June 1945, Japan was waging a desperate and lonely war against over forty-odd Allied countries. Since the end of that war, Japan has profoundly regretted the ultranationalism and militarism it unleashed, and the untold suffering the war inflicted upon peoples around the world and, indeed, upon its own people.

As the only people ever to have experienced the devastation of the atomic bomb, in Hiroshima and Nagasaki, the Japanese people have steadfastly called for the elimination of nuclear weapons. Nuclear energy should be used exclusively for peaceful purposes; it must never again be employed as a means of destruction.

We believe that all living things—humans, animals, trees, grasses—are essentially brothers and sisters, [and yet] our generation is recklessly destroying the natural environment which has evolved over the course of millions of years and is essential for our survival. Our soil, water, air, flora and fauna are being subjected to the most barbaric attacks since the earth was created. This folly can only be suicidal.

Man is born by the grace of the great universe:

> Afar and above the dark and endless sky,
> the Milky Way runs
> toward the place I come from.

7

HANOVER, NEW HAMPSHIRE, EARTH
19 SEPTEMBER 1987

THE SATURDAY AFTERNOON WAS CLASSIC AUTUMNAL IVY League, with a clear blue sky above broad-leaved trees that were just beginning to ignite in their fall colors. Lucille Cartier was glad to be back at Dartmouth, glad that Doctor Bill had agreed to resume counseling her, happiest of all that the damn dreams had gone away with her return to the campus, and that there was yet no sign of subversive mental influence from Remillard's Coterie.

She bicycled to her shrink session, going the long way around Occom Pond and approaching the Mental Health Center via Maynard Street. She arrived with ten minutes to spare, dismounted in a shady spot by the main entrance, and took slow, deep breaths.

I am not resisting therapy. It will help me. I need help and welcome it. I am glad to be here . . .

She lifted her eyes, looked across Maynard, across the big Hitchcock Hospital parking lot, across busy College Street. And there it was, not five hundred feet away, an old gray saltbox building that hulked among spindly birches and dark evergreens like a haunted house out of a Stephen King novel, its windows blank-eyed and sinister.

You won't put me off! I'm not afraid of you. To hell with you and your Coterie. I *defy* you!

Recklessly, she hopped back on her bicycle and zoomed

across the road to stand in the very forecourt of 45 College Street. There were only two cars parked beside the saltbox—Glenn Dalembert's old Mustang with the odd-colored door, and a spiffy new Lincoln with Massachusetts plates, no doubt belonging to some visitor.

You see? I'm back. You couldn't scare me away. I don't need you and I won't let you harass me. You can't recruit *me* against my will like you did Donna Chan and Dane Gwaltney. I'll live my own life, thank you very much . . . and I'll integrate my freak brain without surrendering to ány mind-worm collective!

The saltbox building was utterly still, without telepathic response. And then Lucille realized that she had been using *his* private wavelength, what the mind-worms called a "mental signature," perceptible to him alone. Obviously, he wasn't even here today. Her gesture of defiance was futile.

Or was it? She felt quite a bit better inside! For good measure, she gave Dr. Denis Remillard's laboratory the finger, and then she rode her bicycle back to Maynard Street, parked it in the Mental Health Center rack, and went inside to keep her appointment.

DR. SAMPSON: I'm very glad you decided to resume therapy, Lucille. I presume this means that you've decided to remain at Dartmouth rather than transfer to Rivier College for your senior year.

LUCILLE: Yes. That idea turned out to be a mistake, Doctor Bill.

SAMPSON: Would you like to tell me why you changed your mind?

LUCILLE: We—you and I—didn't seem to be getting anywhere with the therapy last term. And I was miserable here anyway, worrying about Mom having to cope with Dad all by herself besides teaching at the high school. I thought I'd solve that problem and help my own feelings of anxiety and guilt by simply going back home. I could day-hop to Rivier and complete my degree, and help Mom with Dad and the housework just like before. When I went back to Nashua for the summer break I felt pretty good for a few weeks . . . but then the old shit started all over again.

SAMPSON: The anxiety and insomnia?

LUCILLE: [laughs] Don't I wish that was all! . . . Look, Doctor Bill, I've got a confession to make, I haven't been completely honest with you. I didn't tell you all my symptoms.

SAMPSON: Why not?

LUCILLE: I was afraid to. If the college found out, they'd want to bounce me.

SAMPSON: [mildly] You know our relationship is confidential.

LUCILLE: Even so . . . it's so weird, you see. And it would interest—never mind. I didn't think I had to mention it because I hadn't *had* the thing for a long time. Not since I was thirteen, bucking the puberty blues.

SAMPSON: Would you like to tell me about it now?

LUCILLE: I've got to. It's back. Going home again, living with my parents this summer, triggered it. I didn't say anything to them—they would have been scared to death, like they were the other time. You're my only hope now, you see. I won't go to Remillard! I *won't!*

SAMPSON: [nonplussed] Denis Remillard? Of the parapsychology lab?

LUCILLE: It's his fault it's come back! Damn him and his meddling! If he had only let me alone—

SAMPSON: [making a note on his pad] Lucille . . . Stop for a moment and relax. Then let's try to concentrate on this mysterious symptom you neglected to mention.

LUCILLE: All right. It goes back to when I was thirteen. The attacks of creepiness, nerves, anxiety—they really began then. And I also had nightmares. And then . . . the house burned down. I did it.

SAMPSON: You deliberately started the fire?

LUCILLE: No, no! I didn't mean to! But . . . it was a time when I was feeling all mixed up. Nobody understood me, that kind of adolescent bullshit, but something else, too. They really *didn't* understand! I couldn't talk to them . . . Dad was just starting to come down with the sclerosis thing and he was—was hard to live with. I was so sorry for him and wanted to help, but he was so angry all the time and didn't want me around him. Then I started to have these nightmares about fire. I was Joan of Arc and they were lighting the pyre and I was all noble and forgave them and the flames came roaring up to swallow me and my skin would burn and even my bones and I'd be nothing but clean bright sparks flying up to heaven *if only I wouldn't be afraid*. But I was afraid. So the flames hurt horribly because I wasn't Saint Joan at all, and I'd wake up yelling and get the whole house in an uproar, Mom and Dad and my kid brother Mike. It was awful. It was even worse the time I woke up and found my bedroom wall was all in flames.

SAMPSON: Good God! . . . I'm sorry. Go on.

LUCILLE: I got out the door and woke Mom and Mike and we got Dad into his wheelchair and made it outside safely. But by the time the fire department came, the house was too far gone to save much. Dad's piano burned. It was a Steinway grand he'd got years ago, before he was ever married, when he was going to be a concert pianist and studied at the New England Conservatory in Boston. It cost thousands of dollars and he kept it even when he gave up his classical ambitions. Then, when he got sick and couldn't do lounge gigs or even give lessons anymore he wanted to sell it, to help out the family. But Mom wouldn't let him. He loved that piano more than anything. And I burned it.

SAMPSON: But you said you didn't start the fire deliberately. Why do you blame yourself?

LUCILLE: My room was right next to the one where the piano was. The fire started in that wall—the firemen could tell. I hadn't been smoking or anything dumb like that, but the whole wall near my bed and the piano on the other side of it somehow caught fire.

SAMPSON: An electrical short.

LUCILLE: There was no outlet on that wall, and only an ordinary lamp near the piano . . . Later on, they thought I might have walked in my sleep and lit a match. I told them it was my fault, you see. That I did it. But I didn't dare explain how! I dreamed that fire. The dream became more and more real . . . and finally, it *was* real.

SAMPSON: What do you mean by that?

LUCILLE: I did it with my mind. My unconscious. I'm one of them—the freaks that Remillard tests over at the parapsychology lab. He hunted me out long before he came to Dartmouth, when I was eleven. Later on, he and his Coterie wanted me to come here to school. I didn't want to, but there was the scholarship and my folks put on the pressure. I came when I was sixteen, and then Remillard really shifted into high gear. I should be grateful all to hell to assist the boy genius in his researches, even if I could only do a little telepathy when the moon was right, and melt ice cubes and jiggle tables. Dumb, useless things! I told him no. He kept on bugging me for three years, though, and so did his mind-worm clique! I told him all

I wanted to do was live a normal life, study a legitimate science like biochemistry instead of waste time on occult nonsense. And I will!

SAMPSON: Excuse me, Lucille. You're an intelligent young woman. Don't you see any contradiction in what you've been saying?

LUCILLE: Remillard and his people give me the creeps—and I won't be experimented upon!

SAMPSON: I understand that. You want help. But why do you think I'm the one who can give it to you—rather than Remillard?

LUCILLE: It's a psychiatric problem. It really has nothing to do with parapsychology except—in its manifestation.

SAMPSON: You are convinced that this incendiary faculty is a genuine paranormal phenomenon?

LUCILLE: [laughs] There's even a name for it in folklore: fire-raising. Look it up in any compendium of witchcraft. You'll find true stories about people who start fires without any equipment—produce it out of thin air. Some of them even manage to burn themselves to death.

SAMPSON: You only did this once, when you were thirteen?

LUCILLE: I'm . . . not sure. We had other house-fires, small ones, when I was younger. There always seemed to be a natural explanation.

SAMPSON: The piano burning might have had one. A freak lightning strike, for example.

LUCILLE: It was me! My resentment of poor Dad. He only had time for his illness and the damn piano and never any time for me . . .

SAMPSON: Let's suppose your self-analysis is correct. Why do you think you're playing with fire again now, at this particular time?

LUCILLE: *I don't know!* That's why I came to you in the first place, when Denis Remillard's badgering got me so edgy last February and I couldn't sleep or study. I thought you'd just prescribe some Valium, but instead you got me into this analysis that didn't seem to help at all.

SAMPSON: You never spoke to me about being harrassed by Remillard or his people.

LUCILLE: I didn't want you to know. I thought . . . oh, *hell*. Now you do know. Can't you help me? What if the fire nightmares start up here at Dartmouth like they did at home this summer?

SAMPSON: They haven't yet?

LUCILLE: No.

SAMPSON: You suffered from anxiety and depression here at school last spring, and yet the really serious warning from your unconscious only came to you when you tried to return home. Does that suggest anything to you?

LUCILLE: I had to come back here. To *you*. That's what my mind was telling me.

SAMPSON: Are you sure?

LUCILLE: Yes.

SAMPSON: I want to help you, Lucille. You must believe me. But you do understand that your analysis presents unique problems. All humans carry within their unconscious a load of destructive wishes left over from early childhood. You've studied psychology. You know what I mean. The mother takes the nipple from the hungry baby's mouth and it becomes enraged. A little child is punished for being naughty and wishes its parents were dead. We all had feelings like this once and we repressed them, and sometimes this guilt or something similar resurfaces in later life to give us psychic pain. But a toddler is too weak to murder its parents. And an adult who still unconsciously resents her father's neglect will not normally harm him physically. The unconscious may rage, but unless the person is psychotic it remains outwardly impotent and must find other outlets for its revenge.

LUCILLE: But my unconscious isn't impotent . . .

SAMPSON: Evidently not. And one might ask whether your *conscious* mind is similarly empowered.

LUCILLE: God. What am I going to do?

SAMPSON: The only useful answers in psychoanalysis are the ones you see clearly for yourself. I can guide you, but I can't force you to set your deep fears aside . . . And you *are* afraid of your paranormal powers, Lucille. You'd like them to go away so you can be just like normal people—

LUCILLE: Yes. Yes!

SAMPSON: But it seems quite likely that the powers won't go away. So we'll have to predicate our coping strategy on that supposition, won't we?

LUCILLE: [hotly] I know exactly what you're leading up to! And it has nothing to do with mind reading. *Remillard!*

SAMPSON: I haven't had too much professional contact with him, but there are those on the Medical School faculty who think highly of his work. For all his youth, he's a meticulous researcher. His test subjects aren't treated like mental patients, you know. Most of them seem to be Dartmouth students like yourself—

LUCILLE: And just *why* have so many of these psychic freaks come here? Why did I come? There was the scholarship offer, of course—but I felt an unnatural compulsion, too!

SAMPSON: [patiently] Is it necessarily bad to want to associate with others who share your unusual mental faculties?

LUCILLE: [despairingly] But I don't want them . . . I only want to stop burning . . . to be happy . . . to have someone understand me and love me.

SAMPSON: Your unconscious wants you to be happy, too. It wants you to face your dilemma honestly instead of running away from it. The unconscious isn't a demon, Lucille. It's only you.

LUCILLE: [after a silence] I suppose so.

SAMPSON: No one can force you to participate in Dr. Remillard's experiments, Lucille. But you must ask yourself: Might your fear of him be irrational?

LUCILLE: I don't know. I'm all mixed up. My head feels so feverish and my throat is so dry. Can I get some water?

SAMPSON: Today's session is almost over . . . I have a suggestion. Let me find out some specifics of Remillard's research. Let me ask him—without mentioning you—about the general state of mental health among his subjects. Surely some of them must have experienced conflicts similar to yours. When I get more information, we can begin working out your coping strategy.

LUCILLE: But not with him.

SAMPSON: Not if you don't want to.

LUCILLE: He'll want me to join his group. He'll coerce me.

SAMPSON: [laughing] Over my dead body! And I played middle linebacker for the Big Green in '56!

LUCILLE: [admiringly] It figures. And you have the perfect name.

SAMPSON: Uh . . . well, that was long ago and far away. But you can rest assured that no one will coerce you into anything. Now, our time is up for today. Can you come again at the same time next Wednesday?

LUCILLE: Will the Center authorize more than one free therapy session a week for me? I mean, I can't afford—

SAMPSON: That's all right. Your case is unusual. As a matter of fact, it's the most unusual one I've ever encountered . . . But you will sleep with a fire extinguisher nearby, won't you?

LUCILLE: Yes, Doctor Bill. Goodbye.

SAMPSON: Goodbye, Lucille.

8

BERLIN, NEW HAMPSHIRE, EARTH
20 MAY 1989

DON REMILLARD DIDN'T GO TO THE BLUE OX ON SATURDAY nights much anymore, it being a lot cheaper to drink at home. But with Sunny waiting tables on the late shift at the Androscoggin Kitchen this week and Victor gone up to Pittsburg on some mystery errand, the younger brats would be running wild around the place. He'd end up belting a couple of them for sure, and then there'd be a row when Sunny got back—and God knows he had enough trouble with her already.

So he went down to the Ox, settled in at his usual spot on the far end of the bar, and started working through his quota of Seagram's. A few of his old buddies greeted him, but none stuck around to interfere seriously with his drinking. Little by little the place filled up and the tunes played by the jukebox got louder. By ten o'clock Don was almost deafened by the music and the racket made by the roistering mill-hands and loggers and their exuberant ladies. He had downed enough whiskey to be more or less skunk-bit and incapable—and it hadn't done a damn bit of good.

He could still hear the obscene voices inside his head. The goddam telepaths. The ones who were out to get him.

Just look at that pathetic fucker! Can't hardly hold a glass without it sloppin' over. Eyes like poached eggs in ketchup! Skritch-jawed and grubby and wearin' a week-old shirt.

Crazy as an outhouse rat, too. Brains so pickled his power's petered away t'zilch. Won't be long now, he won't be able to shut us out. We'll nail him!

May not have to bother, he screws up again like he did today.

You see the way he tried to clear the throat of the whole-tree hog he let jam up?

Hell, yes. Goddam jeezly bar-toad almost got chopped to red-flannel hash! . . . Hey, stupid! Finish the job next time. Do us all a favor!

Do Victor a favor. What's he need a drunken old fart like you on the operation?

"I taught him everything, dammit. Everything."

Pig's ass. Kid got the outfit percolatin' despite you.

Yeah. That's right!

"I taught him everything! How to use his powers. Never woulda done it without me. Green kid! Shit—I *made* that kid."

You made him what he is.

Whatever that is! Haw haw haw . . .

"Damn right . . . damn right. You tell 'im that."

Hey, Vic! How long you gonna put up with your drag-ass old man? How long you gonna let the old stumblebum bollix up your show? Listen, Vic. Bright kid like you don't hafta put up with shit like he pulls. Lookit today. Feedin' the new Omark the wrong kinda stems. Coulda broke the christly rig! Family loyalty can be mighty expensive. Take our advice. Tie a can to the old asshole. Hire somebody who knows what he's doin'!

I'm considering it . . .

"The hell you are!" Don muttered viciously.

Old Ducky Duquette, who was nursing a bottle of Labatt's a little way down the bar, looked at him with an expression of mild surprise.

Haw haw haw! You think Vic wouldn't get rid of you? Think again!

Tell him, Vic. Tell him why you went up to Pittsburg tonight. Tell him!

. . . I'm putting it up to Howie Durant to come in with us. He's an experienced hand with whole-tree chippers.

Way to go, Vic! Demote the old man to brush-piler. Better yet, get him off the operation altogether. He's an accident waitin' to happen, drinkin' on the job the way he does.

Maybe the sooner the accident happens, the better!

Wipe him out yourself, kid. Tip him over the edge. You don't hafta wait for us. Be our guest!

. . . It might be for the best. Easy enough to rig an accident with programmed incitement. His defenses are negligible now

and his farspeech no longer has the range to alert Denis or Uncle Rogi.

That's right, Vic. Be just another logging fatality. Happens all the time.

Don slammed his shot glass down on the bar and yelled, "Oh no you don't, punk! I'll fry your fuckin' brains out first!"

Ralph Pelletier, the Ox's owner, who was tending bar as usual, called out over the din, "Anything wrong down there?"

Don forced a big grin and shook his head. "All I need's another double, double-quick!" He waved his glass.

Pelletier brought the bottle and poured. Don downed the whiskey and immediately demanded more. The tavern-keeper said quietly, "You've had about enough for tonight, Don. Finish this and then give your liver a rest."

"Don't need your lectures, bonhomme. Just your booze. Un p'tit coup." Don tossed money onto the mahogany. The bills fell into a puddle of spilled liquor.

Pelletier scooped them up with a grimace of distaste. "Drink up and go home, Don. You hear what I'm saying?" He filled the double shot glass again. "I mean it. Hors d'ici." He went away.

Don mouthed silent curses after him. Pelly wanted to get rid of him. *Everybody* wanted to get rid of him! He sipped from the glass and groaned. All around him the Blue Ox patrons laughed and the voices inside his head recited fresh indecencies.

Ducky Duquette edged closer, a tentative smile of sympathy creasing his weathered old chops. "Ça va, Don? Had a rough week?"

Don could only laugh helplessly.

"Trouble out at the chantier, maybe? The logging outfit has growing pains?"

The mental voices chortled at the joke. Don pressed knuckles to his temples until the voices cut off, then lifted his glass with a trembling hand. "My damn kid's gettin' too big for his fuckin' britches. Throwing his weight around."

"Ah!" Ducky looked wise. "Such a clever boy, your Victor. But perhaps impatient? That's the way of the young. Still, he's doing very well, isn't he? I heard about the big new contract he landed with Saint William. Amazing that they accepted the bid of such a youthful entrepreneur, eh?"

"Fuckin' fantastic," Don muttered.

"You can be proud, Don. What sons! First Denis le Mirobolant—and now, Victor, with his own logging company at the age of nineteen."

"And I'm such a lucky bastard, Ducky. I get to work for my own wiseacre kid! I taught him everything. And now he wants to kick me out." His face lit up in a sour smile. "But he won't get away with it. I know where a few bodies are buried . . . like how a shoestring operation like his is able to field so much expensive rolling stock."

Fold your face, you drunken blabbermouth!

Vic—you gonna let him keep this up?

Ducky had gone wary. He lowered his voice. "Tell you the truth, Don, there *has* been some talk. Lot of people wondered how Vic could afford that new Omark chip machine so soon after getting the second feller-buncher. Equipment like that don't grow on trees."

"Lemme tell you something, Ducky." Don draped an arm around the old man's neck and spoke in a coarse whisper. "Any ol' wood rat knows that logging machinery does, too, grow on trees. All you hafta do is know what trees to look under. And when."

Will you shut up, you peasoupin' lush?

He's gonna squeal, Vic. Don't say we didn't warn you. It's his fuckin' conscience, see. Confession's good for the soul, he thinks. Go ahead and confess, Don—we got the final absolution all ready!

We'll show him what happens to finks! . . . Give him to us, Vic. Come on! What're you waitin' for—a posse of county mounties goin' over your stuff with a magnifying glass and an electronic sniffer?

Don tittered. "Wouldn't find diddly. Got every damn ID number and beeper-trace fixed. Told you my Vic was smart. And I taught him everything." The injustice of it all overwhelmed him and his voice broke. "Everything, Ducky. Not just the mind-powers but the business, too. Vic was nothin' but a high school punk when they pink-slipped me at the mill. It was my idea to go into the woods and start cuttin' pulpwood."

And you'd still be a low-bore stump-jumper operatin' with two chain saws and a pick-em-up if it wasn't for Vic!

You taught him? He taught you!

Who coerced the first big contract? Who rounded up the gear? Who found the right men, the ones who know how to keep zipped lips? Who keeps the whole show chargin' ahead in the black? Not you, you washed-up alcoholic cuntlapper.

"No gratitude," Don moaned. "From any of my children."

Ducky blinked and began drawing away. "Tough luck . . ."

"I know what Vic's planning," Don shouted. "But he won't get away with it! None of 'em will!" Heads were turning and he felt the pressure of hostile eyes delving after his dangerous secrets. Could the patrons of the Blue Ox hear the taunting voices, too? No—of course not! They were only in his head. They were only imaginary! What was wrong with Ducky, then, looking so shit-scared? . . . God! How much had he blabbed to the old fool?

"Where the hell you think you're going?" Don grabbed Ducky by the front of the shirt. The old fellow yelped and pulled back, and his bottle of beer tipped and burbled onto the bar.

Ralph Pelletier, his expression thunderous, called, "Goddammit, Don—what'd I tell you?"

He knows! They all know! They'll tell Vic! Tell the cops! You spilled your guts just fine this time, fink!

Don shook Duquette until his dentures rattled. "You won't tell! I never said anything about Vic's equipment. You hear me?"

"He's crazy! He's crazy!" Ducky gibbered, hanging in Don's grip limp as a spawned-out salmon.

Choke the lyin' sonuvabitch! Shut him up!

Lute Soderstrom, who stood six-six and had once punched a hole in the radiator of a Kenwhopper, stepped up behind Don and took hold of his arms. A couple of other Blue Ox habitués pried Ducky loose.

Don's howl was agonized. "You won't get away with it! You're all in it together, aren't you? All working with Vic and the others to finish me off!"

"Ease him outside," Pelletier said.

The jukebox was pounding a raucous dirt-rock tune. Women squealed and men shouted jocose advice to Lute as he wrestled his burden toward the door.

"They're waiting for me out there!" Don screamed. "Waiting with Vic!" He tried to coerce the Swede: hopeless. He tried to trip Lute up by knocking over chairs or tables with his psychokinesis: he hadn't a glimmer. He was impotent. He was nothing. A carousel of light and noise and pain spun around him, slowly dissolving to black, and the jeering mental voices receded to a far distance. Don was a dead weight in Lute's powerful arms as they came out into the soft May night.

Lute dragged him around back to the Ox's dark parking lot, picked him up bodily, and dumped him onto a folded tarp in the bed of a little Nissan 4 x 4. "You gonna be okay, Don." He spoke soothingly. "You stay here, get a little air, maybe sleep. I come back in just a little bit and drive you home, okay?"

Fais un gros dodo, ordure! Haw haw haw...

Don made an inarticulate noise. Lute nodded and went off.

You can't stay here.

You dassn't go to sleep!

Vic knows what you said. You gotta get outa here!

"Je suis fichu," Don mumbled. "Pas de couilles... mon crâne... ah, Jésus..."

Pretty late in the game to be calling on him, shithead.

He can't help you. Nobody can. Nobody cares what happens to you, you drunken freak. Nobody!

Nobody... nobody... nobody...

"You're wrong." The words were slurred, tainted with the bile that had risen in his throat. He clutched at the side of the pickup's cargo bed, summoned strength, and heaved himself up and over. Then he lay on his face in the dirt for a long time, stunned.

Something crawled across the back of his neck and he opened his eyes, lifted his head, and grinned at the Nissan's left rear wheel. His senses were reeling but he was no longer a man without hope. The voices were wrong! Somebody did care. Somebody who would help him, who would even fend off Victor...

"Merci, mon Seigneur. Merci, doux Jésus!"

He struggled to his feet, fighting off nausea. His head seemed to be in the grip of iron tongs and he had to lean against the side of the Nissan until the pain subsided and he could see. He peered about anxiously among the parked cars and trucks for signs of the enemy. Nobody was there. Not *yet*. They were waiting for Vic, and it'd take the kid time to get back to Berlin from Pittsburg, sixty miles away via two-lane blacktop.

When he was steady he thumbed his wristwatch. The lighted read-out showed just a little past eleven. She'd have to work until one on Saturday and it was only a mile to walk, along well-lit Main Street and then Riverside Drive. She had her car. He could sit in it and wait, get coffee and sober up. It would be all right.

Pulling himself together, he shuffled onto the sidewalk and came around to the front of the tavern. The music and laughter were louder than ever. They'd forgotten all about him. Lamenting the callousness of it all, he set off north on Main, heading for the Androscoggin Kitchen restaurant and Sunny.

Don went to the take-out window and ordered a large black coffee from Marcie Stroup, and asked her to have Sunny bring it to the car.

"Gee, Don, I dunno." The girl eyed him dubiously. He was a filthy mess, reeking of alcohol, and he had caused scenes before at the Kitchen that had nearly cost Sunny her job.

"Please, Marcie. I'm not here to make trouble. It's really important. Tell Sunny that."

The girl finally said, "Okay," and went off. He shambled over to Sunny's battered '81 Escort that was parked at the far side of the big paved lot, and got in on the driver's side after opening the door with his own key. The Andy K was bursting at the seams on this fine spring night. The lot was jammed with vehicles coming in and out and cruisers stopping for take-outs. The place was far too brightly lit for those murdering bastards to chance coming after him, so he leaned back and closed his eyes, feeling safe for the moment. The long walk had helped to clear his brain but his head ached worse than ever. It didn't matter. He welcomed the pain because it kept the voices at bay. Not that he really cared about this taunting anymore. They couldn't touch him without Vic's say-so, and Sunny would take care of *him*.

"Don?" She was standing beside the open window, face drawn with worry and shadowed by the overhead illumination of the vapor lamps. She held a large container of coffee. The loving concern that radiated from her mind struck him like a sword in the heart. Poor Sunny. She was only forty-one, and she was old. Like him. He had put her through so much.

He smiled crookedly. "Come sit with me."

She handed him the coffee. "Don, you know I can't. We're busy. I only came because Marcie said—"

His mind took hold of hers in an old familiar way, like a hand slipping into a glove. "It's important. Just for a few minutes."

She sighed and came around to open the passenger door, then slid in beside him. "What is it?" Apprehension made her voice unsteady. She still had one hand on the door handle.

He downed a gulp of steaming liquid. "I was at the Ox tonight. Making a nickel-plated jackass outa myself."

She turned away miserably. "Oh, Don. If only you—"

He interrupted her. "Listen. I made up my mind! If you just help me, I'll give up drinking for good. I'll do what you been asking me to do."

She looked at him, incredulous. "You'll go to Denis? Let him check you into the detox clinic at Project Cork?"

Don gritted his teeth. Even the mention of the quaintly titled but nationally famous institute for alcoholism study at Dartmouth got his back up. Project Cork! Enough to make a grown man puke. But locked away in its stern sanctuary with Denis's powerful mind to shield him, no enemy would ever be able to get hold of him. Not Victor. Not the fiends of his own engendering.

"I'll go to Denis," Don vowed. "Tonight, if you like. Call him up and tell him I'm on my way."

Tears filled Sunny's eyes. "You really mean it this time?"

"I swear to God!" His eyes shifted. Was that something moving in the trees beyond the edge of the lot? Were they out there, listening? Don set the coffee on the dashboard and clasped his wife's hand. "But I gotta go *now*. I need help now, Sunny. You understand?"

"You're in no condition to drive that far. I'll call Denis, and then when Victor comes home he can—"

"No!" Don seized her by the shoulders. Her eyes dilated with fear and he hastened to say, "Victor's gonna be gone God knows how long. I can't wait! I've gotta go now or never!"

She took a resolute breath, detached his hands. "I'll drive you myself. I'll call Denis and ask him to meet us on the road."

"Good idea! Then you won't have to leave the kids alone too long." He gulped more coffee and thought hard. "We'll take Route 2. Ask Denis to meet us at the Saint Johnsbury Rest Area on I-91. Go call him, Sunny. Hurry."

She stared at him, searching. "You're sure?"

His mind cried: Sunny for the love of God *help me*!

She opened the car door and slipped out. "I'll be right back." Then she was hurrying toward the gaudy lights of the restaurant and he was alone, limp with reaction and relief. He reached over, locked the righthand door, and rolled its window fully closed. He secured his own side as well. The car was stuffy and the windshield partly fogged by coffee vapor, but he was safe. His mind seemed to slip in and out of gear, focusing on one menace after another: Victor. The hostile voices. His brother Rogi, that backbiting weasel. Even Denis, remote, ice-hearted, intolerant of a hard-working father's human weakness . . . God, how he dreaded

having to submit to Denis! He knew he'd have to come clean—
tell Denis about the voices and the way they'd drawn Victor into
the conspiracy, maybe even tell about the stolen equipment that
had triggered the whole fuck-up in the first place. Denis would
despise him more than ever! But he'd have to stand by his father
nonetheless. Sunny would see to it. Wonderful Sunny...

And then Don caught sight of the black customized Chevy
van. It was poised in the turn lane out on Route 16, signals
blinking, waiting for a break in the heavy northbound traffic so it
could enter the parking lot.

He's finally here.

It's about time!

Over here, Vic! Over here!

"No," Don whispered. "No, God."

At least four other cars were trying to get out of that exit. The
van was momentarily blocked. Sunny!... But she was probably
still on the telephone. Could he make a break for the restaurant?
It was too damn far away. The van would surely cut him off
before he made it to the door—

And now it was making the turn to enter!

Frantically, Don switched on the ignition of the Escort. There
was another way out, a dirt track that bumped over waste-ground.
He floored the pedal and went ripping down a lane of parked
vehicles. He clung to the wheel as his car careened over the
rutted track and onto the highway. He swerved to avoid being
rear-ended by a furiously honking station wagon, jinked onto the
shoulder, then regained control. In the rearview mirror, he saw
the black Chevy van trapped in the restaurant lot by a tangle of
cars in front of it and behind it.

Vic! Vic! He's gettin' away!

In your mom's car. Northbound!

Don laughed at them. He checked the fuel gauge: nearly full.
The traffic was heavy in both directions. Victor's farsight was
lousy and his coercion didn't reach beyond a stone's throw. He
could lose the kid in the maze of logging roads up the Androscoggin River beyond Milan, then double back and pick up
Sunny.

You'll never get away!

We'll keep Vic on the trail!

You're finished, sucker.

Give up. We'll help Vic nail you!

Don was laughing so hard he nearly choked. "You're not real! You can't hurt me! Go to hell!"

Oncoming cars were blinking their brights at him. He panicked for a moment, then realized that he was driving with only the parking lights on. Giggling, he flicked the headlight switch. Then he settled down and sped north along the river road toward the deep woods.

Sunny wept in Victor's arms, sitting beside him on the front seat of the black van. "He was still very drunk. He's sure to have an accident! Victor, what are we going to do? How will we ever find him?"

He held her tightly. "Hush, Maman. Let me think . . . There's Denis. He could try using his seekersense on Papa."

She broke away and cried, "Yes, of course! Hurry and telephone! He may not have left Hanover yet."

The young man sprinted for the front door of the restaurant, dodging departing diners. Sunny sat with her face buried in her hands, trying to summon from latency the telepathic power she had used so long ago when her eldest son was a baby:

Denis stay home. Don't leave home yet. Stay Denis stay . . .

After an interminable time, Victor returned, alight with triumph. "Caught him! He was on the way to the car, but he dropped his keys—and then he heard the phone ringing and came back."

"Oh, thank God. And he'll—he'll search? And tell you where to find your father?"

Victor started the engine of the van. "Denis will track Papa down, then call me at home. He said there may be some difficulty because Papa's aura tends to be suppressed by the alcohol. But you're not to worry. We'll find him. And now I'm taking you home."

"But I'll have to speak to Mr. Lovett first," Sunny protested. "He'll be furious—"

"I've already spoken to him." Victor's smile was invincibly reassuring. "He's not furious, he understands it's a family emergency. It's going to be all right, Maman." He took a tissue from the console dispenser and wiped her tears, then bent and kissed her cheek with warm lips.

Sunny felt herself relaxing, giving over volition to this tall, masterful son who was so like the strong, youthful Don she had married twenty-three years ago. She said, "I know how hard it's been for you lately, Victor. You're bitter. I understand why. But you must help your father, if only for my sake."

The black van was moving slowly forward. Victor gripped the wheel and stared straight ahead. "Just leave everything to me," he said. "Now fasten your seat belt and we'll go home."

An excruciating thirst, a tight bladder, and a skull-piercing chorus of woodland birds woke Don.

His rheum-clogged eyelids opened with reluctance to misty dawn. Every joint above the waist ached and every joint below was numb. His brain was swollen too large for its fragile bony case and was on the imminent verge of exploding. He cursed, invoked a compassionate God, and asked himself aloud where the hell he had ended up *this* time.

It was the usual Saturday night blackout. The usual Sunday morning hangover. But he was in Sunny's car, not his own. What the hell? . . . Oh, yeah. His heap was in the shop. He must have taken hers.

The windows of the Escort were curtained in condensation. He rubbed a clear space and tried to focus his bleary eyes. There were giant shapes around him, yellow and blue, with jointed arms held rakishly akimbo. The nose of the little car was snuggled up to the flank of a monster machine. Another, even larger, confronted him with threatening insectile jaws. On its back was a cab bearing the legend:

REMCO PULPWOOD LTD., BERLIN, N.H.

Don cursed anew, then fell back into the seat. The thing with the jaws was Victor's new feller-buncher, a self-propelled tree harvester capable of shearing two-foot trunks in a single bite. Grouped around it were other pieces of heavy equipment: the hydraulic boom loader, the whole-tree chipper he usually operated, the tree-length delimber, the second feller-buncher looming out of thick mist.

He was out in the forest at their logging site up the Dead Diamond River. He was hiding from Victor.

He remembered very little of the previous night. His last clear recollection was when he passed through the town of Errol thirty miles north of Berlin after a nightmare flight through the back country around Cambridge Mountain. Goaded by the voices, he had been afraid to return to Sunny at the restaurant. Instead he had decided to head west and work his way down to Hanover and Dartmouth via the roads along the New Hampshire–Vermont border.

But somehow he hadn't. Obviously he'd driven north out of Errol instead of west. God knew what had impelled him to come to the family logging operation . . .

He opened the car door and just managed to catch himself before falling out. The shack! There was water there, the white-gas stove and coffee makings, maybe a few Pepperidge Farm cookies left in Victor's private stash, maybe a half bottle of brandy in the first-aid box. Scorning the Sanikan, he relieved himself against one of the tires of the Omark tree-chipper that had nearly taken his arm off yesterday. That'd show the bastard!

He was fumbling with the padlock on the shack when he heard the sound of an automobile engine.

Terror-stricken, he froze—only to be spotlighted by twin beams that stabbed suddenly out of the fog. The approaching vehicle was dark and blocky. The KC spots mounted on the roof glared at him but no other lights showed at all. It was Victor's black van.

Don heard his son's mind-voice:

Hold it right there, Papa.

The coercive grip and the light held him like a hypnotized moth. The van stopped about twenty yards away and Victor got out.

Don said: They sent you here, didn't they! They told you how to find me! They turned you against me—after I did everything for you!

Victor said: You imagined them. The voices. You're sick. You've been sick for years. Your mind wasn't strong enough to adapt.

Don said: Don't come near me! I know what you're planning. You heard me shooting my mouth off in the Ox!

Victor said: Yes. You wanted me to.

Don said: You're as loony as I am! Why the hell would I want you to hear me call you—to hear me—

Victor said: To hear you call me a thief?

Don said: You are dammit you are! I taught you everything—but I never taught you that. *They* did.

Victor said: You're pathetic. No use to anyone. You hate

yourself so much you want to die. But you're too much of a coward to kick off like a man, so you try to drink yourself to death.

Don said: You're all against me Rogi Denis you we're all freaks together but you shut me out of your minds left me alone to suffer left me alone with *them*.

Victor said: They're you, Papa.

Don said: Bastardsonuvabitchfuckingcocksuckerbrat . . .

Victor said: The voices are you. All the filth. All the accusations. All the threats. The mutation broke you, Papa. You're one of evolution's throwaways and it's time for you to go. You really are too dangerous now, and Denis will be here soon. Neither one of us could get a fix on you until you woke up, you know. Fortunately for me, he drives cautiously on dirt logging roads. Unfortunately for you . . .

Don said: What—what are you going to do?

Victor said: What you want me to do. It'll be an accident. A drunken man playing suicidal games.

The dark silhouette disappeared as the blinding yellow lights shut off. Don crouched in the shack doorway, rubbing his eyes. He saw Victor get into the van and drive away. In his mind, the terrible voices spoke together.

Now.

The big diesel engine of the new feller-buncher coughed into life. Its shear, mounted on a twenty-six-foot knuckle boom, lifted into the air with a hiss of hydraulics. Then the whole rig came lumbering toward him on caterpillar treads, the grab-arms and the blades that could sever a two-foot tree trunk in a single bite held open at the height of a man's chest. The machine's cab was empty. Before Don turned to flee, screaming, he saw the control levers moving by themselves and heard silent laughter.

9

FROM THE MEMOIRS OF
ROGATIEN REMILLARD

SINCE THAT SUNDAY PROMISED TO BE A HECTIC ONE, WITH TWO convention banquets and a fund-raiser dinner-dance scheduled at the hotel, I went to the 6:30 A.M. Mass at the little church in Bretton Woods. It was a rustic place, dimmed by stained glass windows in abstract patterns. Hikers, golfers, and other resort employees like myself made up most of the somnolent, thinly scattered congregation. I arrived a few minutes late, so I slipped into a rear pew back in a dark corner. For this reason it was not immediately noticed when I died with my brother.

It happened during the sermon. My mind was wandering and I had become aware of an increasing sense of unease, only partly dulled by my semiwakeful state. The foreboding may have been an aspect of precognition; but I had no real intimation of catastrophe until I abruptly lost my hearing. I saw Father Ingram's lips move but no longer heard his voice. In place of the background noises of shifting bodies, coughs, and rustling prayer booklets there was a great hush, hollow and portentous. I snapped into alertness.

Then came an appalling noise, a deep grinding rumble laced with a more shrill, undulating sound, like brasses wailing in dissonance or howls from a chorus of lacerated throats. It built to a thunderous crescendo as though the earth itself were being rent open beneath me. I was immobilized by shock. I remember wondering why the priest was oblivious to the tumult, why the other worshipers kept their seats instead of leaping up in panic, why the church roof remained firm when by rights it should have been tumbling down around my ears.

Any notion I had of being caught in an earthquake was disabused when I went blind. At the same time it seemed that a band of red-hot metal clamped about my breast and squeezed, stopping my heart and breath in an explosion of agony. I thought: a coronary! But I was only forty-four, in perfect health—and hadn't the Family Ghost told me that I had a long life ahead of me? Lord, it's a *mistake* . . .

The shattering racket and the pain cut off simultaneously. My body seemed immersed in a thick and swirling medium. All around me was darkness, a liquefied void that was neither air nor water. Then I realized that the black wasn't empty at all; pictures were flashing in it, appearing and disappearing with subliminal rapidity almost like single-frame cinema projections displayed on dozens of small screens encircling me. I recognized early childhood scenes with Tante Lorraine and the young cousins, school days, Don and I blowing out candles on a joint birthday cake, Onc' Louie walloping the pair of us for some transgression, Christmas caroling in deep snow, fishing in the river, an embarrassing freshman high school dance. The vignettes whirled faster and faster and I realized at last that they were memories, the accelerating replay of a life.

But not my life. Don's.

For the first time I experienced real fear in place of stunned astonishment. The riot of images was acquiring a full sensory and emotional input and I seemed caught in an insane mélange of sights, sounds, tastes, smells, visceral and tactile sensations. My mental voice cried Don's name and I heard him babbling an incoherent, furious reply. All of the remembered scenes were showing *me*. And the emotional transfer revealed that my twin brother despised and hated me to the very depths of his being.

Why, Donnie, why?

The only reply was rage. The visions were drenched in it. I seemed to be at the center of a psychic tornado with Don's mind flailing at me from every scene, hurt and degraded. His wife, his children, his friends flickered past, all wounded by his soul-sickness, all diminished, their attempts to help him rejected until it was too late. And he blamed it all on me.

But I don't understand why!

I felt myself standing firm in the center of the vortex while he whirled, helpless, remembering the very worst of it: his rejection of Denis, his corruption of Victor, the torment he had heaped on Sunny and the other children during the years of alcoholism, his seduction of Elaine in a calculated desire to hurt and humiliate me. To my amazement I saw that he was desperately sorry for all those things, and had been for years. What lingered was the source of the sins, his abiding hatred of me. In the final scene of his life he punished himself for it, but the action was one of severance and not remorse.

Donnie, I don't know why you hate me. But it's all right. I've never hated you.

He said: You should have.

He controlled the machine with his own psychokinesis. I screamed, begging him not to do it, but of course it had already happened. The blades that cut him in half cut him free of me at last.

I opened my eyes. Bill Saladino, the limping old church usher, was nudging me with the collection basket and grinning. I fished inside my jacket for the envelope and dropped it in. Bill winked at me tolerantly and stumped away, carrying the little basket of offerings up to the altar to be blessed.

Don's funeral was a big one, attended by scores of Remillards together with nearly two hundred others who had grown up or worked with him. He looked fit and handsome in his casket after the local croque-mort performed his duty; and the eulogy delivered at his burial Mass proclaimed God's unsearchable ways as well as his compassion for the brokenhearted, to which category Don indubitably belonged. There was a good deal of sotto voce reference to "blessed release," and the pious aunts reassured one another that alcoholism was a disease one simply couldn't help. Sunny, supported by husky Victor at her left elbow and the slight but commanding Denis at her right, bore up well. Her eight younger children stood about her dry-eyed at the gravesite while the cousins and aunts and female neighbors wept.

The official verdict on Don was death by misadventure. Denis and Victor had driven their cars simultaneously into the logging site just as the runaway feller-buncher, with Don's severed body still held in its grab-arms, struck a large stump with one of its tracks and tipped over into a ravine. The resulting mangle, and a double dose of coercion aimed at the green-faced investigating deputies, made plausible to anyone but an experienced logger the final report on Don's demise. One of the witnesses, at least, was of unimpeachable reputation.

* * *

Denis and I were at the same motel, and the morning after the funeral we breakfasted together. He would be staying to help Sunny wind up Don's affairs while I was heading back to the White Mountain Resort and the pre-Memorial Day rush. The coffee shop was crowded and noisy, but noise is immaterial when the conversation is largely mind-to-mind. The pair of us might have been father and son: a gaunt older man in a good summer worsted three-piece, thumbing through the *Wall Street Journal*, and a vaguely undergraduate-looking youth in a navy-blue jogging outfit whose extraordinary eyes were blanked out by dark glasses.

Denis lifted the plastic pot. "More coffee?" *I think I've solved the mystery of my young siblings' nonoperancy.*

I said, "Half a cup, maybe." *Victor's certainly at the bottom of it—and maybe Don, too. It's impossible that not a single one should have inherited telepathic ability, given the fact that your mother has occasionally shown flashes of the talent. Jeanette and Laurette were telepathic as infants but then seemed to lose it. I'm not sure about the others—*

"Sugar?" *It was the same with the other six. They were born with higher faculties but had them deliberately suppressed by aversion-conditioning: mental punishment. I got hold of the youngest, Pauline, who's seven. She was vulnerable through grief and shock and it was easy for me to—to—I suppose you'd call it hypnotize—render her receptive to my command that she regress to babyhood and describe her impressions of Victor and Papa. It was clear what had been done. Poor little Paulie! But Papa had nothing to do with it, thank God. It was all Victor.*

The ruthless young bastard! . . . But how was it possible? He would have had to suppress the babies when he was still just a kid himself! How old was he when the girl twins were born? Four? And then Jackie and Yvonne and the boy twins coming bang-bang-bang and George just after you bachelored at Dartmouth in '80 that'd make Vic ten—and he would've been twelve when Paulie arrived my God my God no innocent kid could do such an evil thing—

[Detachment.] I'll have to show you some of my juvenile psychiatric case histories. He could do it, all right. Nothing is more self-centered than a toddler. Why do you think some of them have tantrums? They want the world to turn around them.

Most children outgrow that mind-set and discover altruism. It's useful for survival, actually. But there are exceptions: sociopaths. Vic certainly seems to fit the profile. At first he acted to secure his position as Papa's favorite. Later, his motives would have become more complex. Power-oriented. You see the way he's going. He's an uneducated man, just as Papa was. A shallow thinker with a stunted conscience and tremendous drive and over-weening conceit. Papa had those attributes, too, but he lacked self-confidence because he was afraid of his psychic powers. Also, he'd been inculcated with moral values from earliest child-hood, which Vic hadn't, and guilt warred with egoism, leading to ultimate destruction. Vic is a much tougher nut than poor Papa. Even without higher faculties he'd be something to reckon with. I have a feeling that being a pulpwood tycoon is only the beginning of his ambition . . .

"Want to pass me a little more strawberry jam? Thanks." What the devil are we going to do?

He mind-screens like the Chase Manhattan Bank vault. I can't see into him and I can't budge him a millimeter with coercion. I'm virtually certain he's used his powers in shady ways for self-aggrandizement. Those logging contracts, for instance, and the big bank loan for capitalization of the company. Pure coercion. And there are rumors that at least two pieces of his equipment were acquired via moonlight requisition. Watchmen and guard dogs are no problem for an operator like Vic. (They wouldn't be to me!) And God knows enough logging gear gets stolen by purely *normal* thieves . . .

"Interesting article here in the *Journal*. Want a look? Seems Senator Piccolomini's narcotics bill has a good chance of pass-ing."

Do you mean to say there's nothing we can do to stop that young freebooter?

"Let's see. Hey—bad news for the pot smugglers!" Getting legal proof of his wrongdoing would be very difficult. And what's to prevent him from coercing a jury even if we did get the goods on him? A Homo superior criminal has the odds in his favor. And if one tries to counter him using his own weapons . . . well, you saw what happened to Papa.

I exclaimed out loud, "Doux Jésus—you can't be serious! I told you the way it was. I shared it!"

But I was *there*. With Victor. He's a terrific screener, but he let the triumph leak. I was standing there spewing my guts out and he was crowing!... Papa was a morbid and self-hating man, like most alcoholics, but that night he'd been scared into asking for help for the first time. He wasn't sunk in despair, he was reaching for a way out. Taking a first step onto a very shaky bridge across a black canyon. And somebody cut that bridge somebody sabotaged his newborn hope somebody planted a powerful coercive incitement to suicide that reinforced his own underlying tendency toward death: *Victor!* He knows I know. He knows I can't do a thing about it.

Can Victor... hurt you?

No more than Papa could. [Concern.] But I'm not so sure about you, Uncle Rogi. Your mind is pretty transparent, especially about emotion-charged matters. Your sharing of Papa's death... if Victor found out, he might think you were a threat. I've been considering ways to protect you.

I pushed away my plate. "I don't think I'll finish these hot cakes after all. Waitress! Will you give us our check, please?" Christ Denis what a crock of shit maybe Don was right after all powers cursed—

A long time ago you said that what you'd really like to do is open a bookstore in a quiet college town.

... You're right. I'd almost forgotten.

You're a topflight convention manager. You could probably get a job in hotel management somewhere else in the country. But Hanover really needs an antiquarian bookshop, and if you were there you wouldn't be *alone*. There are nearly forty of us working at Dartmouth now, research assistants and subjects in my lab. You could help us. And I'm certain we could protect you.

"Somehow," I said, smiling. "I don't think I'd be in serious danger here. I have a strong belief in guardian... angels."

"Don't be a fool!" Even through the dark glasses I could see Denis's eyes blaze and feel the searing force of his mind that took hold of me like a puppy. He released me instantly as I reacted with fear and astonishment. His mental speech was anguished:

I should have been able to save Papa from Vic! I ran away from the situation at home shut out what I knew was happening did it to survive and because I believed my work more important than my biological father's life but I *should* have saved him *should* have loved him and didn't and I'll always blame myself always feel him dying dying lost in despair and I won't lose *you* the same way damn you Rogi can't you understand?... One day

I'll find a way to checkmate Vic. Until then the powers *are* cursed and perhaps we are too but I'll find a way to redeem us and if that isn't megalomania I don't know what it is maybe I'm crazier than Vic and more futile than Papa but I must go ahead. I must! Please help please understand please know who you are to me why I need you . . .

"Denis," I said, reaching across the table. "Tu es mon vrai fils."

Tears were streaming from behind his dark glasses. At my touch he lifted his chin and the drops of moisture vanished. "That's creativity," he said softly in response to my start. "A psychic power we've just begun to investigate, perhaps the capstone for all the rest. Let me show you, Uncle Rogi. Join us."

Love and a sudden inexplicable revulsion warred behind my mental barricade. Prudence dictated that I safeguard myself from Victor. But as for becoming closely involved with Denis and his crowd of youthful operants . . . no. By no means.

The waitress handed me the check. I calculated the tip and fished in my wallet for bills. Denis and I headed for the cashier.

You must come with me to Hanover! His coercion was poised. Ordinarily, I could fend him off readily (as I had been able to fend off Donnie and Victor) but there was a chance that if I drove him to extremes he might feel compelled to bludgeon me down. For my own good. I couldn't let that happen.

So I smiled over my shoulder at him.

"I think," said I, "that I'll call the shop The Eloquent Page."

10

SUPERVISORY CRUISER NOUMENON
[LYL 1-0000]
26 APRIL 1990

FOUR LYLMIK MINDS WATCHED FROM THEIR INVISIBLE VESSEL AS the last civilian evacuees from the American space station boarded the commercial shuttle Hinode Maru. The smaller American orbiters were still mated to the station's half-completed drive-unit while their crews completed the demolition arrangements.

The vector of the meteoroid that had struck the manned satellite might have been calculated with diabolical precision. The impact had killed the orbital velocity needed to keep the structure circling the Earth at its temporary altitude of five hundred kilometers, as well as killing six workers. The twenty-three other persons aboard the station survived because of the airlock system connecting the "Tinkertoy" units. These had suffered only minimal damage; but the power-plant that might have restored the velocity of the station was unfinished, and kicking such a huge satellite back into orbit by means of auxiliaries would have taken more booster engines than the Western world, Japan, and China possessed. The addition of Soviet boosters would have sufficed to save the station. However, in addition to its multinational commercial facilities, research labs, and astronomical observatory, the American station had also included a module with functioning military surveillance apparatus. The Soviets had declined to assist in the salvage; and now the elaborate station, only a few months short of completion, traveled a rapidly decaying orbit that doomed it. Rather than await the inevitable reentry and fall to Earth, the United States had decided, for strategic and safety reasons, to blow it up.

"The waste, the dashed hopes," Noetic Concordance mused. "The discrepancy between the promise of this great station and its abortion, brought about by a mere chunk of nickel-iron coated with ice . . . The situation is fraught with nuance. I shall compose a poem."

"You'd better wait until I finish analyzing the disruption of the probability lattices," Homologous Trend warned. "This event may have a truly nodal significance."

"Then perhaps I'd better plan an elegy."

"A dirty limerick, rather," Eupathic Impulse suggested, "dedicated to the low-orbit proponents at NASA. If they'd been satisfied to build a smaller station at high orbit, as the Soviets did, a hundred meteor hits couldn't have knocked it down. But this close-in structure *was* more economical—assuming that no large object disrupted its delicately maintained low orbit during construction. One concedes that the odds were all in the Americans' favor! But, let's see:

The engineers trusted to luck,
Since they wanted more bang for the buck . . ."

"*Please*," Homologous Trend admonished.

Asymptotic Essence said, "I think I perceive some sources of your anxiety, Trend. The new détente between the United States and the Soviet Union is lamentably fragile. In spite of their joint Martian Exploration Project, the ancient political dichotomy persists. The loss of this American station will be viewed by the stategists of both nations as a disruption of military parity."

"Oh, well, of course," Eupathic Impulse conceded. "One need only analyze the psychological dynamics at work. The Americans knew that their space station was immensely superior to the Soviet one from a standpoint of technological sophistication, and it was also to be a showcase of international goodwill. This made the Americans chockfull of condescending magnaminity. (They love being Grandfather to the world even more than we Lylmik do!) The Soviet-American Mars expedition was intended to be only the beginning of a new era of scientific, economic, and cultural intercourse between these two powers. Now, however, the Americans stand humiliated. The impetus toward camaraderie in outer space is disrupted. Worse, the Soviets will have a strategic advantage—at least until the Americans put up a new space station. (Two years? Three? The American economy is already strained.) One hopes that Trend's computation does not point toward the death of détente, but one must also keep in mind that we are dealing with ethical primitives."

"Logically," Essence said, "the Americans should not feel threatened. There are any number of robot surveillance satellites that can be co-opted as backup spy-eyes—and Omega knows both nations still have parity in nuclear weaponry. But the space station was a symbol of national pride as well as security, and the Soviets will certainly exult over the disaster while the Americans will feel naked to hostile scrutiny. And when has human warfare ever been logically motivated?"

"Listen to this," Noetic Concordance broke in. "An experimental apostrophe, but having possibilities: *O Meteor! Frost-cauled detritus of primordial cataclysm, fatal vagrant* . . ."

"One detects a soupçon of bathos," said Asymptotic Essence with regret.

Eupathic Impulse was less charitable. "You certainly can't use the meteor as the subject of the poem. It was a Pi-Puppid. How can one possibly compose an elegy on a Pi-Puppid? Now if the thing had belonged to a meteoric cloud having more intrinsic grandeur—say, if it had been a Beta-Taurid or even an Ursid—"

"I have the revised probability analysis," Homologous Trend declared, displaying it without further ado.

Asymptotic Essence voiced the mutual dismay. "A threat to the Intervention Scheme? Surely not!"

"Beyond a doubt," Homologous Trend affirmed, "if one carries the proleptic analysis to the eighteenth differential, as I have done. The cuspidal locus results from my injection of the character of the American President. His background and his marketing genius link him inescapably to the destiny of the (at base) commercial orientation of the failed space station. Now his bellicose, jingoistic opponents will prevail. The next American station will be austere—and entirely military. With the dire consequences that you see in my projection of events for the next twenty years."

Eupathic Impulse strove for neutrality of tone and failed. "One might ask why the Supervisory Body failed to investigate the critical nodality of the space station earlier—and why we didn't take steps to protect the precious thing?"

"In the first case," Trend said, "it is the responsibility of Atoning Unifex, acting with us in Quincunx, to define situations susceptible to such investigation. In the second case, overt protection would have violated the Scheme as it stands: Shielding the space station against meteoroids of consequent mass would require use of a sigma-field (which the Earthlings would surely have detected with their radio-telescope array); or else a preprogrammed hyperspatial matter trap (which as we know is unacceptably hazardous in a solar system having significant casual interplanetary traffic); or else we should have had to deploy a guardian vessel authorized to zap, deflect, grab, or otherwise dispose of intrusive space flotsam (which would grossly contravene the Oversight Directives)."

"Well, now what?" Eupathic Impulse asked.

Trend said, "The event requires contemplation by all five entities of the Lylmik Supervisory Body, acting in the aforesaid Quincunx."

"Anyone know where It is today?" Asymptotic Essence asked.

Noetic Concordance shrugged mentally. "Either extragalactic or lurking about that college again. We'd better call."

The four combined in metaconcert: Unifex!

One responds.

[Situational image] + [probability analysis].

Serene preoccupation. *Oh, yes. The collision was today, wasn't it?*

Reproach. One might have shared one's prescience.

Well, I didn't exactly use prescience . . . but I do apologize. There is no need for concern or action on your part with respect to this situation.

One disputes the probability analysis of Homologous Trend?!

Not at all. I plan to cope with the matter personally.

![Forbearance.] Indirectly, one presumes, rather than through rescue of the space station.

Oh, yes. The station's nodality hinges upon its use in weaponry surveillance. I shall simply render the entire concept of spy-eye satellites obsolete. Metapsychically. The planetary Mind has already evolved the capability. Bifurcation is imminent. I do not violate the planetary Will in this but, as it were, anticipate the determination.

One of your esteemed Remillards?

No. The Scottish connection has been working on this particular speciality. Given a gentle nudge, there should be a satisfactory manifestation within the critical time-period, restoring the original coefficients of the sexternion and putting our Intervention Scheme back on the rails.

Comprehension. Most gratifying—and ingenious.

I really should have contemplated the matter with you prior to the space-station disaster, however, in order to have spared you needless distress. My absent-mindedness is getting to be a scandal. I become rapt in nostalgia, to say nothing of my joy in the unfolding of the metapsychic World Mind at long last . . . Now you must excuse me.

"Gone again," Asymptotic Essence said. "Ah, well."

"One notes how confident It remains," Homologous Trend remarked.

Noetic Concordance said, "It has a unique perspective."

"One hopes," Eupathic Impulse added astringently, "that It knows something we don't know about these contentious larvae, validating Its confidence in them . . ."

"The probabilities are in Its favor," Homologous Trend said, "as one might expect."

The four entities shared certain ironic retrospections. Then they waited. Eventually, Eupathic Impulse said, "There goes the destruct signal for the space station."

"O Fireball!" declaimed Noetic Concordance. "O perished pride of rigid circumstance—"

The other three Lylmik settled back to study the spectacle while the poet's mind continued its commemoration.

11

CHICAGO, ILLINOIS, EARTH
2 MAY 1990

HE HAD COMPLETED THE MENTAL EXERCISES THAT HE WAS ACCUS-tomed to perform at the start of each business day, and now Kieran O'Connor stood in front of the floor-to-ceiling window of his office and let his mind range out. His aerie was on the 104th floor of the Congress Tower, Chicago's most prestigious new of-fice building, and from its vantage point he could oversee thou-sands of lesser structures, hives of concentrated mental energy that invigorated his creative mind-powers at the same time that they stimulated his hunger. Kieran had known other great cities —Boston, where he was born in poverty and educated in Har-vard's affluence; Manhattan, where he had apprenticed in a law firm having a sizable Sicilian faction among its well-heeled clien-tele—but the effete and tradition-bound East was an unsuitable home base for a unique upstart such as himself. Instinctively he had come to the dynamic heartland of North America, to this city notorious for its cavalier misprision and polymorphous get-up-and-go. Chicago was the perfect place for him; its commerce was thriving, its politics disheveled, and its morals overripe. It was a coercer's town with bioenergies that matched Kieran's own, not suffering fools but welcoming bullies with open arms—a bot-tomless wellspring of novelty, hustle, and clout.

From his high place Kieran looked out across a bristling forest of skyscrapers, a grid of crowded streets, green bordering park-lands along the Lake Michigan shore that flaunted lush tints of spring. Countless cars ant-streamed along the multiple lanes of the Outer Drive. The lake waters beyond were a rich iris-purple, paling to silver along the eastern horizon. Outside the breakwater was a dancing sailboat. On a whim, he zeroed in on it and was rewarded with the ultrasensory impressions of two people making love. He smiled and lingered over the emanations momentarily, not with a voyeur's vulgar need but in dispassionate reminiscence. He had other pleasures now; still, the resonances were good . . .

A chime sounded, pulling him back to reality.

He turned away from the window and went to his enormous desk. The polished surface mirrored a single yellow daisy in a black vase and a photograph in an ebony frame—Rosemary holding the infant Kathleen, little Shannon in a white pinafore clinging to her mother's skirts. Rosemary and Kathleen would never grow older, but Shannon was a moody fifteen-year-old now, resisting initiation into her father's world. The phase would pass; Kieran was sure of it.

The chime sounded again.

Kieran touched one of a line of golden squares inset into the rosewood desk-top. A compact communication unit lifted into ready position. Arnold Pakkala looked out of the screen with his deceptively distant expression. His colorless eyes seemed to study a potted fig tree behind Kieran's right shoulder.

"Good morning, Arnold."

"Good morning Mr. O'Connor. You'll be interested to know that Grondin has checked out and approved two more California recruits. They'll be flying in to the corporate training facility next week."

"Excellent."

"Mr. Finster is standing by on the Washington land-line. However, I must also advise you that Mr. Camastra's car has just entered the Tower parking garage. He must have taken an early flight from Kansas City."

"Hmm. He'll be in a stew so we won't keep him waiting. Let me know as soon as he gets up to the office. There's time for the Finster call, I think. Put him through, full-sanitary scramble."

"Right away, sir."

The communicator screen displayed a sequence of security codes punched up by Kieran's executive assistant. Eventually these dissolved into a close-up of Fabian (The Fabulous) Finster, whose engaging smile featured two large upper incisors separated by a comical gap: chipmunk teeth. Most people were so captivated by that droll grin that they failed to take note of the icy green eyes above it. When Fabian Finster had earned his living as a bottom-of-the-bill mentalist in Nevada casino shows, he had enhanced his naturally striking appearance with neo-zoot suits trimmed in blinking LEDs. Now that he was one of the confidential agents of Kieran O'Connor, Finster strove for a more conservative image and had taken to Italian silk suitings and striped ties, with nary a trace of glitz. But the show-biz aura still clung to him, and he still performed occasionally to keep up a front, even though most of his time was now occupied by more serious and lucrative activities.

Kieran said, "We'll have to make this quick today, Fabby. Did you wrap up Senator Scrope?"

"Tighter than a rattlesnake's ass, chief. You should have seen his face when I mentioned the number of his secret Icelandic bank account . . . Our pipeline into the Armed Services Committee is now secure. Damn good thing, too. Reading politicians' minds is like snorkeling in a sewer. Shit galore—but you got one helluva time finding the one piece you really need before you drown in the utterly extraneous."

Kieran laughed. "Congratulations on doing a super job. I suppose you're worn out with the effort now and ready for a quiet gig at the Hotel Bora Bora."

The mentalist's grin widened. "I can read your mind all the way from here . . . almost. You got something interesting cooking, I wouldn't mind giving it a spin. Provided I don't have to stay in Washington. After digging in the brains of these politicos for six months, I'm fed to the teeth. Really makes a guy appreciate the lucid crumminess of the Mob mind."

"What I have for you is an excavation with a good deal more class. How would you like to go Ivy League, Fabby? Do a little investigating for me at Dartmouth College up in New Hampshire?"

"Ah hah. You want me to sniff around that ESP project!"

"So you've heard of it."

"I even read the new book by that Dartmouth prof that hit the *New York Times* best-seller list. It took me two weeks—what with having to look up all the big words—and I'm still not sure the guy said what I think he said."

Kieran's tone was incisive. "I had no idea that parapsychology research was being taken so seriously by legitimate institutions. Jason Cassidy and Viola Northcutt are looking into the work being done at Stanford on the West Coast, but I want you to find out what this man Denis Remillard is up to—especially what practical applications of the higher mental powers might lie behind the theoretical considerations set forth in his book."

"You mean, is the guy up to anything dangerous to *us*—or is he just blue-skying around?"

"Precisely. Remillard's book is a very unlikely best-seller. It's difficult to read and its conclusions are veiled to the point of deliberate obscurantism. He almost seems to be bending over backwards to make his data appear prosaic. Of course he couldn't squelch the inherent sensationalism of the topic completely, even with the pages of dry statistics and the academic jargon. His experimental verification of telepathy and psychokinesis is one of the hottest scientific stories of the century. But I have a feeling that Remillard is holding back. I want to know what other psychic experimentation might be going on at Dartmouth that the good doctor has decided not to publicize . . . for prudence's sake."

"Jeez," mused The Fabulous Finster. "If certain parties start taking mind reading and animal magnetism seriously, what's going to happen to our *edge*?"

"Work me up a complete dossier on Denis Remillard. Get as much information as you can on his close associates as well. I'm particularly interested in how many adept mentalists he's recruited for his research. How powerful they are. How committed."

"You want me to turn head-hunter if I turn up any live ones?"

"Use the utmost discretion, Fabby." Kieran's eyes rested for a moment on the photo of the late Rosemary Camastra O'Connor and the two lovely children. "This is a dangerous game. The government may have infiltrated the Dartmouth project—or even foreign agents. Remillard's book hints at a worldwide network of cooperating psychic laboratories beginning to achieve significant results after years of fumbling and marking time. I want to know if there's any truth in that idea, or if it's only wishful thinking."

"I get the picture."

"One last thing. If Remillard or any of his people show the least hint of being able to probe *your* mind, get out of there fast and cover your tracks."

"I understand," came the cheerful reply. "Not to worry, chief. I won't screw up. I've noticed how people who cross you seem to get these weird cerebral hemorrhages . . ."

"Senator Scrope's wrap-up nets you a cool Bahama million,

Fabby. The payoff on Remillard's organization could be even bigger. Goodbye."

Kieran touched a golden square, breaking the scrambler patch. The screen went dark. Almost immediately, another square inset on the desk began blinking red.

Kieran keyed the intercom. "I'll see Mr. Camastra at once, Arnold." He recessed the com-unit into the desk, performed a brief Yoga transmutation designed to lift his coercive energies to the highest level, and sat back to await the arrival of his mafioso father-in-law.

"You heard, Kier? You heard? *He didn't veto!* I got the word from Lassiter in Washington on the car-phone just as we exited the Kennedy!"

Big Al Camastra stormed into the room. His cyanotic lips trembled in fury and a small driblet of saliva trailed from the corner of his mouth. The two bodyguards accompanying Chicago's Boss wore expressions of apprehension.

"I heard, Al. I've been expecting this." Kieran came around his desk, solicitous, as Carlo and Frankie helped Big Al settle his bulky body into the office's largest leather armchair.

Al raved, "That yellow-belly bastard! That fink! He's just gonna hold the bill until tomorrow without signing it, then it automatically goes into law even without his signature."

Kieran nodded. "The President wants the law but he didn't want to give public affront to its opponents."

"What the hell kinda religious man is he? Goin' against the Catholic Bishops and the Council of Churches and the NAACP and the fuckin' PTA, for chrissake? They all lobbied for the veto. We all knew he'd *have* to veto! How could he do this? God—you know what this means? It's Repeal all over again!"

"Boss, take it easy," Carlo pleaded. "Your bionic ticker... you gotta calm down!"

"A drink!" Big Al roared. "Kier, gimme a drink."

"Al, you shouldn't," whined Frankie, catching Kieran's eye and shaking his head frantically. "The doc in K.C. said—"

Kieran O'Connor lifted one hand in peremptory dismissal. The two bodyguards stiffened and their eyes glazed. Both of them turned, completely docile, and left the room—oblivious to the fact that Big Al had enjoined them only five minutes earlier not to leave him alone with Kieran O'Connor under any circumstances.

The don had forgotten his own order. He was leaning back in the chair, one puffed and blotchy hand over his eyes, muttering imprecations. Kieran busied himself at an antique sideboard where cut-glass decanters sparkled in the sunlight. "A little Marsala won't hurt you, Poppa. I'll have some, too. It's a nice virginale that DeLaurenti discovered and sent in to New York on the Concorde last week. If you like it, I'll have a couple of cases sent out to River Forest."

Kieran took one of the filled glasses and wrapped the old man's tremulous fingers around it. He let healing psychic impulses flow from his body to Camastra's through the momentary flesh contact. "Salute, Poppa. To your health." Kieran lifted his own glass and sipped.

A bitter smile cracked Big Al's pallid features. "My health! Madonna puttana, you should have seen those vultures giving me the eye in Kansas City, wondering if I'd drop dead right in front of 'em so's they they could call off the Commission meeting and the vote!"

"The flight back has tired you out. You should have gone home to rest instead of coming downtown directly from O'Hare. Everything will work out fine. The Commission did as we expected. I won't have to exert mental pressure on them directly." He raised his glass to the old man again and returned to his seat behind the desk.

Big Al watched him with hooded eyes. At forty-six, Kieran O'Connor was still youthful, his dark hair only slightly silvered at the temples and at the distinctive widow's peak above his wide forehead. With his olive skin and dark brown eyes Kieran looked more Italian than Irish—but he *wasn't*, and that should have stalled him in the consigliere niche permanently, no matter whose daughter he had married. Big Al still didn't quite fathom why it hadn't.

"The Commission voted you your seat," Camastra told Kieran. "You're the Acting, as of today, and they give tentative approval for you to take over when I retire. But we're not outa the woods yet. Falcone and his dinosaur faction keep harping on tradition, bitching because you're not a paisan'. They're willing to give you respect—but not to the point of joining your new financial consortium."

Kieran made an airy gesture. "Patsy Montedoro's influence

will keep the younger dons on our side, and the Vegas and West Coast people are solid. Let Falcone and his pigheaded conservatives stew in their own juice for another year. Their racketeering and gambling interests have been on a long slide for over a decade—and now that the Piccolomini legislation is on the books, they're caught by the shorts. The end of Prohibition was a Sunday-school picnic compared to the legalization of marijuana and cocaine, and the decriminalization of other drugs."

Big Al shook his jowls in bewilderment. "How could the President do it? Every piss-poor tobacco farmer in Dixie will be planting pot or coca trees. Little old ladies'll grow opium poppies in window boxes! We'll have a country fulla junkies." He gulped his wine.

Kieran got up and refilled the don's glass. "No we won't, Poppa. The other provisions of the Piccolomini Law will see to that. The educational campaigns against all forms of chemical abuse . . . the compulsory treatment or confinement of hard-narc addicts . . . the capital penalties for outlaw dealing. What the government has done is to say: 'Okay, you low uneducated trash, you unemployables, you losers, you cheap thrill-seekers. Go ahead and smoke yourself into a stupor if you want to—and pay Uncle Sam tax on each joint. Or snort till your nose falls off—but don't bother nice people while you're doing it, or we lock you up and throw away the key. And don't commit a crime under the influence, or recruit underage users, or peddle shit illegally—or you die.' It's a very simple, sensible solution to a nasty problem, Al. The Treasury will recover revenue lost from the declining sales of tobacco and hard liquor, the streets will be cleared of criminals supporting their habit, and the big bad Mafia will have the financial floor cut out from under it once and for all."

"It's indecent," Big Al said. "Sell cheap pot and crack and kids are gonna get it. I don't give a damn about the adult addicts. Let 'em turn their brains to stronzolo! But the little kids . . ."

Kieran resumed his seat with a shrug. "The bleeding-heart liberals and the church people and the social workers tried to tell the President and Congress that. And so did we, of course."

Al stared morosely into his wine. "Thirty percent. We lose thirty percent of our income just like that with the legalization—and we're the most diversified of the Families! New York, Boston, Florida, New Orleans—they're gonna drop fifty percent at least. And California—!"

"The Outfit will have a lean year or two. But those Families who go into my venture-capital pool will eventually end up richer than ever. Chicago is leading the wave of the future, Poppa, and my consortium will provide the impetus for a whole new profit structure. We'll survive, and so will the Families who follow us."

"Follow *you*." Blood-webbed eyes burned for an instant with the old antagonism and fear; but then came a fatalistic little laugh. "What else could they do but follow you, stregone? Sorcerer!"

Kieran's expression was earnest, his coercive faculty working at max. "Al, we can't keep running a two-hundred-billion-dollar business like a gang of nineteenth-century banditti—squabbling over a shrinking pie, eliminating rivals by shooting them and stuffing their bodies in car trunks. Times have changed. In two years, human beings will be walking on Mars. All financial transactions will be fully computerized. Most of the old rackets will be as dead as the peddling of narcotics. Sure, the Mob is rich. But you know what they say about money: if you just sit on it, it might as well be toilet paper."

"Yeah, yeah," the don said wearily. "We gotta invest. I know."

"Invest properly, Al, so that the money makes more money. That's what I've been doing as your consigliere—and what I'll continue to do when I'm Boss."

"Boss of Bosses," Camastra muttered.

Kieran did not seem to hear. "In addition to our legitimate investment corporation for the Organization funds, we now have our own small tank of sharks to work with—three of them, all under my thumb and without the slightest off-color taint to attract Justice Department bloodhounds. We own Clayburgh Acquisitions, Giddings & Metz, and Fredonia International. They're takeover artists, Al, the kind of outfits that specialize in the leveraged buy-outs of troubled or vulnerable companies. So far, our little pets have confined themselves to modest raids of the loot-'em-and-dump-'em type. But now I'm ready to give them the go-ahead for some real action. Once the capital pool is ready, we're going after the biggest money there is."

"What, for God's sake?"

"We'll begin with small defense contractors—the ones whose stock took a dive during the late-lamented détente. With the space-station disaster and hawkish noises starting up again in Congress, those defense companies will come back like gangbusters. When we're ready to tackle a biggie, there's a McGuigan-Duncan Aerospace, the firm that almost crashed when their

Zap-Star orbiting mirror weapon was axed by the Pentagon econ-
omizers. I have a strong hunch that by 1993—when we have a
new President and the Mars Project is recognized for the useless
PR stunt that it is—this country will wake up and realize how far
ahead of us the Russians are in the space arms race. Then those
Zap-Stars may get a new lease on life."

Big Al had gone the color of chalk. "You think there's gonna
be a *war*?"

"Of course not. Only a fresh defense initiative. Once we've
wrapped up McGuigan, we can go after G-Dyn Cumberland, the
submarine builders. And Con Electric is shaky with the Japanese
and Chinese undercutting their domestic products—but they
were the fourth largest defense contractor in the country during
the 1980s, and the Pentagon certainly won't buy missile parts
from Asia."

"Madonna puttana! You really mean it!" Big Al's glass fell
without a sound to the thick beige carpet. Inside his thoracic
cavity, the pacemaker adjusted his heartbeat in response to the
elevated level of adrenalinemia.

Kieran was patient. "History has shown that there is no greater
potential for profit than in a suitably stimulated military-industrial
complex—and the stimulation is imminent. The Soviets don't
really want war and neither do we. But both countries are bound
to slide back into the Cold War groove in response to internal
tensions. We have our high unemployment and monumental national debt. They have their eternal food and consumer-goods
shortages, and Slavic angst."

"What if you guess wrong about a defense build-up? What if
this U.S.-Russian Mars Project makes us all buddy-buddy with
the damn Reds and the disarmament thing gets into high gear?"

"Then it would be Goodbye, Daddy Warbucks." Kieran
waved one hand dismissively. "But we won't let that happen.
We'll protect our investment."

Big Al stared at his son-in-law with the unaccepting disbelief
of a man confronting an impending natural disaster—an ava-
lanche descending, a looming tornado funnel—and then his face
cleared and he began to laugh uproariously. "Jesus!" he wheezed.
"Jesus H. Christ! Wait till that cazzomatto Falcone gets a loada
this action!"

Kieran touched a golden square. Immediately the door to the
outer office opened and his executive assistant appeared.

"Yes, sir?" Arnold Pakkala inquired. His mind added: The two hoods are sitting quietly biting their fingernails, and you have a conference call coming up at ten-thirty with Mr. Giddings and Mr. Metz in Houston, and then an early luncheon with General Baumgartner.

"Mr. Camastra is ready to leave now, Arnold. Would you ask Carlo and Frankie to step in?" Kieran stood in front of Big Al with an outstretched hand and a cordial smile. "Thanks a lot for stopping by, Poppa. Betty Carolyn invited me to bring Shannon to your place tomorrow for dinner, so I'll see you then. If you feel up to it, we can talk over this new financial business in more detail."

Supported by his bodyguards, Big Al surged to his feet. "Sure. We'll talk tomorrow." He was still chuckling but his eyes refused to meet those of the new Acting Boss of Chicago. "You can bring the two cases of Marsala. It's real good stuff. See you, Kier."

Kieran O'Connor turned to the window to look out again over the luminous lake. The sailboat with the lovers was gone. He focused his farsense on a big cabin cruiser moving up the river toward the Michigan Avenue Bridge.

Arnold said: Ten-thirty. Shall I set up the call to Houston?

One person in the cruiser was telling another person a scandalous anecdote about the Illinois Attorney General and a certain labor official.

Kieran said: Give me five minutes to meditate and clear my mind. Then bring on the sharks.

12

MILAN, NEW HAMPSHIRE, EARTH
16 AUGUST 1990

IT WAS THE WORST PSYCHIC STAKEOUT IN HIS EXPERIENCE, FROM beginning to end, bar none.

The damn tippy little rented johnboat! Essential to his night bass fisherman cover, it was dismayingly low in the water, its aluminum hull clanked at his slightest movement, and it stunk from decaying salt-pork bait trapped down under the duckboards.

The damn hot, muggy night! Not a breath of fresh air stirred over the small lake ringed with summer cottages, and after four hours of surveillance, he was sopping wet with sweat and cramped all to hell.

The damn fucking bugs! They really were—mating, that is—and doing it all over *him*. Perhaps it was the seductive stench, or the little boat might just have provided a convenient rendezvous out there in the middle of the lake. Whatever . . . aquatic insects by the hundreds, gossamer-winged and mostly connubially linked, fluttered, crept, and copulated in and about the anchored johnboat. Any shift in posture by the boat's occupant produced a cellophanish crunch.

The damn fish! Smallmouth bass, gourmandizing on the be-sotted bugs, leapt explosively out of the water at unnerving intervals. If he had been a genuine angler, the sight of the noble lunkers would have warmed his heart. But Fabian Finster was a city-bred, sports-hating sophisticate who preferred his fish filleted, gently grilled, and served with lemon-butter sauce. Periodically, when the feeding frenzy in the waters around him disturbed his concentration to an unbearable degree, he would break off the surveillance, muster his coercive faculty, and blast both predators and prey. The fish would hightail it into the depths and the bugs would faint, fall into the lake, and drown. All would be serene for ten minutes or so, until a new swarm of insects arrived and the fish pulled themselves together again.

The real corker, however, the brain-bender supremo of that enchanted evening, was a technical surveillance problem: the subjects were speaking—and thinking telepathically—in *French*. He had encountered this in his nightclub days, too, and learned to fake translations by cracking the linguistic formulation of the thought and extracting its purely imaginal content. (*Ha ha, ugly gringo! Read my mind! Tell me I have six thousand-dollar bills in my money-clip!*) But translating more than a phrase or two of a foreign language was a bitch of a job for a mentalist—analogous to eyestrain. The intense concentration required would leave him physically and mentally pooped, by no means a healthy state for a guy in the espionage and extortion racket. Add to the French translation grief an uncanny premonition of disaster that no psychic could afford to ignore, and Finster decided he had been very unwise to accept the Remillard assignment, no matter how much loot Kieran O'Connor dangled as bait.

Bait!

SCRAM! FUCK OFF! FUCK ELSEWHERE!

Momentarily alone again in the starlight, Finster sighed.

His troubles had started at the beginning of the assignment, when he'd tackled the kid professor, Denis Remillard. Denis was a truly boffo screener of his private thoughts, nobody to mess with. Any probe attempt by Finster would not only have been detected—but its source would have been pinpointed. So he'd settled for crumbs, bits of "public" telepathy Remillard addressed to his friends and associates. Denis spoke only English and his subvocal thoughts were also couched in that language. But what thoughts! The prof ratiocinated on such a rarefied level that poor Finster was totally out of his league, lost in a labyrinth of symbolic logic, gestalts, alatory subintellections, and other horrors. If Denis was working on anything potentially threatening (or useful) to the O'Connor enterprises, it would take a better brain than Finster's to prove it at this stage. He had suggested, and his Boss had concurred upon, a more indirect course of investigation. Finster would leave Denis and his Coterie alone until there were hints of more than theoretical activity, and concentrate his efforts on the young genius's many relatives. One or more of them might provide useful leverage material for future action against the Dartmouth group.

It was when Finster began surveillance of Denis's uncle, who acted in loco parentis to the professor and worked at a big resort in the White Mountains, that culture shock struck. Like most persons who considered themselves one-hundred-percent Americans at that time, Fabian Finster was completely ignorant of the French-speaking minority population of New England. Uncle Roger was a harmless fellow who spoke fluent Yankee—but his thoughts were an untidy mélange of French and English. Sorting them out had consumed a tedious month, during which Finster stayed as a guest at the resort during the high season, eating too many gourmet meals. But there had been a payoff: Uncle Roger was preparing to leave his job because he was afraid! Afraid of Denis's younger brother, Victor, the black sheep of the family.

Bingo.

Finster had zeroed in on Victor immediately, and discovered that the twenty-year-old man was not only a telepath but a powerful coercer as well—certainly stronger than his older brother and perhaps even more compelling than Kieran O'Connor himself. Furthermore, he was a crook, using a legitimate business as a front in much the same way that Kieran did, only on a vastly smaller scale.

O'Connor was very interested.

Finster was instructed to study Victor and his operation, using the utmost caution. He was always to stay out of coercive range, which they pegged at a hundred yards to be on the safe side, more than twice Kieran's sphere of psychic influence. He was to eavesdrop both electronically and telepathically, being especially alert for useful dirt. Each night Finster would fast-transmit the tape of the day's data to Chicago via scrambled land-line, and there would follow consultation and fresh orders from the Boss.

For three weeks, Finster had shadowed the young pulpwood entrepreneur in and around his home base of Berlin, New Hampshire. It soon became apparent that the shady aspects of Victor's operation were expertly papered over; there was no immediate prospect of blackmailing him. He had no wife, girlfriend, boyfriend, or significant other susceptible to outside menaces. (He shared support of his widowed mother and younger siblings with Denis, but seemed to have no real love for any of them.) His financing was tightly secured in two local banks and a third in Manchester. He had logging contracts in both New Hampshire and Maine, and seemed ready to expand into Vermont as well— as soon as he could pin down the appropriate persons to coerce. Given Victor's apparently invulnerable setup, Kieran O'Connor decided he had two options at the present time: He could let Victor be, as he had Denis, filing him in for future reference; or he could invite the young man into his own criminal coalition.

Finster was now completing the feasibility study for the latter alternative . . . and it was looking dimmer and dimmer. In Finster's judgment, Victor Remillard was not only a mental badass, he was probably a nutter to boot. His French-English thoughts were often chaotic, indecipherable. There were dark hints of no less than three murders perpetrated within the last year, together with an indeterminate number of psychic and/or physical assaults. He dreamed of monsters, and most of them had his own face. He hated Denis, and only some deep-lying inhibition constrained him from doing violence to the older brother he both envied and despised.

Fabian Finster had long cherished a salutary fear of Kieran O'Connor; but he had decided that he was even more afraid of Victor Remillard. When he finished up for the night, Finster intended to pass on to the Boss his own urgently negative vote regarding any alliance with Victor. On the contrary, the Mob might give serious consideration to putting out a contract on this kid before he spread his web any wider...

Sweaty, pest-ridden, and disquieted, Fabian (The Fabulous) Finster resolutely stayed on the job, whispering a simultaneous translation and running commentary into a bug-smeared Toshiba microcorder hung on a lanyard around his neck. Meanwhile, on the screened porch of his lakeside summer cabin, Victor Remillard drank cold beer and went about the business of recruiting fresh heads for his growing coven of psychic henchmen. He was concluding an interview with a middle-aged Canadian telepath of dubious moral fiber who had driven down that day from Montréal in a brand-new Alfa Spider.

"Now the two of 'em just sit there chewing things over... Now Vic offers the guy another bottle of Hibernia Dunkel Weizen from the refrigerator on the porch (Jesus!)...Now Vic says out loud in Frog, 'I agree that a merger of our two groups might be advantageous, Roe-bear, but it must be on my terms. I will make the machine march—be the boss.' And Fortyay says, 'For sure, Vic. No—uh—hassle. I have seen for myself who you are and what you are.' And he takes a fast slug of suds, trying to be brave. And Vic leans toward him and smiles just a little and thinks: 'Is it that you are *certain* your four playmates will accept my direction? Without making any doubts? I am not playing kids' games, Roe-bear. I am going to shock the gallery'—dammit! he means score big—'with this mental thing. My Remco pulpwood operation is just—uh—for starters. I'm going to be a big vegetable'—shit!—'big shot and make more millions'—wait, that means *billions*—'than you can count. So will the people who work with me. But you will have to do things my way. Do you understand, Roe-bear? No one makes the cunt with me—uh—fucks around with me and manages cheap—uh—gets away with it.' And the other guy says out loud: 'Good blood, Vic! I told you, anything you say!' And his brain is dripping blue funk like a colander, and he thinks: 'You know why we're anxious to join up with you. Who else knows the music—the angles—of this mind business like you? Up in Kaybeck, me and Armang and Donyel and the rest have been just—uh—spinning our wheels, fooling around with small-beer scams. We know we gotta come South to get where the real—uh—action is. And that means joining your outfit. Why do you think I made my proposition regular?' He means aboveboard. 'Drill in my head all you want. Drill in the boys' heads. You'll see we aren't—uh—bullshitting.' And Vic is all charm now. He says, like: 'Swell!' They both laugh. The thought-patterns are formless friendly—only underneath Roebear is still trying not to wet his pants and Vic's sub-basement has a gleam like *your* steel tiger-pit, Boss . . ."

Finster hit the pause button of the recorder and shifted position. Inky ripples spread out in circles from the johnboat. The water was now littered with insect bodies and the bass, sated, had retired for the night. Finster prayed that soon Victor would, too.

He whispered a few more translations and comments as the young man led his visitor down the front steps of the cabin and walked with him to the Alfa Romeo. A next meeting was set up, to include the other members of the Canadian gang. Then the Spider's headlamps flashed on, making two paths of wavering light on the lake that stopped short of Finster's boat. The car backed, turned, and drove off along the shore road.

Victor Remillard's mind was strangely aglow. He stretched, yawned, then walked down the path to the small dock in front of the cabin, where he stood looking out over the lake with his arms folded.

Finster's boat began to move slowly toward him, dragging its sash-weight anchor.

"Oh, shit," muttered the mind reader. "Shit a *brick*."

He lunged for the three-horse outboard mounted at the stern and yanked the starting cord, producing pathetic burbling sounds. He yanked again and got a few apologetic pops. Cursing, he fumbled the small oars into their locks and flailed desperately at the water while the boat picked up speed, moving in the opposite direction.

"Turn me loose, dammit!" There were other cabins on the shore, some with lights. He yelled: "Help! Help! . . ." But his voice died away to a croak, lost in the summer chorale of frogs, crickets, and katydids.

Nothing left to do! The tall silhouette at the end of the dock was barely ten yards away. Finster ripped buttons from his soggy sportshirt to get at the .357 magnum Colt Python in its underarm holster. He lifted the gun with both hands and tried to aim, but the Colt seemed to have a life of its own and the blood-hot metal fought to squirm out of his grip, and when he clung to it, it became heavy as the lead sash-weight anchor and tried to break his wrists, and then he saw that the barrel was pointed at his right kneecap and his finger was tightening on the trigger, and he screamed and flung the thing sideways and it fell overboard and Vic laughed.

I'll jump out! his mind howled. And I can't swim but I'd rather drown—

He was drowning.

Drowning in his own vomit that had flooded up his throat and into his windpipe. He made a terrible noise as he crashed against the low aluminum gunwale, his head and upper body hanging over the side, his eyes wide open beneath the dead-black water. And the mental voice:

Don't be any more stupid than you've already been. Not until we have a chance to talk.

Talk? . . .

He was sitting upright, wet only with his own perspiration, and the boat glided smoothly up to the dock and stopped. A hand was extended to help him climb out.

He looked up. The zillions of stars in the summer sky outlined a tall, good-looking young man with dark curly hair. His mind was a simmering blur.

"Talk?" Finster repeated out loud, a wan chipmunk grin trembling on his lips.

"Come up to the cabin," Victor told him curtly, and turned his back to lead the way off the dock. When the mind reader hesitated, something seemed to clamp his heart with red-hot pincers, making his knees buckle; but in a split second the pain was gone and he stood upright again, and the damn frog growled over his shoulder, "Grouille-toi, merdaillon!"

Finster needed no translation. In fact, he was inclined to agree with Victor's rude assessment of him. It was the royal screw-up of his life—what was left of it—and he was a certain goner. Once this realization came, Fabian Finster's spirits paradoxically lifted.

"Sit there," Victor ordered, when they came through the screen door onto the cabin porch. Finster lowered himself into a wicker chair with cretonne cushions. Did he dare ask for a beer?

Something awful lit up behind Victor's eyes. "I could squeeze your brain like a grapefruit, Finster. I could force you to tell me everything you know about the ones who sent you to spy on me, then kick your ass out of here with nothing but scrambled eggs left inside your skull. I've already done that to a couple of snoopers. One was a Russian—can you believe it?—offering me three hundred grand to get him into my brother's laboratory. I took his money very gladly and he disappeared without a trace. The woods are lovely, dark and deep, Finster. You could go the same way . . . or maybe not. You've got a certain familiar smell about you."

And he lifted his mind-screen to give the barest glimpse of reprieve.

"All *right!*" Finster shouted, breaking into a guffaw of relief. "I dig what you're thinking, amigo! Do I ever!"

"Oh, yeah?" Victor's voice was like ice, and the tantalizing image the mind reader had grasped so desperately did a chameleon shift and faded to imminent doom. Finster sat up straight, waiting for it.

But Victor was smiling. "You're not one of my brother's stooges. You're not from the government. You're not a Red. Your mind's spread open like a planked salmon, Finster. I know exactly what you are."

"I'm a crook, Victor," Finster said. "Just like you. And I'm here following orders from another crook—who is definitely *not* just like you. He's big. Maybe the biggest, pretty soon. You reading my mind?"

"Better than you know. Tell Kieran O'Connor exactly what I say, Finster . . . Stay away from me. If your people try to interfere with me, I'll send them back to O'Connor's office in Chicago to die, right in front of his fancy desk. But you also tell him that I have certain plans. If he lets me alone, here in my home territory, maybe the day will come when the two of us have things to say to each other. It won't be soon. But when one of us *really* needs the other, I'll talk to him . . . Do you think you can remember my exact words, Finster?"

The mind reader shrugged, hooked one thumb around the lanyard that hung from his neck, and pulled out the Toshiba microcorder. "You're on the record, Mr. Remillard."

"Then get out of here." Victor turned away, heading for the interior of the cabin.

"No beer?" Finster ventured.

"No beer."

"Figures," Finster said. He went out the screen door, closed it very carefully, and headed for the dock.

13

FROM THE MEMOIRS OF
ROGATIEN REMILLARD

As a bookseller, I have noted a curious thing: There are certain scientific books of epochal importance, titles recognized by every educated citizen in the Galactic Milieu, that nevertheless languish unread by modern people. One thinks of Darwin's *Origin of Species*, Freud's *Interpretation of Dreams*, Wegener's *Origin of the Continents and Oceans*, Weiner's *Cybernetics*, and other works that provoked controversy in their day—only to subside into banality once their contents had passed the test of time and merged with the common body of human knowledge.

Denis Remillard's towering work, *Metapsychology*, is another that suffered this ironic fate. Now, 121 years after its publication, only a few scientific historians bother to read it. But I remember the uproar attending the book's appearance early in 1990, when it sold nearly 250,000 copies in hardback format during its first year and become the common coin of TV talk shows and articles in the popular press—an amazing performance for a highly technical work, bristling with statistics, written in a dignified and daunting style. *Metapsychology* presented for the first time an integrated scheme encompassing all forms of mental activity, normal and supranormal, with an emphasis upon mind's interrelation to matter and energy. In a detailed and elegant series of experiments, scrupulously verified, Denis demonstrated how the so-called higher mind functions are inherent in the mental processes of *all* human beings. He showed how every mind contains, in some measure, powers both ordinary and extraordinary. His keystone theory explained the unusual activities of psychic adepts in terms of operant metafunction, and the deficiencies of "normal" people as an aspect of metapsychic latency—where operation of the higher powers was either inhibited by psychological factors or precluded by a limited talent.

Metapsychology provoked intense discussion—and a certain dismay—within the scientific establishment, since it presented hard evidence that the higher mental functions were genuine phenomena and not merely dubious conjecture. Psychic researchers (and there were many besides Denis), after enduring decades of condescending tolerance or out-and-out ridicule from their conservative peers, basked in a new and unprecedented atmosphere of respect as they found themselves courted by the media, by sundry government agencies, and by commercial exploiters scenting a new growth industry that might eventually rival aerospace or genetic technology. Numbers of hitherto clandestine operants "came out of the closet" as a result of Denis's book and became involved in serious research projects. There were also legions of quacks—astrologers, tea-leaf readers, spoon-benders, and practitioners of black magic—who enjoyed a brief heyday riding the coattails of the legitimate metapsychic movement. The public was entertained for months by debates and squabbles among the mixed bag of opposing psychic factions.

Denis himself remained largely aloof from the altercations his book had spawned, distancing himself from popular journalists, television interviewers, and other purveyors of mass titillation. He had not yet publicly revealed that he himself was one of the principal subjects of his experiments, nor were other operant workers at his Dartmouth laboratory identified by name to nonprofessional investigators. Attempts to make an instant celebrity of the author of *Metapsychology* were doomed by Denis's humorless and erudite manner, his penchant for quoting statistics, and his total lack of "colorful" personality traits. Media snoops found lean pickings at the scene of his researches, a drab old saltbox on College Street in Hanover, across from the Hitchcock Hospital parking lot. The metapsychology lab's personnel was loyal and close-mouthed, giving superficial cooperation to reporters and interested VIPs while making certain that no really sensational data came under outside scrutiny.

Fortunately for the disappointed newsmongers, there were plenty of less diffident psychic researchers at other institutions who were more than eager to fill the metapsychic publicity gap. These basked in the limelight and hastened to publish their own researches—as well as their critiques of Denis's magnum opus. Since most ordinary people have a gut belief in the higher mental powers, the public at large reacted positively to the opening of the new Metapsychic Frontier. There were surprisingly few commentators, in those early days, who envisioned any problem in having an elite population of operants living and working among "normal" humanity...

Late in 1990 when the Mind Wars scandal broke and it was revealed that the Defense Department of the United States had attempted to pressure psychic researchers into undertaking classified projects, public opinion experienced its first anti-meta shift. But this was destined to be swept away in the fresh furor that came the following year, when Professor James Somerled MacGregor of Edinburgh University revealed to a stunned world the first truly practical application of mind-power. MacGregor's demonstration was a total vindication of Denis's theories. It was also responsible for opening a rift in the human race that not even the Great Intervention would heal completely.

To digress momentarily from the earthshaking to the jejune, I must note that 1990 was also the year that I started my bookshop, The Eloquent Page. Nowadays the place has quasi-shrine status, but I continue to resist attempts by various busybody groups to institutionalize it. The shop persists under the original proprietor at its address of 68 South Main Street, Hanover, New Hampshire. For the sake of Galactic tourists, I have a section devoted to works by and about famous Remillards. (I even have for sale a few fragile copies of the first edition of *Metapsychology*, exorbitantly priced. Inquiries are invited.) However, my stock in trade remains, as always, one of the largest collections of rare science fiction, fantasy, and horror books in New England. My shelves hold no modern liquid-crystal book-plaques; every volume is printed on paper—and a goodly percentage of them are still sturdy enough to be read. I welcome browsers of all races, even Simbiari, provided they utilize the plass gloves I keep available and refrain from dripping green mucus on the stock.

The choice of the bookshop premises was not mine. I had initially decided to rent a place farther north on Main Street, closer to the Dartmouth campus, where there was much heavier foot traffic and where my business instincts assured me that trade would be brisk. This intention, however, was thwarted by an old acquaintance.

I remember the sunny autumn day that the rental agent, Mrs.

Mallory, took me on a round of inspection. Even though I had already expressed my preference, the lady insisted on showing me one last vacant property.

"It's such a pretty place, Mr. Remillard," she told me, "the corner shop on the ground floor of the historic Gates House building, across from the post office. A marvelous example of the Late Federal style, absolutely the ideal ambiance for a book-shop! The premises are a tad smaller than the location down by the Hanover Inn—but so much more evocative. And there's a lovely large apartment available on the third floor."

I agreed to look the place over, and it was everything she had promised. The apartment, in fact, was virtually perfect. The store itself, however, seemed far too small for the type of establishment I was then contemplating, a combination of used books and current hardbound and paperback volumes. I told Mrs. Mallory that I found it charming but unsuitable.

"Oh, dear! I really thought you'd like it." She gestured at the old beamed ceiling, the frowsty little nooks at the rear. "The atmosphere of antiquity—can't you feel it?" And then she smiled conspiratorially and said in a lowered voice, "It's even *haunted*."

I paused in my inspection of the bay display window, polite incredulity on my face. "Interesting. I'm sure having a ghost in one's bookshop would be quite a novelty, especially since I plan to specialize in fantastic literature. But I'm afraid the place really is too small, and too far from the campus to attract much evening trade—"

And then I felt it. Without conscious volition, I had let my seekersense range out, the weak divination faculty I had been practicing under Denis's tutelage with a view toward guarding myself from intrusions by Victor or other undesirables. I had managed to learn how to detect the distinctive bioenergetic aura of fairly strong operants, such as Denis, Sally Doyle, or Glenn Dalembert—provided that they were within a radius of ten meters or so and not shielded by thick masonry or some other barrier.

And now, scanning this old frame building's empty corner premises, I farsensed the presence. I stood rooted to the spot, sweat starting out on my forehead.

Mrs. Mallory was chattering on: ". . . and if you're sure you'll need more space, we might talk to the owner, since the little coffee shop next door might not renew its lease and it might be possible to double the square footage available . . ."

I seemed to hear someone say: Tell her you'll take it.

Who's there? my mind cried. Whothehell *is* that?

"I beg your pardon?" said Mrs. Mallory.

I shook my head. *It was in the back room.*

"I know!" she exclaimed brightly. "I'll just let you stay and look the place over at your leisure, both the store and the apartment, and you can drop in at my office later with the keys and let me know what you've decided."

"That will be fine," I said. The sound of my voice was distant, dimmed by my concentration on the detecting ultrasense. *It was coming out of the back room into the main part of the shop.* Mrs. Mallory said something else and then went out, closing the street door firmly behind her. Dust motes eddied in the brilliant sunbeams shining through the display window. As I began slowly to turn around for the confrontation, an idiotic extraneous thought flickered across my mind: In late afternoon, I would have to make some provision so that the strong sunlight would not fade the books.

There's an awning. All you have to do is lower it.

"Bordel de dieu!" I spun around, exerting my farsense to the utmost, and detected an all-too-familiar aura. It had no form, nor was there anyone visible in the shadowed rear of the shop.

The Family Ghost said: It's been a long time, Rogi. But I had to be certain that you took this place and not the other.

"Ah, la vache! I might have known . . ." I stood with one hand braced against the wall, laughing with relief. "So you've been haunting this shop, have you?"

The previous tenant was a trifle reluctant to vacate and I had to insure that the lease would be available. Sometimes it's perplexing, trying to determine precisely which occasions require my personal attention. My overview of the probability lattices is by no means omniscient, and after such a long time my other faculty is unreliable.

"So! You've made up my mind for me and I'm to be forced to rent this place even though it's too small. Is that it? My poor little Eloquent Page and I will go broke just to satisfy your ineffable whim."

Nonsense. You'll do well enough if you stock antiquarian books and forget about the cheap ephemera. The clientele will seek out your establishment and pay suitably high prices for collector's items, and you can also do mail-order business . . . Be that as it may, it is not your destiny to achieve commercial prosperity.

"Well, thanks all to hell for the good news! As if my morale isn't low enough, changing careers at the age of forty-five and playing lab-rat for one nephew while another contemplates offing my ass."

Victor is otherwise occupied. You need not worry about him.

"Oh, yes? Well, you'd better keep him in line!"

I may not influence him or the other Remillards directly. It would violate the integrity of the lattices. You are my agent, Rogi, because you *have* been influenced. You must live and work here, in this place that is appropriate, only two blocks away from the house at 15 East South Street.

I was totally mystified. "Who lives there?"

At the present time, no one who need concern you.

I snarled, "Oh, no you don't!" and pointed a determined finger at the volume of air that seemed to radiate the aura of le Fantôme Familier. "I'm not standing still for any more of your mysterious directives from Mount Sinai! You cut the crap and give me a damn good reason why I should rent this shop instead of the other one—or find yourself another patsy."

There was a cryptic silence. Then:

Come with me.

The front door opened and I was firmly impelled out onto the pavement. I heard the locks click. A couple of coeds sitting at a sidewalk table in front of the little restaurant next door eyed me curiously. I let the Ghost shepherd me around the corner. It said:

Walk east on South Street.

All right all right! I said rebelliously. For Godsake don't make a public spectacle out of me!

I—or perhaps I should say we—walked along the quiet side street. It was only two blocks long, and near Main Street were a few commercial structures and widely separated old homes converted into offices and apartments. There was very little traffic and only sporadic bits of sidewalk, so I strolled along the edge of the street, past landscaped parking lots and mellow frame residences, and crossed Currier Place. There stood the Hanover public library, a modernistic pile of red brick, concrete, and glass-wall framed in enough greenery to allow it to blend unobtrusively with the more classic buildings around it. Immediately east of the library was a large white clapboard house with dark green shutters, a modest portico, and third-floor dormers, set well forward on a thickly wooded lot that sloped toward a deep ravine in the rear. On a weedy and unkempt lawn lay an abandoned tricycle. A football and a yellow Tonka Toy bulldozer decorated the porch, along with a sleeping Maine Coon cat that resembled a rummage-sale fur piece. Two hydrangea bushes flanking the steps still carried pink papery blooms. No people were in evidence.

I stood under a scraggly diseased elm and stared at the house that would one day be famed throughout the galaxy as the Old Remillard Home. The Ghost said: You will note its convenient proximity to the bookshop.

I didn't say anything.

The Ghost went on: Six years from now, Denis will buy this house for his family. Many years later it will be Paul's home—

"Paul?" I said out loud. "Who the devil is Paul?"

Denis and Lucille's youngest son. Marc and Jon's father. The Man Who Sold New Hampshire. The first human to serve on the Galactic Concilium.

Starlings were yammering up in the elm and the golden autumn sun heated the asphalt pavement and gave a faint pungency to the air. The pleasant old house—as solid and homely a piece of New Hampshire architecture as one could imagine—seemed to be drowsing in the late-afternoon calm of this little college town. I looked at it stupidly while my mind took hold of what the Ghost had said and tried to digest its import. The "galactic" bit was too bizarre to penetrate at first, so I seized on a more down-to-earth improbability.

"Lucille? Marry Denis? You've got to be kidding."

It will happen.

"Admitted, she's one of his most talented psychic subjects. But the two of them are hopelessly incompatible—fire and ice. Besides, I happen to know that she's in love with Bill Sampson, a clinical psychiatrist at Hitchcock. It's an open secret that they'll marry as soon as her analysis is complete and there's no ethical conflict."

The Ghost said: Lucille and Denis must marry and produce offspring. Both of them carry supravital alleles for high metafunction.

"Tu parles d'une idée à la con! They don't even *like* each other. And what about poor old Sampson?"

An unavoidable casualty of Earth's mental evolution. His wounded heart will recover. The deflation of the Cartier-Sampson liaison will be one of your most critical tasks in the months ahead. When Lucille is free, she will naturally gravitate to Denis, her metapsychic peer, and the genetic advantage of their union will become self-evident to her. If it is not, you can discreetly press the point.

"Me? *Me?*" I was sandbagged by the casual arrogance of the Ghost. "You think this girl's some kind of computer I can reprogram?"

You'll find a way to work things out. You *must*. Sampson is hopelessly latent, an unsuitable mate for this young woman who is so highly endowed with the creative metafunction. It is unfortunately true that she and Denis have clashing temperaments, but this is not an insuperable barrier to a fruitful marriage. Lucille will be an ideal professional partner for Denis as well. Her drive and indomitable common sense will counter his tendency to brood and vacillate. There will be continuing tension between them, especially in the later years. It is then that your own supportive role—and your fortuitous proximity—will be most advantageous.

"I'm your mole, you mean! Put into position for continuous meddling with people who aren't even born yet—isn't that it?" I pulled myself together. Although the street seemed to be deserted, it would hardly do for local residents to look out of their windows and discover a middle-aged loufoque haranguing an elm tree. I walked on to the east, where the street curved into Sanborn Road and the wooded precincts of the Catholic church.

Sternly, I addressed the Ghost in mental speech: I see very well the role you intend for me. I am to be your agent provocateur, interfering with upcoming generations of Remillards like some evil genius in a goddam Russian novel!

Nonsense. Your influence will be entirely beneficial. You will be needed. Your qualms are understandable, but they will fade as the importance of your mental nurturing manifests itself.

If I refuse the commission—?

I cannot coerce you. If your compensatory influence is to be effective, it must be freely given. The unborn Remillards needing your help are not ordinary human beings, however, and your sacrifices on their behalf will have far-ranging consequences.

How . . . far?

Rogi, vieux pote, I have already said it—but you refused to accept the implication. And so I will be explicit, so that you will know exactly what is at stake. You are a member of a remarkable family: one that will one day be the most important on Earth. Denis and Lucille's children and grandchildren are destined to become magnates—leaders, that is—of the Human Polity of the Concilium of the Galactic Milieu.

"C'est du tonnerre!" I cried, aghast, and my mind asked the halting question: Are you telling me that we . . . the planet Earth . . . will become part of a galactic organization *within my lifetime*?

There was a furious honking and a sarcastic voice that called, "Howsabout it, Charley? You gonna stand in the street till you grow roots?"

I snapped out of my daze to see a laundry van two feet away from me in the middle of Sanborn Road. There must have been something in my face that turned the young driver's impatience to concern. "Hey—you feeling all right?"

I lifted one hand and hastened onto the sidewalk. "I'm okay. Sorry about that."

The driver eyed me uncertainly, then shrugged and drove on.

The Ghost said: My dear blockhead.

You, the entity who reads this, will doubtless think the same of me. Had not the Ghost told me long ago that it was a being from another star, that its intentions were benevolent and our family was of crucial importance? A man possessed of the least modicum of imagination might have deduced *some* design behind these uncanny maneuverings—always supposing that the spectral puppet-master was real and not the perverted manifestation of my own unconscious.

I made an attempt to gather my scattered wits. "When will this . . . invasion of extraterrestrials happen?"

Never! Rogi, you are a prize idiot! Le roi des cons! Why should we invade your silly little world? The starry universe is our domain and our cherished responsibility, and we come to a world only when we are called.

"Elaine and her people called you," I muttered bitterly. I reverted to mental speech when I noticed a workman cutting the lawn of the church across the street: Why didn't you respond to Elaine's appeal, mon fantôme? All her people asked was that you bring us the blessings of your galactic civilization before we're destroyed in a nuclear holocaust. Wasn't that a good enough reason for you to bestow your cosmic CARE packages on Earth?

The Milieu does not dare to contact a developing world until the planetary Mind attains a certain maturity. Premature intervention would be hazardous.

To *whom*?

To the planet . . . and to the Milieu.

Well, don't cut it too fine! Détente's on a fast track to hell again and every other tin-pot nation in the Third World seems to have an atomic bomb ready to defend its honor. You wait too long and your flying saucers might land in a radioactive slag heap!

The likelihood of a small nation detonating a nuclear weapon is unfortunately high. But the prospect of full-scale nuclear war between the great powers is infinitesimal at the present time. The danger seems destined to escalate with the passage of time, but my prolepsis indicates that the Great Intervention will almost certainly take place before your civilization destroys itself.

Well—when *do* you land, for chrissake?

When there is worldwide recognition of the higher faculties of the mind, and when those faculties are used harmoniously by a certain minimal number of humans.

Are you talking about the kind of thing Denis is working on?

Denis and many others. Metapsychic operancy is the key to lasting peace and goodwill among disparate entities—human and nonhuman. To know the mind of another intimately is to understand, to respect, and ultimately to love.

Then all of the citizens of your Galactic Milieu have the higher mental powers—telepathy and psychokinesis and all that?

The spectrum varies from race to race and from individual to individual. But all Milieu minds share telepathic communication and our leadership enjoys formidable insight. In matters of gravity there can be no duplicity among us, no misunderstanding, no irrational fear or suspicion.

No wars?

We have never experienced interplanetary aggression. Our Milieu is far from perfect, but its citizens are secure from exploitation and institutionalized injustice. No individual or faction may flout the will of the Concilium. Every citizen-entity works toward universal betterment at the same time that it is encouraged to fulfill its personal potential. Ultimately, the goal of our people is to obtain that mental Unity toward which all finite life aims.

"Grand dieu," I whispered. "Ça, c'est la meillure!" Without thinking, I had turned left onto Lebanon, a major thoroughfare. My heart soared like that of a six-year-old on Christmas morning. I had thrust aside all my doubts as to the authenticity of the

Ghost. If it was a figment, its delusions were comforting ones. I asked:

How many planets belong to this Milieu?

Thousands. Our present coadunate population includes some two hundred thousand million entities—but only five races. This is a very young galaxy. Eventually, all thinking beings within it who survive the perilous ascent of technology's ladder will find Unity with us. My own race, which was the first to attain coadunation (the mental state leading to Unity) has the honor and the duty of guiding other peoples into our grand fellowship of the Mind. Nearly a quarter of a million juvenile races are currently under observation, and six thousand of those have a high civilization . . . but you humans are the only candidates approaching induction.

Jesus Christ! When I tell Denis—

You will tell no one, least of all Denis. These revelations are for your own encouragement, given because you demanded of me good reasons for your continuing cooperation.

Denis deserves to know!

He would be distracted from his great work. He must go on his own way for now, assisted by you in secret. His trials—and there will be many—will be *his* incentive.

God, you're a cold-blooded bastard! Suppose I tell him in spite of you?

Denis would not believe you. You are being very silly, Rogi. Your obtuseness wearies me.

"Sometimes," I whispered with a certain malicious satisfaction, "I get pretty sick of me, too! Poor Ghost. You picked a weak reed for your galactic shuffleboard game."

There was a spectral chuckle: I myself have had my own ups and downs . . . but here we are in front of the real-estate office. Mrs. Mallory awaits your decision on the bookshop rental.

I felt in my hip pocket for the two keys she had given me, one for the Gates House store and one for the apartment upstairs. The two pieces of brass were cool in my hand. God knew what they would unlock in my future.

The Ghost said: I have a small token for you. Look in the gutter.

I did, and there among the leaves and pebbles and gum wrappers was a gleam of red. I picked up a dusty little key ring. At the end of its short silvery chain was a novelty fob, a red glass marble of the type we kids used to call "clearies," enclosed in a wire cage.

Well? asked the Ghost.

Don't rush me, dammit! I said. Then I opened the office door and went in to sign the lease on my haunted bookshop.

14

HANOVER, NEW HAMPSHIRE, EARTH
22 DECEMBER 1990

THE TEST CHAMBER WAS HEAVILY INSULATED AGAINST SOUND, temperature change, and extraneous electromagnetic radiation. Its air was filtered and its lighting dim and blue, which latter turned the ruddy color of the kitten's fur to grizzled gray and its amber eyes to smoky topaz. In the ceiling were video and ciné cameras, radiation detectors, and other environmental monitors, focused on the cat and on Lucille Cartier. The young woman, wired with body-function electrodes, sat in a chair at one end of a heavy marble balance table. The kitten perched opposite her on the table top; the twin EEG transmitters mounted near the inner base of its ear were only two millimeters in diameter and almost completely concealed by the fur. On the table between Lucille and the cat was the ceramic platform of a hermetically sealed, ultrasensitive recording electro-balance. It looked rather like a medium-sized cheeseboard with a glass dome cover.

Vigdis Skaugstad's telepathic voice said: Ready Lucille?

Lucille said: Steady&ready. Minou too.

The kitten said: [Play?]

Lucille said: Soon now wait be good.

Vigdis said: Systems running scale hot GO.

A white baby spot flashed on, illuminating the glass-covered balance plate. Simultaneously the blue lighting faded away, leaving most of the room in darkness. Lucille began to hum monotonously. She was still only imperfectly operant in creativity and the music helped to suppress her insistent left brain and induce the necessary lowering of the intercerebral gradient. She stared at the dazzling balance plate, trying not to "will" too forcefully, urging the primal power that resided in her unconscious mind to flow toward the controlling conscious. In this way primitive humanity had summoned its gods, worked its magic, achieved transcendence, even compelled reality: by bridging unconscious and conscious, right brain and left, in this subtle, quasi-instinctual way that had been all but lost with the advent of the conquering word. Verbalization, a left-brain function, had given birth to human civilization—but at a price. The ancient creative powers were repressed, and lived on mainly in the archetypal guise of muses, those flashes of artistic inspiration or illuminating insight that welled up from the soul's depths almost without volition. And the old magical aspects of creativity, the ability to direct not only the "mental" dynamic fields but also the fields generating space, time, matter, and energy, were relegated to the dreamworld in most individuals.

It had been so for Lucille Cartier until four months earlier. Then, bowing at last to the counsel of her analyst, she had agreed to undertake training at the Dartmouth Metapsychology Laboratory that would raise her latent mind-powers to operancy. "The faculties are part of you," Dr. Bill Sampson had told her, "and you'll have to accept the fact. And learn to control them—or they'll control you."

So she had come at last to the gray saltbox building. To her great relief, Denis Remillard had assigned her a congenial and nonthreatening mentor. Vigdis Skaugstad was a visiting research fellow from the University of Oslo, a specialist in psychocreativity. She was thirty-six, pug-nosed and rosy, with very long flaxen hair that she braided and wound about her head in a coronet. Vigdis's own psychic talents were unexceptional, but she was a gifted teacher; and her tact and empathy had led Lucille to overcome most of her deep-seated repugnance toward the research program—if not her dislike of its young director. Working with Vigdis, Lucille had learned telepathy very easily. This most verbal of the higher powers quickly assumes a "hard-wired" status in the brain of a talented person, as do most of the related ultrasenses. But Lucille's other significant faculty, creativity, had required a tedious, almost Zenlike regimen to raise it to the operant level. It was still far from reliable. Lucille took training exercises almost every day from Vigdis, and at the same time worked toward her doctorate in psychology. Thus far she had sedulously avoided socializing with other operants, except for an occasional lunch with Vigdis.

The laboratory cats, on the other hand, were her dear friends.

The animals were used in many different experiments, especially those involving telepathy, a feline long suit. Lucille's special affinity with the cats had at first provoked jokes among the staff about witches and their familiars; but the joshing had cut off in short order when Lucille seemed to establish a genuine mental linkage with one particular kitten, leading to an apparent creativity manifestation that was having its first controlled test today.

"Ooh, Minou," Lucille crooned aloud. And to the cat: Let's do it baby you and me let's do it together again ... together Minou!

The kitten's large ears swiveled and its pupils widened as it stared fixedly at the shielded balance platform. It saw the image in Lucille's mind and it knew what she was trying to accomplish.

So it helped.

"Minou, Minou, ooh-ooh," sang Lucille.

The little animal's whiskers cocked forward in anticipation. It uttered a barely audible trilling sound, the hunting call of the Abyssinian breed, and its black-tipped tail twitched. Except for its relatively large ears and eyes, its conformation and color were almost exactly those of a miniature puma.

"Ooh-ooh-ooh." Here it comes kitty here it comes ...

The insubstantial image, brought forth from Lucille's memory. [Amplified by kittenish predatory lust. Oh, fun!]

A smudgy cloud had begun to form above the center of the ceramic balance pan. It was ovoid, smaller than an egg, with a pointed anterior and a humped posterior.

"Ooh!"

[JumpjumpNOW!]

Impatiently, the kitten darted forward and batted the glass dome. The psychocreative image shimmered as woman and cat faltered in their mental conjunction, then sharpened as they drew together again.

"Ooh-ooh, naughty Minou, not yet wait until we're through." Good baby yes work with me sit still help MAKE IT keep it under the glass don't let it get away until it's *here* stay stay work with me ...

[Mouse!]

Yes.

[MOUSE!]

The form was still translucent, in the early stage of materialization that Vigdis Skaugstad had called "ectoplasmic Silly Putty." But the mousy shape was entirely plausible and becoming more detailed with passing seconds. Snaky little tail. Jet-bead eyes. Tiny ears and whiskers—shadowy, yet, but placed where they belonged. (And how many patient hours had Lucille spent beside the cage in the critter room of the Gilman Biomedical Center, committing those anatomical details to memory so that her mind's eye and creativity function would be able to resummon them whenever she commanded it . . .)

The illusion became opaque. It settled onto the ceramic balance platform beneath the glass dome. It had four feet with claws, a fur-clothed body that shone sleek under the bright spotlight.

[Warmth of MOUSE smell of MOUSE twitchy allure of MOUSE!]

The kitten crouched, waggling its rump, stamping its hind feet in preparation for the spring—

"Nooh-ooh, ooh-ooh." Not yet Minou not yet wait baby you can't get at it under the glass wait soon soon . . .

Abruptly, the read-out on the electro-balance went from zero to 0.061 µg. The mouse simulacrum began to move, its eyes sparkling and its nose sniffing. It scuttled obliquely off the pan and went through the thick lead glass of the dome cover, heading for the table edge.

The kitten sprang.

Squeee!

[Gotcha!]

The psychocreative mouse vanished.

Lucille Cartier sat back in her chair and sighed, while the room lighting brightened to normal incandescent and the Abyssinian kitten bounded about, searching for its elusive prey. The test-chamber door opened and Vigdis Skaugstad came in, all smiles.

"Wonderful, Lucille! Did you notice the mass gain?"

"Not really. I was too busy making the mouse squeal. Minou is so disappointed if it doesn't." Lucille reached into the pocket of her flannel skirt and took out a little ball with a bell in it, which she threw to the kitten. Her face was weary and her mind dark.

Vigdis began to disconnect the body-function monitors that had been pasted to the human subject. The kitten abandoned the ball to mount an attack on the dangling electrodes.

"No no, kitty," Vigdis scolded. "Behave yourself—or maybe next time we wire *you*."

"Minou wouldn't cooperate then," Lucille said, disentangling the small paws. "She won't perform unless the experiment is fun. I should be so lucky."

"It was hard on you?" Vigdis's kind, china-blue eyes were surprised. "But you said doing the materialization was always an amusement for the two of you—and your heart and respiration level were not significantly elevated during the activity."

Lucille shrugged. "But now we aren't just playing. The mouse isn't just a pounce toy, it's an experiment with the data all recorded for analysis."

"But the experiment was a great success!" Vigdis protested. "And not just the materialization—although it was the best you have ever done—but the fact of the metaconcert! This is our first experimental confirmation of two minds working as one. Your EEG and the cat's were like music, Lucille! I shall write a paper: 'Evidence of Mental Synergy in a Human-Animal Psychocreative Metaconcert.' "

"That's a new term, isn't it? Metaconcert?"

"Denis coined it. So much more stylish than mind-meld or tandem-think or psi-combo or those other barbarisms you Americans are so fond of, don't you think?"

Lucille only grunted. She stood up, transferring the kitten to her shoulder.

Vigdis said, "We shall have to repeat the experiment, and similar ones. Eventually, we will want to try the metaconcert with you and a powerful human operant, such as Denis."

At the door, Lucille whirled around. "Not on your life!"

"But he would be the best," Vigdis said, gently reproving.

"Not him. Anybody but him!"

"Oh, my dear. If there were only some way I could help you to overcome your antagonism toward Denis. It was all a misunderstanding, your earlier feeling that he was trying to force you to participate—"

"I have the greatest respect for Professor Remillard," Lucille said, heading out into the hall. "He's brilliant, and his new book is a masterpiece, and he's had the good taste to let me alone during most of my work here. Let's keep things that way . . . Now I'll take Minou home, and then I'm off to finish my Christmas shopping."

Vigdis followed as Lucille headed for the Cat House, an opulently furnished playroom where the resident animals ran free. "Lucille, I'm sorry but there is something you must do first. I didn't want to upset you before the run, but it is very important that you speak to Denis before you leave for the Christmas break. He is waiting for you in the coffee room."

Oh *Vigdis*!

Lucille you must. Please.

"If he has any more friendly admonitions about Bill, I'm going to be awfully pissed, holiday season or not!" Lucille stormed. "I've had enough flak from my family without Denis adding his contribution."

"The conference has nothing to do with Dr. Sampson. It is an entirely different matter."

"Good," said Lucille shortly. Then she relented at Vigdis's hurt reaction to her asperity and apologized. "Don't take me seriously. I'm still tensed up over the experiment . . . Did I tell you Bill wanted to give me a diamond for Christmas? His late mother's ring. But I refused. As long as I'm still his patient, there mustn't be even a hint of—of our commitment. But the analysis is nearly complete."

She opened the Cat House door and bent down to put Minou inside. The place harbored five Maine Coon cats, three Siamese, and two other Abyssinian kittens, all breeds noted for metapyschic precocity. The animals lounged on carpeted ledges and shelves, peered from padded lairs, slept in baskets, clambered up feline gymnastic equipment, and lurked amid a well-chewed jungle of potted plants. Minou ignored the lot and made a beeline for the feeding station.

"Is it your family's disapproval of Dr. Sampson that makes you so downhearted?" Vigdis asked, bending to scratch the head of a Siamese that had come to caress her ankles.

"They're being very pigheaded, and it's so damned unfair! I thought they'd be happy when I told them Bill wanted me to marry him."

"A psychiatrist and his patient," Vigdis murmured. "There are ethical considerations—"

"To hell with that! And that's not what's bugging Mom and Dad. They don't want me to marry *anyone*." They don't understand they only know their own stupid fear and Bill the doctor was supposed to cure me of it exorcise it make me normal like them and instead he *loved* it loved *me* and they can't stand that it

proves them wrong and proves me good and lovable and them
wicked because they hate and fear me and they'll be sorry Bill
and I will make them feel so small so ashamed make them burn
with shame burn burnburn *BURN WITH SHAME*—

The cats shrieked.

As if some switch had been thrown, the room exploded in a
clamor of tormented kitten squeals, full-throated Siamese yowls,
and the lynx-roars of frenzied Coon cats. The women dashed out
into the hall and slammed the door.

"Uff da!" said Vigdis.

Lucille had gone white. "I'm so sorry! The poor little things!
God—will I ever get this thing under control?"

Vigdis put an arm about the trembling girl. "It's all right. Your
creativity was energized inadvertently. You must expect that to
happen sometimes when you are tired or stressed. The cats were
not harmed, only frightened."

Lucille repeated dully, "I'm sorry. I'm sorry." Sorry my mind
is perverse sorry my folks don't like Bill sorry they fear me *does
Bill*? sorry they don't love me but just let *him* love me—

Lucille be strong. You want to be loved of course so do we
all.

I think . . . he may be afraid too.

Yes. He may. You must face that. Your Bill is a normal.

He understands!

He is twice your age an experienced clinician yes he very
likely does understand and I am sure he loves you very much
even if he is also afraid. But normal! Oh Lucille my child I
should tell you . . . but how can I? Your parents may have known
in their hearts loved you more than you realized . . . but how can I
tell you how—

What?

Lucille . . . I loved a normal man. We married before my faculties became operant under the tutelage of Professor MacGregor
but then afterward the difference the terrible difference I did not
want to believe what the wisest operants warned me about I knew
my love would be strong enough but in the end Egil divorced me
the price paid for becoming operant is permanent alienation from
normal human attachments.

I don't believe it!

It is true.

It can't be . . . the way you said. Bill loves me! He knows
exactly what I am and he loves me.

He cannot know you. Your mind is closed to him. Your true self will always be unknown and you can only love him rejecting lying—

"No!" Lucille said aloud.

The cats had fallen silent and the old building creaked in the blustering wind. Somewhere in an empty office a telephone rang five times before being switched to the answering machine.

Vigdis said, "It's getting late—nearly six. I must go back to the test chamber and finish up." Her mind had veiled itself, withdrawn from the younger woman's defiance. "Please don't forget to meet with Denis before you leave."

Vigdis hurried away and Lucille stood there for several minutes, seething with resentment, before going downstairs to the room on the main floor that had once been the kitchen of the saltbox and now served as a coffee room for the research staff. It had been furnished with castoff furniture. To honor the holiday season, there was an eighteen-inch spruce tree decorated with multicolored LEDs sitting on an old lab cart in front of the window.

As Lucille entered the room, Denis Remillard turned away from the coffee machine near the Christmas tree, holding two steaming cups. Of course he must have known exactly when she would arrive . . .

"Good evening, Professor Remillard," she said stiffly. "Dr. Skaugstad said you wanted to see me."

"Sugar?" Denis lifted one of the cups. "The half-and-half is all gone, I'm afraid."

"Black is fine." As if you didn't know!

As always, his mind was fathomless below its socially correct overlay. He was dressed for the weather in a red buffalo-plaid shirt, corduroy pants, and Maine hunting shoes from Bean's—an incongruously boyish bête noire who held out the coffee mug to her with a noncommittal smile. His awful blue eyes were averted, watching the snow outside the window.

"They say we'll get another eight inches before tomorrow. It'll be rough for travel."

Lucille said, "Yes."

"I'm glad that your creativity run was successful. The implications of the mass pickup on the simulacrum are almost more intriguing than the metaconcert effect."

"Vigdis has staked out the metaconcert paper," Lucille said sweetly. "That leaves the mass gain for yours."

Denis nodded, still looking out the window. "You might be interested in an article in the current issue of *Nature*. A man at Cambridge has suggested a mechanism for the psychophysical energy transfer, based on the new dynamic-field theory of Xiong Ping-yung."

"No doubt the Chinese Einstein will connect us mind-freaks to the real universe in due time, and the Triple-A-S will heave a great sigh of relief. But if you don't mind, I'll give the six-dimensional math and lattice-construct theory a miss for now. Too many other things to think about." She set her coffee down, untasted. "Just what was it you wanted to discuss with me, Professor?"

"A certain problem has come to light." Denis spoke slowly, keeping his tone casual. "At parapsychology establishments in California, New York, Virginia, and Pennsylvania, workers have been approached and offered enormous salaries as an inducement to join a secret unit being formed at the Psychological Warfare School of the Army Research and Development Center at Aberdeen, Maryland. Persons who declined—and we believe most did decline—were then subject to great pressure by the Army representatives. In several cases, the pressure amounted to virtual blackmail. The more polite decliners were urged to set up a psychic-research data pipeline to the Pentagon. The military is particularly interested in the areas of excorporeal excursion, long-distance coercion, and the psychocreative manipulation of electrical and electronic energy."

"The bastards!" Lucille exclaimed. "It's the atomic weapons thing all over again! Whether we like it or not, we're going to be used—"

We are not.

She gaped at him. He turned from the window so that his eyes caught hers for an instant like a cobra mesmerizing a rabbit. An instant later he lowered his gaze and she was left floundering.

He said, "The human mind is not a docile piece of machinery, Lucille—especially not the mind of an operant metapsychic. Perhaps some time in the future we operants may learn to disguise our thoughts so thoroughly that we can deceive one another readily in moral matters—but that time hasn't come yet. Any operant sympathetic to this insane Mind Wars concept will be expelled from our research projects. Sent to Coventry. Thank God the point is moot thus far."

"You're positive nobody's gone over?"

"Nearly so. However, if certain overzealous Pentagon types discover just how close we really are to psychic breakthroughs of global importance, they may resort to more dangerous tactics. The advent of excorporeal excursion alone will turn foreign policy on its ear... So we won't be able to remain passive in the face of this threat. The people at Stanford are going to blow the whistle on the dirty recruitment tactics—especially the attempted extortion. When the scandal breaks, public and Congressional outrage will dig the grave for the Army's Mind Wars scheme."

"And then they'll leave us alone?"

"I'm afraid not. I'm certain that the military will continue to try to penetrate our research groups for intelligence purposes. But I'm determined that this will *not* happen here at Dartmouth, where so many strong operants are concentrated. So far, we seem to be secure. Very few normals outside of the college administration are aware of what we actually do, and I've examined all of our workers and operant subjects without finding a single person who was suborned by Pentagon headhunters. That is—I've examined everyone except you."

"Well, nobody's tried to buy me or dragoon me. God help them if they tried!"

"I have to be sure of that," said Denis.

"You—what?"

The eyes took hold of her again.

"I must be quite certain."

He set his coffee mug down beside the little Christmas tree and closed the distance between them. His psychic barricade, that wall of impregnable black ice, was dissolving now and she could see for the first time a hint of the mentality that lay behind. It was even worse than she had feared. The coercion was impossible to resist, as cold and impersonal as the northeast wind driving the blizzard. What a fool she had been to think that he had tried to coerce her before! He'd done nothing—only *talked*, exerted ordinary persuasive force. She had been left free, then, to make her own choice.

Now there was no choice.

Dissolving, berating herself, helpless before his invasion, she could only watch as he posed the questions and read the replies her mind passively delivered up. Humiliated, too supine even to rage, she found herself suddenly alone; and her only memory was of a mind-voice, as unexpected as a razor cut:

Thank you Lucille. All of us thank you. We're very glad that you are one of us ...

The window drew her like a magnet. She pressed her nose against the frosty pane and looked out into tumultuous white. The snow-bleared red of his Toyota's taillights shone at the exit of the parking lot and then disappeared.

She was all alone in the laboratory building. A curl of vapor arose from her neglected coffee cup, sitting beside the empty one Denis Remillard had left behind. The Christmas tree blinked against the backdrop of the storm.

One of them.

Am I one of them?

Lucille turned out the room lights, leaving the little tree lit, and went upstairs to make her peace with the cats before going to supper.

15

EDINBURGH, SCOTLAND, EARTH
11 APRIL 1991

A CLASSIC SCOTCH MIST FELL ON THE TENEMENTS AND CLOSES OF Old Town, rendering the quaint streetlighting even more inadequate than usual, but the two persons who stalked Professor James Somerled MacGregor had no difficulty at all keeping track of him. His gangly figure was a blazing beacon to the psychosensitive as he tramped through the murk, haloed by a raging crimson aura lanced with occasional fresh bursts of white indignation. His subvocal thoughts, more often than not, were broadcast heedlessly on the declamatory mode.

Two million quid! The bloody cheek of it!

Oh, aye! He'd been expecting something like this to happen once the EE work reached the critical transition from theoretic to practical. He'd alerted the other metapsychology research establishments actively studying the function to keep a sharp watch for attempts at subversion. And now this! The low, furacious skites hadn't made their move in America or India or West Germany—

they'd tried it *here*, in Scotland, on his very own patch that he'd taken such pains to secure!

Of course loyal Nigel had told the CIA where to stuff their fewking proposition. Whereupon the spooks had piled insult upon insult by telling him that he couldn't hope for a better offer from MI5, who were hamstrung by recent budget cuts. Then they'd hinted that he would enjoy life a lot more in a nice Maryland condominium than in a guarded compound in the Negev Desert or a GRU facility on the outskirts of beautiful metropolitan Semipalatinsk!

Small wonder that Nigel's creative metafaculty had run slightly amok at that point, setting the Yanks' attaché cases on fire and prompting their hasty withdrawal. Nigel had bespoken his boss at once, and he and Jamie had held a council of war in Nigel's Canongate rooms, with the windows open to disperse the stench of scorched cordovan, and tumblers of Laphroaig to calm their righteous ire. Now that the security of the Edinburgh Parapsychology Unit was compromised, there seemed little hope that they could continue on the cautious schedule of action championed by Denis Remillard and Tamara Sakhvadze and the other operant conservatives, who advocated delaying the public announcement of EE capability until there were at least a thousand adept practitioners scattered around the world. This move on Nigel by the CIA meant that other intelligence agencies would soon be homing in on the EE workers. Once the world militarists became aware of the advanced state of EE, they might risk a neutralization scheme of draconian scope in order to preserve the strategic status quo.

The only thing for it was to do a media demonstration just as soon as possible.

Once the news was out, the risks would be diminished—if not quite eliminated. World opinion would help safeguard the adepts from any blatant pogrom or conscription attempt. Yes . . . that was the only way to go. There'd be resistance from Tamara and Denis to overcome. Their timetable had been carefully reasoned. And Denis would certainly balk at participation in a demonstration, since he'd stuck his neck out so far in the publication of *Metapsychology*. Right, then—Jamie would gladly put his own cock on the block. They'd do the media demo right here at Edinburgh University. Probably take until autumn to set it up. Meanwhile, they'd all have to take precautions, just as young Alana

Shaunavon had urged that very afternoon. Curious, her having that premonition of danger...

As Jamie squelched along, cogitating, he was oblivious of other pedestrians on the High Street. There weren't many, since it was nearly one in the morning and the mist was thickening to drizzle. Normally, he would have taken a bus from Nigel's place to his own home a mile away in the northern New Town, but he'd wanted to give his anger a chance to cool, besides mulling over what would have to be done next. Set up safeguards for his own people in the morning. Then excurse to America and tackle Denis. Or should he do that as soon as he got home? What time was it in bloody New Hampshire, anyhow?...

He was just short of North Bridge when the two superimposed mental images struck him like a physical blow.

Alana!

And the Unknown.

...Alana Shaunavon, his most talented EE adept, shivering with her witch-green eyes full of apprehension after a perfectly harmless jaunt to Tokyo, gripping the arms of the barber's chair white-knuckled and confessing that she'd had a flash of dire foreboding. Impending disaster. He'd reassured her, then forgotten the matter until Nigel Weinstein alerted him to the attempted subversion. And now Alana's face sprang to Jamie's mind again—from his memory or from somewhere else—projecting a second warning...

...that was savagely blotted out by the mental override of the Unknown. A man, physically present nearby, strongly operant.

Turn right MacGregor into the next close.

The compulsion was irresistibly exerted. The intent was murderous.

Jamie was both stunned and incredulous. An *operant* enemy? But that was impossible! Both Denis and Tamara had flatly assured him that their governments had no operant agents. Denis had checked Langley many times with his seekersense and Tamara had subjected the files of both the KGB and GRU to remote-view scrutiny.

"Who's there?" Jamie called. And then telepathically: *What do you want? Where are you?*

Come in here under the archway.

Helpless, Jamie turned off the High Street into the entry of the close, one of those narrow urban canyons peculiar to Edinburgh's Old Town that gave access to the warrens of tenement blocks.

The corridor was nearly pitch-dark in the mist. Jamie had no penetrating clairvoyance that would spotlight the way, no dowsing ability that might identify the mentality coercing him. He stumbled on irregular pavement and nearly took a header, then managed to orient himself by looking up at the sky, which shone a faint golden gray above the silhouetted roofs and chimney pots.

"Who are you?" Jamie demanded. American? Russian? *Sassenach?!*

Keep walking.

His footsteps splashed and echoed in a narrow alleyway. He came out into a broader courtyard where there was a bit of fuzzy illumination from a building on the right and saw an insubstantial figure, standing still.

Come closer to me.

What the devil do you want?

Let's just get this over with.

Jamie battled the coercion, reeling like a drunken man, but his betraying legs carried him on toward the waiting Unknown. He tried to shout out loud, but his vocal cords now seemed paralyzed. Strangely, he was not afraid, only more than ever furious. First Nigel—now him!

The Unknown held a narrow tube, no larger than a biro, with a faint metallic gleam. He pointed this at Jamie.

Closer. Closer.

Don't be a bloody fool! Jamie's mind shouted. You won't stop EE by killing me . . .

In retrospect, Jamie was never quite sure what happened next. Strong arms suddenly grasped him from behind and hauled him off his feet. He got his voice back and uttered a bellow that rang up and down the close. The Unknown swore out loud, crouched, and thrust out the cylinder. Jamie heard a sharp hiss. Then he was wrenched violently to one side by the person who had seized him and fell in a heap onto the slippery stones, striking his head. Roman candles popped in the vault of his skull and he heard running footsteps receding into the distance.

"How're you doing, man? Did he hurt you?"

Dim flame of butane cigarette-lighter. Deep-set eyes and touseled fair hair glistening in the drizzle. A burly man wearing a duffel coat, bending over him. A wry but friendly smile.

"I think I'm all right," Jamie said. "Bit of a bump."

His rescuer nodded, extended a big hand, and helped Jamie climb to his feet. Although he was not young he was built like a stevedore, and he topped Jamie's six feet three inches. He held the lighter high, and its blue flame gave a surprising amount of light.

"Your friend the mugger seems to have run off. Did he get your wallet?"

"No." Jamie used his handkerchief to dry his wet hands and explored the lump on his head with caution. "Thanks very much for your help."

"Good thing I happened along. Now and again I use this close as a short cut. Want me to hunt up a policeman?"

"No . . . it wouldn't do much good, would it? As you said, he's gone. I'd rather go home."

"Whatever you say." The lighter snapped off. "But take my advice and stick to lighted streets after this. Better yet, take a taxi. You'll find one back there on the High Street."

"Yes, well—"

The man in the duffel coat started off in the direction taken by the fleeing Unknown, calling over his shoulder with conventional good humor, "Get along now. We'd really hate to lose you."

"A suggestive remark, that," Jean commented.

"And with that he was off." Jamie drew her more tightly against him, the palms of his hands enclosing her breasts as though they were talismans through which the healing magic flowed. "And it's only now, when I'm able to think clearly, that I realize how odd it was that he was able to see that I was in mortal danger. It's not as though the operant mugger had a gun or a knife. There was only the wee tube thing there in the dark. *I* was certain it'd be the death of me because the bugger's mind assured me of the fact—but how did my Good Samaritan know?"

Tell me the answer, said his wife's mind.

My rescuer was an operant too he must have been and that means . . . of course it's only logical that there should be others but good God that they should be *watching us*!

"You aren't inconspicuous," she said, laughing softly. "As you said, it's logical."

They lay together, naked before the fire, on a rug she'd made herself of pieced black and white Islay sheepskins. When he had come home, raging with worry and fear, she had closed her mind to him and not permitted him to tell the story until she had administered the great sovereign remedy there in the dark library, their private sanctum. Then she'd listened calmly.

He said, "We'll have to work out some ways to guard ourselves, until the public demonstration can be arranged. All of the EE adepts will be at risk. Aside from the mysterious assassin, there are the government agents lurking about. The CIA for certain—and if the two who talked to Nigel are to be believed, there are Russians and Israelis and even British agents to worry about . . ."

"You think they might try kidnaping if other recruitment tactics fail?"

"It's a possibility," he said somberly.

She kissed his wrist lightly. "What you must do then is steal a march on the lot of them. For Whitehall, a preview of coming attractions, demonstrating how an EE adept would react to involuntary sequestration by going out of body and raising a hue and cry among his colleagues. For the Yanks, a suggestion that Whitehall pass on the good word, with a judicious warning against poaching. For the others, a more devious approach. You and your colleagues will have to descend to cloak-and-daggering. Excurse into the appropriate embassies in London—and perhaps in Paris as well—and find out whether there are any nefarious schemes being planned against you. If there are, take the aforementioned steps."

Jamie gave a delighted laugh. "Damn, but you're a cool one!"

She grabbed him by his Dundrearies and pulled his face close. "Only because I don't think the intelligence people want to harm you. They don't know enough about you yet, my dear, for that. But your mystery man, the operant mugger, is something else altogether. He frightens me, and I have no notion at all how you can protect yourself from a person like that. He came from nowhere and vanished back into it. You know nothing of his motives. He may even have been a madman—"

"No," said Jamie. "He was sane."

"Then perhaps he's been frightened off by the other one. We can pray that it's so. And you can follow your rescuer's advice and take care not to travel in lonely places."

"Not while I'm in my body, at least," he said, and he kissed her lips, and they lay together for a few minutes more watching the fire die, and then went off to bed.

16

ZÜRICH, SWITZERLAND, EARTH
5 SEPTEMBER 1991

THE ELEVEN MEN AND ONE WOMAN WHO CONSTITUTED THE PRD, the banking regulatory board of Switzerland, watched without emotion as the confidential agent known as Otto Maurer showed his videotape of the photographed documents that verified the nature of Dr. James Somerled MacGregor's researches.

"It is now confirmed beyond a doubt," Maurer said, "that the psychic procedure for remote clairvoyant viewing is reliably practiced by no less than thirty individuals connected with the Parapsychology Unit at Edinburgh University, plus an undetermined number of other persons in other parts of the world who have made use of the mental programming techniques for this— uh—talent, as perfected by Professor MacGregor and his associates. Pursuant to my instructions, I have assembled other documentation from the Psychology Department, the Astronomy Department, and the Office of Media Relations for the Medical School of the University of Edinburgh. This material confirms that on or about twenty-two October of this year, MacGregor will hold a briefing for world media announcing . . . *and demonstrating* this psychic espionage technique."

The twelve banking directors uttered varied cries of dismay. Maurer lowered his head in a momentary gesture of commiseration, then said, "It is needless to belabor the obvious. MacGregor's researches effectively write 'finis' to the confidentiality of the Swiss banking system. Additionally, widespread utilization of psychic espionage will trigger chaos in every stock market, commodity exchange, and financial institution throughout the world, opening virtually any transaction to the danger of public scrutiny . . . This concludes my report, Messieurs and Madame, and I await your questions and instructions."

The woman asked, "This MacGregor—has he any radical political affiliation? Is he a Red? An anarchist? Or simply an ivory-tower academic unaware of the potentially disastrous consequences of his actions?"

"He is none of these things, Madame Boudry. MacGregor is a Scot and a fierce idealist. It is military secrecy he seeks to demolish by introducing this psychic spy technique, thinking thereby to preclude the possibility of nuclear war. The collapse of the world financial structure would seem to him a small price to pay for peace."

There was an appalled silence.

A stout, placid-looking man asked, "You have explored avenues of—of influence that might deter him from his demonstration?"

Maurer nodded. "I have, Herr Gimel, but without conspicuous success. He is fearless, in spite of an attempt upon his life last April and intensive surveillance by a number of state security agencies. He would be affronted by any attempt at bribery. His position at the university is impregnable, and his professional status is beyond reproach so there is no chance of his work being discredited before or after the fact."

"His personal life?" Gimel inquired.

Maurer spoke in English. "Squeaky clean."

The bankers chuckled bitterly. A frail, ill-looking man with burning eyes leaned toward the agent and quavered, "Are you telling us that there is no way of stopping this man?"

"No licit way, Herr Reichenbach."

The invalid clasped the edge of the mahogany table with skeletal hands. "Maurer! You will have to think about this matter urgently. It is of paramount importance to us, to your country's continuing prosperity. Find a way to stop this demonstration—or, failing that, a way to delay it. MacGregor himself is the key to the problem! Do you understand me?"

"I'm not sure, Herr Reichenbach . . ."

"It is privacy that this psychic madman threatens. A fundamental right of humanity! This thing you have shown us, this technique of spying, is a nightmare out of George Orwell that any right-thinking person would repudiate with horror. You say MacGregor hopes for peace. I say MacGregor is the greatest menace civilization has ever known. Think of it. Psychic overseers scrutinizing every action of business, politics, even our personal lives. Think of it!"

Maurer's eyes swept around the board-room table. The other

eleven PRD members were nodding their heads in solemn affirmation.

"Do something," old Reichenbach whispered. "Think very carefully, then do something."

17

FROM THE MEMOIRS OF ROGATIEN REMILLARD

THAT FIRST YEAR OF MINE IN HANOVER WAS VERY DIFFICULT. There is inevitably a lot of hard work involved in getting a new business off the ground, and my Eloquent Page bookshop was strictly a one-man operation. Early in 1991 I traveled a lot, hitting sales and thrift shops and jobbers all over New England as I gathered the basic stock of used fantasy and science-fiction titles that were to be my specialty. I ordered new books as well—not only fiction but also science nonfiction of the type that I thought might appeal to my hoped-for clientele. When spring came and the shop was pretty well filled I opened the doors to walk-in customers and began to prepare catalogs for the mail-order trade. Denis and his Coterie were faithful patrons. They even sent their student subjects along through subtle application of the coercer's art.

My nephew was always urging me to participate in this or that experiment at his lab, but I invariably declined. The place crawled with earnest young students, all gung ho for the advancement of metapsychology, who made me feel like a scapegrace fogy when I refused to share their enthusiasm. And then there was the Coterie. Except for Sally Doyle, who was earthy and nonjudgmental, and her husband Tater McAllister, who had a wacko sense of humor in spite of being a theoretical physicist, the Coterie did not consist of folks I would have freely chosen as drinking buddies. They were fanatically loyal to Denis and his goals and did not suffer the heretical mutterings of the Great Man's uncle with equanimity. My reluctance to sacrifice myself on the altar of mental science was viewed as semireasonable by Denis's chief associate, Glenn Dalembert, by Losier and Tremblay, who ran the main operancy test program, and by the mystic medicine man, Tukwila Barnes. Colette Roy, Dalembert's wife, reacted to my negativism with the perky hopefulness of a camp counselor confronting a recalcitrant eight-year-old. But she moved me not a whit more than did Eric Boutin, the strapping ex-mechanic, whose toothy grin did not quite conceal his itch to whip me into tiptop mental shape, for my own good as well as the good of the cause.

"No thanks," said I, not giving a flying fuck that I was thereby letting the side down. I would not accept operancy training. I would not let them measure my overall PsiQ. I would not even submit to a simple assay of my metafaculties. (Researchers now tended to classify the mind-powers under the headings of Ultrasenses, Coercivity, Psychokinesis, Creativity, and Healing—later broadened to Redaction.)

Maybe someday, I said, lying in my teeth. But not now.

The publicity splash generated by the publication of Denis's book finally petered out, to my relief, and the media abandoned Hanover to cover more newsworthy events such as the Mars Mission, the African plague, and the never-ending Middle Eastern terrorist attacks. The mysterious researches of my nephew became strictly stale potatoes, journalistically speaking—until the Edinburgh bombshell exploded late in October.

Denis knew it was coming. In spring, MacGregor had tried to enlist the cooperation of the Dartmouth group, in addition to that of the Stanford team, for his upcoming demonstration. Denis turned him down flat, and he tried hard to convince the Scot to postpone the press conference—or at least make the EE demonstration a private one for a select group of United Nations representatives. I only found out what was in the wind by accident, when Denis let anxiety over what he felt was a premature disclosure leak into the vestibule of his mind, where I picked it up—and was aghast. If MacGregor and his people came out into the open with a demonstration of their powers, linked to a patently political proposal, other metapsychics would also feel constrained to do so. Denis's group, beyond a doubt! They would acknowledge their operancy in support of the idealistic proposal of their fellow researchers, and when they did my own protective coloration would be destroyed.

MacGregor had confided to Denis his reasons for deciding to

go ahead; but Denis did not at that time reveal those reasons to me. I only saw that my nephew had apparently caved in to the pressure exerted by his older colleague and had abandoned a carefully orchestrated scheme that would have revealed the existence of operant minds to the world only after a period of careful preparation.

Instead, it was to be: Voilà! Like us or lump us.

I was as furious with Denis as I was frightened for myself. We had a flaming row over the matter that led to our first serious estrangement. I cursed myself for ever coming to Hanover, where it was inevitable that I would be drawn into whatever ruckus attended Denis. My original reason for coming, Denis's fear that Victor might try to harm me, now seemed to be without foundation. I had seen Victor only at the Christmas and Easter family gatherings, and he had been distantly cordial. It looked as though the real danger to me, ironically enough, was going to be Denis himself! And I was trapped. All my money was invested in the bookshop and it was too late to set it up elsewhere. I would have to stay in Hanover.

However, I distanced myself from Denis and the other operants almost completely from April, when the Edinburgh matter came to a head, to October. Swaddled in midlife depression, I overworked, trying to distract myself and force my infant business into the black. I stayed open until midnight. I wrote reams of letters to specialty collectors proffering my wares and inquiring about rarities. I went to conventions of science-fiction and fantasy fans and peddled my stuff, making friends and contacts who would be invaluable in later years. I nearly managed to forget what I was. A mental freak? Not I, folks! I'm only a humble bookseller. But if you're into the occult, I might have just the title you're looking for . . .

It was Don who put an end to the charade.

Throughout the early fall, as my anxiety about the upcoming EE demonstration increased, I slept very badly. I would awake stiff with terror, my pajamas and pillow soaked with sweat, but unable for the life of me to remember the content of the nightmare. Then October came and the hills flagged their scarlet warning of approaching winter, and the petunias in the decorative tubs out on the sidewalks died with the first touch of frost. In the misty dawn, when I lay in bed in that odd state between sleep and full wakefulness, I began to feel again the familiar touch of my dead brother's mind. He had wanted so desperately to be free of me . . . but now, without me, he was lost.

I tried to blot out my irrational fantasies in the time-honored family fashion, just as Don and even Onc' Louie had done before me. Sometimes the drinking helped. As a side effect I suffered a drastic "psi decline" (for few things are as detrimental to the metafaculties as overindulgence in alcohol), and this brought reproaches from Denis, along with tiresome offers of help. I refused, even though I was quite aware that I needed some sort of therapy. Somehow I had conceived the notion that to seek psychiatric help would be to "give in" to Don. I told myself that he was only a memory. He was dead, prayed over by the Church, buried in consecrated ground. Thoughts of him could hurt me only if I let them—and I would not! In time I would conquer him and the fears we had shared. Time would heal me.

But the bad dreams and the depression and the feeling of hovering doom that the French-speaking call malheur only sharpened as the day of the Edinburgh press conference drew nearer. I could no longer get to sleep at all without drinking myself into insensibility. A certainty took hold of me that I would end as Don had, a suicide, and damned. In earlier years I might have prayed. I still went through the arid formalities of religious practice, but only to ward off additions to my already intolerable spiritual burden. My prayers had the thin comfort of habit, but lacked the trust in divine mercy that compels the probability lattices . . .

One day, rummaging through a recently arrived shipment of used books, I came upon a title that I remembered Elaine burbling over, a study of yogic techniques. I had smiled when she told me how the book had "helped her resolution of the death-space." (Death had been the furthest thing from my mind in those days!) The exercises she had described seemed to be mumbo jumbo, Eastern balderdash. But now in my extremity I took the book up to my untidy apartment and devoured it in a single reading. The states promised to the adept seemed analogous to the "astronomical consciousness" of Odd John, that supreme detachment that had made both the conquest of the universe and death become irrelevant to him.

So I tried.

Unfortunately, I was not very good at the meditations. They were too inwardly directed, too chilling to the sanguine Franco soul. Still I blundered on, for if the yogic exercises failed as the alcohol had failed, what hope was there? The inevitable day would arrive, and the exposure, and then I would be drawn along with all the rest of them to the inevitable end.

At the start of his research, Denis had told me that there was only one assured way that operants could escape the Odd John Effect, the potentially fatal dichotomy between Homo superior and the less favored mass of humanity. It lay in giving the "normals" hope that someday they—or their children or their children's children—might also attain the higher mind-powers. Much of the current work at Dartmouth was directed toward this end, and it was to be the subject of Denis's next book. Other research groups in other parts of the world were also studying the problem, trying to bridge the gap, to demonstrate that metafaculties were a universal fact of human nature.

Given time, these preparatory efforts might have defused the normals' perfectly rational fear of us. But there was no time.

18

EDINBURGH, SCOTLAND, EARTH
22 OCTOBER 1991

HIS MENTAL ALARM CLOCK WOKE JAMIE MACGREGOR AT PRE-cisely 4:00 A.M., and he began the most memorable day of his life with a queasy stomach and aching sinuses. The first could be attributed to stage fright and a lingering anxiety over the spooks, who might still be entertaining notions of kidnaping him before he let the EE cat out of the bag. The second was evidence that his prayer for just one more day of beautiful October weather had gone unanswered; the low-pressure trough that had lurked coyly above the Orkneys for the past week now sat astride Britain, charging the atmosphere with inimical ions. That might mean that the demonstration could be adversely affected. Under laboratory conditions the matter could easily be remedied through artificial neg-ion generation—but any such fiddle was out of the question during the public experiments, where the EE faculty had at least to *seem* invincible.

Ah, well. If Nigel or Alana experienced problems he would

simply step into the breach himself, and professional modesty be hanged.

It was still very dark. Lying there beside Jean, whose mind cycled in the serene delta waves of deepest sleep, Jamie MacGregor addressed the first order of business: banishing the sinus headache. He relaxed, adjusted his breathing, then summoned a picture of the front of his own skull in cutaway. He let gentle insinuation become a firm command: *Decrease histamine production shrink membranes inhibit mucus secretion initiate sinus drainage LET THERE BE NO PAIN.*

It happened.

He savored relief for a few moments, listening to the faint ticking of sleet against the windowpanes and his wife's gentle snores. Her strongest faculty was the healing, and she had taught it to him and to their two children and to numbers of their colleagues at university. The gift was widespread among Celts and many Scots possessed it suboperantly, with its practice requiring only strong will power and never a modicum of doubt. It did not seem to matter whether or not the healer's perception of the ailment's source was scientifically accurate. Experiments with their own young Katie and David had proved that—and Jamie had to smile as he recalled certain bizarre visualizations by the children. Yet if a person sincerely believed that tiny demons with hammers were the true source of sinusitis, wishing the evil creatures dead would work a cure just as surely as his own explicit redactive commands had done . . .

Outside in Dalmond Crescent an automobile engine whirred to a reluctant start and settled into a rough idle. The car did not drive off and Jamie's uneasy stomach reasserted itself. Damn them! Who was it this time? He cursed his inability to identify individual auras at a distance. Those lucky enough to possess that faculty, seekersense adepts such as Denis Remillard or the Tibetan Urgyen Bhotia, who headed up the Darjeeling establishment, did not have to fear being stalked or ambushed by human predators. But Jamie was blind to mental signatures. There was only one way he would be able to find out which foreign agent or British spook had spent a dreary night on station outside his house and now suffered predawn demoralization that required the comfort of a car's heater.

Jamie let his mind go out of body.

He seemed to ascend through the bedroom ceiling, through the loft, through the roof. He hovered above leafless trees tossing in the wind and streetlamps glimmering on the dark granite paving setts. One of the autos parked along the crescent, a Jaguar XJS HE, had twin plumes of vapor rising from it. Jamie swooped down to peer inside and saw Sergei Arkhipov, the London KGB resident, wiping his streaming nose with a sodden handkerchief before sucking a tot from his nearly depleted flask. The stereo was playing "Fingal's Cave." This solitary vigil by an agent of Arkhipov's high rank undoubtedly meant that the Russians had finally ruled out a kidnap attempt, even as the Americans had. Sergei was probably standing by only to make certain that no other faction—especially the GRU, Soviet military intelligence —got reckless.

Were there other spooks about? Jamie rose high again and began to search for signs of the Yanks or MI5; but the other parked cars on the street and in the adjacent mews were empty, and the only wakeful persons in the neighborhood besides himself and Arkhipov were Mrs. Farnsworth and her fretful infant and old Hamish Ferguson, insomniac again, watching *Deep Throat* on his VCR.

Jamie's upset stomach responded now to self-redaction and he returned briefly to his own body to prepare for the principal excorporeal excursion. Jean, sensing his tension, half woke and sent out a little nonverbal query. He told her: No no it's nothing sleep lass sleep not quite time to rise for the Big Day...

Then he was off again through the freezing dark, a soul that would girdle the globe before returning to its physical anchorage. But first, before crossing the Atlantic, he'd stop at Islay, for Gran.

Storm winds out of the northwest smote the shoulder of the island squarely, shoving mountainous waves into Sanaigmore Bay. The farmsteading in its hollow seemed to crouch like a patient, sturdy beast, back to the gale. To Jamie's mind's eye, refined by the EE faculty as it never was during short-distance attempts at clairvoyance, the Hebridean darkness was as lucid as day, except that there were no colors and the lack of shadows gave the scene a peculiar flatness. The area lights that usually lit the farmyard at night were out and the house looked unilluminated as well, alarming Jamie. But when he glided down and came close he saw the glow of a paraffin lamp through the kitchen window and a smoky thread blasted horizontally from the chimney of the ancient, peat-burning hearth. His older brother Colin and his wife Jean and their grown son Johnnie, who worked the farm now, were still abed, enjoying the last precious half hour of rest. But Gran was up getting breakfast, as was her custom. He heard her humming as she put another peat on the fire and stirred the porridge.

Jamie said: Gran it's me.

Dear laddie you took the time to come! said she.

For your blessing now that we're ready to show our secret to the world . . . I see your electricity's gone out in the storm.

Aye and the fancy cooker and the lights and the closed-circuit telly to the barn and all the other modern thingamajiks useless until Colin wakes and starts the Honda generator but he and Jean and Johnnie will wake to hot food naetheless I cooked over peat for fifty years and I don't mind doing it now it's a comfort to know the old ways still have their worth.

. . . And now some of the oldest of all to be new again Gran.

Affection! To think I'd live to see it! Eighty-one years but not even my Sight gave me a hint of how it would *really* be and I'm so proud so proud.

Well I still have misgivings. If only we could have waited until there were more as adept at the soul-travel as Nigel Alana and I.

No you could *not* wait not with Them skulking about Godbethankit you've been unmolested you must get it into the open then you'll all be safe.

If the demonstration succeeds.

Now stop that. What have I taught you man and boy for thirty-nine years but that doubt's the mind's poison causing the powers to sicken and wane? Shame on ye!

I expect it's all this science that's spoiled me.

Laughter. Now don't be afraid. I See that your showing will bring about a new world and it's Mother Shipton's joke you see: *The world then to an end shall come in Nineteen Hundred and Ninety-One*.

! So that explains *that* . . . still I wish I had the Sight like you and Alana and your confidence. When I remember what happened back in April my narrow escape I still get a cald grue if it hadn't been for that big chap who came along by chance—

So it was chance was it!

Ah Gran.

Ah Jamie. Stop fashing yourself laddie just do what you've prepared yourself and Nigel and Alana for don't think of the cold world watching with its mechanical moonlet eyes pretend it's the first soul-trip just like long years ago a natural thing if a wonder an old thing cherished in spite of doubts and oppression and now it's time we showed it proudly and how will you like being a famous man my own wee Jamie?

You're a cruel old woman to laugh at me when I'm all in a flaughter but I love you. Now charmbless me in the Gaelic for I must be off to California and the Antipodes to make sure that all's ready.

Very well: Cuirim cumerih dhia umid sluagh dall tharrid do vho gach gabhadh sosgeul dhia na grais o mullach gu lar unid ga ghradhich na fire thu i na millidh na mhuaih thu . . . I put the protection of God around you a host over you to protect you from every danger the gospel of the God of Grace from top to ground over you may the men love you and the women do you no harm.

Amen! Thank you dear Gran goodbye.

Farewell Jamie my own heart.

As he waited with the throng of journalists to be admitted to the auditorium of the University of Edinburgh's George Square Theatre, Fabian (The Fabulous) Finster amused himself by ferreting out others like himself who had crashed the event with forged credentials.

The exercise was not difficult. All intelligence operatives live their waking hours wrapped in a miasma of hair-trigger vigilance and subacute anxiety. A sensitive like Finster perceived this "loud" mind-tone as easily as if a neon sign were being worn on the forehead of the emanator. So far, he had spotted spooks from France, East and West Germany, Britain's domestic intelligence service MI5, the Israeli Mossad, the CIA, and (rather strangely) the Swiss Banking Regulatory Bureau PRD. Four Soviet GRU agents were among the sizable press corps from TASS. There was also a lone KGB man playing a clandestine game whom Finster had contrived to stand next to. This Russian was a squat, fair-haired man with a nasty head cold and rumpled clothing. He wore a lapel badge identifying him as S. HANNULA—HELSINGEN SANOMAT.

There was a flutter of action near the theatre's main entrance.

"Look at that!" Finster exclaimed to the counterfeit Finn. "They're going to let the TV crews into the hall ahead of the working press! It happens every goddam time."

A rumble of indignation went up from the less favored media

representatives. Their protests were partly appeased when some
two dozen young people wearing University of Edinburgh Psychology Department sweat shirts came out a side door and began
passing out press kits.

The alleged Hannula growled, "Now maybe we will get a clue
about the kind of circus these academic publicity-hounds are
planning."

Considerately, he handed one of the thick information packets
to the little squirrel-faced American next to him, whose ID badge
read: J. SMITH—SEATTLE POST-INTELLIGENCER. As the Soviet
agent opened his own packet he was thinking:

But surely it cannot be significant EE breakthrough not coming from here this oldfashioned ridiculous place they couldnot
have kept data secure most likely merely another crude stunt
suchas MacGregor described literature but if demonstration not
crucial then why CIA crablice pursuing him&associates try lure
to America HolyMother what awful stuffed head fever perhaps I
come down pneumonia this prickish Scottish dampness at least
GRU donkeyfuckers aborted lunatic scheme kidnap MacGregor
conscript into RedArmy psiresearch overcome KGB advantage
Alma-Ata . . .

Finster studied his press kit for a few minutes, then asked the
KGB man, "Is there much interest in psychic phenomena in Finland?"

"Oh, yes. That kind of thing is part of the national tradition.
We Finns have been accused of practicing witchcraft by Swedes
and other superstitious people from time immemorial." He
sneezed and cursed and made use of a stained handkerchief.

"Gesundheit," Finster told him cheerfully. (He was getting
very good with other languages.) "How about your neighbors to
the east? Would you call the Russians superstitious?"

"Hah! They are perhaps the worst of all." Hannula became
very absorbed in the handout material.

"Not much useful stuff here," Finster noted. "Will you look at
this, for chrissake? *A History of the British Society for Psychical
Research, 1882 to Present.* Did my editor send me halfway
around the world for that kinda shit? And this bio-sheet on Mac-
Gregor is hardly anything except summaries of the guy's publications. How's this for a grabber? 'EEG Beta Activity Correlates
Among Six Subjects During Short-Range Excorporeal Excur-
sions.' Jeez!"

The Soviet agent managed a perfunctory chuckle. He thought:

Shortrange it *must* be shortrange source New Hampshire assured us remoteviewing still unreliable but if so *why* Americans offer so much money Weinstein *who* try assassinate MacGregor April *when* idiots allow us enter hall begin sodding demonstration?

"Any minute now," Finster said absently, still studying the press-kit material. "Say—here's a choice bit. Did you know that MacGregor's official title here at Edinburgh University is 'Holder of the Arthur Koestler Chair of Parapsychology'? This Koestler was a famous writer, an ex-Commie who wrote about the abuse of power in the Red Bloc. When he died he left a pile of money to found this psychic professorship. Wouldn't it send up the Russkies if MacGregor has discovered something big? We all know the Reds have been trying to develop Mind Wars stuff for twenty, thirty years. Lately, there've been rumors that they're close to succeeding."

Hannula was blank-faced. "I have heard nothing about that."

Finster flashed his chipmunk grin. "I'll just bet you haven't." He folded the information packet lengthwise and tucked it into the Louis Vuitton shoulder bag that contained the tools of his trade—audiovisual microcorder, cellular telephone with data terminal, and the seasoned reporter's indispensable steno pad with three Bic pens. Only the most careful scrutiny would have revealed the illegal comsat-scrambler hookup on the phone and the needle-gun charged with deadly ricin concealed within the Bic Clic with the silver cap.

"Look!" Hannula cried. "Something happens!"

The doors of the auditorium were opening at last. A ragged cheer arose from the media people waiting in the lobby and the mob surged forward in a body. Finster called out to Hannula, "Stick with me, buddy! I always get a good seat!" And somehow the throng did part minimally to let the dapper little American pass through. The KGB agent hastened to follow, and the two of them raced down the center aisle and plopped breathlessly into seats in the third row. "What'd I tell you?" Finster bragged. "Best seats in the house."

Hannula groped beneath his own rump. He extracted a placard that said: RESERVED TIME MAGAZINE. Consternation creased his brow.

"Relax," Finster told him. He took the Russian's sign, together with one from his own seat that said: RESERVED CORRIERE DELLA SERA, and tore both sheets to bits. Reporters milling about in search of their proper places were open-mouthed. Finster's eyes swept over them. "We have a perfect right to sit anyplace we want. Versteh'? Capisce? Pigez? You dig?"

The other journalists looked away, suddenly absorbed in their own affairs.

The hall was jammed with more than a thousand people, and some of those lurking about the fringes were plainclothes police officers. Finster pretended to jot down items on his notepad as he relocated the other spooks. Only the CIA, masquerading as an SNN Steadicam team, and the TASS crew were more advantageously placed than Finster and his Soviet acquaintance. The Brits were clustered fifth row far left. Both sets of Germans were way in back with the luckless standees—who now included a distinguished Italian science editor and a hopping-mad *Time* stringer. The Israeli agent and the lady from the Direction Générale de la Sécurité Extérieure were side by side, chatting chummily. But what had become of the Swiss bankers' spy? Ah. Somehow he had wormed his way to the very front of the theatre, to the area between the seats and the platform edge, where he stood focusing his Hasselblad in the midst of a crush of television technicians. The fellow's mind was wrapped in feverish excitement, but because of the distance, it was impossible for Finster to sift out coherent thoughts. Obscurely troubled, Finster frowned.

"Ah," breathed Hannula. "It is about to start."

A white-haired woman in a heather-colored suit had come out onto the platform and stood expectantly, holding a cordless microphone at the ready. Behind her was a simple small table with another microphone, and a wooden chair. Hung upstage against a curtain backdrop was an impressive GPD video screen that measured four meters by five. It had been flashing enigmatic test patterns while the audience settled down, but now it had gone blank except for the digital time display in the lower right-hand corner that indicated 09:58. No other apparatus was in evidence.

Ready-lights on the TV cameras surrounding the platform began to wink on like wolves' eyes glittering in fireshine. Technical directors muttered into headsets, giving last-minute instructions to their colleagues who manned a great gaggle of satellite-transmission vans massed outside on George Square and Buccleuch Place. A few still-cameras clicked and buzzed prematurely and print-media people whispered establishing remarks into their microcorders. At precisely ten o'clock, the university spokeswoman cleared her throat.

"Good morning, ladies and gentlemen. I am Eloise Watson, the director of media relations for the Medical School of the University of Edinburgh. We would like to welcome you to this special demonstration and press conference organized on behalf of the Parapsychology Unit of the Department of Psychology. Immediately after the demonstration, questions will be accepted from the floor. We must ask that you hold all queries until then. And now, without further ado, let me present the man you have been waiting to meet—James Somerled MacGregor, Koestler Professor of Parapsychology."

She withdrew, and from the wings shambled a tall and loose-jointed figure. His jacket and trousers of oatmeal tweed were baggy and nondescript, but he had compensated somewhat for their drabness with a waistcoat cut from the scarlet MacGregor tartan. Still-cameras snapped and whirred and TV lenses zoomed in for close-ups of a lean and wild-eyed face. MacGregor's beaky nose and thin lips were framed with extravagant Dundreary whiskers of vivid auburn. His hair, unkempt and collar-length, was also red. He clutched a sensitive dish-tipped microphone with big bony hands, holding it up as though it were the hilt of a Highlander's claymore presented in defiant salute. When he spoke his voice was gruff, with the barest hint of a lilting western accent.

"What we're going to show you today is a thing that people of a certain mind have been doing for hundreds of years—perhaps even thousands. I learned it myself from my grandmother in the Isles, and I've managed to teach it to numbers of my colleagues. You'll be meeting some of them today. The phenomenon has been called out-of-body experience, remote-viewing, astral projection, even soul-travel. Lately, psychic researchers have taken to calling it excorporeal excursion or EE. I'll stick to those initials during the demonstration for the sake of simplicity, but you journalists can call it anything you like—just so long as you *don't* call it magic."

There were scattered laughs and murmurs.

Jamie's fierce, dark eyes glowered and the audience fell silent. "EE isn't magic! It's as real as radio or television or space flight! . . . But I didn't invite you here today to argue its authenticity. I'm going to show it to you."

He half turned, indicating the huge video screen at the rear of the platform. "With the kind assistance of the University's Astronomy Department and the GTE Corporation, we have arranged for several live television transmissions to be beamed exclusively to this theatre from other locations. I will be able to speak directly to the persons you will see, using this microphone—but they won't see me. All they will receive from me is an audio signal, like a telephone call... Now I think we're ready to begin."

At a gesture from MacGregor, a balding bearded man in his forties came on stage, saluted the audience with a wave, and seated himself at the table. Jamie said, "I'd like to introduce my old friend and colleague of twenty years, Nigel Weinstein, Associate Professor of Parapsychology here at the University. He will explain his role in a few minutes. But first—may I have the California transmission, please?"

A color picture flashed onto the screen. A smartly dressed woman and an elderly man sat in easy chairs before a low glass table. Opposite was a long settee and behind them potted plants and a window that appeared to overlook moonlit waters spanned by an enormous suspension bridge. City lights starred the surrounding hills. The display in the corner of the screen now read: SAN FRANCISCO USA 02:05.

The woman said, "Good morning, Professor MacGregor—and all of you members of the world media there in Edinburgh, Scotland! I'm Sylvia Albert and I host the Late-Late Talk Show here on KGO-TV, San Francisco. We're coming to you live via satellite in a special closed transmission that was arranged at the personal request of Dr. Lucius J. Kemp of Stanford University. Dr. Kemp is no doubt well known to you all as a distinguished brain researcher and a Nobel Laureate in Medicine... Will you tell us, Dr. Kemp, why you're participating in this demonstration?"

Kemp had been staring at his clasped hands. Now he nodded very slowly several times. "Numbers of my colleagues at Stanford have been involved in parapsychology research for some twenty-three years. I've watched their progress with great interest, even though my own work involves a different area of study—one that you might say is more conventional."

He looked directly into the camera and leveled an index finger at his viewers on the other side of the world. "*You* might say! I say parapsychology is as respectable as any other branch of psychiatry. Now I study brain cells, things you can see and touch and measure. But the brain is a peculiar piece of matter that houses the mind—which we scientists most definitely *cannot* see or touch, and which we are only incompetently able to measure. The nature of mind, and its capabilities, are still nearly as mysterious as outer space. It wasn't too many years ago that the majority of educated people—scientists especially—dismissed parapsychology as nonsense. Things aren't that way today, but there are still skeptics in the scientific establishment who will try to assure you that paranormal psychic phenomena are either non-existent or else freakish effects without practical value. I am not one of those scientists . . ."

The screen in the Edinburgh lecture theatre was now filled with the Nobel Laureate's face, copper-brown skin stretched over high cheekbones, black eyes narrowed with the intensity of his emotion, a few drops of perspiration trickling from the snowy wool of his hair onto his broad forehead. Then he flashed a brilliant smile.

"Because of that, the parapsychology researchers at Stanford nailed me! They asked for my help with this experiment, and they got it. That's why I'm here in the wee hours of the morning along with Miss Albert and the director and crew of her show and the three impartial witnesses we've asked to assist us."

The camera pulled back again and the talk-show hostess rapidly explained how the experiment was going to work. The three witnesses had each been asked to bring a small card with a picture or a few lines of writing. The subject of the card was to be known only to them, and they had sealed it inside three successive envelopes. The witnesses now waited in the TV studio's green room, where guests assembled before being taken on stage for their interviews. There were no cameras in the green room and the monitor there had been disconnected.

Now Jamie MacGregor asked, "Miss Albert, is it true that there is no means of outside communication in this green room? No telephones or radio equipment?"

"None whatsoever," she said.

"Very good. I want to be sure that the journalists with us here in Edinburgh understand that. Go on, Lucius. Tell us what your own part in the experiment will be."

"I'll wait," Kemp said, "until you tell me that your colleague, Dr. Weinstein, is ready to undertake a remote-viewing of those cards the three witnesses have hidden away on their persons. When you give me the word, I'll go to the green room and stand in the doorway. I'll ask the witnesses to take out the envelopes and hold them up, unopened, for two minutes. After that they'll

accompany me back here to the cameras, envelopes still unopened. And then we'll see, won't we?" He smiled.

"Aye, we certainly will," Jamie said. "Thank you, Lucius."

The audience in the theatre let out a collective sigh. Seats
creaked as many of them hunched forward. Jamie was holding a
whispered colloquy with Nigel. The KGB agent turned to Finster
and whispered, "If this works—great God, the repercussions!"

"You can say that again," the Mafia's man agreed. "In Fin-
nish."

Nigel picked up his own microphone. He was still seated at
the table, while Jamie had withdrawn to the left side of the platform.

"I'm afraid," Weinstein said, his expression mischievous,
"that your worst suspicions are about to be confirmed. I'm going
into a trance."

Tension-relieving laughter.

"Usually we do this EE business in a soundproofed room to
avoid distraction. We relax in a kind of glorified barber's chair
equipped with monitoring gadgets that tell what our brains and
bods are up to while our minds go soaring through the blue
empyrean . . . but that wouldn't do today. We want you to see how
ordinary EE can be. But I warn you—don't cough or drop your
pencils or crack chewing gum while I'm off, or I just might
crumble to dust before your eyes like Dracula in the sunlight."

More laughter. Then total silence.

Nigel had closed his eyes and was breathing slowly and
deeply. Up on the giant video screen the American scientist and
the talk-show hostess waited.

"Ready," said Nigel in a flat voice.

Jamie spoke into his microphone. "You may go to the green
room now, Lucius."

The California camera followed Kemp into the studio wings,
where he vanished amidst a clutter of equipment. Then it swiveled back to Sylvia Albert and held. Twenty-six seconds clicked
by on the digital display.

Nigel's eyes opened. "Got it," he said simply.

Jamie went to the platform edge. "Would one of you be so
kind as to pass up a sheet of paper and something to write with?"

A BBC technical director thrust up a yellow sheet and a pen-
cil. Jamie nodded his thanks and passed them on to Nigel, who
scribbled energetically for a few minutes. Then he gave the sheet

back to Jamie, who returned it to the BBC man, saying, "Hold on to that. We'll want you to read it shortly."

Almost nine thousand kilometers away, the two minutes having passed, Dr. Kemp was returning to the talk-show set leading two women and a man. The newcomers sat down at the glass table and placed their sealed envelopes in front of them.

Sylvia Albert said, "May I present our guinea pigs! Lola McCafferty Lopez, Assistant District Attorney for San Francisco County; Maureen Sedgewick, Associate Editor of the *San Francisco Chronicle*; and Rabbi Milton Green of the B'nai B'rith Hillel Foundation of the University of California at Berkeley . . . Now, will you tell us what results you have, Professor MacGregor?"

Jamie leaned down to the BBC crewman. "Sir, would you please read out what Dr. Weinstein wrote?" He reversed his microphone so that the tiny parabolic receiving dish at its tip was aimed at the technician.

"First card," came the man's voice clearly. "From a Monopoly game: GO DIRECTLY TO JAIL, DO NOT COLLECT $200."

The audience roared as on the screen, the attorney ripped open her multiple envelopes and showed the card. The cartoon face peering through bars loomed in an extreme close-up.

"Second card," the BBC man read. "Handwritten quote from Shakespeare: 'To be, or not to be: that is the question.' "

The Edinburgh audience was murmuring loudly. As the California camera zoomed in for the second confirmation the noise swelled to a clamor. Jamie lifted his arms. "Please! There's still Rabbi Green's card."

The BBC man read, "Picture postcard of planet Earth taken from space with handwritten note on back: 'Let there be light.' "

Instead, there was bedlam.

The false reporter from the *Helsingen Sanomat* covered his face with his hands and groaned, "Yob tvoyu mat'!" Finster appended, "In spades, tovarishch."

While the hubbub quieted, Jamie gave brief thanks to the California participants and the screen blanked out. Almost immediately it was replaced by a new image, a stark newsroom desk backed by a station logo: TV-3 AUCKLAND. A comfortably homely man and a blond young woman with an abstracted Mona Lisa smile sat close together at one end of the desk. The time was 20:18.

"Good evening, Professor MacGregor! Ron Wiggins here,

with your graduate student Miss Alana Shaunavon, who flew in on Air New Zealand SST from London earlier today. Alana, tell us just a little bit about yourself."

"I'm a doctoral candidate in parapsychology at Edinburgh University, where I work with Professor Jamie MacGregor. There are thirty-two of us at the Unit, in various stages of training for EE—excorporeal excursion. I was chosen to come here and attempt to view a message written by a member of the audience there at the Edinburgh press conference."

Ron Wiggins gave a worldly chuckle. "Well, we'll give it a fair go!...And here to keep a sharp eye on things are Bill Drummond of the *Auckland Star*, Melanie Te Wiata of the *New Zealand Herald*, and Les Seymour of the *Wellington Evening Post*."

The camera panned over the scribes, who sat at the opposite end of the desk, looking aloof. Wiggins said, "As I understand it, Alana will leave her body here in Kiwi Land and attempt to project herself more than eighteen thousand kilometers to Scotland—"

"Excuse me," the girl interrupted firmly. The close-up showed eyes of a magnetic emerald green. Her voice was low and cajoling as she contradicted Wiggins. "It's really not like that, you know. Subjectively, I may feel as though I were traveling, but I don't—any more than we travel when we dream. Current metapsychic theory holds that the EE experience is a type of sensory response, like long-distance sight. Farsight. But it's not mystical, and my mind certainly doesn't leave my body."

"Mm," Wiggins said. "Be that as it may, let me assure our witnesses here and overseas that we have no electronic means of viewing events there at the Edinburgh press conference. Furthermore, we aren't broadcasting this transmission to our national audience. It's a coded impulse beamed solely to Scotland via satellite. We are recording here for a later presentation, however, in conjunction with the material we expect to receive from our people on the scene in Edinburgh...And now, Alana, are you ready to begin?"

"Yes."

Jamie spoke once again to the BBC man who had read Nigel's results aloud: "Sir, will you please select a colleague in your immediate vicinity to write our sample message for Alana?"

"Right," said the Beeb technician. "How about this Swiss bloke over here with the Hasselblad?"

There was a brief wrangle when the Swiss seemed reluctant to cooperate, apparently perturbed when camera lenses were aimed in his direction by the TV crews of several dozen nations.

Fabian Finster felt the skin along his spine tingle with the same uneasy premonition he had experienced earlier. He whispered to the KGB agent, "You know anything about that guy? Otto Maurer, his badge says, photographer for the *Neue Zürcher Zeitung* . . . but I have reasons to doubt that he's legit."

"He would not have been admitted without a computerized credential check. He is surely a bona fide journalist. As legitimate as you or I."

"Idi v zhopu," scoffed The Fabulous Finster. The thunderstruck Russian gaped at him.

Meanwhile, the Swiss had evidently complied with the request to pen a brief message. Jamie MacGregor was saying, "Thank you, Herr Maurer. Now if you will place the sheet of paper on the floor, face down. None of the people around you have seen what you've written? . . . Good. You must try not to think of it, either. EE seems to be an ultrasense quite distinct from telepathy. It also seems inconsequential what position the target object may be in, or what barriers of matter may lie between the target and the percipient. What we seek to demonstrate is that EE makes it possible for trained persons to remotely view virtually anything in any part of the world."

A wave of incredulous exclamations swept the hall. Somebody called out, "But if that's true, it means—"

"Please!" Jamie held up his hand again. "Let us have the demonstration first, then the questions."

"I have already read the paper," came the amplified voice of Alana Shaunavon. Her young face was enormous on the screen, the brilliant green eyes fixed, wide open, blinking slowly. "He has written a verse in German:

> Die Gedanken sind frei,
> Wer kann sie erraten?
> Sie fliegen vorbei
> Wie nächtliche Schatten.
> Kein Mensch kann sie wissen,
> Kein Jäger erschiessen.
> Es bleibet dabei: die Gedanken sind frei.

I can translate it rather freely: 'Thoughts are free, who can discover them? They fly past like shadows of the night. No one can know them, no hunter can shoot them down. When all's said and done, thoughts—' *My God, look out! His camera! It's a weapon!*"

A wild fracas broke out on the floor and there were shouts as the Swiss attempted vainly to rush away. But too many bodies and too much equipment hemmed him in and he went down, tackled by two intrepid Canadian Broadcasting Corporation telecasters. The lethal Hasselblad was wrested away and smashed by a soundman of the Fuji Network. Plainclothes police officers materialized and camera crews leapt about balletically recording the capture.

As Maurer was being hauled away, he screamed, "Fools! Crétins! Er hat Sie alles beschissen! Don't you know what's going on here? What this MacGregor has done? Um Gottes Willen . . . Pandora's box . . . ruin . . . chaos . . . anarchy . . . Weltgetümmel . . ."

The uproar subsided slowly. Jamie spoke into his microphone and the screen was wiped clear of the New Zealand transmission. There was a burst of video clutter and then the simple advisory:

OVERSEAS TELEPHONE MESSAGE READY
AUDIO SIGNAL ONLY

"Jamie? Jamie? I could not wait!" A woman's voice, speaking heavily accented English, came through a hiss of interference. "I saw everything—but then I became so excited that I lost the sight! Tell me—is everything all right?"

The confusion subsided and the attention of the crowd of newspeople was drawn once again to the platform. Jamie MacGregor tugged at one of his Dundreary cheek-whiskers. His expression was resigned. "All is quite well for the moment, lass. But I think this wee carfuffle's only the beginning of what we'll be seeing anon."

"Yes, that's true . . . Are you ready for me to speak? I must not waste any time. We may be cut off at any moment if my little bypass of the monitored circuitry is traced."

Jamie said, "Just wait for a moment, while I ask our Edinburgh University communications people to show the journalists in our audience where this telephone call is coming from."

The loudspeakers trilled a brief electronic aria and the video display printed an advisory:

ORIGINATING: 68−23−79 ALMA-ATA USSR
VIA SKS-8 + EUS-02 GTE/BT 4−3

The female voice said, "I am Tamara Petrovna Sakhvadze, Deputy Director of the Institute for Bioenergetic Studies at Kazakh State University, and a member of the Kazakh Academy of Sciences."

"Nevozmozhno!" A pained whisper escaped the false Hannula. Others in the lecture theatre seemed equally unbelieving and they sprang to their feet shouting questions.

"Silence!" Jamie roared. Then he spoke gently into the microphone. "Tell us why you've joined the demonstration today, Tamara Petrovna."

"I am a person who loves my country and its people. I am also a scientist, dedicated to discovering truth. And finally, I am the mother of three small children whose minds are just beginning to flower. I have worked in the field of parapsychology since 1968, when I was only a young child. My late husband, Dr. Yuri Gawrys, was my close associate. Like Jamie MacGregor, I have specialized in the phenomenon of excorporeal excursion, along with clairvoyance and certain other metafaculties. On several occasions, I have . . . met with Jamie and with certain other scientists in other parts of the world. When Jamie told me he was determined to demonstrate EE, I agreed with his decision. The work we are doing here in Alma-Ata falls under the highest security classification, and this telephone call is a technical violation of Soviet law. And yet I make it with the full consent of every one of my colleagues here at the Institute, in the interests of all humanity.

"You people, listening to my words being beamed to you via many satellites, try to understand! You Americans, especially, listen! The whole world will benefit from what we do today. To my fellow citizens of the Soviet Union who hear me, I say: Eto novoye otkrytiye prinesyot polzu vsyemu chelovyechestvu! An extraordinary door is opening, and from behind it shines a light that does away with all state secrets. There can be no more clandestine weapons research, no surprise military actions, no first-strike capability. The people of the Soviet Union need no longer fear attack by the USA, and Americans need no longer fear us.

We can now work to resolve our differences without the threat of accidental or deliberate nuclear war. Our children can look into the future with hope again. My children can ... and Jamie's ... and yours."

The voice paused, and the immediate response of those listening was like the upsurge of a tremendous rising wind, wordless, laden with emotional energy. But before the sound wave could crest, Jamie cried out, "Wait! Let her finish!"

She said, "I was there with you, a witness to one man's despair. I saw his violent reaction when he realized what changes we must expect when the higher mind-powers come into common use. He was afraid. He warned of Pandora's box, and perhaps his warning is justified. 'Die Gedanken sind frei' ... thoughts are free, but with freedom comes responsibility. There will be great difficulties to overcome if we are not to exchange one kind of danger for another. But the door is opened and nothing can close it! A new age of the mind has dawned on our planet and all of us must enter into it. We must face this terrible new enlightenment courageously, together. As a first step ... I invite you, my dear Jamie, and all of the scientists in the world who study the higher mind-powers to come to a meeting—the First Congress on Metapsychology. I invite the journalists of the world also. Come to Alma-Ata next year, in September when the fragrance of ripening apples fills our lovely city. Come and let us take the first step toward mir miru—a world at peace."

"Tamara, my lass, we'll be there," said Jamie MacGregor. Then he bowed his head to the tumult of shouting that erupted in the theatre and waited patiently until order was restored and he could begin answering the questions.

After the press conference was long over, two foreigners with press ID badges still pinned to their raincoats sat together in Greyfriars Bobby's Bar, making steady inroads on a bottle of the Macallen. The astonishing news had spread like wildfire and the place was packed, rocking with song and jollification as students and other celebrators marked the arrival of the new age of the mind with an impromptu ceilidh that showed signs of escalating into a riot.

"I never knew 'Comin' Through the Rye' had words like that." The Fabulous Finster was slightly scandalized.

"Hah," said the KGB man. "You should hear the unexpurgated version of 'For A' That.' Or 'Duncan Gray.' Or 'Green Grow the Rashes, O!' Yes, the Scottish hero poet, Robert Burns, wrote very earthy songs. We are very fond of him in my country. He was truly of the proletariat." He brought his glass down onto the tiny table with a thud and caroled in a raspy basso:

> "Green grow the rashes, O!
>   Green grow the rashes, O!
> The lassies they hae wimble-bores,
>   The widows they hae gashes, O!"

The patrons gave a yell of approval. Somebody with an accordion tried to drag the Russian from his seat; but he shook his head violently, red-rimmed eyes gone wide, and croaked, "No! I will not sing! I cannot sing!"

Nobody took it amiss. Usquebalian dejection is no novelty in an Edinburgh pub. The musical gilravagers directed their attention elsewhere and Finster refilled his companion's glass. "Drink up, Sergei, old hoss. I know why you're feeling low. To tell the truth, I'm a trifle shook-up myself. Talk about a bombshell! My Boss back home'll be farting flames. Yours, too, I betcha."

The Russian agent tossed down the dram and began to pour another. "You are talking nonsense. And my name is Sami, not Sergei."

Finster shrugged. He reached out, clamping the other man's hand tightly to the bottle, and leaned very close. His face was so friendly, so droll. With that gap between the large front teeth, the face seemed like that of a saucy squirrel in a cartoon show for children. Who could feel threatened by a squirrel?

"Tell me honestly, Sergei. Do you think that dame in Alma-Ata will be able to pull it off? The open-door psychic congress? Or has she bought herself and her bunch a quick ticket to the Gulag?"

It was not a comical squirrel asking such questions. It was not even a reporter from Seattle, U.S.A. Who was it? Why was it so necessary to answer this funny little man?

"She was devilishly clever . . . Deputy Director Sakhvadze . . . just like a damned Georgian . . . knowing our countries still officially embrace détente . . . and *we* must uphold noble world-image . . . next year Diamond Jubilee Revolution! . . . Sakhvadze all but confesses she and her cohorts are involved in Mind

Wars research . . . just as your scientists are also, belka! . . . What a joke on both our countries . . . we must fulfill the world's expectations of us now, like it or not . . . Die Gedanken sind frei und wir stehen bis zum Hals in der Scheisse . . ."

The squirrel did not seem willing to believe this. "Do you mean your government is going to let her get away with it?"

The tipsy KGB man laughed, then blew his nose resoundingly. Finster's coercion was no longer needed. "Little squirrel, she has *already* got away with it. In that lecture hall were perhaps forty television cameras, trained on MacGregor and his video screen. Sakhvadze's words and their origination were broadcast live to our people as well as to the rest of the world. We cannot claim her message was a hoax because its source in Alma-Ata can be verified easily by the computers of British Telecom. Doubtless this verification will also be trumpeted to the world via the free satellite transmissions . . . Oh, yes! The lovely Tamara Petrovna has caught both the Soviet and American governments by the balls, and she is on a downhill slide. The Cold War is over, thanks to the Scottish Professor. You and I are washed up, Amerikanskiy. You are not CIA—but whatever you are, you are finished. The soul-travelers and the mind readers will expose the most closely guarded secrets of our two nations as easily as cracking hazelnuts. There is nothing left for us but to become friends . . . just as Robert Burns wished. Yes, little squirrel! The proletarian poet of Scotland was a great prophet! Do you know what he said?

> For a' that, and a' that,
>   It's comin' yet, for a' that!
> That man and man the world o'er
>   Shall brothers be for a' that."

"Sure," Finster agreed, smiling. "Sure, Sergei. One for all, and all for one. At least until we get rid of our mutual enemies."

19

FROM THE MEMOIRS OF
ROGATIEN REMILLARD

WHEN THE LIVE TELECAST FROM EDINBURGH ENDED AT 7:00 A.M. Eastern Time I was in a state of near-mortal funk. I downed a neat tumblerful of Canadian Club sitting there in my armchair in front of the blank television screen while my brain kept replaying that scene of the crazed Swiss photographer screeching his Cassandra warning as the Scottish police hauled him away.

Pandora's box! Oh, yes, indeed. It was opening wide to an amazed and fascinated world, and what was inside was *us*.

I had to call Denis. I told myself it was to find out what plans he and his people had. On my first three tries, his home phone was busy; then I only got his answering machine. I called the lab and reached Glenn Dalembert, who had come in early to make a videotape of the Scottish demonstration.

"Yeah, I got detailed for the scut-work while everybody else watched the big show in comfort at home. This afternoon we'll do a replay for the full Medical School faculty, together with learned commentary by yours truly and homegrown EE talent displays by Colette and Tucker. With Denis gone, I'll be in charge. Want a freebie ticket?"

"Denis has gone where?" I demanded.

"Down to West Lebanon. They're sending an Air Force chopper to shuttle him to Burlington International where the Washington flight will be held for him—"

I cut Glenn off. *"They?* D'you mean those Mind Wars bastards roped Denis in after all?"

My nephew's associate gave a strained laugh. "Oh, no. Nothing so picayune as the Army or the CIA this time. The President himself called Denis at home right after the telecast. Seems he read the book and was very impressed, and now he's pegged

Denis as the guy most likely to give him the straight poop about the authenticity of MacGregor's block buster."

"Oh, shit," I groaned. My nephew—the Kissinger of meta-psychic realpolitik! He would be asked to help recruit American operants for MacGregor's noble scheme. He would certainly reveal his own operancy. Or would he?

Glenn had turned solicitous. "Roger, is there something wrong?"

"*Everything's* wrong."

"Listen—come to the faculty meeting and we'll talk. Better yet, join Colette and me for lunch—"

"No thanks. You folks have a good time at the show-and-tell. I'll be just fine." I hung up, then took the phone off the hook.

Denis. He was the only one who could help. I could try to reach him at the airport by telephone . . . but that was no good. I wouldn't be able to *say* what was wrong . . .

Farspeak him, then. Make the appeal mind-to-mind.

I slouched over to the bedroom window and stood there in my pajamas and grubby old terry-cloth robe trying to marshal my booze-addled wits. It was not going to be easy to attract Denis's attention with the all-important telepathic "hail." My mind was weakened and Denis would surely be preoccupied with the enormity of MacGregor's gamble and by the upcoming Oval Office meeting. Furthermore, the bulk of Crafts Hill lay between me and the West Lebanon Regional Airport, four miles south of Hanover. I would have to muster up sufficient strength to "flow" my mental shout around the hill and puncture my nephew's brown study. Once alerted, he would have no difficulty tuning in to my puny thought-beam.

But how was I going to manage that initial hail?

An idea slowly formed. One of my yogic exercises featured a spiral focusing of body energies spinning centripetally in toward the heart, which certain psychic authorities proposed as the vital center of the modern human being. This so-called in-spiraling chakra meditation had tended to promote feelings of comfort and power even in my beleaguered soul. I could do it. The reverse form of the exercise, the out-spiral, had carried a cautionary note for novices. It was alleged to have more drastic effects in the focusing of energies and was more difficult to control. Since additional psychic trauma was the last thing I had needed during the awful summer and fall, up until now I had given this particular form of meditation a firm miss. But it might just offer me my best shot at reaching Denis.

I assumed the appropriate posture, one I had dubbed "Leonardo's X-Man," still standing there at the window. I closed my eyes, shielded myself from external stimuli as best I could, and concentrated on the region of my heart. Far more than a mere blood-pump, the heart is also a gland whose secretions help in the regulation of the entire body. I tried to visualize it as the focus of my being, a receptacle of life-force and love. When there was a distinct knot of warmth behind my lower breastbone, I coaxed it out to begin a slow, tight, flattened curve. It moved to the left and downward, traversing my solar plexus. Gaining strength and speed, it spiraled smoothly up to the branching of the trachea and the thymal remnant, then arced left within the body's frontal plane. It dove down through my spleen, illuminated the suprarenals, and swung back up toward the thyroid in my throat—for the first time passing outside my body as the spiral widened. A long curve brought the still-meager ball of energy to the root of my spine, where lay the chakra that yogic tradition deemed one of the most vital. I felt a great influx of fresh power enlarge and accelerate the ball. It swung upward, seemed to blaze behind my closed eyes, and began its final swift circuit through the elbow of my extended left arm, through my left and right knees, through my right elbow. I was waiting as it flew toward the crown of my head and branded it with the impress of a single mental signature, adding a dollop of heavenly appeal as a sop to the faith of my fathers. Then I hurled it away from me, that cri de coeur véritable:

DENIS!

Simultaneous with the farspoken hail came a terrific neural ignition, part orgasm and part high-voltage shock. My body convulsed and I fell heavily to the floor.

[Images: Full-color 3-D Denis face stunned. Air Force helicopter open door blades windmill tearing fog fabric colored runway lights yellow Toyota Land Cruiser.]

???GoodGodUncleRogi??? What'sWRONG?

. . . sorry . . . trying hard get your attention . . .

! You almost blasted me off my feet whatinhell you upto I suppose Glenn told you WhiteHouse summons . . . !!! . . . HOW DID YOU DO THAT?

[Image drenched in sheepishness.] Outspiral chakra Leon-

ardo's X with cyclotronic kundalini embellishment . . . worked a little better than expected . . .

Fuckingidiot! Don't you know that could be dangerous?

Yes.

Acute anxiety. Dammit bon sang d'imbécile you leave that stuff alone until we go over it together I really *mean* what I say!

Yesyesyes but had to reach you had to . . . [image].

Concern. EdinburghDemo provoked fear? Explain.

[Concatenated images.]

Uncle Rogi . . . what you need I can't do at a distance. But you must believe me when I tell you it will be all right. *[Airman beckons inside chopper Denis nods ducks blades scurries into aircraft door shuts airman orders seat belt signals pilot upup&away.]*

Denis . . . what President want?

You can probably guess: my analysis assessment Scottelecast. Legit? Practicable solution armsrace? Howmany EEops potential US/USSR/Scotland/Elsewhere? When online? Anychance Russ have jump on us already emplace their Psi-Eye?

Psi-Eye?

Prexyname ever the GreatSalesman. Fortunately can tell him Russ EEprogram controlled by Tamara [kiss!] she deceived Politburo re her project readiness so not emplaced. Russ EEops all peaceniks group purged of GRU/KGB/opportunist/fanatic heads last decade. Now Russ operants tend antiestablishment because "elitist phenom operancy" remains suspect under Marxist dogmatism. Tamara will see to honest observer team setup. There will be no war.

That was never my worry. Too selfish . . .

Then?

[Projected image: Screaming figure waving camera disappears beneath bodycrush hauled up handcuffed dragged away.] Pandora's box ruin chaos anarchy and worse OUR EXPOSURE OURS DENIS!

Difficult days yes there will have to be economic summits global cooperation in many other psychaffected areas—

You don't understand yet what I've driving at! We will be pawns manipulated hated the coercers willbe offered power over others—

This won't happen. Do you think we haven't anticipated such a thing? It was dealt with in the longrange plan that had to be scrapped but we will preserve our freedom and dignity. President wants set up MetaBrainTrust. Public. Plan for best use other operant faculties besides EE goodofcountry goodofworld. Guess who invited to be chairman?

! You had to write that goddam book.

Relax. My forte research not administration. I'll decline with humblethanks let Brawley of Stanford or The Astronaut sit in Washington metahotseat.

How can you not listen when 900-lb canary sings?

Laughter. Now you know why I had no photo on bookjacket *Metapsychology*. All President has to do is take look at me [image] would YOU entrust Third Millennium diplomacy to half-baked egghead twerp? . . . I'm safe plan propose myself special advisor sortof GrandYoungMan metapsychology.

Denis . . . are you going to tell him that you're operant?

Yes. I'm sorry Uncle Rogi . . . for your sake. But soonerorlater we have to come out with it.

Despair. Later. Much later.

Yes . . . I argued JamieMacGregor pleaded caution wanted postpone until operants numerous more organized for selfpreservation and my training normals-operancy proved feasible. But MacGregor cited increasing peril globalwar . . . and another factor. He said: We are all members humanrace survive or perish together no Homosapiens vs Homosuperior only Homoterrestris. Earth Man.

Resignation. Bitterness. Still terrible gamble Godsake nobody seriously believes Russ planning launch WorldWarIII—

That was not deciding factor. I told you there was something else. Someone tried to kill Jamie in April. He was afraid his whole group endangered so decided to go to ground do demo soonest. His attacker not KGB/GRU/CIA/XXX. *He was another powerful operant.*

Jésus Christ.

Man coerced Jamie into darkalley physique metarendered fuzzy aimed tubething at paralyzed Jamie apologetic implacability just then muscleman in duffelcoat came scared off assailant was not affected coercion nextday Jamie examined alley found needle later analyzed coated deadly poison ricin favorite assassins no other clue attacker . . . or rescuer. Damn worrying.

Operant crooks in Scotland! So NewHampshire doesn't have monopoly afterall. [Familiar image quickly erased.]

Jamie says coercive ability assassin formidable. Disguising of appearance interesting jibes with my currentstudies creativity—

The mysterious power to cloud men's minds. The Shadow knows! . . . Or are you too young to know that nonsense?

I've heard classic radiotapes. But apparently attacker not really invisible or passerby might not have saved Jamie. Affair peculiar. If not metagovernmentagent (impossible we would *know*) then who?

Wild card. Odd John had one. Psychometa.

Jamie positive attacker sane.

You intend tell President metavillains atlarge?

Will mention possibility. But this minor compared to prospect end nucleardeterrent.

MacGregor figure he's safe now?

He thinks now Psi-Eye scheme revealed danger minimal. Actually SwissBankAgentfakephotographer had best motive for offing Jamie. Perhaps metassassin another of theirs. Governments not only ones with valuable secrets.

Be sure you tell President that. Eventually we'll need bodyguards and they come expensive.

Hogwash.

Pauvre innocent! Go go carry out great mission pray Goodness triumphs . . . Were other academiclights also summoned President?

He said no. Maybe later.

Hah. So that's wayofit. By time you return Dartmouth you famous inspiteofself President will see to it whetherornot you agree head BrainTrust.

Humor. It was the book. Talking heads come&go but if you write book you are AUTHORity.

Laughter. Easing.

. . . Uncle Rogi we're approaching Burlington International. Please try not to worry. When I get home you must let me try to help you. (Yes yes I know how could I not tu es mon père!) Other Remillards all over US&Canada will find selves in your position after I exit metacloset. Most of them will cheerfully admit they haven't a metafaculty to save their lives. You can too. But it would be best if you didn't conceal your powers. Best for you for all operants as well. We must hurry day when operancy commonplace as musical/artistic/intellectual talent similarly unthreat to normals—damn!—there I go we're just as *normal* as they are aren't we?

Pour sûr. [?]

Nonoperants will realize in time that they have nothing to fear
from us.

But they do.

Oh Uncle Rogi.

. . . and we have even more to fear from them. We're outnum-
bered.

Exasperation. If you spent some time with us at the lab you'd
know we're finding ways to . . . neutralize . . . antagonists. Peaceful ways. You and your oneman stand! You don't have to face
this alone can't you see the only way is through solidarity even
nonoperants know a lonemind is doomed there must be two or
three or more loving for Love to heal and initiate transcendence
please please monpère don't shut us out—

We'll discuss later. Smallthing compared momentous events
demanding your attention. You must not be distracted.

We are landing . . . Please Uncle Rogi please join us. [Guile.]
You will ease my mind.

Will think over carefully. Bon voyage et bonne chance mon
fils.

I stood looking out the window. Outside, the morning mist
was burning away and the streetlights had gone out. I was
hungry, very nearly cheerful, but still perversely determined to
best my inner demons in single combat. I would certainly have to
find out just what self-defensive maneuvers Denis and his people
had discovered, but as to joining with them—letting Denis into
the secret parts of my mind—it was impossible. A Franco father
cannot stand naked before his son.

As I stared at the passing cars below and the students hurrying
up Main Street toward their early classes a mundane thought stole
into my skull. If the presidential favor did confer fresh notoriety
upon my nephew, there would surely be a great new demand for
copies of *Metapsychology*. If I called the jobbers in Boston with a
rush order, I could get a leg up on the competition at the big
Dartmouth Bookstore down the street. And when Denis returned,
I might prevail on him to do a signing session. He had never
autographed copies of his book before, but he might agree to help
me out.

Just as I was turning away from the window my eyes focused
upon the glass itself. I swore mildly. Some damn kid with a
BB-gun must have been taking pot shots at squirrels. There was a

small hole neatly drilled in one of the upper panes. But it was a strange hole, lacking the typical halo crater produced by the impact of a missile, and there were no cracks radiating from it. It was about a quarter of an inch in diameter and the edges were not sharp, but smooth. Perplexed, I studied the tiny opening, which was above my eye level. Then I went to a drawer in the kitchen and got a tape measure.

The hole was six feet two inches above the floor, my exact height in bare feet. I felt a blob of warmth begin to form again behind my ribs. Wondering, I touched the top of my head.

Surely not. But on the other hand . . .

Denis would no doubt be eager to test it. Should I agree? Why not, provided the rest of my mind was left inviolate? I chuckled at the thought of the consternation this "mind-zap" power would provoke among the academics. Nothing in any of my readings on parapsychology had prepared me for an effect such as this, nor had there been any mention of it in the lengthy catalog of higher mental phenomena in Denis's book. Not only was my zapping new, it was also fraught with possibility . . .

How d'you like *them* apples, Donnie? Maybe you better rest in peace if you know what's good for you, mon frérot!

I went to the telephone. It was after 8:30 and the book jobber in Boston would be open. I decided to triple the order I had originally decided upon. Denis would beef about the autograph session, but he'd cooperate.

Now I was certain of it.

20

ALMA-ATA, KAZAKH SSR, EARTH
24 OCTOBER 1991

ANY OTHER GENERAL SECRETARY WOULD HAVE COMMANDED HER immediate presence in Moscow before a Star Chamber tribunal. It was a mark of this man's populist style, and his shrewdness in dealing with the often nonconformist scientific element, that he came to her. He dismissed his hovering aides, sat casually in front of her desk in the small corner office of the Institute for Bioenergetic Studies at Kazakh State University, and chatted about the weather.

Tamara served him tea without hurrying. Afterward she did not resume her normal seat behind the desk but pulled up a side chair next to him. They could both look out the window and see the high Tien Shan's white rampart in the south. The day was brilliant, but the first storm of the season was forecast for tomorrow. He would decline the proferred hospitality of the Kazakh Party Secretary and fly back to Moscow tonight.

"And tell the comrades of the Politburo your elucidation of the Edinburgh Demonstration," he concluded, sipping the tea. "Delicious."

"I have prepared a précis of our work on excorporeal excursion." She smiled winsomely, a plump, dark-eyed woman whose shining red hair was worn in a tidy knot, and indicated a sealed portfolio on the desk. "It also contains recommendations for the speedy establishment of a corps of psychic observers. I will be honored to cooperate in its deployment, of course."

He eyed her over the rim of the tea glass. "Of course. I daresay we couldn't do without you . . ."

She shrugged. "I know my people and their capabilities. This EE business is often more of an art than a science. You understand that the operants will require congenial working conditions in order to do their work properly. They are loyal Soviet citizens —you have my word of honor on it—but fully committed to peace."

The General Secretary sighed. "This is going to be difficult."

"For us," she said, "it has been difficult for twenty-five years."

The General Secretary finished his tea and took up the portfolio. Unsealing it, he leafed through the papers. After a few minutes of silence, he said, "You were not at all surprised to see me come here, Comrade Doctor."

"I confess that I was curious about the reaction of the Politburo to the Edinburgh Demonstration, as were all of my people. We did not think you would panic, but we had to be sure."

"Radi Boga! You spied on us!"

"And on the American President and his advisers, and on the leaders of the People's Republic of China, and on the Pope."

"The Pope?" The General Secretary was taken aback. "What did he do?"

"He wept, Mikhail Semyonovich."

"And so did Comrade Dankov of the KGB," the Secretary muttered. "You will be interested to know—if you don't already —that the ever-vigilant comrades on Dzerzhinsky Square were foreskinned to a marked degree at your personal participation in the Edinburgh Demonstration. Dankov demanded the immediate liquidation of you and your entire cadre of wizards. It seems you have deceived your KGB sponsors rather spectacularly."

"It was a matter of survival..."

"As you know, Dankov was made to see reason. There was greater difficulty with the Defense Council. Marshal Kumylzhensky pushed for a pre-emptive nuclear strike. This is still a serious option if we do not have a competent EE inspection team to balance that in the West."

"We have sixty-eight EE adepts, most with global faculties. It is an adequate number. The combined EE adepts of the West number more than eighty—over thirty in Britain, perhaps forty-five in the USA. There are also scattered groups of neutralist percipients in other countries. Their numbers will grow, as will our own."

The little office was becoming chilly with the close of day, but the General Secretary's balding head had a gleam of sweat. "The militarist lunatics were voted down resoundingly for now. The Politburo knows that the present euphoric mood of our people would never countenance a first strike—no more than it would allow the psychics to be harmed. The people demand—demand! —that MacGregor's proposal be implemented."

"There was dancing in the streets of Alma-Ata," Tamara said.

"And in Moscow. And everywhere throughout the Soviet Union! By allowing them to view that telecast—and we are investigating *that*, too!—we have indeed opened the door to a new age. But that age may not be golden, as you and your idealistic associates hope, Tamara Petrovna. You know that I have been striving for years now to upgrade our faltering economy, to instill a new spirit of industry and progress into our people, to control military adventurism, to fight the ingrained corruption, the laziness, the despair infecting our youth...And now, suddenly, there is this! Our enemies all around us will be thwarted in aggression by the psychic observers. The people will expect drastic disarmament initiatives. They will believe that reductions in our huge defense budget will bring about improved domestic conditions. For a while, they will wait patiently for this to come about.

Perhaps they will wait as long as a decade, distracted by our travels to Mars and other wonders. But then . . ."

"I read your subvocal thoughts, Comrade General Secretary. We are not a unified nation. Discipline and right order have up until now been preserved among our disparate ethnic elements primarily through the Great Russian bureaucracy, and the people's determination to stand fast and defend the Motherland against the common enemy."

Smoothly, he took up the skein of his own thoughts again. "But without that enemy to distract us, the masses will look more critically at the kind of life they live—at the inefficiencies of our system, at the often unjust decrees of the central power structure, at our economy based upon obsolete philosophic principles that falls further and further behind the other industrialized nations of the world . . . Look into your crystal ball, Tamara Petrovna, you and your psychic colleagues with your shining dream of peace for the future! Will we have that peace in the Soviet Union? Will we be able to adapt fast enough to avoid catastrophe?"

She turned her face away abruptly, lips tightening. "I don't know. Sometimes I *do* see the future. And far away . . . years from now . . . there is a great change, a time of expanding horizons, when our people will help to colonize the stars as we now seek to colonize Mars . . . But the near future? I do not see that, Comrade General Secretary. Thank God I do not. The job of guiding our nation through the last perilous years of this twentieth century is yours, not mine—and I also thank God for that. Now take the portfolio with the details of the psychic-oversight scheme, and do what you must."

"While you watch," he said.

She rose from her chair, turning her back on him, and looked out at the gleaming mountains. "While the world watches."

21

FROM THE MEMOIRS OF
ROGATIEN REMILLARD

THE SPECIFICS OF THE EE MONITORING PLAN WERE PROMPTLY DE-
livered to both Washington and Moscow, and a Summit was
scheduled. The much-battered Strategic Arms Limitation Treaty
was dusted off, updated, and promised to an exultant world as a
Christmas present.

In the United States, the emplacement of Psi-Eye was considered a fait accompli by the general public—and the White House
did nothing to discourage the impression, nor did the Soviets.
Most people were happy to believe that vigilant American EE
adepts (inevitably dubbed pEEps) had settled in on the job immediately following the Scottish telecast. There were "Big Brother
Is Watching You" jokes and voyeuristic editorial cartoons, however, and a tentative panic on Wall Street that was quashed by the
President in a brilliant personal appeal. Some nay-sayers recalled
the madman who had tried to shoot MacGregor with a camera-
gun, whose identity was released to the press by the British only
after a question had been raised in Parliament. By and large,
however, the United States reacted with happy exuberance to the
Psi-Eye scheme. It was seen as a virtually foolproof reprieve
from nuclear doomsday. The identities (and the numbers) of the
pEEps were kept secret, of course; but everyone knew that they
were en garde night and day, keeping a mind's eye out for potential Kremlin button-pushers—at the same time that their noble
Russian opposite numbers scrutinized the U.S. Joint Chiefs sulk-
ing impotently in the Pentagon war-room.

In actuality, neither the American nor the Soviet authorities
achieved a working psychic monitoring effort for nearly three
months, until early 1992. There were endless niggling details to
be resolved, the most critical of which was: Where do you look?

317

As in the classic BEWARE OF THE DOG sign ploy, however, the mere proclamation of Psi-Eye was as good as its actuality. Neither of the superpowers was willing to risk being caught out trying to steal a march on the other—and although the Americans and Soviets might have had doubts about each other's Psi-Eye capability, they had none whatsoever about Scotland's. At the close of the Edinburgh Demonstration, Jamie MacGregor had remarked offhandedly that the University's independent psychic surveillance team of thirty-two EE adepts was already at work, and would be issuing regular press releases of selected U.S. and Soviet military secrets. The team's revelations were far from sensational; they were not intended to be. But they did provide a continual reminder to the world that excorporeal excursion was a reality, and inspired the two superpowers to get on with the right stuff. Both the Soviet Union and the United States behaved with unblemished probity throughout the Summit talks, the SALT signing and ratification, and the initiation of nuclear disarmament. The threats to world peace came from entirely different directions.

Here in the United States, a groundswell from burdened taxpayers called for an immediate halt to military spending. The few remaining Congressional hawks, the fundamentalist Red-haters, and the as yet insignificant numbers of meta-skeptics had their objections steamrollered into oblivion. The President, shrewd as ever in his response to consumer demand, hailed Tamara Sakhvadze's call for a World Congress on Metapsychology, and then proposed that the United States host a sister international conference on shared high technology. The Soviet General Secretary said that his nation would eagerly participate in both meetings. Then he suggested that Professor Jamie MacGregor be nominated for the Nobel Peace Prize.

My nephew Denis was closeted with the President for nearly a week, briefing him on virtually every aspect of current metapsychic research. He also testified before the House Committee on Science and Technology, the Senate Armed Services Committee, and a full meeting of the Cabinet. He would accept only an advisory appointment to the Presidential Commission on Metapsychology, but promised to consult with the Meta Brain Trust on a regular basis.

Figuratively crowned with laurel and trailed by belling newshounds, Denis returned to Dartmouth intending to get back to his researches. It was a vain hope. Post-Edinburgh and post-Washington, he and his little establishment became very big news indeed. Now prestigious foundations stampeded to Dartmouth's door, proffering endowments; and these, unlike the tainted Pentagon grants that Denis had helped to discredit during the Mind Wars scandal, were accepted "for the good of Dartmouth College and for the advancement of metapsychology as a whole."

There would be no more dodging of the media, either. Submitting to the inevitable, Denis put his associate Gerard Tremblay in charge of the lab's public affairs. At that time, the vivacious former granite-quarryman was thirty-one years old and had taken his M.D. just three years earlier. In spite of his Franco heritage, he was the member of the Coterie that I liked least. He was a fiery, good-looking fellow with intense presence; but I had always thought him a bit of a brown-nose, suspecting that his obsequious manner might be compensation for an unconscious envy of my nephew. My suspicions were to be eventually confirmed. But until he precipitated the disastrous Coercer Flap during President Baumgartner's second term, Tremblay did an outstanding job coping with the media, with curious politicians, and with the many national and international organizations that suddenly focused their attention on the shoestring research establishment at 45 College Street, Hanover, New Hampshire.

Tremblay's first PR triumph took place in November 1991, with the interview of Denis by the investigative news program *60 Minutes*. CBS was prepared to devote the entire hour-long telecast to metapsychology's Wunderkind. The interview would be combined with a tour of the Dartmouth facility and would show the actual testing of operant subjects, who would remain anonymous. Denis's lab was a prime media target because it had always remained off-limits to journalists during the blizzard of publicity attending the publication of *Metapsychology*. Heaven only knows what kind of Frankenstein shenanigans the *60 Minutes* people hoped to uncover. As it happened, the program was destined to be nearly as memorable as MacGregor's Edinburgh shocker... only this time *I* was there, doing my thing in front of the network cameras, and daring the world to make something of it.

22

FADE IN
BG STILL SHOT (MATTE) EXT DARTMOUTH RESEARCH
FACILITY A picturesque, rather dilapidated three-storey New
England saltbox building, dark gray; resembling a barn on side of
wooded hill, it looms almost ominously above a stretch of rain-
wet pavement and is framed by bare-branched trees. In FG of
MATTE stands reporter CARLOS MORENO, whose hard-hitting
questions, mobile woolly-bear eyebrows, and divergent squint
have often provoked unexpectedly revealing responses from even
the most guarded interviewees.
TITLE AND CREDIT ROLL

> *SUPERMINDS AMONG US?*
> *Produced by Jeananne Lancaster*

CARLOS MORENO
(addressing viewers)
Tonight we conclude our special three-week investigation
of the startling new developments in psychic research by
meeting a scientist who is acknowledged throughout the
world to be one of the most influential in the field. He
heads this laboratory at Dartmouth College in New
Hampshire . . . a place that has been, up until now, completely off-limits to reporters. *60 Minutes* will be taking
you inside this deceptively modest building, the workplace
of the man who was described by the President of the
United States as "the most awesome person I have ever
met, an authentic supermind" . . . But first, let's meet him
in a more conventional setting . . .
INT BOOKSHOP
Begin with ECU of DENIS REMILLARD, with downcast eyes;

320

then SLOW REVERSE ZOOM to a FULL SHOT of him sitting at table in ELOQUENT PAGE BOOKSHOP signing volumes for a crowd of CUSTOMERS who include students in Dartmouth sweat shirts, professional types, working-class types, retirees. Remillard is slight of physique, blondish, with a pleasant, shy smile. He wears tweed jacket with shirt and tie, exchanges inaudible comments with his fans during MORENO VOICE OVER.

MORENO (VOICE OVER)

Denis Remillard looks more like a graduate student than an Associate Professor of Psychiatry at an Ivy League school. He is only twenty-four years old and he has always shunned publicity—even after his book, *Metapsychology*, leaped to Number One on national best-seller lists last year. Unlike the other psychic researchers we've interviewed during this series, Denis Remillard doesn't concentrate on narrow areas of mind-study. Instead, he's a theoretician who has tried to fit the puzzling higher mental powers into a larger context.

CU REMILLARD

REMILLARD

I think my book was a success because people are very open to new ideas now. Things that our grandparents would have called absurd—like traveling to Mars—are reality. But the New Physics shows us that even *reality itself* isn't what common sense says it ought to be!

(quizzical boyish grin, eyes averted)

The universe isn't just space and time, matter and energy. You have to fit *life* into a valid Universal Field Theory— and *mind* as well. That's basically what my book is all about. Theoretical physicists and life-scientists have known for quite a while that the old view of the universe as a kind of supermachine just doesn't work. It doesn't explain the natural phenomena we experience, and it especially doesn't explain the higher mind-powers, which have never fitted into a conventional biophysical format.

INT BOOKSHOP—CLOSE SHOT MORENO

Remillard and his fans visible in BG as CAMERA MOVES BACK.

MORENO

(addressing viewers)

As he autographs copies of his book here in Hanover, New Hampshire, in a little shop owned by his Uncle Roger,

Denis Remillard hardly seems to fulfill one's expectation of a world-renowned psychologist—much less a supermind. But he was the first person summoned to be a presidential consultant on psychic affairs following the sensational Edinburgh Demonstration. He declined the chairmanship of the President's recently organized blue-ribbon Advisory Commission on Metapsychology... But he *has* agreed to head the American delegation to Alma-Ata in the Soviet Union, where researchers from dozens of nations will meet next year to discuss the practical applications of mind-power... And last week, Remillard's lab was singled out for a ten-million-dollar grant from the Vangelder Foundation. The allocation has been earmarked for an investigation into ways whereby ordinary people—people like you and me—might someday be able to learn the amazing mental feats that Denis Remillard has studied and written about... feats that *he himself* performs.

MEDIUM SHOT—REMILLARD, UNCLE ROGER, FEMALE FAN

Remillard's CONVERSATION with his Uncle, who has brought over a fresh supply of books for autographing, and the young Female Fan is audible at LOW VOLUME under MORENO V.O.

MORENO (V.O.)

Yes... it's true. Vouched for by no less an authority than the President of the United States. Not only is Professor Denis Remillard a distinguished psychic researcher, but he also possesses extraordinary mind-powers himself!

REMILLARD

(looks up from book to Fan)

Well, it's not the kind of thing one brags about or shows off in bars. But... yes, I am what we call metapsychically operant.

FEMALE FAN

(hesitantly)

Do you mean... can you *read my mind?*

REMILLARD

(laughs)

Certainly not. Not unless you deliberately try to project a thought-sequence at me. However, I *am* aware of the general emotional tenor of your mind. That you're not hostile,

for instance. That you're fascinated by the idea of higher
mind-powers.

FAN

Oh, I am! It would be marvelous to do things like soul-
traveling or telepathy or that mind-over-matter thing . . .
whatchacallit?

REMILLARD

Psychokinesis.

FAN

That's it. Just imagine being able to go to Las Vegas and *clean
up*!

The rest of the CUSTOMERS laugh and murmur at this.

REMILLARD

(patiently)

But I can't, you know. Even if I were dishonest enough to
try to manipulate slot machines or dice or a roulette wheel
with my mind—how long would it take the casino owners
to catch on? I'd be tossed out on my ear . . . at the very
least.

More laughs and murmurs from CUSTOMERS.

FAN

But . . . then what *good* are the powers?

REMILLARD

You might ask Professor Jamie MacGregor that . . .
Actually, I find my own metafaculties most useful in con-
ducting experiments. I can compare my own reactions to
those of the test subjects in psychokinesis training, for example.

FAN

(interrupts, gushing)

Ooh, Professor, do you suppose—? I mean, would it be an
awful imposition if you *showed us*? I mean, I've seen it
done on TV by those Russians, but to see you do it *live* . . .

CUSTOMERS

(ad lib exclamations)

Hey! . . . Wow! . . . Would you? . . . Super! . . . Please!

REMILLARD

(indulgently)

And Mr. Carlos Moreno told you to ask me—right?

FAN

Uh . . . I'd really appreciate it.

CU REMILLARD looking sardonically into camera. For the first time we see that his eyes are effulgent blue, almost glowing within their deep orbits.

REMILLARD

Your camera crew is quite ready? . . . Well, PK is one of the least significant metafaculties, so I guess I don't mind doing a small demonstration. After all, we can't let the Scots and the Russians garner all the kudos . . . Why don't I use these copies of my book?

MEDIUM SHOT. Remillard takes a volume, turns it so that front cover faces camera. He balances book precariously on one corner of its cover, takes hands away, and leaves book poised sur la pointe.

Now it's impossible to balance a book like this, right? Defies the law of gravity.

He balances another book on top of the first, also on its corner. The books do not tremble or totter; they are rock-solid.

And if we balance another book on that . . . and then a third . . . and then a fourth . . .

He does so.

. . . You know I must be either holding the books up with mind-power, or else I'm some kind of a [BLEEP]ing magician. And if I then extract the bottom book . . .

He does so, leaving the three upper books hanging in thin air.

. . . and the top trio remains there, then you have to be positive that something rather out of the ordinary is going on.

CUSTOMERS

(ad lib exclamations, applause)

How about that! . . . Sheesh! . . . Eat your heart out, Houdini!

Remillard shrugs. The three books in the air tumble to the table with a clatter. His UNCLE ROGER, the bookshop owner, a beanpole with graying hair and a youthful face, steps forward looking humorously indignant. Camera CLOSES ON HIM.

UNCLE ROGER

Is that any way to treat books? All you have to do is write them. I have to sell them!

He extends his hands and beckons solicitously. All four books fly off the table to him. He grasps them and forms them into neat stack.

CUSTOMERS

(ad lib shouts, a feminine squeal)

God! . . . Holy [BLEEP]! . . . You see that? . . . Sonuvagun!
UNCLE ROGER
You didn't know? Sorry. My nephew should have told you
that it runs in the family.

[SCRIPT PAGES OMITTED]

TWO SHOT—STEADICAM FOLLOWING MORENO AND
REMILLARD
Emerging from TELEPATHY EVALUATION CHAMBER, they
walk down HALLWAY toward Remillard's OFFICE, continuing
conversation begun in chamber.
REMILLARD
Only persons who already possess strong latencies for metafunctions can reasonably expect to develop into operants
after training. It's like any other kind of talent: singing, for
example. One must first be born with a proper set of vocal
cords. Then the person might become a talented amateur
without training. Usually, however, the voice must be
trained. The singer practices for years, and with luck a
great singer might result. But nobody can make an opera
singer out of a person who lacks the right vocal cords, or
who is tone-deaf. And you can't make a really competent
vocalist out of someone who hates to sing, or who suffers
from terminal stage fright. . . . It's a similar thing when you
work to raise a latent metafunction to operancy. Some will
fail to make it, and some—we hope!—will sing at the
Met.
MORENO
(frowning)
Then all human beings don't have the potential for developing these higher mind-powers?
REMILLARD
Of course not—any more than all people can become great
opera singers. This is why my proposal to test all Americans for latent mind-powers is so important. The powers
are a national resource. We must discover who among our
citizens have the potential for becoming operant—then
give them proper training.
MORENO
Sort of like the Astronaut Program?

REMILLARD

Yes . . . but enrolling both children and adults. Let me try to clarify the concept of latency for you. Our studies have shown that everyone is metapsychically latent to a certain extent. The strength of the latency may vary from power to power. Dick may be strongly latent in telepathy and weak in the healing faculty, while Jane is just the opposite. With hard work, we may make an operant telepath of Dick and an operant healer of Jane. But their weaker latencies may never amount to anything.

MORENO

Suppose I was a latent telepath. Could you make me operant?

REMILLARD

Maybe. Keep in mind that there's no hard and fast line between latency and operancy, though. Maybe you're a natural—what we call a suboperant. All you need is a bit of practice and you're able to broadcast telepathically to the Moon. But suppose your potential is weak. We might train you till your skull warps—but discover that your operant telepathic radius is only half a meter in diameter. Or you can only broadcast at night when the sun's ionization of the atmosphere is minimal, and even then only when you're completely relaxed and rested. You'd be an operant, technically speaking, but your metafaculty wouldn't be very useful. Except possibly for pillow talk.

MORENO

(smiles briefly)

You mention factors that can inhibit operancy, like ionization. Does this mean that there are ways to screen out telepaths—or stop them from using their powers?

REMILLARD

We're only beginning to discover ways to do this. It's very hard to foil the ultrasenses, such as excorporeal excursion and telepathy, that don't seem to require much expenditure of psychic energy. Things like psychokinesis, on the other hand, can be rather easily frustrated by external factors. And *internal*, subjective factors can be even more inhibitory.

TRACK INTO REMILLARD'S OFFICE

Angle favoring door as Remillard ushers Moreno inside. The office furniture is old, academic-shabby. Extensive wall bookcases

overflowing with books and papers. Computer terminal. Wall ho-
logram of human brain. Painting of Mount Washington, New
Hampshire. And everywhere—on desk, shelves, brackets, floor
—PLANTS growing luxuriantly.

MORENO
(looking around)

Quite a conservatory you have here, Professor. You must
have a green thumb.

REMILLARD
(examining droopy plant on desk)

Actually, it's more like a green mind, I guess. Now this
poor little Paphiopedilum really needs mental TLC, so I
keep it close by and let it share my aura as well as the
occasional healing thought.

He sits down and motions Moreno to a seat.

MORENO
(puzzled)

Your aura?

REMILLARD
(seeming vaguely annoyed with himself)

The bioenergetic field that surrounds my body—and that
of every other living thing. Plants included.

MORENO
(nods, as if suddenly recalling)

It seems to me I've read that certain people can even *see*
the aura that surrounds others . . . Can you see auras?

REMILLARD

Yes. If I concentrate on it.

MORENO

What do auras look like? What does *mine* look like?

CU REMILLARD

He is cupping his hands about the sick orchid plant and staring at
it with mild intensity.

REMILLARD

Auras look something like glowing, colored halos that
pulse and change. Healthy plants usually have a golden
halo. Animals and people have more varied colors. Operants have halos that look bright to another operant who
concentrates on viewing them. Since you're latent, Mr.
Moreno, your aura is quite faint. It's reddish, shot through
with flashes of violet.

MORENO (V.O.)

Does the color of a person's aura have any significance?

REMILLARD

We haven't worked out precise correlations yet. The individual aural coloration tends to vary according to mood, health, and the kind of mental activity being engaged in.

MORENO (V.O.)

Any particular significance to my red and purple?

REMILLARD

(looking blandly into camera)

I'd prefer not to comment on that today.

TWO SHOT—MORENO AND REMILLARD

Favoring Remillard and taking in the striking hologram of the brain.

MORENO

(in brisk mood switch)

We were discussing things that can inhibit the operation of the higher mind-powers . . . I suppose things like liquor, drugs, fatigue, illness—they'd all have an adverse effect on operancy, wouldn't they?

REMILLARD

Oh, yes. If anything, the higher faculties are even more sensitive to such things than the lower ones. But there are all kinds of other factors that can diminish one's operancy as well. For example, what the lay person calls mental blocks.

MORENO

Can you clarify?

REMILLARD

Let's take a more common mind function like memory. We've all experienced forgetfulness. Suppose I'm sitting next to a lady at a dinner party and I can't remember her name. Now why is that? Am I eighty-seven years old—in which case my forgetfulness is to be expected? No, I'm young and compos mentis. But no matter how much I exert my will power, I just can't remember. A psychoanalyst might come up with any number of reasons why. Perhaps the lady is an old flame who jilted me many years ago. Perhaps her name is the same as that of my Internal Revenue Service auditor! Or perhaps the problem is simply a very difficult foreign name that I failed to concentrate on when the lady and I were introduced. Any one of those rather subtle factors could inhibit memory. Metafunctions can be inhibited similarly.

MORENO

How about emotions? Anger, say. Or fear. If a person with strong metafunctions was afraid of the reactions others might have—afraid of hostility—could that make his powers go latent?

REMILLARD

It's possible. A strongly hostile or skeptical group of observers can also inhibit displays of metafunction.

MORENO

Have *you* ever experienced a diminishing of your own mind-powers because of emotional influences?

REMILLARD

(hesitating)

No. If anything, the adrenalin released by my body in response to such emotions would tend to reinforce my metafaculties. But then, I've been using the powers all my life, from the time I was an infant. When we begin training small children to operancy, we'll probably find that their higher faculties will remain usefully operant under all but the most extreme inhibitory conditions. After all—you yourself are seldom too shocked to speak. Or to see or hear. Or even to react in an emergency.

CU MORENO

MORENO

This testing and training program you advocate. Some people might say it had certain dangers. We'd be setting up a kind of elite mind-corps, wouldn't we? One that might eventually feel justified in seeking political power on the basis of their superior mentality.

TWO SHOT

REMILLARD

I don't think there's any danger of that.

MORENO

Oh? . . . Do you mean these operants would think politics was beneath them?

REMILLARD

(impatiently)

Certainly not. But there are so many other jobs to do that operants would find more satisfying. Einstein didn't run for President, you know.

CU MORENO

MORENO
(suddenly)

Do you, as a powerful operant, feel superior to normal people?

CU REMILLARD

REMILLARD
(again looking at plant, frowning)

The way you've phrased that question is somewhat inimical. Does a concert violinist feel superior to the audience? Does a mathematician feel superior to a cordon-bleu chef? Does a librarian with an eidetic memory feel superior to an absent-minded professor who won a Nobel Prize?

(lifts eyes and speaks deliberately)

Mr. Moreno, we all do things we know are wrong . . . like harbor prejudices to boost our insecure egos. One can suffer from shaky self-esteem no matter how well educated or how poorly educated one happens to be. Even television journalists can show bias for or against people they interview . . . I don't *think* that I look down upon persons without operant metafunctions. I'd be a fool if I did. I have certain talents, yes. But I lack so many others! I can't play the violin or sing or even cook very well. I'm not good at drawing pictures or playing tennis. I'm a terrible driver because I'm always off in the clouds instead of paying attention to traffic. I tend to shilly-shally around instead of making decisions promptly. So I would be an integral idiot to think of myself as a superior being . . . and I don't know of any other operants who think that way. If they do exist, I hope I never meet up with them.

CU MORENO

MORENO

How about the flip side of that question, then? Do you ever feel threatened by nonoperants?

TWO SHOT—REMILLARD FAVORED

REMILLARD

When I was much younger I kept my mind-powers completely under wraps because I didn't want others to know I was different. I wanted to be just like everyone else. You've interviewed a number of other operants for your television series, so you know that such protective coloration activity is the usual thing for youngsters who grow up with self-taught metafunctions. Minorities who seem to be a threat to majorities make the adaptations they must in order to survive.

MORENO

Then you admit that operant psychics *can* pose a threat to normals!

REMILLARD

(calmly)

I said *seem to*. Persons who are different from others in marked ways are often perceived as threatening. But it doesn't have to be that way. That's what civilization is supposed to be all about—resolving differences maturely, not acting like bands of frightened children. The gap between operant and nonoperant is only the latest that modern society has faced. We also have technology gaps, economic gaps, cultural gaps, the generation gap, and even a sexual gap. You can refuse to cross the gap and throw rocks at each other, or you can cooperate to build a bridge to mutual betterment.

INTERCUT STOCK SHOTS—MONTAGE

Riotous scenes at London and Tokyo stock exchanges; mobs besiege banks at Geneva and Zurich; Monte Carlo Casino with sign: RELÂCHE/GESCHLOSSEN/CLOSED UNTIL FURTHER NOTICE; *Time* magazine cover: DEFENSE STOCK DEBACLE; newspaper headlines: RUSSIA DUMPS GOLD, OIL LEASE CHAOS, COCA-COLA FORMULA REVEALED, OFFSHORE TAX REFUGES SELF-DESTRUCT; *Newsweek* magazine cover: WHO WILL WATCH THE WATCHERS?

MORENO (V.O.)

But we've seen the turmoil that rocked the world stock and commodity markets following the Edinburgh Demonstration. And you must know that certain financiers and businesses that depend upon secrecy for their operations look upon telepathy and excorporeal excursion as deadly menaces. Other very serious problems are just beginning to crop up. Operants aren't numerous enough yet to pose much of a threat to society or to the global economy, but what about the future, when the superminds you propose to train begin to invade every walk of life?

TWO SHOT

REMILLARD

Operants aren't invaders from outer space, Mr. Moreno.

We're only people. Citizens, not superbeings. We want just about the same things that you want—a peaceful and prosperous world for ourselves and our children, satisfying work, freedom from prejudice and oppression, a bit of fun now and then, someone to love . . . This invasion of yours: Do you realize you could be talking about your own children or grandchildren? Our preliminary studies seem to show that the human race has reached a critical point in evolution. Our gene pool is throwing up increasing numbers of individuals with the potential for becoming what you call a supermind.

MORENO
(looking slightly shaken)

My children?

REMILLARD

Or those of your cousins and uncles and aunts . . . or neighbors, or coworkers. In years to come, all humans will be born operant! But that's a long way off, and we poor souls are going to have to endure life in the transition zone during the foreseeable future. I won't minimize the fact that we may have a tough time. Adjustments will have to be made. But all throughout human history society has had to confront revolutions that overturned the old order. In the Stone Age, metal was a threat! The first automobiles frightened the horses and doomed the buggy-whip makers. But what one group sees as a threat, another group may hail as a blessing. Not to belabor the point . . . but did you notice that the latest issue of the *Bulletin of the Atomic Scientists* has turned back the hands of its doomsday clock from two minutes before midnight to half past eleven?

MORENO
(permitting himself a wintry smile)

Is that how you operants see yourselves, Professor? As the saviors of humanity?

CU REMILLARD

REMILLARD
(sighs, fingering the plant)

Sometimes I wonder whether we might be the first scattered spores of the evolving World Mind . . . and then again, we might be only evolutionary dead ends, the mental equivalents of those fossil Irish elk with the six-foot antlers that were gorgeous to look at but losers in the survival game.

He looks at the plant, which seems noticeably perkier. Opening a desk decanter, he pours a bit of water into the pot.

MORENO (V.O.)

(incredulously)

A *World Mind*? You mean, some kind of superstate, like the Marxists envisioned? Operancy will lead to that?

TWO SHOT

REMILLARD

(laughs heartily)

No, no. Not a bit of it! No chance of our evolving into a metapsychic beehive. Humanity's individuality is its strength. But, you see ... with the telepathy, especially, you have the potential for vastly increased empathy: mind-to-mind socialization on a level above any we've ever known ... And it would be such a logical and elegant survival response, the World Mind. A perfect counterpoint to our increasingly dangerous technical advances.

MORENO

I still don't understand.

INTERCUT MYXOMYCETES NATURAL HISTORY SEQUENCE—paralleling Remillard's VOICE OVER.

REMILLARD (V.O.)

Perhaps an analogy will help. There's a peculiar group of living things called Myxomycetes—or, to give them their more prosaic name, slime molds. A slime mold is either an animal that acts like a plant, or a plant that acts like an animal. Officially, it's a type of fungus. But it's capable of independent movement, like an animal. In its usual form, the slime mold is like a tiny amoeba, flowing here and there on the forest floor engulfing and eating bacteria and other microscopic goodies. It eats, it grows, and in time it splits like a genuine amoeba into two individuals. In a favorable forest environment there will be thousands or even millions of these little single-celled eaters going about their individual business ... But sometimes, the food supply gives out. Perhaps the forest dries up in a prolonged drought. In some way the individual cells seem to realize that it's "unite or die" time. They begin to come together. First they form blobs and then rivulets of slime. These flow toward a central point and combine into a multicelled mass of jelly that becomes a real *organism*, sometimes more than thirty centimeters in diameter... and it creeps along the ground. Some creeping slime molds look like pancakes of dusty jelly and some look like slugs, leaving a trail of slime behind. The organism may travel for two weeks, looking for a more favorable place to live. When it stops migrating it changes shape again—often to a thing like a knob at the end of a stalk. In time the knob splits open and releases a cloud of dusty spores that fly through the air. Eventually the spores come to earth, where warmth and moisture turn them into amoebalike individuals again. They take up their old life—until the next time things get rough and Unity becomes imperative...

TWO SHOT—REMILLARD AND MORENO—STEADICAM FOLLOWING—

We discover them as they are approaching the exit of the RESEARCH FACILITY. Moreno is leaving.

MORENO

And you really believe that human minds will have to come together in somewhat the same way in order to survive?

REMILLARD

The idea seems very natural to a telepath, Mr. Moreno. It's only a higher form of socialization, after all. To a tribe of primitives living at the clan level, the notion of a complex democratic society seems hopelessly bizarre. But primitives transplanted into industrial nations have often adapted very successfully. Think of some of the Southeast Asian hill folk who came to America in the 1970s and '80s. A World Mind is quite plausible to operants, and of course it would include nonoperant minds as well.

MORENO

I don't see how!

REMILLARD

Neither do I... at the moment. But that's the payoff that some of us metapsychic theoreticians envision. A society of the mind evolving toward harmony and mutualism that still lets individuals retain their freedom. That's one of the topics we'll be discussing in Alma-Ata next year, at the First World Congress on Metapsychology. We'll deal with practicalities first, but then the universe is the limit! It may take a few thousand years to accomplish a World Mind, but

I like to think of the meeting there in Kazakhstan as the first little blob of amoebas flowing together into a true organism. The creature is still tiny and not very effectual... but it'll grow.

CUT TO MORENO CU—AGAINST PROGRAM LOGO (MATTE)

MORENO
(addressing viewers)

Denis Remillard's vision is an amazing one—but then he is an amazing man. Perhaps, as the President said, a supermind. Right now there are at most a few hundred others like him scattered around the world. But tomorrow, and next year, and in the twenty-first century fast approaching, those superminds among us will multiply. And as they do, they'll change the world. How they change it remains to be seen... I'm Carlos Moreno for *60 Minutes.*

FADE TO COMMERCIAL BREAK

23

FROM THE MEMOIRS OF ROGATIEN REMILLARD

WHY HAD I DONE IT?

What perverse compulsion had led me to top my nephew's display of psychokinesis with one of my own, thus revealing my most closely guarded secret on a television program beamed around the globe?

Oh yes, I had been more than a little drunk at the time, having given in to the need to fortify myself against the invasion of my bookshop by Carlos Moreno and his squad of muckrakers. But to show my power so flippantly, with such cornball insouciance! I had to be cracking up.

After the fatal taping session in the shop, when we had all had our giggle and it occurred to me what a piece of lunacy I had perpetrated, I went on a towering binge. I missed the actual *60*

Minutes telecast that took place on Sunday, three days later, as well as the debriefing party afterward that was given at the Metapsychology lab, where Denis and his Coterie celebrated having thrown their bonnets over the windmill. Apparently only one person missed me, out of all that supposedly psychosensitive lot, and wondered where I had disappeared to, and figured things out, and had the compassion to come and ring the bell to my apartment and shout telepathically until I was roused from my stupor and coerced into opening the door. . .

Lucille.

"I knew it!" she exclaimed, pushing inside. "I just knew you'd done something stupid. Look at you! Roger, what are you *doing* to yourself?"

"Good question," I mumbled, grinning down at her. But my drunken insolence quailed in the face of her terrible charity. I must have looked like a sodden scarecrow, half conscious and filthy; but she had helped tend her invalid father for years and had no trouble at all coping with me. She forced me to take a shower, dressed me in clean pajamas, and pummeled my brain until I swallowed a vitamin-laden milkshake. Then she put me to bed. When I woke up ten hours later she was still there, dozing in a chair in the parlor, and my hurrah's nest of an apartment was now spotless and my entire stock of booze had been poured down the drain.

With my head throbbing like a calliope at full steam and my knees awobble, I looked in hung-over wonderment at the sleeping young woman, trying to think why she, of all people, had come to my rescue.

Her eyes opened. They were brown and very stern, and I couldn't help remembering how she had sent Denis and me packing when we had first dowsed her out eleven years earlier.

"Why?" she said quietly, echoing my telepathic question. "Because I know just what came over you when Denis did his thing and you knew the jig was up. Poor old Roger."

She stretched, then got up from the chair and looked at her wristwatch. "Quarter to eight. I have a seminar at nine this morning, but there's time to scramble some eggs." She headed for my kitchen.

"What d'you mean you know?" I croaked, shuffling after. "*I* don't even know! And what the hell right do you have coming up here and interfering with me? Don't tell me the fuckin' Ghost sent you!"

She began to crack eggs. The sound was like ax-blows against my tortured eardrums. I lurched and her coercion reached out and coolly tipped me into a kitchen chair. I let out a groan and caught my head before it bounced on the freshly polished maple table top. A few moments later she was shoving a cup of coffee under my nose.

"Microwaved instant, but strong enough to etch glass," she said. "Drink." Coercion locked on, stifling my instinctive refusal. I drank. Then she produced a nauseously aromatic plate of eggs with buttered toast. My guts cringed at the loathsome prospect.

"Eat."

"I can't—"

YES YOU CAN.

Bereft of will power, I dug in. Lucille sat down opposite me and sipped tea, keeping the compulsion firm by maintaining eye contact. She was not a pretty woman but her face had that high-colored attractiveness indicative of a formidable character. Her dark hair was cut in a simple pageboy with the bangs just touching thick, straight brows. She wore a scarlet turtleneck sweater and jeans, and her hands were raw, the once polished fingernails damaged from the heavy housecleaning chores she had undertaken on my behalf.

As my stomach filled and my aching head deflated to a size approximating normality, I felt ashamed of my surly ingratitude and more than ever mystified that she should have been the one to think of me. She had been an occasional customer at the bookshop, showing a rather regrettable penchant for fantasy books featuring dragons. Her mind had always closed primly at my avuncular jests and resisted my attempts to put her into a more sophisticated style of escapist literature. Lucille knew what she liked and stuck to it with Franco stubbornness. She was not even a full-fledged member of the Coterie, but only one of the more talented experimental subjects—a mere student—which made her assertion that she understood my mental state all the more improbable.

"But I do understand," she said, reading my subvocalizations. "You and I are really quite a bit alike. Both of us are still trying to adapt, asking questions about ourselves that desperately need answers."

I glared at the nervy little chit, mopping my plate with the last of the toast. Her coercion slid aside as I managed to prop my mental barricade into position.

She only smiled. "There's a person who's helped me to find some answers, Roger. I think he could help you, too. I'm going to come back here this afternoon at three o'clock and take you along with me to meet him."

"No, you aren't," said I. "Don't think that I'm not grateful to you for shoveling me up and putting this place back in order after my lost weekend—but I'm quite all right now. I don't need any help from your friend. And don't think you can force me. You'll find I'm not nearly so susceptible to coercion when I'm compos mentis."

She leaned toward me earnestly. "I wouldn't coerce you to come. That wouldn't be any use. But you must, Roger! You know that you're seriously in need of help. Everybody knows."

I laughed. "So I'm the talk of the town, am I? A disgrace and an embarrassment, sans doute, to my nephew the distinguished supermind! And which one of his brilliant young colleagues have you pegged to drag the black sheep out of his alcoholic wilderness?"

"None of the Coterie. I want you to talk to my own analyst, Dr. Bill Sampson. He isn't an operant at all. But he has more insight—more caring competence—than that whole damned labful of superior metapsychic pricks. Denis included."

Oh my God. I squeezed my crusty eyelids shut.

She babbled on. "When I felt how deeply afraid you were there in the bookshop, with the TV people closing in and Denis put in the position of having to demonstrate his PK, I was just appalled. Then you *defied* it! I knew right then that I'd have to do something to help you. Take you to Bill. He helped me lick my dragons and he can help you—"

Lightning struck.

Now I knew why I had made that lunatic gesture in front of the TV cameras, why I had berated myself so that her mind's ear overheard, why I had admitted her to my squalid sanctum, asking if my own special dragon had sent her.

It had.

Poor little kindhearted Lucille! Let me reinforce my mindscreen, hiding from you the blaze of certainty. It had been more than a year ago that I was admonished to break up your love affair with Dr. Bill Sampson, and I put the notion completely out of my mind. But synchronicity is not so easily denied . . . and here we are, and there the inevitability awaits us.

Once again I am not a man but a tool. And how is the dirty deed to be done? (Neither she nor Sampson are fools, and any blatant action, such as reporting the prima facie breach of doctor-patient ethics, would tend to solidify their liaison rather than sever it.) No, I would have to be both subtle and direct.

All that is really necessary is to show old Sampson the truth.

The psychiatrist is a normal, but he is clearly enthralled by the metapsychic phenomenon in his beloved. Show him how he has played the romantic hero, rescuing a malleable young Androm-eda from the mental rock where she chained herself as dragon-meat. The princess is tender and grateful now; but her chains can be taken up and worn again at any time—and they can be stretched to fit two minds as easily as one when reality inevitably intrudes on the glamour. Then she will destroy the mortal lover as well as herself, surrendering to her dragon's fire . . .

Does he think that love will transcend? Then show him what operancy really means—what a mature operant can do—what *she* will be able to do someday! Now, blinded and gentled, she shrinks from prying into the deeper layers of his mind. But pry she will, and she'll find the petty, cruel, and unworthy thoughts that flit through every human mind, no matter how loving, and in her hurt she'll fling them into his face. Show him how easily it's done! And then coerce him. Show how his darling will be capa-ble of violating his sovereign will, should the mood come upon her. Show him the PK! Give him just a hint of the healing fac-ulty's flip side! And then the clincher. Project the image that every operant, even the most noble, holds deep in his heart when he compares himself to lowly normals. Show him Odd John's truth.

"I was living in a world of phantoms, or animated masks. No one seemed really alive. I had a queer notion that if I pricked any of you there would be no bleeding but only a gush of wind . . ."

Learn the truth, Dr. Bill Sampson. Then find a normal woman to love and leave Lucille Cartier to her metapsychic destiny. Learn the easy way, from somebody who learned the hard way.

"Roger," Lucille said. "Please come with me this afternoon. It will all be for the best."

"I hope so," I told her. "God, I hope so."

24

SUPERVISORY CRUISER NOUMENON
[LYL 1-0000]
4 JUNE 1992

WHEN THE FANATICS SUCCESSFULLY SMUGGLED THE SECOND OF the Armageddon devices into place, and that place was the Israeli nuclear weaponry works at Dimona, the portents were such that Homologous Trend felt impelled to consult with its three fellow entities.

"One must admit," Trend told the others, "that my anatomization of the probability lattices is somewhat disorderly—but that's Earth for you. However, the resultant inevitably leads to still another global crisis capable of disrupting the planetary sexternion—and Intervention."

"One's sensibilities churn," Eupathic Impulse said, upon viewing the analysis. "From this one locus proceed conflicts not only in the Middle East, but also in South Africa, Uzbekistan, and India."

"One is chagrined," Asymptotic Essence said, "given the worldwide flowering of goodwill after the Scottish Demonstration, to note that the group instigating the atrocity stubbornly persists in its ancient tribal hostility mode. Other Earth populations at higher and lower levels of sociopolitical organization experienced positive transformational nuances as a result of MacGregor's ploy. What's wrong with this bunch?"

"Status Three indigenes," Noetic Concordance observed sadly, "are a perverse and difficult lot, more likely to stall in metapsychic development than other classifications. Status Threes vest authority in puppet rulers dominated by a powerful priestly caste. The intellectual establishment is subservient, and upward mobility of individuals is limited according to their profession of orthodoxy. The higher mind-powers—even elementary creativity—tend to be repressed, except insofar as they serve the narrow religious objective. The mind-set is intolerant, reaction-

340

ary, xenophobic, and more than a little silly. Fanaticism is a prime activator of psychoenergies and the view of consequents is minimal. Even this impending catastrophe is seen by the perpetrators as a glorification of the All."

Eupathic Impulse said, "One has a sneaking suspicion that this particular terrorist group wants to get its licks in before the inspection teams of the UN Nuclear Nonproliferation Agency include persons adept in farsensing."

Trend waved all this thought-embroidery aside. "You three agree with my dire prognosis. Do you also agree that the gravity of the situation demands that we summon Atoning Unifex for a contemplation?"

"One regrets having to disturb It," Concordance said. "But if Earth is to be spared this profound trauma, overt action will have to be taken."

Asymptotic Essence permitted itself the barest hint of vexation. "Another deliberate skew of the noögenetic curvature? That will make three inside of fourteen months, including the rescue of MacGregor from the Mafia hit-man and the augmentation of the Alma-Ata group's coercion of the Soviet TV net. How long must we keep this up? If Earth's Mind were treated in a normal manner, it would never achieve coadunation!"

Eupathic Impulse was inclined to agree. "Intervention in due season is one thing: continued interference with significant nodalities on the evolving mental lattices is quite another. If it were any entity save Unifex commanding this most atypical wet-nursing, one might have the most serious misgivings."

"One of the most notable incongruities is our own physical presence here," Noetic Concordance reminded the others. "One questions why the Supervisory Body does not simply work through the Agent Polities who are more than a little scandalized by our participation."

"One may question," Eupathic Impulse noted wryly, "but one doesn't necessarily get straight answers."

Homologous Trend said, "One *must* trust Unifex."

Eupathic Impulse said, "If It would only share Its prescience!"

Noetic Concordance said, "Of all our vague and absent-minded Lylmik race, It is the most terribly preoccupied. And weary. One intuits that It would transfer the burden of Galactic mentorship and submerge Itself in the Cosmic All in a trice, were It not faithful to some great overriding dynamic—"

"Which It declines to share," Impulse said.

"We must trust It," Trend reiterated, "as we have since the dawn of the Milieu, when It selected us four from all the eager Lylmik after manifesting the Protocol of Unification. Unifex *has* shared . . . as much as It has been able to do so. You know our racial Mind's limitation as well as its strengths. We are ancient and tending toward stagnation, conservative and over-fond of the mystical lifestyle. Unifex's great vision of a Galactic Mind was able to electrify us, to send us beyond the Twenty-One Worlds in search of other, immature Minds that we might shepherd toward coadunation. Toward Unity. *That*, if you will, was the great outrage Unifex committed: the initiation of the Milieu. You younger entities have let the memory of it slip away in your earnest contemplation of present anomalies."

"Yes," the three admitted. For some time they filled their minds with the Milieu's essence and drifted, serene.

But Trend recalled them. "The two Armageddon devices are in place. Action, if it is to be taken, must be taken soon. Let us summon Unifex."

They called in metaconcert.

And It was there with them, glowing in the liquid-crystal films of the star-cruiser's innermost heart, emanating Its familiar emotional mix of affection and crotchety longanimity.

The Quincunx formed. The problem was set forth.

Unifex told them: "One may take no preventive action. This awful event happens . . . as it must and as it has."

"May we ask why?"

"To unite the World Mind more fully in pain, as it has failed to unite in joy during the past seven months of premature celebration. This calamity is only one in the ultimate educative series leading toward the climax: pain upon pain lesson upon lesson ordeal upon ordeal."

"We suggest, in all respect, that the teaching process might be less radical. As you saw from your contemplation of the problem as formulated, there is a distinct probability that the United States and the Soviet Union will abandon their newborn rapprochement and be drawn into a fresh posture of hostility. The operant human minds will no longer be viewed as an assurance for peace, but rather as a hindrance to necessary war!"

"Nevertheless, we will not forestall the detonation of the Armageddon devices." Unifex's mind-voice was sorrowful, but It declined to reveal the thought-processes—proleptic or otherwise —that had led to Its judgment.

The four subsidiary Lylmik entities came as close to out-right dissent as they had ever done in the two-million-year life of the Quincunx. "We suggest that it may be unloving of you to fob us off on this grave matter without resolving some aspect of the paradox. Do you base your decisions upon analysis of the probability lattices, as we do, or are you privy to some recondite data-source that influences your special treatment of the planet Earth?"

"I may not tell you that... What I may tell you is that the lessons to be learned by the Earthlings must be learned most especially by the operant minds. It is these, not their contentious latent brethren, who must mature in Light if there is to be an Intervention. The majority of the operants must decide freely that their mind-powers must never be used aggressively. Never. Not even in a cause that their intellects perceive as good. And because this truth is counter to one of the deepest imperatives of human psychology, its apprehension will be attained only at a fearful price... a price that will not be fully paid until *after the Intervention*."

The four were aghast.

Unifex said, "O my friends, I admit that I have not been sufficiently forthcoming since our Earth visitation began. I admit that I have reserved data and allowed myself to be submerged in perplexity. But I have forgotten so much and the chasm between the human mind and our own is so vast... You are aware that Earth's nodalities are more critical to the future of the Milieu than those of any other world—and yet our own role in its mental evolution remains unclear to me. Often I must act through feeling rather than through logic! This world, unlike the worlds of the Krondaku, Gi, Poltroyans, and Simbiari, does not occupy a place clearly defined in the larger reality. I have been able to penetrate its mystery only partially myself, by processes outside of intellection. So I can only beg you to bear with me... and in return, I shall offer you a species of metaphor. If you attend to it, certain aspects of the Earthly paradox may be clarified."

"We are eager to experience your metaphor."

"Very well," said Unifex. "We five will contemplate it together, but as individuals and without any metapsychic penetration of the human participants in the drama. We will empathize with the Earthlings to the fullest, and view the spectacle as much on their simple level as is possible for us. Please accompany me mentally now to Japan, where a baseball game is about to be played . . ."

It was the final contest of an exhibition series: the first East-West Championship ever organized, and one of numerous goodwill enterprises that had been undertaken in various parts of the world in the joyous aftermath of the Edinburgh Demonstration. For a few brief months, the planet had given itself over to a carnival of hope, reacting to decades of nuclear anxiety. There had been festivals of music and dance and drama and poetry, and there were seminars of knowledge sharing, and there were games. Seven countries had participated in the baseball series, and now it had all come down to a last championship game between the mighty New York Mets and the formidable Hiroshima Carp. The teams were tied at three games apiece in the seven-game series.

The players, clad in colorful close-fitting suits, enacted the deceptively simple contest before an audience of more than 150,000 fans, who had packed the vast Hiroshima Yakyujo to the topmost tier. Those who viewed the game on television numbered nearly a billion—some twenty percent of the global population—and included many who, like the fascinated Lylmik, were more interested in the symbolic than the sporting aspect of this particular match-up.

It was a multilayered event: physical, psychological, mathematical. There was even an elusive musical element in its alternation of violent action with intervals of pregnant ennui. Atoning Unifex imparted to Its fellow entities an instantaneous knowledge of the rules, the attributes and eccentricities of the players, and the strategic theories employed by the team managers during the previous games of the series.

"There are actually a number of metaphors being manifested here," Unifex said. "As we watch, let us also synthesize and strive to apply the essential wisdom to the larger reality."

Then the game began, and for more than two hours the exotic beings were caught up in the symbolic conflict. The game was closely fought until the seventh inning, when the Mets leaped ahead, 4-2. They kept their lead through the bottom of the ninth, and the Carp came to bat for the last time facing a make-or-break situation.

The Mets pitcher, the celebrated Zeke O'Toole, was no longer in the flush of youth and obviously tiring, but it was out of the question that he should be replaced. Instead, he adopted an excessively cautious technique designed to frustrate and anger the opposition. He posed, ruminated, and eyeballed the Carp players on deck and the waiting batter in an insolent and intimidating manner. The tactic resulted in two strikeouts, and wails of dismay arose from the Carp partisans in the stadium. Their desolation was transformed into fresh hope, however, when the next batter hit a single, and the one after him doubled.

"Now the climax of the drama approaches," Atoning Unifex said. "The next scheduled batter is the Carp pitcher, an untalented ball-walloper who will undoubtedly be replaced by a pinch hitter. Yes. Here comes Kenji 'Shoeless Ken' Katsuyama, a redoubtable but somewhat erratic man in the clutch situation. The Carp manager takes a monumental gamble sending him in. If this massively muscled young slugger can connect with the ball, he may very well hit it into the hyperspatial matrix! He would score himself on a home run, and bring in the men on second and third, winning the game for the Carp. To avoid this outcome, one might expect the wily veteran pitcher, O'Toole, to give this dangerous rival a walk to first base. This might set up a double play if the men on base attempt to steal, wiping the Carp out and winning it for the Mets. Or, even if a single Carp should score on the walk, it seems virtually certain that the unagile Katsuyama would be tagged for the third out on a subsequent play, also giving victory to the Mets. Another possibility, more perilous for the Mets, is that with Ken taking first on a walk and the bases loaded, the next batter up might put the Carp into an advantageous scoring position. O'Toole and Katsuyama are both in what humans call the hot seat."

"The Japanese fans certainly do not concede defeat," Noetic Concordance remarked.

"See how they plead for a home run," said Eupathic Impulse, "exerting all their collective coercion! What a pity the metafaculty has such a large suboperative component."

Homologous Trend displayed statistics on the powerful young batter's past performance. "This Shoeless One does not seem to know the meaning of the term 'strike zone.' One notes that he has been known to flail away at bean balls. This may influence O'Toole's style of play."

"The batter is impatient with the dilatory tactics of the elderly pitcher," Asymptotic Essence said. "The men on second and third base hold back, wary of the American's reputation as a butcher of base-stealers."

Zeke O'Toole was dawdling conspicuously on the mound, but he was given the benefit of the doubt by the Japanese plate umpire. Meanwhile, Katsuyama glowered, pawed the earth, and gripped his Mizuno bat in a strangle hold.

Atoning Unifex said, "Play ball, you dragass Irish grand-stander!"

Now the catcher was sidling to the right, obviously expecting a waste pitch thrown wide. O'Toole shook his head minimally. A split second later he hurled a sizzling knuckleball high and inside, barely crossing a corner of the plate.

Strike one.

There were more delays. O'Toole sketched a series of cryptic signals, then finally threw one very wide for ball one. Katsuyama stomped about, twirling his bat and grimacing. He took his stance and waited. And waited. When the pitch came, curving and slow, he swung heroically. He missed.

Strike two.

The Lylmik were aware of Shoeless Ken's mounting fury. He stood in a kind of sumo crouch while a fastball came zinging in, deliberately wide, for ball two.

O'Toole chewed his cud of spruce gum, nonchalantly cupped the return behind his back, swiveled his head to spear the men on base with his pale and ornery eye, then seemed to bow his head in prayer. The fans hooted and screamed but the complaisant umpire merely waited. At last the pitcher wound up and delivered wide and junky for ball three.

"This is called a full count," Unifex said. "One notes that the veteran O'Toole remains cool while Katsuyama is livid."

The men on base were ranging out desperately. O'Toole wasted no time but wound up with barely legal celerity and threw a wide pitchout to the waiting catcher. It was intended to be a fourth ball, walking Katsuyama and nailing the man creeping along the base line toward home plate, but it barely scraped the edge of the strike zone and . . .

Kwoing!

Crowding the plate, uttering a martial shout, Shoeless Ken swung his bat in a flattened arc at that hopelessly wide pitch. The connection came perilously close to the bat's tip; but so heroic was the swing that the ball took off like a blurry white meteor into the remotest coign of left field, topping the fence. A tsunami of ecstatic sound engulfed Katsuyama as he ceremonially encircled the bases. He bowed to the crowd. Then he bowed to Zeke O'Toole, who still stood on the pitcher's mound with folded arms.

The huge electronic display posted the final score:

HIROSHIMA CARP 5
NEW YORK METS 4
HIROSHIMA CARP WIN PLANET SERIES
4 GAMES TO 3

In the Lylmik cruiser invisibly orbiting Earth, the supervising entities studied the baseball game in its totality, frozen in the spatiotemporal lattices like a fixed specimen on a slide, viewed under a microscope at extreme magnification.

"One observes the obvious historical parallel," said Homologous Trend. "The old antagonism ritualized."

Asymptotic Essence said, "One notes that, in sharing this sublimation with their fellow humans, the two powerful nations speed coadunation of the World Mind."

Eupathic Impulse said, "One perceives that you, Unifex, knew the outcome and educational potential of this obscure contest before it began. This reinforces my own hypothesis of a great Proleptic Peculiarity in the planet's sexternion—nodally determined by yourself!"

The poet, Noetic Concordance, was silent for some time. Its contribution, when it finally came, was almost tentative. "One observes that the American sports fans in the stadium cheered the Carp victory even more fervently than did the Japanese . . ."

Atoning Unifex let Its mind-smile embrace the four. "Well done. Hold the collection of metaphors deep in your hearts. Return to it from time to time to assist your contemplation of Earth. And tomorrow when the atomic bombs destroy Tel Aviv and Dimona, mourn with humanity. But remember that the probability lattices are not certainties. They can be moved by fervent acts of will. Both love and evolution act in an elitist way. And now, farewell."

THE END OF
PART TWO

INTERVENTION
WILL CONCLUDE
WITH BOOK TWO

THE METACONCERT

TO BE PUBLISHED IN FEBRUARY 1989 BY
DEL REY BOOKS

APPENDIX

THE REMILLARD FAMILY TREE

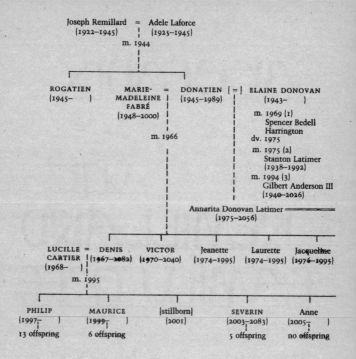

Joseph Remillard = Adele Laforce
(1922–1945)   (1925–1945)
m. 1944

ROGATIEN
(1945–   )

MARIE-
MADELEINE
FABRÉ
(1948–2000)

= DONATIEN [=] ELAINE DONOVAN
(1945–1989)   (1943–   )

m. 1969 (1)
Spencer Bedell
Harrington
dv. 1975

m. 1975 (2)
Stanton Latimer
(1938–1992)

m. 1994 (3)
Gilbert Anderson III
(1940–2026)

m. 1966

Annarita Donovan Latimer
(1975–2056)

LUCILLE = DENIS   VICTOR   Jeanette   Laurette   Jacqueline
CARTIER (1967–2082) (1970–2040) (1974–1995) (1974–1995) (1976–1995)
(1968–   )

m. 1995

PHILIP   MAURICE   [stillborn]   SEVERIN   Anne
(1997–   )   (1999–   )   (2001)   (2003–2083)   (2005–   )

13 offspring   6 offspring   5 offspring   no offspring

THE REMILLARD
FAMILY TREE

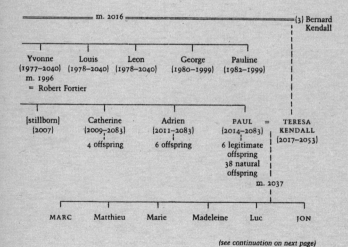

(see continuation on next page)

O'CONNOR GENEALOGY

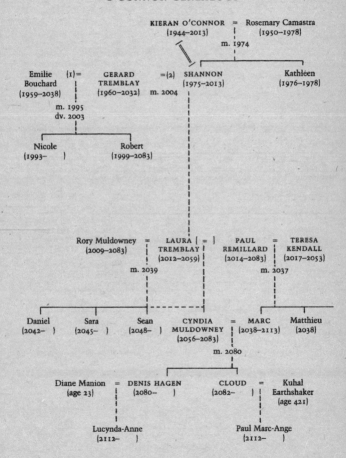

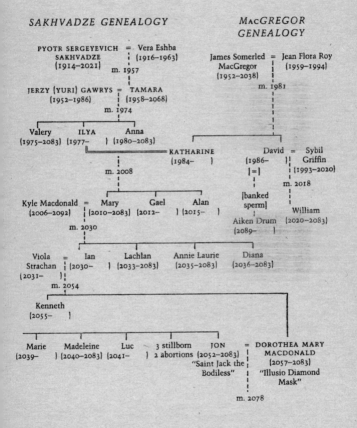

SAKHVADZE GENEALOGY

MacGREGOR GENEALOGY

PYOTR SERGEYEVICH = Vera Eshba
SAKHVADZE   (1916–1963)
(1914–2021)
                m. 1957

James Somerled = Jean Flora Roy
MacGregor   (1959–1994)
(1952–2038)
              m. 1981

JERZY (YURI) GAWRYS = TAMARA
(1952–1986)   (1958–2068)
                 m. 1974

Valery   ILYA   Anna
(1975–2083) (1977–   ) (1980–2083)

KATHARINE
(1984–   )

David = Sybil
(1986–ǁ) Griffin
(=)   (1993–2020)
           m. 2018

           m. 2008

[banked
sperm]

Kyle Macdonald = Mary   Gael   Alan
(2006–2092)   (2010–2083) (2012–) (2015–)

                m. 2030

Aiken Drum
(2089–   )

William
(2020–2083)

Viola   = Ian   Lachlan   Annie Laurie   Diana
Strachan   (2030–) (2033–2083)   (2035–2083)   (2036–2083)
(2031–)
      m. 2054

Kenneth
(2055–   )

Marie   Madeleine   Luc   3 stillborn   JON   = DOROTHEA MARY
(2039–)   (2040–2083) (2041–) 2 abortions   (2052–2083)   MACDONALD
                                                   "Saint Jack the (2057–2083)
                                                   Bodiless"   "Illusio Diamond
                                                                    Mask"

                                                            m. 2078

ABOUT THE AUTHOR

JULIAN MAY's short science fiction novel, *Dune Roller*, was published by John W. Campbell in 1951 and has now become a minor classic of the genre. It was produced on American television and on the BBC, became a movie, and has frequently been anthologized. Julian May lives in the state of Washington.

Julian May's

SCIENCE FICTION SERIES:

The Saga of Pliocene Exile

Available at your bookstore or use this coupon.

___ THE MANY-COLORED LAND (Volume I)	32444	$4.95
___ THE GOLDEN TORC (Volume II)	32419	$4.95
___ THE NONBORN KING (Volume III)	34749	$4.95
___ THE ADVERSARY (Volume IV)	35244	$4.95

BB **BALLANTINE MAIL SALES**
Dept. TA, 201 E. 50th St., New York, N.Y. 10022

Please send me the BALLANTINE or DEL REY BOOKS I have checked above. I am enclosing $............. (add 50¢ per copy to cover postage and handling). Send check or money order — no cash or C.O.D.'s please. Prices and numbers are subject to change without notice. Valid in U.S. only.

Name _____

Address _____

City _____ State _____ Zip Code _____

08   Allow at least 4 weeks for delivery   TA-218